HAIR-TRIGGER SMILE

HAIR-TRIGGER SMILE

DANIEL JAMES

PROLOGUE

T HE TWO WEARY FIGURES CAME to a stop upon the bluff. Before them stretched a landscape as harrowing and unpleasant as the trudging march they had thus far endured. The living of the pair sighed with exhaustion, but his gaze remained steely. Konstantin Kozlov had seen enough wonders and horrors in his time here to drive lesser mortals to the brink of madness before pitching them right over the edge into a screaming abyss.

Kozlov was no lesser mortal, but his body ached under his filth-soaked necronaut armor, a protective suit designed with enough sigils to ward off any unwelcome souls seeking a free ride. He offered a small, sweat-dampened smirk to his companion, a pale specter bedecked in his own sigil-laden armor and bearskin, but his were immaterial with a ghostly cast. The spirit was the last Arkhitektor of the now destroyed Rising Path sect, and Kozlov's one-time monk superior. Kozlov's smile was returned to him tentatively from within the wild growth of the Arkhitektor's beard.

Spreading out from the base of their bluff towards the edges of this latest infinity lay another kingdom as challenging as any infernal circle Dante ever faced. To Kozlov, these new, untamed lands were substantially more crazed than any the poet had imagined, like those of a mad child's jumble of hellish toys and fates and traps. To their "left"—if standard directions had any meaning in this chaos—lay a titan's grinning mouth set deep within the lambent cracks of the earth, a crescent moon of teeth, quivering and cackling like a loon, loud enough to rumble the ground and be heard from even up where Kozlov and the Arkhitektor stood. To their right was some type of medieval carnival, a torture town hosting a number of ritualistic sacrifices to the sky. And everywhere in between were sacked temples and churches and curious menaces too numerous to count.

Kozlov found it impossible to choose the safest route through this infernal maze. Each path would take them through a menagerie of adapted and crafty beasts hungry for refugee souls or the living flesh of foolhardy trespassers. Whatever this particular domain was, it was virgin territory to him, and he didn't know anything about the monarch who ruled it or the types of souls they laid claim to.

As a former military man, a once thoughtful and critical mind for the KGB, Kozlov prized intelligence and situational awareness, but if there was one thing the latter years had taught the old dog, it was that he could learn new tricks. He had learned to survive the dangers of the last kingdom, that of the House of Fading Light, which had killed the mortal body of the Arkhitektor and many of Kozlov's brethren, and he would now learn to survive the fresh dangers of this one.

Kozlov knew it was worse for the Arkhitektor. Though most Earthly dangers had stopped being a concern for him the moment he had died, lacking a physical form here in the afterlife of Erebus offered no protection. And being soul-bound to his old pupil Kozlov, a state that had kept him from being a wandering spirit fighting to survive in these violent and endless wilds, only meant he worried about Kozlov's flesh and bone rather than his own. No, they were both in the wilds here, and living flesh and intangible spirit alike were fair game in this sadistic jungle.

'Straight as the crow flies?' Kozlov asked his companion.

'We're familiar enough with these blighted lands to know that safety is no guarantee,' the Arkhitektor replied.

Waiting at the very edge of this ludicrous tableau was a fortress of suitably deranged function and design. The details were too difficult to accurately discern from this vast distance, but Kozlov's keen eyesight noted its appropriately haphazard geometry. 'That looks like some form of keep,' Kozlov said. 'The best lead we've had in a while.'

They had been wandering these violent lands in search of hope. To them, and the now-eradicated Rising Path sect, hope was the Firmament Needle. A mythical item from the slain race of divine protectors, crafted to stitch a brand new paradise from the ashes of the old; those ashes were long cold and scattered now, leaving only these barbaric kingdoms ruled by the remaining Houses of the Order of Terminus. Victors of a metaphysical war between death-worshippers and champions of life.

The Arkhitektor glanced behind them, all around them, taking in the landscape and the toxic vaults of the sky, likely searching for any hungry nightmare creatures. 'Then let's not wait around to become an easy meal.'

With a careful step, checking for sure footing, Kozlov started his descent.

1

FORTY MILES SOUTHEAST OF ALBUQUERQUE, New Mexico, life went on as normal as you please. The sweltering desert heat had subsided considerably since the last time Clyde was here. He didn't even know parts of New Mexico received snow like festive shotgun blasts from the sky. Otherwise, it seemed the same. Roadrunners zipped along the surrounding plains, avoiding the noisy, crushing metallic monsters zooming along the slushy highways, and the skies over the barren plains of Valencia County were still scraped clean by the wings and rotors of jets and helicopters returning to Darnell Air Force Base.

But Clyde didn't hear any jets or military choppers from where he sat. He only heard the soulful sounds of Motown on the jukebox. The Midnight Vulture was a slice of 1950s Americana, a roadside diner situated between Indigo Mesa—the government-funded spook-watch central and high command of Hourglass, hidden deep within the red-rock canyons to the northeast—and Darnell AFB to the northwest. Built upon an invisible ghost road adjacent to the interstate highway, the charming diner was mystically cloaked to any road-weary civilians, only serving Hourglass employees who knew where to look. And Clyde Williams was no longer a civilian, even if a small part of him wished otherwise.

Clyde started on his second cup of coffee, staring tiredly at the papers from the open file spread before him on the countertop. He had first read

5

them three weeks ago, and they continued to bother him. But he found, with each subsequent read, his brimming curiosity was slowly offsetting his initial anger. Before this file landed in his hands, Clyde had spent his short career as an Hourglass agent believing himself to be a mere Level I necromancer, meaning he'd barely registered as a blip on Hourglass' radar prior to recruitment. By way of this limited talent, he had accidentally bound the soul—or Post-Life Entity (PLE), in company lingo—of his deceased best friend Kevin Carpenter to his own. Through subsequent training, this automatically elevated him above the standard gunplay and tactics of regular agents, allowing him to forge a very effective partnership with Kev's spectral telekinesis, and qualifying them for the most dangerous assignments.

But to Clyde's dismay, Spector, his specialist talent coach, had been keeping some pretty big secrets in relation to Clyde's true asset capabilities. Clyde considered it lying but knew the tight-lipped bureaucracy of the agency brass would prefer to call it need-to-know omission.

However, Clyde's agent status had yet to be reclassified because, professionally, he remained an unknown quantity. But what he now knew was that the source of his novel and unpredictable abilities was rooted in the past exploits of his father's run-in with a dream parasite. His father was long dead, and even while living had been estranged from his son, yet Clyde felt haunted by him as much as or more than he was by Kev.

The only reason the agency had decided to disclose the troubling revelation of his father's unlooked-for inheritance to Clyde was because of circumstances surrounding his last assignment. The Cairnwood Society, a cabal of wealthy and infernal sorts, human and non-human, had acquired the decimated remains—one large eyeball, to be exact—of Charon, deposed monarch of the House of Fading Light, once a mighty force in the Order of Terminus but long assumed destroyed. However, enough of the dead king's power had remained in that solitary eye to not only create a series of monstrous soldiers for Cairnwood but also kindle to life a scintilla of untapped dark energy stored deep within Clyde's blood. This had resulted in Clyde's recurring visits to the Median, the dreaming kingdom situated halfway between sleep and the undead vistas of Erebus. It was a sacred place. A forbidden place. And a place no middling Level I necromancer should be habitually wandering into each night without invitation. And without Spector acting as his authorized chaperone, Clyde's accidental dream walks into the Median had begun to trouble the slumbering realm's mysterious powers-that-be.

And all because Marine Corps Sergeant Richard Williams, KIA, had stumbled into a chance encounter with the object in the photograph Clyde was now studying.

It was a small stone fetish, the camera's flash accentuating the darkness of the cave around it. Eight inches tall, the statue exuded sinister intentions. The lithe figure boasted enough beady eyes to shame a spider, an elongated and curved torso more suited to a question mark than functional mobility, and six slim arms—two of them protruding like long hooks from its back-bent torso—arranged as if caught in some mesmeric display. Each appendage was bound in what appeared to be woven threads, the paintwork of which had dulled with age.

The report identified the stone idol as the Coma Weaver; that was the closest English translation, at least. An opportunistic predator, it was known for illegally slipping into the Median between the heartbeats of sleepers like a viper slithering through tall grass, with a feasting hunger for the ubiquitous soul threads that stitched the entire realm together.

The Coma Weaver had been vanquished a very long time ago by the Median's ruling council, the House of the Glowing Reel, but statues of dreamscape interlopers such as this one remained imbued with a lasting force.

Clyde closed the file with a sigh and stared blankly at the U.S. Marine Corps seal on the front. It was pure happenstance that his father's squad had come across the long-lost temple that housed the statue during an attempt to chase down one of Saddam Hussein's top advisors. The man had quite literally gone underground, and they finally pinned him down in the lost and nameless temple. From the pictures and notes Clyde had examined, it was a place that would drive archaeologists to their knees in giddy excitement, full of old pillars embossed with mysterious pictograms and walls covered in ancient symbols, all worn smooth by the slow passage of time. The squad's lieutenant had found little interest in anything beyond the capture of their target, but Sergeant Richard Williams had spotted the fetish and picked it up, perhaps thinking to pocket the artifact as a souvenir. Something about its touch had compelled him to hastily set it back down. Or so subsequent interviews with the surviving squad members had established in the reports Clyde had obsessively perused.

That fleeting touch had been enough to awaken the diminished essence of the Coma Weaver. Like a disturbed spider, it had stung the hand that held it. And thus Richard, himself entirely unaffected, had unknowingly come to bear an insidious genetic marker that somehow skipped his firstborn son, Clyde's older brother, Stephen—like their father a U.S. Marine and also like him KIA—and settled on his second. Thus had it come to be that Clyde Williams, one-time Level I necromancer, was currently unclassified on the necromantic spectrum.

Spector had explained to him that it might take some time, perhaps Clyde's whole life, to understand the full extent of the Coma Weaver's effect on his soul. The situation was fluid. And Clyde was worried. Worried that some other nasty little surprise might present itself. Worried how much more his waking and sleeping life might change. He had seen and done a lot in six months, moving from frightened and confused civilian to official Hourglass agent, his powers shared and harnessed with his best pal, Kev, in a lethal symbiosis of telekinesis, guns, and departmental resources. And now every time he nodded off, he risked his life and soul by sinking too deeply, cascading through the kaleidoscopic outer layers of memory and fictional dream works into the Median, the shining light at the threshold of death. Provoking its quiet authority.

Clyde sipped his coffee, glanced around at the otherwise empty diner, and listened to the Isley Brothers' "Work to Do." He thought about the top-secret file, scared at what it all might mean for him in future. But being scared was just part of the job at this point.

Caught in that antsy place between concentration and daydream, he sought out the piece of blue twine he kept in his pocket, something he had started carrying on Spector's instruction, his fingers snaring complex macramé patterns as his eyes lazily hovered over the face of the redacted report. The macramé was ostensibly to clear his mind, shunt any distractions, and help him achieve some control over his unpredictable sleeping habits. While that might sound like nothing more than a psychic placebo and some wishy-washy nonsense to the unfamiliar, Clyde had found that the task did seem to help him focus. Of course, the advanced dream studies he was undergoing were much more than fooling about with twine. Predominantly, the sessions involved Spector politicking at length to the Median's ruling council on Clyde's behalf, and Clyde being educated on how to be a savvy and respectful tourist of the dream kingdom, which mostly consisted of him being hit with a few historical or geographical factoids and being explicitly warned of exactly where he could and could not go should he trespass on the realm without Spector at his side.

Clyde knocked back the coffee dregs and set down the mug. A stone hand swung a coffee pot into view to top him off. This appendage didn't belong to Spector. Spector was human in appearance, at least in the waking world. No, the stone hand belonged to a stone arm, which in turn became a full stone approximation of a man. But the stone man still took pride in wearing his G-man suit. Director Trujillo, the founder of Hourglass, was once a man but was now something much more, the facts of which Clyde knew little. What he knew for certain was that Trujillo was the top of the agency totem pole but only a small pebble—literally—in comparison to the faceless, lumbering rock giants that resided in the bedrock basement of this very diner. These creatures were known as the hoodoo, guardians of the mortal worlds, the makers and keepers of the gigantic eponymous Hourglass below Clyde's and Trujillo's feet, and ancient allies to Trujillo's Native American ancestors. Otherwise, they were a complete mystery to Clyde and the rest of his team. Need-to-know again.

Clyde might have waved off the coffee refill, but it felt rude to walk away from his superior's generous hosting, and it was cold as a penguin's ass outside. He looked at Trujillo, finding his brown and very human eyes embedded in the craggy stone face.

Clyde felt the awkwardness between him and the director had lessened a little over the past weeks. But only a little. He still felt conflicted about his service within the agency, having recently learned, during the Charon assignment, that the operational performance of him, his team, and the entire agency was largely an exercise in redundancy. The reason? Because every living soul on every world, good, bad, or ugly, were all destined for Erebus since heaven had been razed long ago in the beforetime of a secret history. But Clyde had learned this at the start of his training, and as deeply depressing as it was, this wasn't the revelation that had triggered a small rift between his team and the agency. Rather, it had been the unauthorized snooping of Kev and fellow teammate Savannah Barros into private Hourglass files—snooping that had unceremoniously revealed the Firmament Needle was real. And it was out there somewhere in the vast wastes of Erebus—or the Null, as the agency triggerpullers called it. But Trujillo had no intention of pursuing that goal, deeming it too risky. The Order of Terminus had won the war for the fate of all mortal souls, but there remained enough powerful forces on the side of the living—including the hoodoo—to keep a precarious balance. A truce had been formed long ago, one very much in favor of the Order's otherworldly monarchs. Mortals had their brief lives to enjoy; after that, the dead kings were waiting to collect their due.

The stalemate had forced Hourglass and all international and otherworldly counterparts into the same tired old holding pattern of protecting the living from malevolent forces despite knowing that for all their hard work and bravery and sacrifice, the souls of the living would all ultimately be dropped down into the Null.

The Firmament Needle's veracity remained a trade secret outside of Clyde and his team, which was for the best, at least professionally, since it would very likely cause a great number of Hourglass personnel to deem their occupations pointless and their employer at best an accessory to a kind of afterlife genocide.

That alone had been a punch to the gut for Clyde, but the fact that Director Trujillo had been keeping a secret file on his father's encounter with an artifact of arcane origins had been the finisher in a formidable one-two combination.

Clyde sipped his fresh coffee and nodded his thanks. He knew it would take a bit more time to get over the hard feelings, confusion, and mistrust, but there was more at stake than gripes about departmental bureaucracy.

'Not sleeping well?' Trujillo asked. Clyde assumed it to be a wry remark, but the sandstone face was limited in expression.

'I'm probably sleeping too much. Seem to be spending most of my days dropping down to the Median with Ram-man.' Ram-man was Clyde's chummy abbreviation for Spector's other self, the dream-walking avatar known as Ramaliak. 'This thing, the Coma Weaver,' Clyde said, tapping the file, 'how big a deal did it used to be?'

'I'm old as rocks, but I'm not *that* old.' Trujillo managed a smirk, which was like watching a stone face eroding on fast-forward. The rocky flesh preserved his age well, with the man having come up through the Army and then very briefly through the earliest days of the CIA before founding Hourglass in 1948. 'The Glowing Reel have had dealings with plenty of such primordial leeches. Beings such as the Weaver should never be underestimated, but in this instance any damage it could do, it has already done.'

'You sound pretty sure about that,' Clyde said. The Weaver was long dead according to Spector, but that didn't change the fact that some lingering presence or essence of it had been severely hindering Clyde's beauty sleep for the better part of a month.

'Are you referring to your increased potential?' Trujillo asked. 'Because depending on what form that will take in due course, it's more a matter of perspective.'

What form that will take? Clyde thought back on how he had defeated the Hangman, the Charon-enhanced killer who'd had the New York branch sweating over a heap of dead strike-team members. Clyde, somehow, had astral-projected from his body, reaching deep into the Hangman's head, phasing through physical matter and the material world to enter, inexplicably, almost instinctually, the Median in the exact spot where the brainwashed killer's soul thread lay. By restoring the Hangman's volition, Clyde had liberated the man from the monster, though the man was monster enough before Charon ever got to him, being a fearsome gangland enforcer with a fondness for barbed wire. Spector had so far been unable—or unwilling?—to elucidate how Clyde had pulled off that feat, other than linking it to the vague prowess of the Coma Weaver. Either way, Clyde had been unable to help wondering how invaluable and dangerous such a talent would be if he mastered it.

The distant rumble of a long-haul truck speeding along the highway's black ribbon returned Clyde to the present. He casually turned to watch it pass by the window of the invisible diner and glugged more coffee.

'How are we doing here, Clyde?' Trujillo asked. The strain of their fractured trust still permeated the atmosphere every time they were in the same room, which was why, Clyde assumed, he had seen much more of the director now than he had since joining the agency; and it wasn't just because he had been posted to the New York office. It felt like Trujillo was actively taking an interest in him. Hence these near daily diner hangouts the director had initiated.

'Professional relationships thrive when there is trust between all parties,' the director said without irony. 'And in our line of work, a lack of trust, a lack of focus, can be a dangerous thing.'

Clyde agreed. He had spent most of his life hating all things military-industrial complex on account of a dead older brother and dad, so it pissed him off that the first time he'd found a place in such a world, that same place had quickly pulled the rug out from under him. It sometimes felt like a big cosmic joke. The universe asking him, *Well, what did you expect?*

'I want to trust this place, and you,' Clyde said. 'To believe that what we do on this earth matters, makes a difference. But that's difficult when you hear how your employers have known all along about a way of ending this whole raw deal between life and death and choose not to act on it because it's a little risky.'

'Too risky.'

'Everything we do is risky. So instead, we waste time waging shadowy wars with smaller competition. Small-picture stuff.'

'We've been over this at length, Clyde, with me *and* Meadows.' Deputy Director Meadows, the head of the New York branch, the Madhouse, and Clyde's immediate boss.

'I know, but I still find it hard to square away,' Clyde said bluntly, fidgeting with his coffee mug. 'Someone in your position, I know you're no stranger to doing the sneaky covert shit. I still don't see why you can't—*won't*—authorize sending spies into the Null to help Kozlov locate the Needle.'

Unlike his pal Kev, Clyde had never met Konstantin Kozlov personally, but he'd had a tangential encounter with the Russian necromancer's activities during his first assignment, learning of Kozlov and the Rising Path's obsession with finding the Firmament Needle.

'Yeah, it's risky, but only for the agents being sent over,' Clyde continued. 'If they're killed, that's a professional hazard we all face daily. And if they're caught by any of the Order's forces, make sure they have some old-school shit like a cyanide tooth or something. The monarchs wouldn't be able to pin it to any direct action from us, and the treaty stays intact. They might think the intruders are just a bunch of people big on extreme outdoor pursuits.'

'Cyanide tooth, bullet to the head; their physical bodies would die, but seeing as how they would already be Null-side, their souls would still be up for grabs by those same forces,' Trujillo countered. 'Now let's say these living spies are caught, and they commit suicide in the presence of a monarch, or a lieutenant of theirs, one capable of wrangling intel out of their souls by way of torture. The Order would then know that our organization is actively undermining the treaty by performing operations against them in the hopes of securing a power grab. The *ultimate* power grab. The Needle could wipe them out of existence if the person holding it wished it.'

'Everything we do is risky,' Clyde repeated, knowing it was pointless.

'And would you be volunteering for this blatant act of suicide?'

Clyde glanced out the large window, watching snow flurries and the brass-button sun struggling to peer through a ragged swath in the dense clouds. The shadows were already beginning to stretch across the snow-swept desert. His memories dredged up some of the horrible things he'd witnessed in his very short stint in the Null. It had been one hell of a way to bust his official Hourglass cherry. He turned back and gave Trujillo an unflinching stare.

'Why not?' Clyde said flatly. 'Some of the stuff I've been involved in so far has only been a hair away from suicide. I just came back from helping take down one of those monarchs of the Order. That could have ended very badly for all of us.'

Trujillo smirked again. 'Don't take this the wrong way, but you and your team took down Charon when he was in a very weakened state. It would have been like fighting him when he had both arms tied behind his back. And even so, you barely escaped with your lives. The rest of the Order won't go down so easily.'

'They would if we found the Needle. I know it could take forever, but what else are we doing that's so damn important?'

'Any of a hundred problems. All the bloodthirsty things. Helping the living enjoy their short times here on Earth. Stopping the psychopaths and the idiots with a little power or knowledge but no moral compass.

The cults and the demons. And let's not forget, Cairnwood are still making problems everywhere they go.'

'I'm not saying we should ignore those issues. All I'm saying is I'm sure you can sacrifice some willing agents to search the Null. Seed some spies throughout the place to find it, steal it, whatever it takes. No matter how long it takes. Maybe the Rising Path had the right idea.'

'And look what happened to them. No, this isn't the right time, Clyde.' Trujillo's tone was as hard and final as his mineralized complexion. 'I won't ask you to trust me on this, just to acknowledge that I'm making this decision on sound intelligence.'

Clyde slapped his fist into his palm, but it was half-hearted, more tired than angry.

'Finish up here with Spector,' Trujillo said. 'See if you can find a yardstick to measure your power, or at least a way to not piss off the Glowing Reel. They're as politically neutral a House as you can find within the Order, and you upsetting them is another forest fire we would do well not to start. After that, return home. See your teammates. Focus on the things you have the power to change: helping the little guy.'

Clyde was missing Kev and his teammates. And his mom. And Nat. 'My ankle's healed. Suppose I'm due some field work.' The scar, a souvenir from his last encounter with the Hangman, was still ugly, but it could have been a far sight worse. The pain had subsided, and it was only the itching that bothered him now. 'What about Kev?' Clyde delivered the question like it was a concealed knife, swift and unsuspected.

Still, Trujillo must have sensed it coming. He cleared his throat with what sounded like two flat rocks sliding across each other. 'What do you think I should do?'

That sounded like a test to Clyde. Fuck it; pass or fail, he knew how he would always answer. 'I'd say he messed up, but he did it with noble intentions. And if he hadn't done what he did, me and my team would be just another bunch of company goons operating in the dark, clueless to the fact that the Firmament Needle isn't just some myth.'

'And you think that's a positive thing?' Trujillo asked. 'Raising a lot of difficult questions, harming the trust between your team and the old pen-pushers such as myself?'

'I'm still here, aren't I? You could argue that all Kev did was ensure that you have to trust us as much as we trust you.'

Tension balled itself up in Clyde's gut as he held Trujillo's dark inspection. For a moment he thought he might have pushed a bit too far. It felt like a rock wall was threatening to fall on him, and here was Clyde, currently lacking Kev's telekinetic prowess to push it back. And there were worse fates than collapsing rock walls. The agency had black sites not only reserved for useful targets but for agents with a renegade streak.

'I've already spoken to Meadows,' Trujillo said with a calm and impersonal air. 'Seeing as how you and Kev are a package deal when it comes to active duty, I've decreed that his return to service is to commence upon your return to New York, but not a minute sooner. And it will be probationary. He'll be observed closely. If I, or Meadows, catch even a whiff of something treasonous, then his ankle monitor and revoked status will seem like a kindness.'

'I'll keep an eye on him.' Clyde pushed off from his stool and drained his coffee. 'I better head on back. Spector's waiting.'

Trujillo scraped up Sergeant Richard Williams' redacted file, holding it tight to his lint-flecked suit. 'Then I suppose I should bid you good night.'

Clyde pushed through the polished-chrome-and-glass door into the stinging cold air, leaving the pleasant heating and sounds of Motown behind him. He climbed into the unmarked jeep, flexed his healed ankle a couple of times, and reversed out of the empty lot, leaving the mirage of the Midnight Vulture to blur out of existence behind him. Then he cut across the hard-packed snow and followed the road northeast towards the flat, snowy peaks of the Manzano Mountains and Indigo Mesa therein.

2

T HE MAN WITH THE DISFIGURED face felt a cold, damp mass drop on his shoulder. The night was freezing, the air still, with no gusting wind to disturb the hard snow coating the red maple's highest branches. The cause of the snowfall, he knew, was one of the snowy owls perching in the boughs, taking a brief respite from its reconnaissance. The scar-faced man had been handsome once, but never vain. His name was Edward Talbot. Whilst his disfigurement had healed significantly over the past weeks, at a rate impossible for a human man, there remained a noticeable strip of rubbery and discolored burn tissue along one side of his drooping mouth, and half-knitted gashes across his cheekbones, nose, and brow. A lesser being never would have survived the explosion. And his eyes worked perfectly fine. He watched the resting owl's quiet vigil for a few seconds before it alighted to rejoin its companions for a final pass of the forest clearing. The flying hunters reared back in formation, gained elevation, and banked sharply, their razor-keen yellow eyes taking in the large timber buildings and farming machinery. The scene looked ordinary enough to Talbot. Just 200 acres of well-tended farmland and the ubiquitous century-old maple trees vital to a seemingly innocuous maple syrup farm.

Nothing extraordinary.

Syrup season was long over, and though the bustling enterprise for those with sweet teeth never truly closed, the owl squadron's aerial recon saw things beyond the scope of common snowy owls, for the piercing gaze of this particular breed was sensitive to wavelengths of certain energy signatures. And they saw through the syrup farm's façade. What seemed a pleasant and rustic industry was anything but. It was a specialist facility for one of Hourglass' most vital offices.

Shin-deep in snow and breathing in the crystal-pure air of the southern Ontario wilds, Talbot leaned patiently against one of the many towering spruces crowding the property's outskirts. His eyesight was not as sophisticated as that of the enchanted owls, but it was nothing to be sniffed at. He watched two of the black-and-white hunters gliding across the starry sky with lethal speed—80 kph according to their master, and *his* master too, he sullenly reminded himself—before vanishing into the cover of trees and shadows. This secret installation operated under the truism that hiding in plain sight is often the safest method of concealment. But as Talbot knew, few things were truly safe in the realms of intelligence and counter-intelligence, and even less so when the confounding elements of mysticism and secret arts were in play, because the more complex a system became, the more prone they were to error and circumvention.

Case in point: the "Syrup Farm" had been a rumor on certain occulted black-market tongues for quite some time now and had only remained in the unsubstantiated ether with the buyers and sellers of such knowledge due to their lack of interest—or the brazen will—to validate and act upon the rumor. Not so for the people Talbot served in the Cairnwood Society. They were very sizeable fish in these bloody waters, with ways and means available only to the titans of underworlds and shadows. And as Mr. Gabriel's voice had just confirmed in Talbot's earpiece, his winged pets had proven the validity of the rumor mill.

Talbot thought about Gabriel sitting comfortably miles from here in the warm luxury of a private jet while he himself was about to do something that could very well succeed in doing what even the explosion hadn't managed. Talbot had lived too long, knew too much, to think easily about what awaited him after death.

Exhaling a hoary breath, he fingered the rather dull silver band girding his gloved right index finger, topped with a gray stone flecked with veins of fiery orange. When he stared at it, it appeared to smolder and swirl like a miniature clay oven. Known as Leberecht's Maquette, it was one of Gabriel's many antiquities. It was also too ostentatious for Talbot's tastes. Too gaudy. But it wasn't a fashion accessory. It was actually a ruthlessly dangerous weapon.

Talbot was never one to be overly impressed by card tricks either, being no backwoods rube, but the deck of fifty-two in his pocket was much more than a novelty for parlor tricks and hocus-pocus. The ring and card deck were peculiar weaponry for sure, but Talbot was glad to have them, being under no illusions about how much he would need them for what came next.

He was nervous, which rankled him no end. He was above this level of degrading grunt work. Or had been. But a couple of professional mishaps, and now here he was, freezing his arse off in some rural Canadian boondock as a glorified foot soldier. It wasn't fair. Even Gabriel's sodding owls would be warming themselves on the blood of some small mammals by now, their work complete.

With a quiet crunch of snow, Talbot stepped out from the tree line. His natural—or unnatural—reflective lenses shone like greenish pennies in the dark. Beyond the farm's metal fence, the facility looked quiet. Reputedly, this place didn't house a regional Hourglass task force. It existed for an entirely different function.

But that didn't mean it would be easy pickings. Raising his hand almost daintily, he signaled the phalanx of Cairnwood thugs waiting amidst the trees. Now they emerged, moving in clusters towards the main chalet-styled barn and the various outbuildings.

The owls had done well enough to determine this rustic slice of heaven as the target site, but they hadn't been able to spot the presence of any armed resistance.

Talbot watched the Cairnwood stooges hop over the fence and take cover behind transport trucks or piles of lumber.

Without warning, angry declarations of gunfire erupted from various points around the main chalet, short accurate bursts that tore into the Cairnwood invaders, splashing their colorless blood across the snow; Cairnwood's rank-and-file troops looked human enough, but they had all shed that aspect of themselves. This had advantages under most circumstances, such as being able to handle significant physical trauma.

But this wasn't one of those circumstances. Talbot watched the bullet-wounded sag and fall apart as though they were being rapidly chewed up from within by millions of invisible mouths.

Talbot grimaced at the sight, then smirked at Hourglass' ingenuity.

It appeared the Syrup Farm agents were using ammunition cored with a particular substance, perhaps harnessed from a drusillika brood. The material in question had the unpleasant tendency to release a swarm of ravenous microscopic ticks that were not too choosy about the flesh presented to them. A terrible and inhumane weapon, but one that was effective against a wide variety of inhuman threats. On the upside, drusillika ticks couldn't tolerate sub-zero temperatures and so would be dealt with by the weather as soon as their feasting was over.

Talbot took note of where the Hourglass shooters were positioned. They were everywhere! That was the bloody problem. The odds against him were as terrible as expected. Gabriel and the higher seats either wanted him out of the picture, still held him in surprisingly high regard, or were simply curious to see what he was still capable of after several embarrassing failures.

Crouching behind an unlit fire pit, Talbot noted two Hourglass gunners behind the double-doors of the main building's entrance, each door a series of large, robust logs and likely carved with protective runes covering a steel inner layer. Several other pairs of shooters were keeping low behind three different wooden balconies, and a small army was piling out of the main building's side door as another group rushed in from the outbuilding near the steep, rocky drop-off just north of the property.

Talbot didn't bother checking the status of the Cairnwood henchmen. Their being hardy and stalwart had earned them the affectionate nickname of "coffin nails" amongst Cairnwood's older blood. But coffin nails could still rust and bend, and most of these were currently in pieces, each one little more than a hodgepodge of limbs and chunks of watery gore. Though those still standing remained fearless. Like the good little idiots they were, they would continue marching to Cairnwood's fife, taking aim at the nearest clusters of Hourglass shooters.

But Cairnwood had some nasty bullets of their own, the aptly named Exorcist rounds. Talbot watched as one of his subordinates punched a volley of these into a few Hourglass agents, the souls of whom were destroyed along with their failing bodies. There would be no Erebus for them—a mercy really, Talbot thought—only the big black nothing beyond death.

A few dead agents, however, wasn't quite enough to turn the tide of this battle, as the dead were quickly replaced, and before the coffin nails could push any further, one of them triggered a hidden trap, a concealed device that opened a glyph-laden portal, an eye-searing beauty that quickly dilated, unleashing a large slazarian claw that mangled the blunderer before vanishing along with the portal.

If these bastards wanted to compare light-shows, then that was just dandy with Talbot. With his pulse hammering, he reached into the hip pocket of his black thermal jacket and withdrew the pack of playing cards. Circa 15th-century France, a favored amusement of a crazed traveling practitioner named Merlin, they were meant for far more than games of solitaire. Tearing the protective seal on the deck, Talbot felt a sudden rush of energy thrum through his gloved fingers, and the fifty-two cards took flight like uncaged doves. From their lofty fluttering came twelve spectral figures: four jacks, four queens, and four kings, each of whom raised a hand towards the forty other circling cards as if in benediction. After several seconds, the twelve court cards blinked out for parts unknown, leaving the marvel and wonder of the spinning cards to become a savage spectacle. Ten of the cards shot out piercing diamonds, the projectiles accurately shredding a number of the Hourglass agents whose tactical armor proved unable to withstand the eldritch attack.

Ten of the cards grew large, man-sized, and became doorways for a series of heavy clubs, with each one speeding out to bludgeon the tactical helmets of Hourglass' army, cracking the skulls within. Ten more cards unleashed a procession of large shovels, their black blades hitting, slicing, and then speedily unearthing the frozen ground to scoop the wounded but still alive troops into shallow freezing plots. It was all over in less than a minute. Talbot grinned at the muffled screams of the buried and dying. Magic gimmickry had its uses, and with some satisfaction he deemed his selection from Gabriel's collection as worthy. The first wave of expendable meat had been disposed of, but Talbot knew better than to think the hard work was over with. A place this important to Hourglass would depend on more than some jazzed-up bullets and sneaky perimeter traps.

That was when his shining eyes caught movement: a woman of indeterminate age standing in the doorway of the main building. One second she was there, and the next she wasn't. But then Talbot found himself on his back with a flash of light in his eyes and an achy numbness in his jaw. The woman stood over him, hate in her eyes. She was young, late twenties maybe, rosy-cheeked from the cold, her slim frame bound in a thermal figure-hugging suit, much like an alpine skier, Talbot mused through his near-concussion. That would make her Sugar Rush, or Maddie Blanchet, one of this division's regular agents, according to Cairnwood's sources. Most notably, she was a Spark, one of the mysterious and formidable race of divinely enhanced humans, respected and feared amongst even the most powerful of Cairnwood's elite.

Personally, Talbot despised the lot of them, with his recent run of bad luck partially attributable to at first one, and then two, Hourglass-backed Sparks.

Swollen jaw aside, he had no prior dealings with this particular Spark. But his intel explained her silly sobriquet, a self-coined combo of her post at the Syrup Farm and her ability to instantaneously move faster than a Formula 1 car at top speed.

Talbot knew she could kill him before he even thought about getting back up. But with no shortage of relief, he saw how her large doe eyes started to brim with a warm depth of love, filling up like tea in two hazel cups. His gambit had worked. Floating overhead, the remaining hearts cards of his deadly deck pulsed with amatory power. She was his now, a love slave.

'Take me to the seer,' Talbot commanded. 'Protect me.'

Sugar Rush reached down to gently help him up. The Spark moved swiftly ahead with just enough speed to put a safe distance between Talbot and any further security measures within the compound. He watched while she shut down the runic anti-intruder system protecting the main doors, the glyphs shining ember-hot for a brief moment before going cold and dark.

Enough chaos had already been wrought, though, and even with a pet Spark at his beck and call, Talbot was under no delusions about how tenuous his situation remained. Though he was relatively confident he and Sugar Rush could handle the second Spark intelligence had identified as a likely presence, he knew reinforcements were already on the way.

Inside, the compound maintained its faux-rustic aesthetic of expensive ski chalet seasoned with subtle touches of sleek modernity and advanced technology. Sugar Rush held up a warning hand. Talbot paused, listening for whatever it was she had sensed. A good thing too, because seconds later an axe, glowing with a yellow luminosity, whooshed across the length of the massive main room, spinning end over end like a hatchet towards Talbot's face. Sugar Rush blurred and suddenly was halfway across the room, snatching the axe out of the air with one hand. Talbot was still processing the likelihood of Leberecht's ring, the Maquette, working from this range, when Sugar Rush, without pausing, hurled the axe back in the direction from which it had come. A husky older man, broad of shoulder and wrapped in a thick blue-and-black plaid shirt, stumbled from the shadows. Talbot's intel referred to him as Lumberjack.

'Maddie...?' Lumberjack gasped, his returned weapon embedded deep in his chest, fizzing with energy.

'Sorry, friend. I think she loves me,' Talbot said smugly.

Lumberjack went down like a felled tree, the axe dissipating into a cloud of luminous particles.

Sugar Rush gave Talbot a look that he had only previously seen in photographs of young girls gazing devotedly at pop stars.

'Carry on, my dear,' he said, gesturing for her to precede him. Ever the gentleman.

He stepped over the corpse of the dead Spark and followed her into a wide rotund lounge at the rear of the lodge. Sugar Rush stopped at a camouflaged terminal set in the varnished wall and used her access clearance to shut down whatever the next combination of scientific or mystical deterrents were. Wooden panels slid aside to reveal a steel vault door. It swung open silently, and Talbot entered an impressive domed room that reminded him of a planetarium. There was, however, only one seat, a large and comfortable recliner positioned near the middle of the room. Beside the chair was a sturdy side table with some scientific apparatus consisting of a boxy piece of circuits and microchips—not available on the open market—wired up to a sleek black plastic headband being worn by the frail elderly woman occupying the seat. This, he knew, would be Estelle Page, otherwise known as the Astronomer. Beams shone from her eyes to track across the domed ceiling like twin spotlights, summoning a constellation of gently blinking lights within the familiar outlines of a Mercator map of Earth's continents. Next to each small, flickering light was a sequence of squiggled impressions, a language Talbot could recognize only as not of this world.

He watched as the alien symbols were quickly translated into English, not French—while this was Ontario, Hourglass remained a product of the United States—before being recorded by the machine. The data was the tally of names and current coordinates of all the Sparks in the world, each detected by the old woman's remarkable ability. A truly divine gift, and one she had been using to track newly awakened Sparks since the 1950s, helping to bring them in from the cold, where they could put their unique talents to good use, or at least learn to assimilate to ordinary life as very extraordinary people. Some people discovered they had power and became scared of using it, while others managed to go through their entire lives without realizing they had it at all. And then there were those with more volatile natures. Here was the raw material from which Hourglass had recruited its Sparks for decades now.

Talbot slowly padded down the wide steps into the sunken chamber, ensorcelled by the information silently blinking overhead. Across all six continents there appeared to be dismally few Sparks, not quite the dense nebula Talbot and his employers had been anticipating. Of course, the small number was only limited in the grand scheme of seven-billion-some souls, so in truth, the count wasn't too bad. Not too bad at all. Perhaps several hundred eligible candidates. And more would always be born.

He retrieved a small, rolled-up sheet of paper, ancient and sepia-tinted, from his insulated inside pocket and gently removed the black ribbon that bound it, then pulled the parchment taut and held it up to the ceiling, all the while visually honing in on the East Coast of the USA. The Sparks suddenly vanished from view, leaving the domed ceiling a black, barren cosmos.

The reclining chair creaked gently as the Astronomer sat up, the headband's wires trailing across her knitted wool sweater. The woman was somewhere in her late nineties, brittle and thinned by a largely sedentary occupation as much as age. The shining beams were gone from her eyes, leaving only a stern challenge in their stead.

Irritated, Talbot lowered the parchment. 'Could I trouble you to restart the show?' he asked, briefly turning his attention from the ceiling. 'I don't have time to dawdle.'

The Astronomer looked at Sugar Rush in confusion, but the young Spark had eyes only for Talbot. The swarm of cards pulsed redly overhead.

She directed her attention back to Talbot. 'Who the devil are you?'

'Just a man trying to make a living.'

Her eyes became hooded with hatred. 'You're Cairnwood.'

'Yes, I suppose I do wear it on my sleeve. My employers always have an eye for new markets and talent. It surprises me they haven't recruited you before now.' He nodded towards the dark ceiling again like a salesman wrangling a skittish client. 'If you would be so kind . . .'

'Did you consider the possibility that your employers are trying to kill you?'

Talbot shrugged. 'It has occurred to me. Especially after the warm welcome I received outside. But this is a job without glass ceilings, so being daring pays off. Now, I'll ask one more time politely. Can you please light it up again?'

The Astronomer uttered a word that seemed ill-suited to an elderly lady of such genteel appearance.

Talbot sighed and turned to Sugar Rush. 'My dear, if you would?'

'Maddie, no!' The Astronomer's voice was commanding, that of a grandmother scolding a beloved grandchild about to do something unwise. But the vacancy in Blanchet's eyes told her that this wasn't her Maddie anymore.

Before the Astronomer had time to blink, Sugar Rush was there, her hands pressing on either side of the old woman's head, forcing her gaze back to the ceiling. Perhaps deep down, what was left of Maddie had some awareness of what she was doing. The pain she was inflicting. The betrayal. Talbot certainly hoped so.

The Astronomer fought, but it mattered little. Her anguished gaze flickered for a few seconds. Then a strong picture projected onto the ceiling, coinciding with a moan from Estelle that sounded to Talbot like a creaking floorboard. Calmly, he adjusted the position of the blank scroll, holding it up to the State of New York. Before his eyes, the details of the first Spark began to etch themselves upon the parchment letter by letter, as if set down with fine penmanship by an invisible hand; the name and general locality were offered along with an illustration of the Spark, but not their skillset, which Talbot found irritating, but then realized it just made it more exciting. When the first candidate's details were complete, the second began: one letter, two—

A deafening bang caused Talbot to flinch. The constellation of sparks vanished, leaving a black void. Talbot turned to see smoke slowly rising from the side of Estelle's chair. A small revolver dangled from the index finger of one limp hand. Talbot was both angry and impressed. Despite everything, the Astronomer had possessed the strength of will to put a bullet in her own head rather than allow herself to become a tool in the hands of Cairnwood. She could have shot Talbot in the back. She could have shot Sugar Rush. But she did not know the extent of Talbot's abilities. And she must not have been able to bring herself to shoot her friend. So she had ended herself.

Sugar Rush blinked in confusion, drawing her hands back, her face spattered with the old woman's blood and brains.

'Sneaky old bitch,' Talbot muttered, his face twisting into a feral composition. He wanted to hit something, but he controlled himself. He knew he had screwed up. Again. Gotten too greedy. Too impatient. He should have searched her. But her age and apparent decrepitude had caused him to underestimate her. And the result of his stupidity? An invaluable resource snatched away. And one poxy name for all his trouble. One Spark out of all those hundreds.

'You,' he said to Sugar Rush, whose hands were trembling, as if she were trying to fight off the effect of the cards that still hovered above her, pulsing like vampiric butterflies. 'All that data.' He pointed to the black space of the ceiling. 'There must be back-ups. Recordings.' He jerked his head towards the boxy device beside the Astronomer's chair. 'What about this thing?'

'N-no,' Sugar Rush stammered. 'That sends the data elsewhere.'

'Where?' Talbot asked impatiently.

'Off-site.' She gritted her teeth, and anger flashed in her eyes ... eyes no longer regarding him with the blank adoration of a moment ago. The fluttering heart suit was beginning to fade away like a neglected love. 'What did you make me do?'

Talbot saw his only opportunity. Strike now, while she was still floating through the fleeting vestiges of affectionate euphoria. He pulled the glove from his left hand and lashed out, the pale, dexterous fingers gripping Sugar Rush about the throat. His hand began to change its pigmentation, morphing from white to a slick, deep green mottled with black spots: something fit for a marsh-wading horror. Meanwhile, the Spark's incredible life force flowed through his reptilian hand, filling him deeply with a sensation of lightning and ozone. He gasped with near sexual pleasure. The potency of her Spark bloodline enhanced his own healing abilities significantly, and the scars and burns from the recent bomb blast—which had been no mere conventional explosive—faded more swiftly now.

Sugar Rush must have finally broken free of the cards' malign love spell because her fist moved like a bolt of lightning, punching Talbot in the face once, twice, and then slipping a thumb into his eye and pressing it deep enough to cause an eruption of ichor. Talbot smirked and used her own rapidly dissipating life force to restore his ruptured eyeball.

Sugar Rush swiped for the scroll in his hand, but her amazing speed was gone, and she managed to tear away only a blank strip. Her eyes grew milky, and her lustrous hair turned peppery, then white as cotton, and the withering marks of age appeared on her once-full lips and formerly smooth cheeks.

It was over quickly, and Talbot let the desiccated agent—the snuffed-out Spark—fall dead upon the ground, where she resembled an exhumed corpse from some ancient crypt. His fingers humanlike again, he probed his new skin, delighting in its smoothness. All traces of the explosion were gone. He felt a little better, at least physically, but still couldn't help glowering at the single name upon the otherwise blank scroll. All this nonsense for one sodding name. Hardly a result to catapult him out of his professional rut.

He ripped away the wires that connected the Astronomer's damaged headpiece to the mysterious black box and gingerly picked it up. It was a little heavy, but he could manage. With one irritable parting glance at the erased blackboard of the domed ceiling, he made his exit.

．　．　．

THE PRIVATE JET was waiting for Talbot at the small airstrip, its engines already roaring into the night. The escape from the farm had been hassle-free, apart from lugging the bulky box through deep, snowy forest and the bumpy snowmobile ride back to the helicopter. All this running around was a young man's job—or, rather, a lesser man's job. He used to have lackeys for such menial work as this. Though he couldn't deny it had been exciting. How long had it been since he had been involved in such hands-on affairs? Considering his age, it was surely a long time indeed. It made him recall his last gofer; what was the name of that chap?

Collins!

That was it! Decent fellow. Unpleasant demise.

In fact, as Talbot recalled, the last thing Collins did before meeting his maker was freeze his bollocks off on an errand to a Russian military black site to take custody of Konstantin Kozlov. And what a disaster that had proved for Talbot's credibility. Between them, the bastard Russian monk and Hourglass had left him with one hell of a metaphorical black eye. One that even his enhanced healing abilities were powerless to erase. And his actions tonight would only partly make up for that earlier defeat. How bloody infuriating.

Here he was, Edward Talbot, once the up-and-coming go-getter of Cairnwood's North American operations, stalking across a damp, slushy airfield in a climate colder than a witch's tit, returning with a box that might very well be empty rather than his true target, the Astronomer whose head held riches beyond measure. He could only hope the situation could yet be salvaged.

Mr. Gabriel was waiting for him at the bottom of the jet's carpeted airstairs, tending to his parliament of owls, each one clinging to his arms or shoulders in such a way that Talbot expected them to carry him off into the night, as if he had no need of a jet. For an instant, he imagined their beaks and claws tearing at Gabriel, shredding him like some giant rat. One could dream.

As soon as Gabriel saw him, he turned and retreated up the steps with his uncaged pets. Talbot crossed the slick tarmac, a weary exhaustion beginning to sap him. He knew his coming report wouldn't have Gabriel doing cartwheels. Perhaps if Merlin's card deck had been able to maintain its charm over Sugar Rush, her Spark abilities could have been a great asset for Cairnwood, offsetting the loss of the Astronomer.

Talbot paused at the foot of the stairway and took a breath, noticing the enchanted ring still on his finger. He hadn't had the chance to try it out. He dared amuse himself for a moment with fantasies of testing it on Gabriel, wondering what it might look like in action, before dismissing the idea. This was a cutthroat business, but that would certainly be career suicide. He removed it from his gloved finger and placed it in his pocket. With the Astronomer's black box under his arm, he mounted the stairs, thinking of the single name he had managed to capture before the Astronomer blew her brains out.

David Bentley. Twenty-four years old. Buffalo, New York. An image of the man had been sketched alongside the brief biographical details.

Whatever this Bentley's Spark abilities proved to be, Talbot had to hope they would be enough to get him back in Cairnwood's good graces.

3

IT WAS A PLACE BUILT of dreams, but the creatures that made up the advising council seemed more the stuff of nightmares. They were beings formed of spindly limbs and white-fire eyes, some with silvery flesh and ornately decorated wings pulled tight around slender bodies like royal cloaks, a few with corkscrew horns, catfish whiskers, and even one with a head shaped like bovine udders, a crown of teats.

Despite this bizarre menagerie, it was Clyde, the simple human, who was made to feel like an invasive phantasm. But he knew this had little to do with his anatomy and physiognomy, and everything to do with his blood.

This was the sixth arraignment session in two weeks with the House of the Glowing Reel, and each one so far had mostly played out the same way: Clyde would follow Ramaliak—née Spector—into the palace court and be made to stand before the stern appraisals of the tribunal staring down from their gallery seats.

Clyde stood patiently as the odd creature he had come to think of as the Michelin Man, wrapped in luminous patchwork, held his soul thread taut like a couturier perusing interesting fabrics. This process tended to be quick, quiet, and impersonal, which suited Clyde. The sooner these arraignment sessions concluded, the sooner Clyde could breathe easy. Day-Glo Michelin Man released Clyde's soul thread, the thin blue filament vanishing like a mirage back into his forehead, for the mind's raw material was the birthplace of the soul. The bulky soul reader didn't bother with Clyde after this, turning around with an awkward waddle to give a silent nod to the bristling judges. This silent signal cleared Clyde of any wrongdoing; rather, it indicated that the Coma Weaver was not currently active within his soul, confirming he was no current threat to the Median. Though the Coma Weaver had certainly interfered with his nascent soul, the insidiousness of its effects went no further than making him a sporadic and unwanted guest of the sleeping kingdom.

While the rulers of this plane were sticklers for the law of dreams, deeming that the soul threads that constituted the kingdom were not to be interfered with beyond the accepted activities of the Order of Terminus, and none too lenient on mortal beings dropping by unannounced, Clyde had started to believe Ramaliak when he said the council were not overreacting. This was not classism, or mystical beings turning their noses up—few of whom actually had noses—to a weak and fleeting mortal with the audacity to encroach on their hallowed lands. The Coma Weaver was not something to be underestimated. It was a criminal element that had trafficked in realm trespassing, soul stealing, and the widespread ignition of nightmares. And so, when a living soul erred and found themselves marked by even the faintest trace of such a demon's potential, vanquished or not, it wasn't to be tolerated.

Past experience told Clyde what came next.

Dremel's routine questions. Udder-head. Asshole.

'Clyde Williams, speaking under oath, do you understand that an act of perjury on your behalf is punishable by death?' Dremel asked. His eyes looked like ragged holes cut in a cheap rubber mask to Clyde, the irises as black and empty as an eager executioner's.

'I do,' Clyde replied.

'Have you felt any undue or uncharacteristic malevolent thoughts imposing themselves upon you in your wakeful hours?'

'No.' Same two questions each time.

Dremel stared at Clyde as he always did. Like he was trying to spot a bluff. These appraisals felt more like an excuse to try and make Clyde feel guilty, but Clyde always held udder-head's supercilious stare.

'Dismissed.'

And just like the last times, Clyde would be led outside the courtroom while Ramaliak negotiated further with the judiciary on his behalf, defending him from unjust imprisonment or possible execution, either fate having been a very near possibility had Ramaliak not originally intervened. For that, Clyde was grateful, but part of him was starting to suspect that the House just wanted to kill him. A preemptive measure. Just in case his tarnished soul became something more problematic in future.

He kept a cautious distance from his escort, royal guards robed and hooded, their faces masked in tightly woven neon threads—whether cultural artifice or snippets of real souls, Clyde wasn't sure.

But at least he had one hell of a view while awaiting—he hoped—this latest stay of execution. The court was on the top floor of the palace, and the hallway outside the chamber of which he stood was a lengthy and exquisite balcony looking out across the grounds, the rolling lands beyond, and of course, and most importantly, the giant Glowing Reel for which this House was named. Resembling a staggeringly large fly reel or Ferris wheel, it spun slowly, the march of time an irrelevance as it perpetually drew in each new soul forged from the acts of physical love, or even hate, across all the known worlds, weaving every newborn soul into the expanding luminescence that was the Median.

To Clyde, the lambent soul threads gave the place a somewhat futuristic charm, like a scientific fantasy painted by Michael Whelan. A bizarre utopia cast like one final shining beacon of hope into a dark universe. These playful curiosities would always segue into more banal thoughts as he looked at the sea of threads and wondered which of those souls were currently watching TV or bored at work, sitting in traffic, stressing over Christmas, fucking, fighting, or sleeping, and even now blundering through their own personalized dream fictions of memory, experience, and passions.

He still didn't quite understand it all, despite Spector's best efforts at explaining. It wasn't that it was complicated to understand, or even to imagine—and Clyde had a very active imagination—but the difficulty lay in the fact that all of this was such a fantastical and painstakingly maintained system. That royal council of advisors back there—always minus a monarch, he'd noticed—made all the decisions, but the monumental upkeep and labor that must be involved in trimming away the blackened threads of the truly vanquished souls—those destroyed entirely and beyond even the reach of the Null's horrors—was carried out by creatures Clyde had been told about but still hadn't seen.

The diamond-heads, Spector had called them.

Despite their apparent shyness, these creatures doubled as custodians and security, and Clyde couldn't possibly put a number on how many of them there must be toiling away in this kingdom, just out of sight, hidden deep within the stitching, like lice in a shimmering blanket.

Behind him, the beautifully woven balcony doors opened with a gentle, almost electronic humming sound.

Clyde turned to see Ramaliak staring at him. Clyde couldn't read Ramaliak's expression; anthropomorphic ram-headed deities could be hard to pin down. Clyde grew nervous, envisioning his soul thread being cut, casting him out into the Null without weaponry and without a chance to say his goodbyes.

Finally, Ramaliak raised a hoof in victory.

Clyde was spared, and he felt a sudden looseness unspool through his tense mind.

Ramaliak sauntered over to him, and Clyde, supremely relieved he'd never had a lesser advocate defending him in there, asked, 'Have I got a free pass now?'

'Steady on, cowboy.' Ramaliak dropped his formal tone around Clyde, sounding more like his easygoing human self. 'Far from it. Their decree was that you won't be killed on sight whenever you detour over here. But that's not a backstage pass to poke around the place. So if I were you, anytime you do slip in here, just keep to the outskirts. Don't go wandering around the heart of the city, and certainly don't go sightseeing to the prohibited areas beyond the city. This isn't a tourist trap. And do not, under any circumstances, get any ideas about practicing those new skills of yours, ever.'

Memories of how he'd pulled the Hangman from Charon's control, and then of what he'd done to Charon, the white fire somehow engulfing his hands as he'd destroyed the monarch's disembodied eye.

'I wouldn't know how to if I tried,' Clyde answered honestly.

'And we're going to keep it that way, aren't we? Because that little flare-up you experienced—'

'And used to great effect.'

'Regardless. The power you tapped to defeat Charon was the Coma Weaver stirring in its sleep. Believe me, you don't want to wake it up.'

'No flexing from me, I promise,' Clyde said. 'I have no intention of waking it. My life's fucked up enough already.'

Clyde's look grew wistful as he watched the Glowing Reel, running his palms along the smooth balcony, feeling countless pulses of life pass through the soul threads into his palms.

'What if it happened again by accident?' Clyde asked. 'Let's say I'm on a mission, fighting who knows what, and the next thing I know I'm some astral projection, reaching in here and tearing out some hostile's soul thread?' He didn't look Ramaliak in the eye as he waited for his response, keeping his gaze on the giant reel's slow revolutions.

The pause troubled him.

'I just bought you some leniency in there. Not much, but enough to cover a slight fuck-up should it occur: slap on the wrist rather than sleep death.'

Clyde exhaled. 'Wouldn't want that.'

'But the council knows you only tapped into that latent power because Charon's presence must have been like the smell of coffee or bacon to the sleeping Weaver. We have security measures here in the Median that keep things like the Coma Weaver from feeding, but out there in the waking world, you're like a proxy just waiting to smuggle it snacks. So in future, keep away from any monarchs of the Order or similar-sized power-sets that will make its belly rumble, and you should be hunky-dory.'

'Right. And if not, go mad with power and become a dream god like you?' Clyde smiled cynically, catching something in those big, dark ram eyes, a trepidation only magnified further by Spector's glasses.

'And that's why I want to keep up regular training sessions with you,' Ramaliak said. 'I know you'll be needed back on your team soon, so you won't have to stay here much longer. I can schedule times and dates for us; you use those focusing techniques I showed you to drop down here, I meet you outside the city walls, and we make sure you're not getting too wayward.'

'Hard to refuse with views like this.'

'It is quite a place, isn't it? I used to think I'd never get tired of being in here,' Ramaliak said, leaning on the balcony with a restless vibe, gazing at the grandeur of the Glowing Reel.

'It's something, alright.' Clyde waved his hand an inch from his forehead, the motion temporarily making his own blue soul thread visible. He rolled it between his fingers and then released it, allowing the thread to become invisible once more. 'The rules don't really apply to this place, do they?'

Ramaliak scoffed. 'What tipped you off? If you're comparing this place to the waking world, then no, they don't.'

'For instance, this whole kingdom is stitched together of soul threads, and the Glowing Reel is like one big loom, weaving all the newly minted souls into the fabric. But when dead souls get clipped—I mean the truly dead—the integrity of the surrounding structure doesn't unravel like a cheap sweater. That reel, it's constantly threading in the new souls, but how does each new one get from there to, say …' Clyde's finger made a line from the reel to a random point in the vista, emphasizing a great distance, 'there? Is the reel just symbolic of new life coming into the universe?'

'No, it's quite real. There are forces that guide each new thread to their rightful place within the tapestry. Forces that tax a little something from each new soul in the process—not much, but enough energy to help keep the whole kingdom running.'

Clyde watched the reel and thought about the psychic imagery he had been unexpectedly shot with during his vanquishing of Charon, imagery incited by the Coma Weaver's unasked-for powers.

It was a vision of a strange-looking cult assembled before the Glowing Reel. Details had been hard to discern at the time, but among them was a being with a ram's-head appearance not dissimilar to Ramaliak—an ancient predecessor of Spector's, Clyde now knew—and the others were various shades of monstrous. They had been making some sort of pact.

According to Ram-man, that was the beginning of the new paradigm: the truce between the nine Houses of the Order of Terminus, most of whom were very much in favor of the Null's reigning hellscape, with only a few Houses standing in opposition. Whatever power those few Houses packed, Clyde knew it must be staggering if it had held back the other monarchs for so many years.

Clyde's eyes were briefly drawn away from the Glowing Reel to a more intimidating structure a little beyond it: two pyramids, one shining like gold, the other a winged and nebulous shadow inverted atop it, both of them touching peak to peak, with a cloud of swirling rainbow-streaked plasma circling their tips.

Spector had referred to them as the Gilded Hypnos and Obsidian Extremis but had said little more on the matter. Having first seen this divine and hellish building in the memories of the Coma Weaver, Clyde had naturally pressed Spector for a little more detail, but Spector had told him to admire it from afar and otherwise forget about it. Such instructions told Clyde one thing about the conjoined pyramids: they were clearly aspects of vast power and significance in this domain. And during the course of his drawn-out legal proceedings, Clyde couldn't help but silently fixate on them, knowing nothing good could come of it. Getting too interested in them would only rouse the council's ire.

A hoof patted Clyde's arm, snapping him to attention. 'Come on, let's celebrate.'

.   .   .

'TO A GOOD NIGHT'S sleep,' Spector toasted, a small bottle of apple brandy in his hand. He had picked it up from the liquor store in a small dustbowl town by the name of Cactus Flats, situated north of Indigo Mesa. Apart from the suburbs, there wasn't much else there but a line of stores, bars, and a few outlying farms.

'To not waking up dead.' Clyde knocked back the capful. The smooth fire in his throat matched the inferno of colors igniting the snowy horizon. Everything burned, and even the coldest winter was helpless to stop it.

They were seated on the tallest of the rock chimneys clustered around the western edge of Indigo Mesa. It was an incredible view at magic hour, and Clyde had whiled away more than a couple of hours sketching it since his return, cold fingers be damned. From where he was sitting, he could stare due west to the lights of Darnell Air Force Base. And the slim-built hoodoo several feet from where he sat emitted its curious energy, allowing him to see through the ghostly bubble hiding the Midnight Vulture from plain view; from this height and distance the diner was smaller than a matchbox.

This was the spot where Rose and Ace had first shown Clyde and Kev the hidden diner, Director Trujillo's unorthodox nerve center; the small nearby hoodoo was just one of the many secreted away by the larger sentient members of their race, acting like energy relays and security measures for the barriers set up around Indigo Mesa, Darnell, and the Midnight Vulture.

Behind Clyde, the large, flat, expansive top of Indigo Mesa was rife with activity: jeeps drove across the tarmac from one building to another; a helicopter prepped to launch from the helipad; a few agents were running errands. And this was only the tip of Indigo's iceberg, with the real activity housed deep inside the mountain, where prying eyes couldn't peep.

Still, the mesa was protected by a no-fly zone enforced by Darnell AFB, and the public hiking trails littering the mountain range were sealed off from the restricted agency routes—however, a big male black bear whose fur color ran closer to cinnamon was lethargically ambling through the agency route, tremendous paws imprinting the virgin snow, paying no mind to the barrage of prominent legal challenges and signposts. Wildlife was welcome to wander from the beaten path. Tourists were not.

Clyde leaned back against the chilly rock to watch the stars perforating the dusk and thought about the bizarre characters who made up the council, with one face starring more prominently than the others—the glaring udder-headed admonisher.

'That Dremel,' Clyde began. 'I still can't decide who he hates more: me or you. Because I did get an impression they all have some beef with you.'

Spector sat there quietly, wrapped up in a handsome wool winter coat and scarf, and took a warming slug of brandy. 'Well, there was a time when we saw eye to eye. You could even call our relations cordial. But that was before I stepped down to help this place, playing secret agent... though thief is more accurate. They don't view stealing dreams from dangerous targets as a worthy use of my abilities. It's sacrilegious, I suppose. They don't meddle in mortal politics and don't approve of me doing it either. They believe the troubles of the wakeful should be left to them. Unless, of course, they're troubles that impact their own power dynamic.'

'You mean like some handsome upstart cursed by a Babylonian dream demon?' Clyde suggested wryly.

Spector's dimples carved deep shadows around his charming smile. 'Something like that.'

Clyde held his hand out for the bottle, which Spector was happy to oblige him with.

'It just never ceases to amaze me how fucked up my life is.' Clyde took a drink and passed the bottle back.

Spector gave a dry laugh. 'You're getting used to it, though.'

'If going numb qualifies as "used to it." Look, this new controversial ability of mine: I get that I've only been pardoned for a minute, and it's the result of a dirty little secret, but…I keep thinking about how I stopped the Hangman, then finished off Charon. And I did that shit while I was still awake.' Clyde was careful with his tone, curious but not wanting to sound too eager. 'Not in the Median.'

'Yes, but everything you did directly affected the Median, whether you were consciously in there or not.'

'I know, but is there definitely no way Dremel and the others will turn a blind eye if I try to practice it? Because tell me that's not a useful skill for fieldwork.'

'I'm not saying that wasn't impressive, and hell, I wish I had been there to see it,' Spector said with some regret. 'But that's the exact sort of action Dremel and the others have expressly forbidden you from doing. You don't even know how you did it. Neither do I. But what I do know is that it's some sort of by-product of the Weaver, and a damn dangerous one at that. One the council don't want you getting familiar with.' Spector took down two fingers of brandy instead of the customary one. 'I just kept you from getting your soul snipped and shunted off into the Null. Don't push it, Clyde. Please. We both agreed I'd try to do what I could to help you understand your situation a bit better, but that's to make sure you don't accidentally do what you did again.'

Clyde thought about how Charon recognized the hidden danger buried inside of him, something capable of inducing fear in a king of the dead. He could still hear its disembodied voice calling him *usurper*, his hands becoming immaterial, blossoming with cool white fire. 'Shame,' Clyde said. 'Not a bad party trick to have. Even if I could bust it out on demand, I'm not saying I'd do it without some warning to the council, or maybe even the Reel's king—*whoever* and *wherever* the hell he is. And they already tolerate you occasionally dipping in and out of the dreams of Hourglass' high-value targets. If I could get my head around this new skill a little, it might be useful for—'

'*Killing* high-value targets?'

Clyde made a sour face, suddenly feeling uncomfortable. 'What, where did that come from?' He sat up a little straighter. 'Just because I'm boogieman black-ops means there can't be non-lethal applications? What I did to the Hangman wasn't lethal. I liberated his dirty little soul from Charon—shit, it even helped us win that fight, if I say so myself. If you could find out how the Weaver did it, try to school me in it, I could probably help others. You never know when some unlucky cat might fall under the sway of another mind-controlling supervillain.'

Spector took a nip from the bottle and passed it back to Clyde, who promised himself that it would be his last swallow. He could already feel the booze circulating through him, giving him a nice and relaxed buoyancy, and he didn't want to be navigating the precipitous rocky trail back to the mesa with a gut full of brandy.

'Your dad has one little run-in with a Babylonian dream parasite and you're marked for life.' Clyde gave Spector an uncertain look. 'Let's put my bright future as a dream assassin on the maybe pile for now.'

A duo of digital chimes rang out like electronic crickets. Clyde and Spector both reached into their pockets to retrieve their phones. It was a priority message from Hourglass intelligence.

Clyde read the brief and put the phone back in his pocket. 'Looks like I'm getting a late flight back home.'

4

H E STARED AT THE CINEMA screen. Content, serene. Cherishing these moments of solitude. Just him, watching the dramas unfold on the big screen, his sneakers propped up on the empty seat in front. Most of the other seats were empty on this early weekday afternoon. But then, the Encore Cinema had been barely keeping afloat for the last three years. An old, rundown, 19th-century theater converted in the 1940s for the fiscally bright future of the silver screen, it now scraped by on a particularly loyal crowd who enjoyed old genre movies and midnight matinees. But this place's days were numbered, and that saddened David Bentley, for whom the Encore was a comfortable refuge. Movies were the only thing that made sense to David. They offered elation and solace, stirring all the wonderful and magical sensations of humanity that he could only experience through a good script, a visionary director, and a cast of talented actors. In Dave's opinion, humanity was at its best in the movies. Their motives were clear, concise, digestible, and understandable. In real life, people only confused him and let him down.

He was picking at a bucket of popcorn that had all the flavor of packing peanuts when he felt the ache right in the pit of his stomach. It wasn't pain; it was a soaring rail of undiluted joy and love and excitement all swirling about in a perfect concoction of adrenalized sentiment, almost coaxing a tear from him as the movie's heroes rallied together for one final push, risking their lives for one another and vanquishing the ruthless villain to a euphoric thematic score. *Scions of Saturn II* was one of his favorite movies—just edging past the original—a pulpy sci-fi fantasy with an anarchistic wit and the sort of unforgettable characters he yearned to match with his own screenplay one day. But despite the goose bumps and the lump in his throat, he wouldn't allow tears. Dave had never been one for external displays of emotion.

Fifteen minutes later, the credits rolled, and just like that, the magic began to fade. He checked the time on his phone—3:15. Plenty of time to get across town for his afternoon appointment.

He ambled out of the screening, ditching his half-full popcorn in the trash. In the lobby he accidentally caught the eye of the young guy at the concession stand—Elijah, according to his name-tag. Elijah had only started working here about a month ago, but Dave had seen him enough times now to offer a polite nod, having learned as a young boy that good manners were a valued custom amongst polite society. Elijah, a cocksure type not even out of his teens, offered a sneer in return. Good manners: it never ceased to surprise Dave how many people looked at him like he was an idiot for practicing them.

He tried to hold on tight to the movie's slipping sense of peace but knew it would have left him completely the moment his shoes hit the pavement outside. Exiting the cinema, he spotted a young woman about to enter and stepped aside to hold the door open for her. She flounced past without even acknowledging his existence, talking as loudly as possible on her cell phone to make sure her inane business was now the world's business.

As a lifelong resident of the city of Buffalo, New York, Dave no longer expected common courtesy, but it still bugged him how rude some people could be.

Dave let the door swing closed, buttoned up his dark trench coat, and adjusted his black beanie against December's crisp bite. He tried to clear his thoughts while walking the couple of frozen blocks to the bus stop. With nothing but a bunch of stops between him and the Blue Sky Wellness Center, it would be an ample opportunity to spill some of his bottled-up bile onto the page.

Screenwriting was his anchor, and in his heart of hearts he knew it to also be his delusion, a flight of fancy for a new life far away from here. But that didn't alter the fact that it was all he had to keep him going.

He didn't even make it to the bus stop before the dregs of his cinematic dopamine fix were rudely obliterated by a heavy shoulder check. Yanked from his thoughts, Dave fought to keep his balance and turned to see the frothing anger of the man he had accidentally collided with. They say bad things happen in threes. The man, a well-built thirty-something in a leather jacket, exuded the sort of intolerant macho bravado that Dave imagined must always leave his clothing peppered with a fine mist of testosterone and excessive cologne. Dave was too shocked to really take in the tirade of expletives being leveled at him, more concerned with keeping the man from getting physical. Dave never was one for fighting. After a few more choice words, the man stormed off, leaving Dave standing there on the sidewalk feeling an inch tall, heart pounding, mouth dry. Dave felt one of his moods coming over him. He had to find a quiet corner, and quick, his hands clenching almost hungrily at his side.

His legs carried him of their own accord towards a filthy alley between a dry-cleaner's and a phone-repair shop and didn't stop until he was halfway down it, out of sight of the street traffic. Breathing like a tormented bull, he tasted the cloying sweetness of ventilated steam and spoilt garbage, and started pacing in circles, limbs shuddering, palsied with rage. Positively brimming. He didn't want to make a public scene. Not again. He was in charge of his anger. Except . . . yep, this episode was slipping his control. It all happened so fast. So rash. So stupid. He lashed out, his knuckles needing to break something, but he didn't have the wherewithal to realize what he was swinging at until the last second.

Denting steel makes a surprisingly muffled thud. His fist was half buried in the back door of the dry cleaners. Horror started to pool between the cracks of his now-spent fury. He wasn't yet processing the fact that he had just hit harder than a sledgehammer; instead, he was anticipating the delayed pain responses of a completely shattered hand and wrist.

Except no pain came, even though he stood there for a full minute, trying to make sense of what he had just done. Pulling his fist from the cratered door, he stared in numb confusion at his unmarked fist and wriggled his fingers. Never felt better.

Suddenly remembering that he had just committed property damage, he hustled out of the alley, back onto the street, his mind a static confusion.

Moving on autopilot, he made it to the bus stop just in time to catch his ride. He found a window seat near the back of the bus, where he sat and clutched his cold, shaking, *undamaged* hand. A light sweat had broken out despite the chill. He had blown a few gaskets in his time, but nothing like this had ever happened before. With a self-deprecating smile, he pushed the event away. There was obviously a rational explanation. He didn't know what it was, but there had to be one. Forget about it. Write.

He unlocked his phone and opened the notepad. Letting the outside world fall away, he continued hacking away at his latest script, the sort of story that gave him hope: a story of bravery in the face of cataclysm, with an endearing bunch of would-be heroes and set-pieces that hopefully wouldn't make any potential producers laugh their asses off at the requisite financial costs. Dave liked his dramatic showdowns. Who didn't? That's when something occurred to him. Something he hadn't thought of until now—but now that he had, he couldn't help but find it amusing. How strange it was that for someone who carried a general dislike of people, most of his scripts centered on saving them. Fiction: it was so much more relatable than reality.

. . .

Dave sat comfortably in Annette Bancroft's warm office, his face a careful mock-up of pleasant amicability. He listened carefully to her as he always did: the warm greeting, the friendly catch-up, indulging her questions about his current mood, whether he had experienced any triggering events since their last session, and if so, had he applied the calming exercises to regain control.

Dave liked Annette, not in a sexual way, as he was a young man in his twenties and she was at least forty years his senior, but she exuded a pacific calm that, combined with her sincere interest in him, made him want to appease her, to show her that he was capable of conquering his temper.

It was because of this that he didn't dare mention what had happened on the way here. Instead, he tried to feign his continued personal growth as a vibrant Zen flower garden. Was his act believable bullshit? He believed it to be passable on occasion, though he never was a good actor; his one foolish, humiliating attempt at a high school play had highlighted that fact, and even to this day it was a memory that occasionally resurfaced out of the blue to shame him. What Annette referred to as an *internal event*: a trigger caused by his own perceived failures and frustrations.

Right now, his nonexistent thespian abilities were surely doing little to disguise the fact that he was only one rude asshole away from a good, solid rage-on. But he knew that Annette knew this. She was a multistate licensed professional counselor, a member of the advisory committee for the American Counseling Association Foundation, a columnist for a counseling magazine Dave had never actually read, and even an author of several successful books on anger management. Annette Bancroft could no doubt see through Dave like polished glass.

His restless eyes skimmed across the framed certificates on the wall behind her desk, stopping on a quote from Jung: "The difference between a good life and a bad life is how well you walk through the fire." Every time Dave looked at this, he couldn't help but cynically reflect on how anyone walking through fire would be burned to a crisp.

'It's okay, Dave.'

Annette's assurance stumbled him. 'Sorry?'

She cut a glance to his erratic finger-twitching—Dave's lifelong anxiety made him prone to finger-drumming and foot-tapping. 'Please, if something is on your mind, liberate yourself of it.'

Dave's hand and foot stopped dancing. He closed his eyes for a moment and took a breath, visualizing himself sitting in Annette's office, the feel of the comfortable chair's contours, the warmth contrasting with the snow outside her window. His gentle breathing. He was in this moment. Living in it. Self-awareness helping to hush the clutter and clatter freighters rattling about his head.

But self-awareness didn't change what had happened in the alley behind the dry cleaners. He knew he couldn't tell her about what he'd done. She wouldn't believe him—he could barely believe it himself. It was textbook *direct aggression*, and then some!

'It's nothing. I think I had a few too many cups of coffee before I got here. I know I should moderate my caffeine intake.' He calmly reached for his glass of water on the small curved table beside him.

'Have you given any more thought to finding an alternative line of work?' Annette's openly patient expression was an island of understanding and tolerance, without a trace of obsequiousness. Not like the types of faces Dave typically had to deal with.

'I'm still looking, but it's hard,' he admitted. 'I am pretty desperate for something new. Get away from the drunks and the noise.'

Salty's Tavern fluttered about his mind like a pestilent fly. He had a shift there tonight, eight till close—close always varied, depending on what dregs of the clientele were present. Whoever it was, they were all similar shades of asshole to Dave: petty thugs, peddlers, skank whores looking for a cheap drink, a line of coke, and a violent dickhead to cling to. Having lost three other bartending jobs—in much nicer bars—in as many months due to his volatile outbursts, Dave now longed for any of his previous employers.

'You're right, it doesn't gel with my personality,' Dave said. 'Too many chances for unwanted external events.' That was putting it mildly, he thought.

'The important part is that you recognize this,' Annette said. 'Remember, the objective of anger management is not to eradicate it completely. Our anger, if regulated and controlled, can be healthy and useful. Our objective is to learn how to curb unwanted acts of direct aggression. To prevent outbursts that can harm others, property, or ourselves.'

Dave thought about the steel door again. Could it be he was now becoming delusional too, because why wasn't his hand in a million itty-bitty pieces? He'd punched a goddamn dent in a steel door without so much as scraping the skin on his knuckles. Luckily nobody had been pissing or smoking in the alley to witness his frustration.

'But I can still be passive-aggressive, right?' Dave smiled, maybe a little too insistently, smothering his own joke.

Annette laughed politely. 'In small doses it should be fine. Now, what are the three types of aggression: Passive. Direct. And the healthiest type…?'

'Assertive,' Dave answered.

'Correct.' She gave him one of her congenial smirks. 'That's what I want you to achieve. Assertive is constructive, not destructive. If we can get any possible future acts of aggression into the assertive category, then it's a rousing success.'

'I was thinking about maybe finding a job in the Parks Department. Fresh air, exercise … not customer-adjacent.'

'That's a good idea,' Annette enthused. 'Healthy. Could help with clearing your head.'

'That's what I was thinking. Cut grass, rake leaves, prune trees.' *Try not to punch my fist through a stone fountain.* 'Doesn't seem too bad a way to get paid.'

Whilst Annette seemed pleased at this, Dave wasn't entirely sure the counselor was buying his plastic emotions.

'Has anything else been on your mind since we last spoke?' she asked.

One court-appointed anger-management course following a blow-up at a previous job that concluded with Dave throwing a bar stool through the windshield of his boss' parked car, and he had to take note of every little gripe and grievance he experienced should he erupt into a frenzy of frothing animosity; if he wasn't working away on the new screenplay, he was scrawling in the notebook Annette had provided him on their first session. Still, at least Annette was doing her job properly by taking this seriously.

'It's just Christmas, you know,' Dave said, feeling very silly, a bashful smile teasing the corner of his mouth. 'I don't know … surrounded by so many people, but it still makes me feel like the last man on earth.'

'The holiday can be a very trying time,' she said. 'Try to remember you're not alone in your loneliness.' Dave wondered which pamphlet she'd dug that pearl from, but knew he wasn't being fair to her; she was the only person who actually pretended to give a shit about anything he had to say. 'Do you have any cousins or extended family or friends who are free over Christmas?'

Dave shook his head, showing her a congenial *It's okay, I'm cool* smile to try and assuage her. 'I'll probably be working anyway.'

Not wanting to fruitlessly dance around how lonely his Christmas was going to be, he brought up a few of his more recurring—and, unlike the steel door incident, believable!—issues.

'I had a few difficult hours the other day. I was in the supermarket, and it was a little busy—it was a little late, but still busy. I was walking down the aisle, and I must have been thinking about something, distracted, but I saw this woman looking at me as she passed.' Dave considered the memory with sullen clarity. 'I don't know, but it happens a lot. I'll be minding my own business, but I feel like people look at me like I'm weird, like I'm giving off a vibe or something. But it bothers me. Makes me self-conscious.'

Annette nodded thoughtfully. 'You said you were distracted. Your mind on other matters. How do you know the woman in the grocery store's mind wasn't on other matters too? She probably wasn't even aware of you. The same for anybody else you might have thought was giving you looks. Most people are so wrapped up in their own lives that those around them on the street, in the store, on the bus, pass right through their consciousness like water through a sluice.'

'I guess so. Yeah.' It made sense to Dave, but his voice still harbored a slim doubt. 'I practiced my self-awareness after that, right there in the store. Reminded myself what I was doing, where I was. Kept the cloud of bees from swarming.' He shook a hand about his head as though shooing away the swarm. 'It helped, but it's tricky sometimes. Hard not to react.'

'It can be a difficult headspace to maintain early on. When there's one angry hand on the steering wheel, it takes focus to keep it from jerking the car from lane to lane, always speeding, always frustrated. But with practice you'll find it much easier to stay in your lane,' Annette promised. 'You will get the hang of it.'

Dave felt a timorous hope rising up inside of him, naively reaching out for a calmer future in which he fit in with the rest of society, where he was the master of his external and internal triggers. Where he might find a small patch of happiness.

'I hope so. Thanks, Anne.' Dave noticed the clock on the wall between a few other psychoanalytical quotes and beat Annette to the punch. 'Same time next week?'

5

CLYDE SAT ALONE IN THE wood-paneled interior of the private jet, listening to the soft hum of the engines. He was currently somewhere over Missouri, but all he could see was pristine clouds and blue sky. He had been anticipating a late-night flight after receiving the alert, but Spector had to first clear him as reliable with Director Trujillo, who was already in the middle of putting out fires with the Canadian and other U.S. agency heads. Clyde didn't know the first thing about Estelle Page or the Canadian facility she had worked out of, but from the atmosphere he'd witnessed last night and this morning, he knew this was the equivalent of a DEFCON 1 situation. From the basics he'd been given, the late Estelle Page had been responsible for locating Sparks, which underscored the seriousness of the situation. He didn't know if the agency had contingencies in place for losing a headhunter of such high caliber, but he tried imagining doing his job without Ace and, more recently, Nat at his side. Was it possible? Sure. But would it be more difficult without them? One hundred percent, and he would probably be dead already.

As of now, being acquainted with Sparks had just become a privilege. And it was all because of the Cairnwood Society.

All because Edward Talbot had finally stepped back out from the shadows. He might not have pulled the trigger, but his actions had forced Estelle to do what was necessary to mitigate his damage.

No one at the Madhouse, New York's Hourglass branch, had really believed Talbot was dead, due to the lack of a body. The working assumption was that he had slithered away at some point during their killing of Charon at Elzinga Asylum, but it was a real shame to be proven right.

Clyde was suddenly very anxious to be back home with his teammates.

With the only other souls on board this plane being the pilots, his distractions were internal. And he insisted on keeping his tired eyes open, not even entertaining the thought of getting a few hours' sleep, despite getting very little the night before; but that was fine with him, all things considered.

After packing his few belongings, he had called Ace, having heard that he had a prior working relationship with Estelle, being both a Spark and a Canadian loaner. The man was a bit drunk and leery, obviously dealing with his pain in his usual fashion, but at least he sounded happy to hear from Clyde. It sounded like he was in a bar, and from the raucous cheers and *oohs* and *ahhs*, he guessed Ace was holed up in a sports bar watching his beloved Maple Leafs. Clyde was glad to hear his voice for the first time in weeks—Ace not being the chatty small-talk type—but it felt weird to hear notes of actual pain and confusion in his voice. He had become a sort of gruff asshole uncle to Clyde, a guy who would glower all day long but reluctantly step up when it mattered.

Clyde had been initially hesitant about calling Rose after that, but she was a teammate. Things were still awkward in the group dynamic. Technically, she had no direct beef with him, since he hadn't been part of Kev and Barros' treasonous breaching of the agency's cyber security, but her hostility towards Kev had naturally pitted him as another potential thorn in her side. He hoped they could get past all that as a team upon his return, but he knew Kev too well, and unless Rose had developed a brand new identity and set of professional sensibilities in the weeks he'd been away, he wasn't confident this would happen.

They had been the difficult calls.

The one after had been the fun one. Nat was very happy to hear his voice.

The aloof yet casual flirtatiousness she had first exhibited towards him during their working relationship had become a sultry smoldering after their last assignment, and even though he'd had to leave for Indigo

Mesa shortly afterward, their nightly phone calls had become something of a sordid pastime. Clyde had never thought of her using her audiokinetic ability in such a way before, but after their pally jibes back and forth, Nat's voice would lower into a sexy, trashy tone as she undressed on camera, free and easy, teasing Clyde with the best canvas he had ever seen, all lithe curves and bright ink, and Clyde would find her converting his words into just the right vibrato to get her off. A whole new dimension to oral sex. The first time she suggested this, Clyde had felt beyond awkward, thinking about who else could be snooping on the line—they worked for an intelligence agency, after all, and in this game everybody was looking over each other's shoulder. What if it was the NSA? Worse, what if it was Hourglass themselves? What if it was Deputy Director Meadows, Nat's close family friend!

But after the first few times, he stopped caring. When you knew the Null was waiting for you one day, it had a certain way of reframing perspectives.

And finally, after their call ended, there was still one more call to make: Kev. It should have been the easiest for Clyde, but it felt like a challenge. Kev had always been quite an internal, reflective guy, ever since they were kids, but recent events had impacted him heavily, pushing him from excited and purposeful rookie Hourglass agent into a sullen recluse, made worse by his current suspension. Clyde's guilt had resurfaced again as a result of this, for he was the one tethering Kev's soul to this mortal plane. One could argue it beat being stuck in the Null, but Clyde knew Kev wasn't scared of that place. On the contrary, he knew Kev would rather be there, chasing after Kozlov and searching for a way to build a new paradise.

Kev had answered his call and sounded surprisingly upbeat. Clyde didn't delve into the attack on the Canadian site, deciding to save that conversation for in-person, wanting to keep the mood light. They had both agreed to meet up in one of their usual seasonal hot spots upon Clyde's return.

He stared out the window at the clouds for a minute more, sipping his water, then returned to the sketch book splayed open on the fold-out table. On the page, Dremel had never looked so smug, and Clyde had initially been tempted to draw him jerking off one or two of the strange udder-like appendages protruding from his head but had decided against it. Live and let live. It was difficult to draw from memory, not to mention dreams, but Clyde had stood before the sneering, righteous looks of the Glowing Reel's representatives enough times to develop some decent impressions. He had drawn them all by now: hideous, nightmarish, divine. He flicked through their portraits, coming to a stop on the few rough drafts he'd made of the Gilded Hypnos and Obsidian Extremis. He found himself studying his renditions as though still seeing the incredible structure in person, his pencil putting a little more emphasis on the god-like dark wings stretching out from the inverted black pyramid, each pinion a midnight sickle. In one hypnotic session he had used colored pencils to try and capture the endless swirl of light and color that girded the pyramids' connecting peaks, all those souls—a veritable ocean—clipped by the hundreds, the thousands, more, so many beings, the ends of their soul threads snipped, leaking their remaining essences out into that black pyramidal drain. Washed out into the Null.

Without realizing it, Clyde had slipped into a fugue as he stared at the pyramids, losing a full five minutes of flight time. He closed the book, zipping it away in his backpack.

He wanted to see his friends.

6

S TAKEOUTS GOT REALLY OLD, REALLY fast, no matter how important
the assignment. Ace sat behind the wheel of a company car, an old,
bland, and nondescript Honda easy to lose in traffic except in mitigating
circumstances where the driver might be forced to unleash the whip-
lash power of the supreme engine hiding under the hood. Right now,
Ace couldn't handle a go-kart chase, forget a reckless high-speed tire-
burner. He'd overdone it on the booze last night. What had started off
as a beer session to watch the game had turned into an unofficial wake
for Estelle Page.

His head was thudding, and caffeine and a bottle of chilled water
were slow-acting medicine.

Nat was in the back seat, one of her earbuds in, soaking up the hard-
thrashing energy of some punk band or other. She was drumming the
back of Ace's headrest, either to keep him alert or to keep him grouchy.
Ace worked best when he was grouchy.

Ace was staring at a crummy apartment building in a rough section
of downtown Buffalo, the blanket of snow covering the street looking
more gray and dirty than white and pure. 'Watching his building now,'
he spoke, not into his comm-channel but into his phone, which rested
on the dashboard. 'Fingers crossed we pull him in before one of those
Cairnwood assholes finds him.'

Ace waited for a reply. When none was forthcoming, he voiced other concerns. 'Cairnwood have never dared try anything so fucking ballsy as to hit a target like Syrup. Fucking Talbot…' He bared his teeth—of which he was already missing a few, courtesy of his amateur hockey days—like a mad dog chained up in the yard. 'I can't believe it. Estelle. She brought me into this job.'

'You and a lot of good people,' the voice on the phone answered. Male, deep, scratchy.

Nat continued to drum either side of his headrest. He tried to swipe her hands away like a clumsy bear pawing at a wasp.

'How's Ike taking it?' Ace asked. 'He's almost as old as Estelle. Lot of shared road there.' Ike Friedman was the senior agent running Igloo, and Ace's former and longest-serving boss.

'As you might expect. Everybody's hurting here. I loved Estelle. She was like everybody's grandma.' The voice on the phone had a caller ID displaying *The Mountie*.

'A grandma who gave the best presents. I mean, shit, how do we continue recruiting Sparks without her?' Ace had known the Mountie long enough to know that his fellow countryman could recognize a rhetorical question. Need it be answered, the answer was vague and bleak: neither of them knew if she *could* be replaced.

'It wasn't just Estelle, though,' the Mountie replied. 'We lost a whole lot of good agents. Some were friends of mine. Maddie and Jack, they were new additions, but they were good.'

'Talbot needs to go under for certain this time. Then we should all focus on doing whatever it takes to fucking crush Cairnwood, bottom to top. Not just back-and-forth shit-slinging. If they're prepared to take such big swings, then we need to repay them in kind.'

Ace suddenly realized that his hands had almost turned the steering wheel into a frozen disc. He used to have a better handle on his ability… . until Charon had tried to get inside his mind and, in turn, his soul. Nat, too, had been subjected to this failed takeover, which was another reason why Ace was hesitant to let her enthusiastically finger-drum his headrest, in fear of her accidentally detonating his skull all over the car's interior. He dusted off the wheel's icy coating.

'It's one thing to say it, another to do it,' the Mountie said. 'They're global players. An organization that well connected, and that insular? Case in point, we don't even know how Talbot arrived over our border. Road, air, or sea? And even if we did, it wouldn't mean much. The ones who operate that high up always have ways of circumventing security. If they didn't, we wouldn't be burying a lot of good agents.'

'You sure know how to take the fun out of impotent smack talk, you know that?' Ace grumbled.

'Anyway, it looks like Talbot's your problem again.' The Mountie took a thoughtful breath. 'Prove me wrong by killing him.'

'It won't be for lack of trying.'

'Good. We're going to be up to our necks in it here,' the Mountie said. 'We've been exposed. All those bodies, having to burn that whole site to ashes. It makes us look weak.'

Ace agreed. 'A lot of other assholes might start getting ideas.'

'That's how it goes.' An inflection in the Mountie's voice signaled that he was now needed elsewhere. 'I got to take care of something. But I hope you find this Bentley guy before the wrong people do. Look after yourself.'

'I will, Duds. Send my best to Ike and the other guys. Tell 'em I miss 'em.'

The call ended, and Ace was back to listening to Nat's drumming.

He glanced at her in his rearview. 'What are you listening to?' he asked her.

'Cro Mags,' she answered. Ace had always been a devout classic rock fan, including hair metal, but in their shared time together they had both started to begrudgingly find some common ground between their respective music camps. 'Is his name Duds? Like Dudley?' *Tap-tap-tap* went her fingers.

'No, it's Tyler. Call him Dudley after Dudley Do-Right.' Ace was once again reminded of the two-decade age difference between him and the twenty-something woman. Though age wasn't the barrier here, not when she was a devout follower of old-school punk rock. It was her ignorance of *Rocky and Bullwinkle*. 'Old cartoon character.'

'Huh. Caller ID said The Mountie. That true, or just another goofy nickname?'

'That's true.' Ace glanced up and down the street, watching the light traffic. 'He's the real deal. RCMP.'

'They still have to ride horses and wear those ridiculous red outfits?'

'No to both.' Ace almost smirked at a memory. 'But he still does.'

'Oh yeah? How come?' *Tap-tap-tap.*

'He's from a bygone era.'

'Huh … I could take that any number of ways. Are all the guys at Igloo of a "bygone era"?'

'Not in that way, but they have their own issues.'

'No one ends up on an Hourglass strike team because they're punctual and polite.' Nat started drumming with one hand; a glance in the rearview showed her guzzling her vanilla latte. 'So, do you think your old boss will call you back over the border? Seems like things are heating up, up north.'

'No. At least not yet. Cairnwood accomplished their goals up there. If Ike wants me back at Igloo, his request will have to go through Meadows, and something tells me things will be warming up down here more than up there.' He rubbed his aching eyes.

'Speaking of, how about putting the heating on?' Nat asked, drumming with both hands again.

'Would you quit the damn drumming? You get so excited and jumpy every time you have your earbuds in, it's like sitting in a car full of fucking nitro.'

'Jesus, old man, okay.' She held out her extended fingers in a pantomime of laying down her drumsticks. 'But in case I was being too subtle with my heating request, I'm trying to keep myself from catching pneumonia. Freezing my fricking tits off back here.'

Ace noticed for the first time that he could see her warm breath. He flicked the heating on and dusted off a bit more frost from the steering wheel. 'I didn't realize. Guess I was getting a bit worked up too.'

Nat wiped a palm across the condensation on her window. She had jumped into the back seat so they could both have full view of David Bentley's building. 'The only parked car visibly freezing up on the inside is a bit conspicuous, huh?'

'I got it under control,' Ace grunted. He just hoped he hadn't sapped the car's battery.

'It catches you unawares, huh?' Nat asked. Ace held her gaze in the mirror. 'The little power boosts. You ever wonder how far you might be able to take it? How powerful the Luminaries actually were compared to a couple of mangy mutts like us?'

Luminaries: the extinct, vastly powerful race of cosmic beings who had warred against the Order of Terminus, those ruthless dead lords who changed their dark underworld to a dark omni-world, controlling the entirety of the afterlife.

'We're not mutts anymore,' Ace retorted.

'We're not pedigree either.' Nat glanced out her window. 'Man, this Bentley kid better show up soon. If I can't drum and stamp my feet, I'm going to talk.' She pulled her single earbud out and shivered under her leather jacket, rubbing her hands for warmth.

Ace gulped his coffee and whacked the heat up to full for her. Battery be damned. If it died, it wouldn't be the worst thing that had happened to him in the past twenty-four hours.

'We're only about ninety minutes away from your hometown, aren't we?' Nat asked.

'Give or take, yeah.' Ace had been born and bred in Mississauga.

'You miss it?'

Ace had never really given it much thought. 'I don't know. It's a nice city, but there's nothing there for me anymore. Sometimes I think about how life might have been if I wasn't a Spark. If I never pinged on Estelle's radar and got dropped in Hourglass' lap. But where does that kind of thinking ever get a person?'

Nat chewed her lip. 'No place good. I wish I'd listened to my parents and joined the agency sooner. Got trained up. Would have saved a lot of dead friends.' Nat's refusal to acknowledge and harness the latent power brewing in her blood had manifested in the worst possible way: soaking up enough throbbing decibels to accidentally explode a warehouse party full of her pals.

'You should stop carrying that around with you,' Ace told her. 'You couldn't have known it would happen like that. You were a stupid kid when that happened. Still are a stupid kid.'

'Old enough to know better. Fuckin' Sparks, man.'

'Fuckin' Sparks,' Ace agreed.

'What do you think this Bentley guy can do?' she asked.

'In a perfect world? Shove Talbot's head up his own ass with the power of thought.'

Nat spoke into the comm channel. 'Anything yet, Rosie?'

'Nada,' came Rose's reply. She was stationed around the rear of the building.

The Astronomer's monitoring hub was observed remotely by all major Hourglass offices, with any new Spark data being recorded, encrypted, and then broadcast by her black box. And according to the CCTV footage, it appeared that Talbot was holding some type of mysterious scroll up towards the ceiling map. The scroll's purpose was unclear, but the working theory was that it was a means of data recording—but could it transcribe the Luminary language? At the time of the Astronomer's death, only a few individuals, including Dave Bentley—who was geographically the closest to Cairnwood's New York operations—were flashing in that broad region, which could be considered fortunate, sparing the agency a lot of frantic guesswork and running around, but true good fortune would have spared Hourglass the loss of Estelle Page. Dave Bentley had no reason to fear abduction just yet, but with Talbot and his handlers soon to be sniffing around him, it didn't hurt to cover all the bases.

'The ISU have performed another sweep," Rose updated. 'Still no sign of him. No bogeys either.'

The ISU, or Intensive Scare Unit, was Rose's trio of former U.S. Army buddies, now deceased. Post-Life Entities—PLEs, or ghosts—had a tendency to draw attention, especially when in such ghastly states as the ISU, but they were adept at slipping through floors and walls to avoid detection, only peeping out when safe to do so.

'You think maybe Talbot already nabbed him?' Nat asked Ace.

He shifted in his seat, wondering how long it would be before he had to take a piss. 'Bentley's bank records and personal files display some pretty OCD behavior.'

'Outright crushingly dull?' Nat asked.

'Works nights Wednesday through Sunday at some shit bar called Salty's Tavern. Mondays and Tuesdays he goes to the movies, gets takeout from the same place, and according to the last four weeks, sees his tantrum sensei at four p.m. on Tuesday. This being Tuesday, he should be on his way back here now.'

Dave Bentley further cemented himself as a creature of habit within the next five minutes when he plodded down the street towards his building, shoulders hunched up against the cold, hands deep in the pockets of his black winter coat. With that coat and his black beanie, he looked to Ace like a refugee from a beatnik poetry reading.

'Rose, I got eyes on him,' Ace said. He had memorized the guy's mug through various photographs from the DMV and the like. He climbed out of the car as inconspicuously as possible for a man as gloomy and mean-looking as he.

Nat slipped out the back, slick as water.

'He's entering the building,' Ace muttered into his comm. 'Stay posted.'

Ace and Nat calmly crossed the snowy street, dodging the traffic with polite ease as Bentley hustled up the salted steps and entered the lobby of his apartment building.

'Dude doesn't look like much,' Nat commented.

'Your boyfriend didn't look like much at first either. Still doesn't.'

'Can't argue with facts.' Nat gave a quick shuffle-step to head Ace off at the entrance. 'Let me do the talking.'

'I can be personable,' Ace protested.

'I'm a hot girl who still has all my teeth.'

Ace grumbled and pushed through the scuffed metal door into the lobby. The lobby's interior wasn't much of an improvement on the exterior. Even the Christmas tree in the corner looked seasonably depressed and as if it might commit suicide before the big day. Bentley was at the wall of mail slots.

'David Bentley?' Nat asked, all sugar and innocence.

Bentley half turned, his eyes regarding them skeptically. Nat was a cute Filipina in ripped jeans—the tears showing hints of colorful tattoos—and a leather jacket, and Ace was a lumbering brute with a dark hockey mullet and handlebar moustache.

'Can we talk in private?' Nat asked.

Bentley squinted. 'Do I know you?'

'Not yet, but I'm hoping we can change that.' Nat lowered her voice. 'We believe you might be in danger.'

Before Bentley could answer, the fire exit behind him crashed inward, banging off the wall like a gunshot. A body came sailing across the damp and dirty tiles, slowing to a stop at Dave's heels. Through the newly open doorway, Ace caught glimpses of Rose flipping, throwing, and pulverizing a huddle of other men dressed as either financiers or funeral mourners.

Bentley put his back to the bars of the stairwell, head swiveling between the wild brawl to his left and the two strangers to his right.

'You need a hand out there, Rosie?' Ace called.

'They with you?' Bentley asked Nat.

The motionless body in the middle of the lobby started to move. Bentley looked appropriately shocked. Its neck was clearly broken, as was one of the arms, and maybe even a leg. The dead man, face blank and utterly unconcerned by his injuries, readjusted the snapped bones, stared at Bentley, and then, after a second's debate, ignored him in favor of Ace and Nat.

'Cairnwood's finest,' Ace said aloud, a weak attempt to maintain some form of friendly communication with Bentley.

'Who?' Bentley asked, eyes bugging. 'What are—'

He broke off as Ace formed a six-inch shiv of ice in his hand and sent it punching through the eye socket of the dead guy. It wasn't blood that dripped down the suit's face but a pale liquid, largely colorless.

'You need to come with us,' Ace commanded.

But Dave had seen enough. He spun on his heel and, more nimbly than Ace had dreamed possible, clambered over the stairwell's railing and sprinted up the stairs.

'Shit! Get after him!' Ace slapped Nat on the back and leapt over the corpse to give Rose a hand outside.

∎ ∎ ∎

Dave careened around the corner of the third-floor hallway and bounced off the wall like a panicked gazelle fleeing a cheetah … only in this case it wasn't a cheetah in hot pursuit but a hot Asian woman wearing sneakers and torn jeans, and calling for him to stop. The hell with that.

There was no way he was going to dead-end himself by entering his apartment, so he flew down the corridor, hitting the crash bar of the fire exit with all the intent of a committed stuntman, cold air sandpapering his face as he braced against the fire escape railing. Below him was the small residential parking lot at the rear of the building, a chain-linked rectangular space containing only a handful of old, worn-out models, but also a pair of incongruous Mercedes, their doors flung open and the occupants—more of those suited guys—engaged in a grunting, bone-crunching, bar-burning slugfest with the big mullet guy and a petite yet inhumanly strong woman with a silver ponytail—Dave was awed again as he watched her pick up one of the dazed suits and launch him at the chain-link fence like a cannonball. Dave heard the thudding sneakers of the Asian woman pounding down the corridor towards him. He had to move! Speeding down the fire escape, his foot slipped on a patch of ice, almost sending him down the rest of the steps on his ass. Leaping off the last landing onto the dirty snow, he chanced a look over his shoulder, finding the Asian mystery woman making good time on the fire escape.

Pissed-off and confused as to who the fuck he was running from, Dave's skeptical mind was ablaze with scientific curiosities: his fist denting a steel door, the big guy with the missing teeth crafting an ice shank out of thin air, that dead guy in a suit repairing his broken neck and limbs as though straightening his tie, a woman who could probably arm-wrestle a grizzly and win, and who knew what this chick chasing him could do?

Was Santa doling out killer gifts to all the boys and girls this Christmas?

He had the sudden mad idea to stand his ground and take a wild swing at the Asian woman. But for the moment, her two pals were preoccupied with the suits.

'Mr. Bentley?' a man's voice, cultured and polite, beckoned from the mouth of the alley that ran parallel to the building.

Dave spun, bewildered, to see another well-dressed man standing there on the street. Unlike the other, this one was very much alive. He appeared to be in his thirties, attractive and slick in a pampered yuppie sort of way. A sleek car, another top-of-the-range Mercedes, was parked at the curb behind him, engine running.

'That garishly dressed man and his female companions are murderers. They and their associates.' The man's voice was level, solicitous. 'I can explain everything in the car, but we need to get you out of here now.'

Dave glanced back at the fire escape. His pursuer was nearing the last landing. Worse, the sounds of fighting had ceased, and Dave saw Hockey-

Mullet and Silver-Hair crossing the lot towards him. The petite but stockily-built young woman might be pretty under other circumstances, but right now her scowl would have given pause to the bouncers at Salty's.

In the blink of an eye, Dave decided to take his chances with the nice car and the man in the expensive suit. He charged down the alley and leaped through the open door to the car's leather back seat, solicitously held open for him by his would-be savior. Righting himself, Dave glimpsed the well-dressed man toss something into the alley before sliding into the plush seat opposite him, dispensing a polite wave to their three pursuers. The trio slid to a stop, the young Asian woman almost slipping on black ice. Whatever had been thrown at them emitted a series of glowing runes that burned briefly in the air, causing the three freaks to leap away. Effervescent bubbles boiled out from the small trinket on the ground, creating a thermal vent of shimmering heat that misted the alley with a scalding hiss. Meanwhile, the car pulled smoothly from the curb.

Dave was still catching his breath as the city slid by through tinted glass. He was trying to connect the dots of a pattern too absurd to make sense.

The man seated opposite swept his hair back with a black leather glove and smiled cordially, extending his other gloved hand. 'Mr. Bentley, Edward Talbot. It's an honor.'

Dumbfounded, feeling as if he had not just passed through a car door but through a looking glass, Dave shook the hand. His mind was awhirl with too many questions to articulate.

Talbot gestured to the stylish minibar built between the two rear-facing seats. 'Eggnog?'

7

THE CROWDS MILLING AROUND ROCKEFELLER Center's ice rink were suitably colorful in warm seasonal wear. This close to Christmas, there was no shortage of eager sorts dressing themselves up like Santa's unofficial workforce. Clyde scanned the shifting walls of people, his eyes zooming about in search of one person in particular. One person who, for once, could bundle himself up in face-concealing scarves and heavy coats without looking suspicious.

Kev was here somewhere.

Clyde squeezed and slid through a few more knots of people before spotting him hanging back by the statue of Prometheus and the sky-scraping Christmas tree. Winter or not, only Kev would be accessorizing with his aviator shades, and he seemed to be in a trance, staring fixedly at the dashing skaters made up of cheerful families, friends, and couples. Clyde had a good idea whom Kev was watching on the ice.

Clyde was edging and weaving his way towards Kev when he felt that itch. With a casual glance, he spotted one of Kev's minders keeping vigil along the upper rim of the sunken ice rink. It was barely perceptible, but he gave Clyde an acknowledging nod. There would be another agency babysitter somewhere close by, and most likely other surveillance resources employed by Deputy Director Meadows that Clyde, and probably even Kev, didn't know about.

Clyde was practically on top of Kev before his friend noticed him, snapping out of his reverie.

'Hey, man!' Kev said with some relief. They bumped fists and leaned in for a quick bro-hug. If Kev hadn't been capable of telekinetically solidifying his clothing, Clyde's embrace would have folded Kev's coat in two to reveal the ghost hiding underneath. 'You're back!'

'Why so surprised? I told you last night I was getting jetted from Darnell.'

Kev shrugged, voice muffled by the thick scarf mummifying the bottom half of his face. 'I thought it might have been too good to be true. You look rested. Spector's hibernation retreat must have done you well.'

'A few bumps and starts, but it's okay now.' Clyde had kept the details of Ramaliak's politicizing to a minimum during their phone conversations, and despite Kev's curious head tilt, he didn't want to recount the whole thing with each team member. 'I'll tell you about it later. I knocked on your door when I got back. Started to get concerned when I found your place empty. Thinking maybe you'd tried to make a break for it. Got dragged before Meadows and a tribunal or something.' A small pause. 'Then I remembered the date.' They watched the clusters of people whizzing by with earmuffs, reindeer antlers, and smiles on their faces. 'Have you spoken to them yet?'

Out on the ice, the joyful quartet of Kev's parents, his younger sister by two years, Rhianne, and an unknown young man were leisurely doing laps of the rink. Rhianne and the presumed boyfriend were holding hands.

Kev shook his head. 'I still don't think I can. But it's good to see them. To know they're okay. It's nice to see that some things haven't changed. I used to love coming here with them. Bit of skating, eat some food, buy some presents. Who'd have thought it? Sociable guy like me.'

Clyde relished the sarcasm. It meant his friend was in a decent mood.

'I remember that one time I came here with you guys and nearly broke my neck,' Clyde reminisced.

Kev gave a throaty chuckle. 'That was classic. What were we, sixteen? First and last time on the rink.'

'Got that right,' Clyde said. 'Just my luck that I end up getting partnered with a sub-zero ex-hockey thug. Who's that dude with Rhi?'

'I don't know, but I'm guessing it's her boyfriend.'

Clyde noticed the mischievous edge in Kev's voice and immediately started to scan the crowds for Kev's other minders. 'Whoever he is, I'm sure his background has been carefully raked over by company intelligence,' he said, wanting to keep Kev from having any "fun" at the expense of Rhi's beau.

'It's okay,' Kev said. 'I'm not going to do any shenanigans. Believe me, I'm sick of the doghouse. But he better not get too grabby with her.'

Clyde smiled. 'Cool. 'Cause I got some good news and bad news for you.'

'I'm a sucker for tradition: good news.'

Clyde gestured towards Kev's ankle. 'By authority of Director Trujillo, that ankle monitor's coming off.'

Kev muttered something that sounded very much like 'thank fuck.'

'An agent will be meeting us later to pop it off. Your suspension's over.'

'Meadows must be over the moon, having to take me back in.'

'We're a two-man ass-kicking machine. He wants me in the field, and he knows I can't do what I do without you.'

'Aww, that's sweet. And I'm betting this connects directly to the bad news.'

'One of our facilities was hit last night.' Clyde hardened his voice a little. 'A place in Canada. Whole staff wiped out, including three Sparks.'

'That couldn't have been easy.'

'I wouldn't have thought so. But I think sometimes it's more a case of having the guts to do something than it is possessing the firepower to do it. Those in the know understand how big of a mistake it is to take a run at Hourglass.'

'Take a run at? Sounds like they ran straight through.'

'It wasn't Igloo. It was a smaller facility, one intentionally trying to stay shrunk to avoid detection. At least that was the idea. But somebody must have known about it.'

'Secrets never last forever.' Kev gazed at one of his watchers with disdain, grew bored, and averted his gaze back to his skating family. '*Hmmm.* Who do we know whose brand is equal parts wealth, dirt, and a professional aversion to Hourglass... Cairnwood?'

'I'll do you one better. Talbot.'

'So he *did* survive. I wonder who Meadows will be sorry to see more: him or me?' Kev gave a cynical chuckle. 'And here I hoped you were going to tell me it was somebody fresh and new.'

Clyde shook his head. 'I'm not quite ready to branch out into alternative large-scale villainy at this time.'

'I feel like you've glossed over something crucial,' Kev said. 'What was this facility?'

'The Syrup Farm.'

'Okay. It's probably a safe bet Talbot isn't opening a chain of pancake houses, so why target that place?'

'Estelle Page.'

Unsurprisingly, Kev looked nonplussed.

'The name means nothing to me either,' Clyde admitted. 'But she was something of a legend and a closely guarded secret. She was an agency vet, and one of the three Sparks. Her ability was honing-in on other Sparks. That's how the agency recruits them, or at least it was. The intel department at Indigo kept a live feed in her monitoring room. The CCTV footage showed that she killed herself before Talbot could steal her whole watch list, but we think he might have gotten the details of a few newly lit Sparks. Most likely a guy out in Buffalo called David Bentley.'

'You think the weasel's trying to poach some potential talent or just keep us from recruiting him?'

'Can't say. But whatever the outcome, it won't be good.'

'What about Ace and Nat? They trying to pick him up?'

Clyde noticed how Kev didn't include Rose's name. 'Now that you mention it, we're meeting them at the Barrel.'

'Okay, cool. So they already brought Bentley in?'

'Nah, they tried, but they had a run-in with Talbot and some of his flunkies. Cairnwood has Bentley.'

This wasn't good news in any conceivable way, but it was clear Kev just wanted something to do other than be constantly observed by his begrudging employers. He cast a parting glance at his gleeful family, looking every inch the outsider.

'Then it looks like we're meeting at the right place,' he said. 'I'm betting Ace is already four beers deep.'

8

T HE BOTTOM OF THE BARREL was a microcosm of old-school punk venom and raucous aesthetic. Clyde cared little for the music, but was learning to tolerate it for Natalie's sake. He had only managed three steps into the bar when Nat came flying at him like a surprised monkey out of a tree, wrapping her legs about his waist and kissing him so forcefully Clyde couldn't tell where his tongue ended and hers began.

After several blissful seconds, she dropped off him, spun to Wasserman, the bartender and owner, and flashed a two-fingered V. Wasserman, a crooked Santa hat hanging over his bottle glasses and spiky skunk-dyed hair, diligently set to pouring two pints of his own local brew, called Riot. It was potent, it was still early, and Clyde wasn't really in the mood to drink, but on the other hand, he hadn't seen Nat in weeks—at least in person—and Ace and Rose were already crowding a booth, several pints deep but talking soberly. He noticed the easy exchange of words between Kev and Ace as Kev took his perch at the edge of the booth, but not so much with Rose; the quiet static between the two of them was almost enough to raise the hair on his neck.

'What's happening with the dreams?' Nat asked Clyde when they were seated at the booth, pints in hand. He felt one of Nat's Converse nudging one of his. 'You like Freddy Krueger with a gun now?'

Clyde sipped his pint, now glad that he had it. 'I don't think so. It's . . . ' His eyes bounced from Nat to Kev hunched over the table's edge. '*Well,*

65

Spector wasn't entirely forthcoming during our first meeting.' The "our" encompassed Kev, since both of them had been introduced to the dream whiz simultaneously. 'It turns out my dad accidentally crossed paths with a stone idol belonging to this parasite—a dream demon called the Coma Weaver. Dad made the mistake of picking it up, and *bam*. It did something to him, and he didn't even know it. But whatever the juju was, he passed it on to me. If I hadn't started taking those uninvited soirées into the Median, I'd probably never know anything about it. Hourglass sure as shit wasn't going to tell me.'

At that precise moment, Clyde felt the booth's atmosphere cramp up a little more on account of Kev and Rose's unresolved issues, sensing how Rose was likely waiting for Kev to shovel a little more shit up against the lip-locked brass of Hourglass' totem pole.

But Kev didn't say anything. He just sat there, a mystery behind shades and scarf, mulling over Clyde's story. Aided by the rest of his strong pint, Clyde went into a bit more detail, elaborating on Dremel and the other regents of the House of the Glowing Reel and their naked distaste for his tainted mortal soul being an irregular house guest.

'I guess you're just going to have to have dirty dreams about me from now on.' Nat winked and drank. 'But do you have better control over it now, the random visits? And what about that little floating immaterial episode you had back at Elzinga?'

Clyde flashed back on that night at the old asylum, his intangible hand reaching through the Hangman's mind, deep, deeper, all the way to the Median's tapestry of souls to shake Charon's pawn awake. And shortly after, his spectral hands blazing with white soul fire, seizing Charon's eye.

'TBD,' Clyde answered. 'But what I did during that episode is a real hot button for Dremel and the others.'

'So apart from a few names and faces of some snooty dream creeps, what exactly did you learn with Spector?' Kev asked.

Clyde pulled out a loose piece of blue string from his pocket and started to make a cat's cradle.

'I don't get it,' Ace said.

'This helps me achieve a calm state of mind.' Clyde calmly focused on the loops, his fingers slow, smooth, and deliberate. 'We're normally so quick to overcomplicate things. Like, I usually have trouble getting to sleep, shutting out the thoughts and letting go. But something as simple as this,' he said, stretching his fingers taut against the trapping of string, 'helps me focus, clear my head, and remain in control, easing into a deeper, more lucid sleeping state where I can choose whether or not I plunge all the way into the Median or stay adrift in the outer layer of unconscious dreams.'

'And that's just a normal piece of string?' Ace asked, using a knuckle to wipe away beer foam from his moustache.

'It's what it does, not what it is.'

'Very fortune cookie. Three weeks in dreamland with sensei Spector and he comes back with a piece of fucking twine.' Ace raised his glass.

A small smile crept along the corner of Clyde's mouth. 'And a brokered parlay with the House to not kill me if I go back there. Hardly an open-door policy, but it's a start.' He untied his fingers. 'And that's me. So what's all this about you guys letting some new Spark escape?'

'It sure sounds lovely and cozy spending three weeks in bed, but we didn't let him escape.' Ace sulked, his big beefy arms crossed over his Maple Leafs jersey like hairy caveman clubs. 'He was spooked from the jump. Can't really blame him. But we could have caught him if he hadn't done a stupid fucking thing like climb into the back of Talbot's car. Nice car, but who the fuck would trust an oily bag of shit like him?'

Clyde chose not to point out the unappealing sight of having somebody like Ace running towards you to "help."

'What I'd have done to him if I'd got my hands on him,' Rose commiserated with a hearty chug of her pint, her hand easily capable of grinding the dense mug into powdered glass. The trio of the ISU were on leave for the remainder of this public social gathering, sequestering in their little bunker located somewhere between Rose's soul and who-the-hell-knew. 'But maybe it's a good job I didn't. You saw the reports on the Syrup Farm?'

Clyde nodded. Kev shook his head, if only to bitterly clarify that he might as well have been on the moon, he was so out of the official loop. Clyde knew Nat had visited Kev at his apartment more than a couple of times, but other than that, he could have been a complete stranger at their booth for all of the palpable awkwardness.

'Talbot's an oily shit bag, but he's an oily shit bag with some juice of his own,' Rose said. 'The way he drained the life right out of that Spark.'

'We knew he had to be more than surface charm and a big piggy bank,' Clyde said. 'Guy's Cairnwood. But now we know he's the sort of problem to be dealt with from a distance. Don't want him touching you.' Rose could flip a Humvee like it was a beer coaster, but getting into a backyard wrestling match with something like Talbot wasn't advisable.

'Let's say Bentley isn't currently in an unmarked grave,' Kev said. 'How big of a problem could he be if he buys the Cairnwood timeshare?'

To Clyde's surprise, it was Rose who answered, but there was still a definite air of distrust in her voice. 'According to Meadows, Estelle Page's compilations never disclosed intel on skill-sets. That was always potluck. But he's a Spark, and that's dangerous enough.'

Rose wasn't wrong. Clyde had noticed the new violet pigments infrequently tracing through Nat's eyes, a feature she'd never possessed before her battle with Charon. And Ace wasn't without his own subtle yet different physical characteristic. His skin seemed a little paler, and Clyde could swear he felt a slight cold spot just by being near him. Clyde had fought some deadly enemies, but he wouldn't ever want to get on the wrong side of Nat or Ace, especially now that their powers had been accidentally tweaked by Charon.

'Then it's a good job you guys have me and Clyde back, huh?' Kev gestured towards his ankle monitor. 'So when's this guy with the key showing up?'

Rose huffed, just a little. She reached into her pants and held up a peculiar doodad, a key that might have doubled as some type of thaumaturgical lock pick. Clyde wasn't sure if Rose's holding of the key surprised him or not: on one hand it made sense, since she could have picked it up from the Madhouse directly, but on the other, he assumed she might be a little irritated at being the one to bring Kev back into the fold.

'Not here,' Rose said. 'We'll do it in the van.'

Kev nodded. 'This mean we're cool?'

Rose gave him a sharp once-over. 'Meadows needs reliable agents in the field to bring Bentley in. I don't mind admitting that we need you and Clyde, but that doesn't mean I'm thrilled to be working with you.

Frankly, I don't understand how I'm supposed to trust somebody who is actively opposed to our agency's aims.'

'You think I'd let something happen to you because of a difference in perspective?' Kev asked.

Rose returned the ankle-monitor key to her pocket and stared deep into the frothy remains of her pint. 'I trust you to have my back when the shit's flying. It's the quiet moments I'm not so sure about.'

Kev leaned forward on his elbows. 'I've spent these last weeks being babysat by moody assholes in suits, unable to do any type of divination beyond a Google search, and even that was stringently monitored. Right now I'm so bored I'd happily follow Meadows and the Hourglass credo as long as it meant I had something to do besides being treated like a terrorist on a watch list.'

'You'll still be under scrutiny.' Rose quaffed the rest of her pint the way a post-pillage Viking might have. 'At first there was even talk of only removing your tag when we needed you in the field. Believe it or not, it was Meadows who decided against that. He thought you deserved the benefit of the doubt.'

'And you don't?' Kev asked, voice flat, body calm and motionless.

Rose leveled her hard stare into his shades. 'Just don't fuck this up.' She made a helicopter twirl with her finger. 'One more round to talk shop?'

Ace and Nat competitively necked their pints in answer.

Nat burped out the side of her mouth. 'I'll go.' Turning to Clyde, 'Helping hand?'

Clyde made a quick read of Kev in a way only familiar to old friends, looking for any little tics or idiosyncrasies that meant it wouldn't be a smart move to leave him here with Rose, with Ace as their only conversational buffer.

'I'm getting a little tired of being watched,' Kev said, turning his attention to Clyde. His ethereal gaze peered over the edge of his aviators. 'Give her a hand. I can behave myself.'

Clyde slid out of the booth and followed Nat to the bar.

9

THE ROAD WAS HARD. IN fact, the road was hardly even a road at all. Kozlov felt the sweat pouring down him, pooling under his cumbersome necronaut armor, his aged body trembling with burning lungs. Somehow even more troublesome, his shorn hair had grown back to an irritable length, long enough to drape into his eyes like mud- and dust-coated foliage.

He stuck close to the narrow canyon wall, keeping his blade gripped tight while his other hand clutched a piece of sharp bone, a remnant of some mysterious creature. With a weary breath, he kept a nervous vigil behind him, wondering if he'd lost the beast. The Arkhitektor remained at his side, his wizened eyes trained for any new threats hidden among the passage's craggy slates. A hoary shattered moon hung dead in the purplish sky, its clusters of meager light doing little to light the way.

Kozlov ventured on quietly, listening for the sounds of the predator pursuing them: the chaotic train of rasps and meaty thwacks as it scrabbled across the terrain. But all he could hear was his own bursting heart.

He and the Arkhitektor shared a look. Safe. For now.

Nearing the edge of the crepuscular chasm, Kozlov noticed for the first time the number of skeletons embedded between the slates of the canyon walls. A million pressed creatures, buried under landslides. He would never know if these towering slate stacks had tumbled from a mountain or risen from a retreated sea, but such peculiarities had long since stopped teasing his academic curiosity. Academia and logic were a thing of the past for him now, locked away in the dusty bureau of his former KGB career. Erebus was a place of horror and hunting. If there were rules to this domain, scientific principles to govern and order, he hadn't found them yet.

Putting such musings aside, he led his watchful companion out of the chasm onto a craggy bluff. Another spectacular vista spread out as far as the eye could see. But the first thing to catch Kozlov's attention was what waited for them at the bottom of the bluff's steep slope: an expansive field of mossy stone blocks, each column gently rising and falling arrhythmically, as though powered by a giant subterranean heart shuddering in the throes of a violent attack. Other than that, the way forward seemed safe enough. The sky was clear of skeels, bodybags, or any of the other airborne terrors scouting for an easy soul or piece of native meat to rip into; in fact, it had been so long since either Kozlov or his companion had laid eyes on those creatures that he suspected they were species native to the previous kingdom.

Beyond the field of rising and sinking columns, the grim, giant palace they were aiming for stood straight ahead.

The distant palace begged for investigation. To eyes less accustomed to the Null than Kozlov's, its design would have seemed laughable, the drunken result of some prankster architect. But nothing about this place could amuse anyone who had survived its terrors as long as Kozlov.

What appeared to be the wreckage of a vast flying saucer was embedded into the highest tower at a near 55-degree angle—whether crashed or intentionally embedded, it was hard to tell. Glowing orbs and radiation-green beams lazily rotated from the saucer. He recalled the great space race between his former country and the USA, and the latter's cultural obsession with alien monsters from outer space, but neither government had ever actually encountered extraterrestrials to his knowledge. Humanity: how little they knew.

The strangeness of the castle didn't deter Kozlov. Something about it called to him, declaring itself as the sovereign base of another monarch of the Order of Terminus.

When the Arkhitektor gestured to Kozlov's left, his gut instinct was validated. For there stood a soul pipeline, just one small part of Charon's expansive soul network.

Even rendered miniature by distance, the snaking pipeline could be seen pulsing with its spectral glow, streaming a steady buffet of fresh souls towards the bizarre imperial holdout.

But what were the appetites of this particular House and monarch? The House of Fading Light, the one-time seat of the vanquished Charon, had gathered the souls of the weakest and infirm. Which unfortunates fed this land?

Finding an answer to this would be no small feat, as standing between them and the strange palace was a wide variety of confusingly ill-fitting landmarks and dangerous ground: a huge sunken arena hosting a rowdy celebration that had all the blood-tinged cries of public executions; huge shipwrecks beached here and there to complement various crashed airliners, blimps, and inhuman aviation vehicles, each of which carried standards, sigils, or statuary; ransacked alien structures with a still-lingering air of the holy or the demonic about them; a distant ruined ghost town of collapsed nuclear reactors and their otherworldly counterparts; and a giant trench of a mouth cut into the earth, from which issued bass-booming laughter that caused the ground they stood upon to tremble.

Kozlov squinted at that giant mouth, wiping a bead of sweat from his eye. It wasn't just laughing, he realized. It was spitting something out. Blood? Spittle? No . . . whatever it was flecking the earth moved and wriggled. It was an odd assortment of beings, too far away to coherently observe from here, but close enough to notice the curiosities in their anatomy and movement.

'Are you ready, friend?' Kozlov asked.

Before the Arkhitektor could speak, a nearby sound stilled them.

Coming from behind.

'No,' Kozlov muttered, his lips cracked and dry.

It was back. It had found them.

It emerged from the dark crevasse behind them, unfolding like a confusing bouquet of white palm fronds. Hands. Abnormally large, a dozen or more, dressed in stained white magician gloves and all connected together at their frilly severed wrists. The tumbleweed of hands pulled and snatched and rolled forth, eager to claim its escaped plaything.

Even with his former military training and all of the fighting experience gleaned from this harrowing realm, Kozlov had no idea how to set about engaging a creature this unorthodox in its movements. A hand could be stabbed, no matter the size. Its fingers chopped off. But a rolling wave of the things, each grabbing from multiple angles, was too erratic to contend with.

Kozlov fled down the shale terrain, mentally cursing the weight of his armor, heading straight for the open plains of rising and sinking stone blocks. The Arkhitektor, drifting several feet off the ground, tried to hold off the jumble of pawing and grabbing hands racing after them like a freakish colony of spiders. Alas, the spirit's efforts were in vain, just as in his previous attempts. The hands wouldn't be stalled, and in fact they pushed back against the ghost, too strong for a mere single soul to overcome. The Arkhitektor changed tack, pulling loose a large piece of shale and smashing it down upon the fingers and knuckles of the closest grasping hand. The shale fragmented before the finger bones did, with several other hands dutifully dusting off the chunks of stone before hurtling the sharp shrapnel after Kozlov's labored retreat.

Chunks of stone scattered about him, one piece crashing off his armored shoulder. The blow almost tumbled him down the incline, but he managed to keep his balance. He felt something lift his boots several feet into the air, and initially thought the thing had seized him before realizing it was the Arkhitektor offering him a powerful gust, his body gliding majestically and fighting the pull of gravity. Throwing a glance over his shoulder, Kozlov saw how easily the wave of hands was keeping pace with them. The slope leveled off into the first row of stone columns, rising ten feet into the air before them—actually floating out of their square plots for a brief time. Several of them sank back down sharply, others more slowly, as if it were no longer a single beating heart that was powering their rise and fall but instead a whole colony of hearts, each throbbing to a different pulse.

Another boost aided Kozlov, lifting him high enough to grip the rising mossy column and clear it. Before him, the succeeding rows continued their random dance into the distance. Kozlov wasn't sure he had the stamina to clear this obstacle course, even with his mentor's assistance.

But seeing how the columns briefly floated clear of their earthen pits gave him an idea.

It was desperate but risky. Still, what choice did he have?

All he needed was to time this correctly.

Huffing, he pushed on, tackling the course with taut muscles and his comrade's boosts, scrambling across column after descending column, needing to reach one still on the rise. He had traversed a dozen or more—mis-timing a couple of closing gaps—when one of the massive hands slapped down bare inches from his boot heel. Quickly, he dropped onto the next column, his legs on fire from exertion. Chains of hands scrambled down the block behind him, and Kozlov caught a fleeting glimpse of his companion straining to hold back the spidery things with his spectral telekinesis.

'There!' Kozlov bellowed, pointing towards the column rising up next to him and the empty hole in the ground left behind by its movement. 'The gap! Knock it in!'

Kozlov ran towards the hole, narrowly avoiding a swiping grab from one of the gloved hands. He almost tripped, lumbering on in a bear-crawl. The column had already begun its descent, smooth and slow, but swift enough to steal his opportunity very shortly.

He ran.

He leapt.

He was thrust forth.

The column, dropping meter by meter, promised to crush him to a pulp at the bottom of the deep hole, like a peppercorn caught between a pestle and mortar.

Kozlov braced, expecting to feel the column's rough stone crack into his head and shoulders. But aided by a boost from the Arkhitektor, he found himself somehow on the adjacent column. The tumbling hands leapt after him, then stalled in midair as though they had hit an invisible barrier—which they had. It was the Arkhitektor, using every ounce of his telekinetic power. One second, two...the descending column smashed the whole lot of them down deep into the hole.

On hands and knees, sucking in ragged breaths, Kozlov watched as the column started to rise again. His heart heaved in anticipation. If that thing hadn't been crushed, he had no better alternatives to fall back on, no hope of escape.

With the Arkhitektor at his side, he watched the column exit the earth. The hole thus revealed was too deep and dark to see the bottom of, but nothing stirred in that black void. Nothing crawled up out of the hole. Kozlov sighed through gritted teeth and stared up at the underside of the rising column. A soupy ichor dripped from it.

As their column neared its peak, Kozlov saw that the distant mouth-spat oddities had coalesced into a mob. There was something about them that brought a circus act to his mind: small figures on stilts, stalking like insects; a human cannonball half hanging out of its own cannon and somehow dragging himself and it across the uneven terrain.

Creatures that could have been suicidal amateur astronauts tied to rockets veered through the sky on air patrol.

'What is this madness?' Kozlov asked as the distant swarm of figures moved off, away from them. Sighing, he climbed to his feet. When the column rose to its apex again, he noticed the last row of the shifting columns was in sight. A mile or so beyond them waited the labyrinth of melted-down nuclear reactors; the decaying cooling towers from a man-made reactor stood prominently amongst the more otherworldly structures. It seemed as good a place as any to continue their search in these lethal lands.

They reached the ruins without incident. All the way, Kozlov heard the ground-trembling chuckle of the giant grinning crevice. Even from miles away, its mirthless joy shuddered the twisted canyons of industrial folly.

Kozlov advanced through a warren of collapsed alloys and mysterious materials, knife in hand, when a careful movement snared his attention. A figure of troubling proportions slowly solidified from the shadowed lee of a sagging structure. It made a creaky rumbling sound, like worn wheels on a squeaking axle. What resembled a huge arachnid dragging a large snail shell slowly revealed itself in the smoky light. It was not a spider per se, but a mechanical, multi-legged conveyance carrying a freakish rider.

Kozlov's tired muscles needed rest, but they tensed, preparing for the challenge. The Arkhitektor took a protective step between Kozlov and the new threat. The mech spider jockey stopped its ride at a respectful distance, seemingly curious rather than hostile. Kozlov didn't know what to make of it. With a mighty chest, long face, and longer ears, the creature before them could have belonged to a race of bipedal donkeys, albeit one with mammalian hands and a snout that ended in what resembled some sort of bulbous air horn. Cinched about its powerful shoulders and trunk were several sets of straps like a race driver's harness, binding it to the spider, while others—and a few electrical wires—were connected to the rear mechanical carriage; the carriage was not like that of a snail, Kozlov realized, but rather a large, half-open clamshell atop four big wagon wheels.

Kozlov's eye was drawn to the creature's face, where a big red smile had been painted over white greasepaint, like it was a mistreated jackass in a cruel circus. The thing leered at them like a lunatic.

'Leave us,' Kozlov warned, not in the mood for a fight and not sure how much of one he could currently put up.

To his surprise, the creature responded in Russian, though not verbally, which was a relief, for he could only imagine the volume of any words issuing from that klaxon of a mouth. Instead, a circular window on its chest harness lit up with a glowing oscillation accompanied by a digital voice.

'I am not your enemy.'

'You speak Russian?' Kozlov asked in his native tongue.

'This device enables me to translate and speak many languages and dialects. It is something I developed under the yoke of the maniac king of these black-humored lands.'

There was an anger in the thing's eyes that reminded Kozlov of the last time he had looked in the mirror. 'You're a monarch's royal servant?' he asked. 'Of the Order of Terminus?'

'Was. No more. Never again.'

'Then what are you now?'

'A rebel, in need of allies.' Its large eyes looked Kozlov and the Arkhitektor over, no longer with fire but with calm appraisal, apparently finding satisfaction in what it saw. 'I have a feeling the fates have aligned our paths. My name is Calkarion.'

Kozlov shared a look with his mentor, finding a weary acceptance. Friend or foe, it was worth a gamble if it meant assistance in this weird world.

Kozlov stated his name and tapped his breastplate, then gestured to his companion. 'My friend, he forsook his birth name many years ago, but his title is Arkhitektor.'

Calkarion made a hand gesture that Kozlov could only assume was some type of formal greeting, an alien equivalent of *Pleased to meet you.*

'Tell me,' Kozlov continued, 'what royal house claims ownership of this hell, and who is this king you rebel against?'

'The Strange Fates is this House's coat of arms. The last stop for fools who perish holding false beliefs. Gods that never existed, stories and powers that could only ever instill short-term hope. Then, in death, they learn their faith has been misplaced. The cruel humor of Kerzix the Imp King knows no bounds.'

Kozlov was confused. 'What of all these power plants and airships? Where do they fit in?'

'Kerzix isn't content to receive only his percentage of souls from the other kings of the Order. Over the millennia, the sadistic tyrant has secretly made a legion of doomed chaos-bringers across the many living worlds. He calls them his Marotte Marauders. Once-ordinary individuals who are atheistic in spirit, who would otherwise bypass his cursed collection, become his jesters, forced to provide a tribute of mass death on Kerzix's whim. Some hijack zephyrs or sink boats; some start fires large enough to blacken whole villages and giant cities. These are re-creations of some of Kerzix's favorite catastrophes carried out in his name.'

Kozlov stared at Calkarion's grotesque makeover, no longer seeing it as tribal paint but a permanent mark of ownership.

'You were one of these jesters.'

The bright-red tattooed smile wasn't deceptive enough to hide how much displeasure Calkarion took at the reminder. 'We should keep moving,' it said. 'The Macabre Applause isn't the worst thing hunting these lands.'

It turned about, backing up its affixed clam carriage like a seasoned rickshaw driver.

'The what?' the Arkhitektor asked.

'The severed hands of the jesters who displeased Kerzix.'

'And what is worse?'

'The Big Top.' Without further detail, Calkarion angled its spidery conveyance in the direction of the sagging cooling towers and alien reactors. 'I have a safe place where we can talk and rest. If you wish.'

'Is this place still radioactive?' Kozlov asked.

'You are quite safe, at least from poisoning.' The malformed horseman held up his palms to the sagging cooling towers and leaking structures. 'These are nothing more than tributes and decoration now.'

'Tributes...' Kozlov weighed up his options, liking none of them. But while he wasn't naive enough to trust this alleged ex-servant of the bastard called Kerzix the Imp King, the creature would likely have some useful intel. Enemy hierarchies, local geography, perhaps even information on the whereabouts of the Firmament Needle. He kept his knife gripped tight, thinking how Calkarion's broad muscular back and neck made good targets if it came down to it. He nodded at the Arkhitektor and followed the cyborg centaur.

10

DAVE STARED IN QUIET AWE at the luxury of his surroundings and thought about what the fuck he was doing here.

Never in his life had he set foot in such a swanky place. Even the air tasted rich, not like that dirty urban stink of Buffalo with its car fumes and piss-splashed alleys and his moldy apartment overstuffed with rejected screenplays, thousands of Blu-rays, and movie posters. He fidgeted in the leather wingback chair, waiting for the enigmatic Edward Talbot to return.

He knew he should be freaking out right now, with all that had just happened to him. Still was happening! But he didn't want to let any negative thinking in—which was much harder than it sounded—so he focused on a few of the cognitive behavioral therapy techniques that Annette Bancroft had shown him: he became mindful, allowing himself to be in the moment rather than running manic laps about his head and trying to outpace his fleet-footed anxieties. That didn't last long, and the moment he thought of that big, rough motherfucker with the icicle and the silver-haired girl who must bleed anabolic steroids, he felt himself beginning to seethe. What the fuck had he ever done to them?

He knew these angry impulses were not good for him or anybody else, and he tried to meditate on something more positive. He thought about his last lay, Carly, the skank bartending co-worker he had made the mistake of fucking after closing the bar one night; she was an asshole, sure, and completely not his type, but that didn't mean it wasn't fun. But those memories connected him back to work, his dipshit manager, Hank, and a whole clientele of drunken lowlife losers who had zero respect for anybody, especially him.

Okay, different tack. He thought about his new screenplay. The latest of his dumb little escape fantasies that would take him away from this sucky life of his. He chastised himself for thinking so pessimistically of the one good thing in his life as something silly and frivolous. Why did he have to describe it to himself as a *dumb little escape fantasy*?

Because it was. Deep down he knew. Not necessarily for lack of talent but because there was no way he would be escaping this suffocating, angry little world of his, with its people he could never connect with or, really, want to connect with.

Nervously fingering and kneading his beanie hat, he couldn't get comfortable in the chair, so stood up and started to walk about the large room, feeling the gaze of a dozen or more of the ubiquitous stone and clay owl statues observing him.

He wondered if he actually was being watched. Like if maybe this was a test or something. Stick the cheap guy alone in a room that could have been pulled straight from a museum and see if he tries to pinch anything, maybe see how much he can stuff into the pockets of his trench coat.

Dave wasn't a thief. And if he had been, he certainly wouldn't rob one of the borderline fetishistic owl statues eerily perched about the shelves and cabinets. What was Talbot's obsession with them? The entire mansion was infested with the things: oil paintings, models, and an enormous mural on the lobby's high ceiling. Dave was starting to think Talbot might be some type of owl fondler.

Pulling his beanie back over his mussed-up hair, he stuffed his hands into his pockets and tried to admire the paintings. They were mostly woodland scenes, moody and depressing, with yet more owls hidden in hollows and on branches, but then he noticed something else and took a curious step backwards: the whole wall of paintings flowed in sequence, each individual work a single frame of a larger picture. Following them along, Dave watched as the dense forest gradually opened up into a marshy glade, full of soupy greens and mossy rock piles. His careful eye caught a minor detail, making him peer a little closer. In the dank wooden heart of the wood was a . . . flame? Dying, too, from the looks of it, unnatural in color. A small party of silhouettes were arranged about the ghoulish phosphorescence, with many glowing eyes staring down from the canopy above them. The assembly was clad in long, dark coats, their number hard to discern, with some concealed more deeply in the tree line than others, but one figure—the leader, Dave suspected from their centralized position in the gathering—was truly bizarre in form and performing some type of obscene ceremony. It appeared as though the leader had opened its body, quite literally, arms spread-eagled, hands propping open its impossibly strange-shaped torso, exposing the innards for all to see around the spectral flame.

The door burst open so promptly that Dave jumped, immediately feeling embarrassed for doing so. It was Talbot, finally back, and still the picture of a gracious host.

'Sorry to keep you waiting, Mr. Bentley. If you would kindly follow me, this will all start to make sense soon.'

'Right.' Dave slowly listed away from the canvases. 'I like your paintings,' he lied.

This seemed to delight Talbot. 'Yes. They're commemorative. Please . . .' He held the door open for Dave.

Dave was led along one enormous wing of the estate into what must have been a collector's room. He didn't know what the hell any of the items were but guessed that the value of the room's contents could fund a small country. Everywhere he looked there was some aged treasure encased in glass on a dark-wood pedestal: jewels, necklaces, some items that looked like potential weaponry, scrolls, armor, and a whole lot more. One item in particular caught his eye: a wooden staff topped with the carved head of an old-timey court jester that wore a creepy, almost lascivious expression.

'Tea?' Talbot had stopped next to a highly polished table loaded with china cups, silverware, and a beautiful porcelain teapot painted with a floral motif.

Dave was never much of a tea drinker. 'Sure.' He shrugged, hands still safely in his pockets out of fear of bumping into something worth more than his life. 'I hope this is some good tea, because I have no idea what's happening here, and it's making me a bit tetchy.'

Talbot smiled politely and gracefully poured two cups. 'Milk and sugar?'

'Sure.'

Talbot was stirring Dave's tea when he said, 'I used to be a beggar. Long time ago. I slept in hay bales and alleys. I'd steal to eat, beg for change, and be kicked into gutters.' He handed the tea to Dave. 'Can you hear how well I speak, my careful enunciations?' Dave took the tea, curious as to what this had to do with anything. 'I used to sound exactly how I was: a brash, poorly educated no-account. But dying a peasant's death in a street strewn with horse shit was not something I aspired to.'

Horse shit. Dave went to sample his tea, but the steam deterred him. *And exactly how long ago was this?*

'So I did what was necessary.' Talbot sipped his tea quietly. 'There was a group of aristocratic chaps who frequented a private club in London. Very posh place. The sort that paid callus-handed men to keep people like me far away from it. But these aristocrats, they had something else about them. Infamous reputations, but not for the typical reasons of scandal and wealth. There was a whiff of devilry that followed these chaps like brimstone. And if there was one thing even the mucky vermin like me knew, it was that devils made deals.'

Dave managed to take a sip of tea. Not bad. Not bad at all. But it didn't do much to improve his situation. Didn't change the fact that he had dented a steel door with his fist, discovered that assholes with powers of their own were apparently hunting him, and that this posh Talbot guy had driven him to an upstate mansion to talk about deals with devils. Should he have taken his chances with that big cold dude and those two ball-busting chicks?

'I didn't have much care for my soul metaphorically—well, mostly. But no, what I cared for was to sleep in the lap of luxury, to know that my belly would be full each day, but predominantly, I wanted to know how it felt to have power for once in my life.' An excitable fire blazed in his eyes for a second, and Dave could have sworn they'd shone like little jade discs, polished and bright. 'So, one evening, I managed to smash a brick over the doorman's head, just when these rumored wealthy warlocks had had their fill of revelry and were retiring for the night. It was quite the scene, I can assure you. But whilst the doorman lay dead on the cob-

bles, I saw how unafraid the noblemen were. If anything, they seemed
to be amused, as though they had just encountered a singing mouse. One
of them, a great man you'll come to meet, by the name of Mr. Gabriel,
whose very home we are both standing in right now, held off the rest of
the security with a gesture as I pleaded with them. It was a lowly thing
to do, groveling. I know. But beggars get used to begging. I told them I'd
do anything they needed of me. Anything. And so Gabriel shared a quiet
word with his fellows, then he clapped me on the shoulder. My stink
didn't trouble him. He saw the diamond in the rough, as the expression
goes. For several weeks he tested me. Doing this and that, some menial
work, some skullduggery, some murder. It was for his and their entertainment, but it was also a test. And I succeeded, for once in my life.' Talbot's
eyes grew cold, causing Dave to straighten his back. 'On the day of my
ascension, they took me to a marshy wood, far from the boroughs of London. And I was initiated.' Talbot tugged gently at his lapel. 'Fashion and
comfort soon followed.'

'Is this about me punching a hole in that steel door?'

Talbot gave him a puzzled expression. 'I'm not aware of any vandal-
ism per se, but in a roundabout manner, yes, I suppose that's correct.
Steel, you say? You have something wonderful in you, David. And it
could pave your dirty streets with gold. Money, power, I can help you
achieve these, but this isn't a charitable foundation. It will require work.'

Dave delicately set his cup down on the table. 'Work, huh? You need
me to knock down a few walls? Hammer some nails? Because they have
construction crews for that.'

'They don't have construction crews who can do what you can. With
a bit of practice.'

Dave was becoming impatient. 'What the hell am I? Just tell me
what's going on.'

'You finished your tea?'

Dave gave his barely touched brew an exasperated look. 'I think so.'

Talbot nodded, with perhaps a slight disparaging look for wasting
the tea. 'Your answers are in there.'

Dave's stare was guided to a central chamber in the middle of the
room, walled-off by a large ring of tall bookcases, with a single aperture
for access.

'But before I take you in there, tell me, are you a happy man?'

Dave had an immediate answer but still took a moment to think about his shitty little life with his shitty little job and his shitty little apartment. And he thought about the much larger problem that couldn't be measured by materials and status: the anger and great sadness that characterized his every waking moment, a miasma without cause or escape.

He didn't even have to answer, for Talbot was quick to assume correctly.

'That's what I thought. I sensed it on you in the car. I can see it in you right now. And it's not your clothing or everyman status.' Dave appraised his old jeans and black trench coat, and his filthy sneakers crusted with barroom and city dirt. 'And it isn't your apartment building, which, admittedly, leaves a lot to be desired. As I mentioned, my beginnings were a far sight worse than yours. What bothers you is a lack of spiritual fulfillment. You need something more. *Bigger* than what you have.'

'I'm already seeing an anger counselor. I don't need a second opinion on my emotional state. I need to know what's happening to me, and why people, yourself included, are after me.'

'Very well,' Talbot said with dignity. 'I'll show you what you need to see. Come, I'll introduce you to Mr. Gabriel.'

It could have been Dave's confusion, but he thought he witnessed a small crack in Talbot's cheery and confident façade as he started them towards the round chamber.

Dave gave the glass case holding the jester-headed staff a final lingering look on his way past and followed Talbot into the inner sanctum. It was occupied by six tall, extravagantly gilded mirrors, five of which held a living silhouette, a shadow council in conversation. But it was whom they were currently addressing that captured Dave's attention: an older-looking gentleman, slender, with sharp, almost avian features and tufts of hair around a bald, veiny dome, and beside him, a second figure whose appearance actually unhinged Dave's jaw: a man—man?!—who Dave initially believed to be wearing a book like some bizarre, ungainly costume until he realized the man's torso actually *was* a large tome, book-spined, aged and battered from wear, with reams of arcane script where bones and vital organs should be. His head was entirely wrapped in yellowing, scrawled-upon parchment, a feature that extended down his neck, across his slim shoulders and arms, right down to his fingers—possibly his legs too, but they were covered by a robe cinched around the waist, just below the bottom of his book-body. It was, Dave realized after a few moments, the figure from the painting.

'Gentlemen,' Talbot said crisply, 'I present to you Mr. David Bentley. Our Spark.'

The council of seven stopped, silent, and gave Dave their full attention.

Dave's mouth went dry, but his palms and lower back tingled with sweat. The mere presence of this book... *man?* had him on edge—the murky figures in the mirrors couldn't even compare. The council's silence dragged on to the point of being unbearable; even Talbot showed signs of strain.

Finally, the tableau broke as the walking tome extended his papery arms, slipped his fingers into the closed text, and parted the covers like he was about to spill his glossary of knowledgeable innards all over the floor. He quickly riffled through the pages of his body as if seeking some relevant passage. It didn't seem possible that the book-man could read any of his pages, seeing as how he would be viewing them upside down and from a terrible angle; did he have some undefined ability to know every word and page by heart simply by exposing them, as though the ink was in his blood, guiding him? Dave could catch only a fleeting exhibition of ink and symbols and diagrams, but then the book-man stopped on a blank page with a strip torn off near the bottom, displaying it to Dave as though it was supposed to mean something to him. Dave stared at the paper-bound head as though he could glean some understanding from the featureless face. When this proved fruitless, he switched to the book-man's cadaverous companion with the hawkish nose, but the impersonal, nigh-analytical look in those ancient eyes provided no information and less comfort. Desperate now, Dave threw a final look at Talbot and, with a twinge of relief, caught a stiff-lipped nod of support from him, one of those chin-up-and-hang-in-there kinds of looks. Before the council's uncomfortable scrutiny withered Dave any further, the book-man slammed his torso shut on the ripped page.

I take great pride in the knowledge held in books, a disembodied voice said. *I do not enjoy seeing harm come to them. Damaging books is for ignorant minds.*

Dave somehow knew the disembodied voice was coming from the book-man's mouthless, manuscript-muffled face. It was a dusty whisper that rustled and cut like paper, tinted with the sort of old European accent that reminded Dave of schlocky Hammer Horror movies. But this was no hammy performance.

I ripped out one of my pages in order to find a battalion of Sparks. Instead, our council only received you. Dave saw a small wave of tension run through Talbot and the older beaky man he now assumed to be Talbot's boss, Mr. Gabriel. *Does this illustrate the importance placed on you?*

Dave was lost for words. Was he actually supposed to answer? Panicky, he had to force himself not to smile nervously, cordially, feeling his anxiety pleading for an end to this moment.

What do you do with your life, Mr. Bentley?

Dave swallowed what felt like a ball of paper and licked his lips. 'Um, I, er... bartender. I tend bar, but I like writing.' An alarm bell gonged in Dave's head the second he said that, not wanting the book-man to quiz him on his reading preferences or assume they shared some commonality. '*Screenplays.* You know... movies. I like writing those.' He glanced in embarrassment at his hosts, including the silhouettes in five of the six mirrors, wondering when the last time they went to the movies might have been. The advent of the "talkies"? Did people like these even watch movies?

I am not familiar. I don't care for modern man's amenities, but aspirations are important for a person. And a person needs to ensure they have suitable power to achieve their aspirations. This pastime of yours is a waste of your very essence. A peasant's aspiration. I made a sacrifice for my cohorts to gather you here. I now expect you to make a sacrifice by setting your aspirations on par with those of Mr. Gabriel and Mr. Talbot.

Dave didn't know about all that. He thought about his still-in-progress screenplay and the computer file full of various other movie pitches and in-progress screenplays, each one another as-yet-unfulfilled wish to propel himself from the confines of his small, awkward life.

They have been disgraced several times recently, the voice continued, *and while these disgraces should sit heavy upon their heads, they also tarnish the name of our whole collective. However, these difficulties with the Hourglass group are becoming a minor objective of mine. There will be a whole new paradigm before too long, rendering all of these mortal skirmishes as redundant. You will be a bit player in the grand scheme, Mr. Bentley, regardless of your in-*

nate Spark. You are here as a way to assist Mr. Talbot and Mr. Gabriel in winning back some of their credit within this society.

Dave felt a leaden weight around his spirit, one that felt like servitude. He saw Talbot, his expression blank and obedient, but there was something else there too. Uncertainty?

'Chairman Sarkozy,' said the vulture-beaked man, presumably Mr. Gabriel, to the book-man, and then, turning to the silhouette collective, 'esteemed colleagues. It is with humility and utmost gratitude that Mr. Talbot and I vow to correct our recent failures. The sabotage of our inroads expansion of Erebus and, of course, the destruction of the remains of Charon, first monarch of the Order of Erebus, continue to burn me with shame. With this unassuming young man here in our midst'—he gestured to Dave—'I believe we have a potential ally who can protect our local interests and, in doing so, restore your trust and demonstrate that Mr. Talbot and I can still be of use to our society's grander aims.'

The mirror forms were mute, but Dave saw several accepting nods.

Mr. Bentley, the book-man—Sarkozy—said. *What do you know of your lineage?*

11

'**S**HOULD BE INTERESTING IF **H**IGHWAY Patrol pull us over,' Clyde said. He was riding shotgun in the van while Kev drove them along the I-495 from Manhattan towards Oyster Bay, doing the speed limit but with his face still concealed.

Kev pulled his scarf down, stuck his ethereal blue mouth against the window, and wagged his tongue at several passing cars. When he saw Clyde wasn't amused, he pulled the scarf back over his mouth. 'Relax. Anything happens, we drop Meadows' name and we're off the hook.'

'You've been reinstated less than an hour, and already you're abusing your authority. Nice.' Clyde glanced at the rest of the team, seated in the back of the van. The liquor had done little to enliven them. Ace was gloomily studying his phone. Clyde hadn't realized how close Ace had been to Estelle Page until the pints had loosened him up a little, but even then Ace still wasn't much for elaborate displays of emotion. Clyde gazed fondly at Nat, watching her discuss something with Rose and the ghoulish trio of the Intensive Scare Unit, then returned his attention to Kev.

He lowered his voice enough that Rose wouldn't hear him. 'Just don't give her another reason to make this more difficult.'

Rose had unlocked Kev's ankle monitor with a minimum of hesitation, but Clyde suspected it was mainly because the order to do so had come from on high.

Clyde saw Kev check the rearview mirror, as if the mere mentioning of Rose's name might have invoked her attention, like some militant folk demon.

'I feel like I'm the scapegoat,' Kev said.

Clyde thought about how he should answer that, his hands idly toying with Kev's PLE ankle monitor. What Kev said held some merit. It wasn't self-pity: acting against Hourglass policy and digging up some very polarizing intel on the larger tenets of its whole functional existence would naturally create staggering repercussions, but the injustice lay in the fact that while Kev had been suspended, Private Savannah Barros of the ISU, the cyber-savvy one who had helped—guided, even—Kev's stubborn renegade activity, had remained fully active. Granted, she was part of Rose's former military life, one of the ISU trio alongside Darcy and Sarge, but where was Rose's hardline attitude when it came to Barros' disciplinary? Kev got suspended. Barros got a slap on her ghostly wrist.

'Rose will come around,' Clyde said, though he didn't know what he was basing that on. They were all a team, sure, but apart from Kev, he hadn't known any of them for more than a few rough-and-tumble months. But they were bonded through the heat of survival and battle, and that had to count for something. 'She will,' he insisted. 'Working together will bring you back together.'

'What are you two ladies whispering about up there?' Ace called out.

Clyde peered into the rear of the van. 'Just saying how much we're looking forward to getting back to work.'

'Fuckin' right on!' Ace thudded his head against the van sullenly.

Kev exited the interstate and guided the van down a long and winding private road, approaching the Madhouse. He stopped outside the heavy gates and flashed his reinstated pass against the stone column's card reader. The gates parted smoothly. Clyde kept an eye on Kev, checking whether he was displaying any signs of hesitancy. He didn't appear to be. That might have been a relief, except Clyde could tell from his friend's sudden slouch that he was in a *fuck-it* sort of mood.

'At least they didn't drag their feet on reactivating my status.' Kev stared at the all-seeing electric eye housed in the stone gate column. He stepped on the gas. 'You think Schulz will have any hard feelings?'

Clyde gave him a dubious look but didn't comment.

The winding asphalt stretched across a hundred acres of snow-covered field towards the large edifice known as the Madhouse. It had been the Baxter Institute back in the 1940s, before a scandalous closure had shut its doors. A few decades later, Hourglass had quietly reopened them. The original shell of the building remained: two sprawling, six-storied, red-brick wings spreading out from the central hub complex, with three additional basements; it was a veritable fortress of covert intelligence and otherworldly paramilitary means.

A helicopter rose from behind the building and whirred off somewhere westward; the peaceful gardens at the rear of the building gradually rolled on to be demarcated by a concrete airfield and a dockyard rising out of the bay and propped up on stanchions.

Kev slid the van into one of the rows closest to the main building. The Madhouse seemed to stare down at the van like an ominous bureaucratic god.

Clyde could see the merest onset of tension in Kev, notable by his clothes "puffing up" due to an increased output of telekinesis.

'Hey, you're good.' Clyde wasn't asking him but telling him.

Kev straightened up and gave him a furtive glance, and then started to ease. 'Yeah … Yeah, let's go.'

Kev locked the van behind them and tossed the key to Ace, who managed to snatch it out of the air despite being six pints deep.

Clyde was painfully aware of the team's divide. Rose had already marched ahead. Clyde, Kev, and Nat hung back a few yards. And Ace hung around somewhere in the middle of the no-man's-land of professional relationships.

There were a lot of eyes on them now. Electronic, zooming, tracking, fixed to light posts and strategic angles of the building's eaves. The eyes of Dr. Martin Schulz, dead, but not a PLE. In fact, none of the resident experts in the various obscure disciplines knew for certain what exactly Schulz had become. But he was an ally, and that's what was important, the digital and techno-mantic eyes, ears, and security of the building, as well as still functioning as the staff psychiatrist when necessary.

A wispy figure reemerged from the wide, powerful back of Rose, decimated, immolated, and horrifying to the unfamiliar. Barros was a double amputee below the waist, courtesy of her explosive death, with some heavy charring around what remained of her, except for her face. She broke away from Rose, waiting for Kev to reach her.

'I talked to him a few times about what we did,' Barros said of Schulz, referring to their coordinated cyber security breach into classified Madhouse—and, ergo, Hourglass—files; a feat accomplished with her computer know-how and Kev's ability to physically move objects, such as keyboard keys.

'He wasn't a fan of mine for a little bit there,' Barros said, 'but he's come around.'

Rose turned on her heel to stare at Barros and Kev. She stayed quiet, but her expression said loud and clear about how much she still denounced their betrayal. Barros must have picked up Rose's continued resentment but chose not to comment. She gave Kev a complicated look: part regret, part pride in what they had done, and perhaps something more.

Clyde saw the black electric eye over the building's ballistic-proof front doors rotate and focus on the team's approach. The doors slid open, and the two agents on guard duty, who looked like tactical-armored insects, nodded them through into the huge lobby. One of the sentries slapped a wad of dollar bills into Ace's expectant palm.

'Same time next week?' Ace asked.

'You know, I don't think poker is my game,' the guard replied.

'You know, I think you're right,' Ace retorted humorlessly.

Nat gave him a bemused look. 'No one will ever back you up if you keep taking their money.'

'Gambling's for dumbasses. Maybe I don't want dumbasses backing me up.'

Clyde decided not to point out the flaw in Ace's logic and glanced around the lobby. He had anticipated finding Schulz standing in the middle of the busy foot traffic, a ticked-off expression on his bearded face, his electrical yellow-white form crackling like sparks from an overloaded power line. But Schulz wasn't there, or at least not in person. Regardless, Clyde was sure the shock doc's mind would be watching them—watching *Kev*—through the cameras.

Kev stiffened with mild tension, and Clyde knew his friend wouldn't completely relax until he got that first awkward encounter out of the way.

Rose kept on marching, and Clyde and the others fell in line.

▪ ▪ ▪

CLYDE HAD BEEN expecting their briefing to be held in the Situation Room, that perpetually busy hub of computers, phones, and endless screens of citywide surveillance. Instead, Rose told them that Meadows had asked to be met in the library. That was a new one. Clyde hadn't even paid a visit to the building's library, having had no prior need of it since his posting here.

So why now?

Déjà vu struck him immediately upon their arrival. The exterior of the library was a pair of steel vault doors, probably capable of withstanding a pretty substantial warhead, similar to the ones protecting the library at Indigo Mesa.

Rose scanned her card across the reader, and the doors opened quietly enough to appease even the strictest of librarians. Everything was going smoothly until Kev suddenly hit an invisible wall at the entrance's threshold. A pair of wards protecting against all spectral ingress had been designed into the robust doorframe.

Schulz appeared in the corridor, his form a fuzzing charge of static, but not so erratic as to muddle his features: middle-aged, a body adapted purely for academia, balding with a philosopher's brow and a naturally inquisitive expression. Currently, this expression also held a hint of overdue castigation.

'Kevin…' Schulz briefly seemed lost for any other words. 'You made a fool of me.'

Clyde, having paused at Kev's barring, watched what was about to unfold.

Everybody else carried on into the library—everybody except Barros, who appeared momentarily hesitant, torn between defending Kev and following Rose. Kev gesticulated to her and Clyde that it was cool to head on in, he'd catch up shortly.

'That wasn't my intention,' Kev said. 'I thought I could have found what I wanted and been gone without you or Meadows being any the wiser.'

'You thought you could have located top-secret files and disappeared before I detected you?' Schulz looked offended.

'I'd say we came pretty damn close,' Kev retorted, causing Clyde to squeeze his eyes shut. Kev's flippancy wasn't conducive to mending fences. 'Look, I had my reasons, and they were well founded. Trying to slip by you wasn't personal. Honestly, you're just something in the middle. I wasn't trying to undermine you, or make Meadows doubt your capabilities. So for that, I'm sorry. And I'd like to move past this if possible.' Kev pulled his ID from pocket to hand as if it were on an invisible string. 'We have a job to do, and even Meadows authorized my return.'

'I'm fully aware of what Deputy Director Meadows has authorized, Kevin. It's on the system. I *am* the system.' A begrudging pause. 'However, I admit that the adult thing to do is accept your apology and move forward.'

'Great.' Kev's card vanished back into his coat pocket. 'Thanks.' He made to enter the library but was once more rebuffed by an invisible wall, one that hadn't impeded Barros, nor Sarge or Darcy, who were both elsewhere, most likely waiting inside their astral bunker. Agitated, he turned back to Schulz.

'I also have a job to do,' Schulz said. 'Meadows doesn't want you anywhere near this facility's bibliography. I'm sorry, Kev. And I hope you can move past this.' Schulz crackled and popped out of existence.

Kev snorted derisively.

Clyde didn't like this one bit. It didn't bode well for renewing trust on either side.

'Man, fuck this bullshit.' Kev wasn't brooding at Schulz's departure; if anything, he appeared to find the whole scene something of a bad joke. 'Go on in. You can fill me in later.'

Clyde's gaze swept slowly between Kev, stuck outside the threshold, and the wide avenue between the book stacks Nat and the team were walking down.

'Hang tight, man,' Clyde told him. Annoyed for Kev's sake and his own, he spun around and jogged after the others.

Nat fell in lockstep with him once he had caught up. 'It'll be cool,' she reassured. 'Uncle Meadows isn't the petty type. He's just being cautious. But I'll try and guilt-trip him, smooth things out a little for Kev.'

Meadows was no blood relation to Nat, but a longtime family friend, which meant he was partially susceptible to certain charms of hers that nobody else on the team could ever match.

To Clyde, the library seemed as imposingly well-stocked as the one back at Indigo Mesa, meaning it was likely big enough to rival the New York Public Library, full of towering shelves, old reading desks, and so many nooks and crannies it seemed entirely possible to become so lost you might never be found again. However, for all of its centuries-past charm and splendor, the invasive signs of modernity could be readily found in laptops, printers, security scanners, and more of Schulz's black, glassy eyes.

In a large corner of the library was what looked to Clyde to be some type of alchemist's bibliotheca, filled with tall candlelit candelabras, old wooden racks housing glass jars of what could be shimmering inks, peculiarly designed pens, and a large walnut and fiery rosewood desk; his mind ran away with high fantasy and D&D tropes, like some of those commissioned illustrations he'd once provided for a couple of role-playing game books. He swiftly brought the tangent to heel. He was a soldier now.

Meadows was waiting patiently at the ornate desk, his posture commanding. Ex-Army prior to joining Hourglass, he was tall and broad, carrying his advancing years well, with short hair turning gunmetal gray over a black face weathering the wrinkles of experience and unspoken traumas.

'Glad to have you back, Clyde.' Meadows' smile was so professionally minor it might have been a mild twitching of the mouth. 'Spector filled me in. I'm relieved to hear I won't be losing a valuable agent to some jumped-up night terrors.'

'Right.' Bit of an understatement, Clyde thought. 'Sleeping easy, sir. And I'm very sorry to hear about the loss of your friend.'

Meadows' calculating eyes stabbed between Clyde and Nat, standing very close together.

'Estelle was a good friend,' Meadows said, sharing an ephemeral look of commiseration with Ace. 'A good woman. I'd like to say she deserved better, but we all get what we're given in this life.'

Clyde thought, perhaps naively, that he would glimpse the merest streak of anguish in Meadows' eyes, but all he found was the man's typical cool detachment. 'What we can do is make sure her death—all of their deaths—doesn't go unpunished. We need to make an example of Cairnwood. Guarantee nobody else mistakes us as having gone soft.'

'This isn't the Situation Room,' Ace groused, 'so meeting here tells me we're in the holding-our-dicks portion of the mission.'

'On the contrary.' Meadows tipped a hand towards what looked like a simple scrap of paper clamped delicately by an iron vise-type instrument on the heavy desk between them.

The parchment had yellowed with age.

'What am I looking at?' Rose asked, peering closer. Sarge and Darcy materialized, joining Barros in all their fatally wounded glory.

'This came in this morning. It was found near the bodies of Estelle and Agent Blanchet. Talbot was using it to copy down the details of Estelle's watch list. It's a scrap from the *Enlightened Xenoglossia*. A very old and believed to be very *lost* book. Accounts state that the paper within has the capability to translate and mimic any known language, code, or inexplicable data into the user's own personal lexicon. An incredibly useful item for any intelligence organization worth their salt. So it's a good job it was found by the erudite members of an Hourglass clean-up team.'

'And how does it help us?' Nat asked.

'Talbot might have accidentally exposed a big cog in the Cairnwood machine. You see, the *Xenoglossia* fell off the face of the Earth when a Hungarian warlock called Soma Sarkozy got his hands on it. Chronologically this predates Hourglass by a significant margin, but our UK and European counterparts in Avalon and the Covenant of Soteria are very aware of him. Sarkozy was a scholar dangerously obsessed with eschatology and various other troubling schools of magic, his desire for hidden knowledge knowing no bounds. According to our allies, he served as an advisor to the Hungarian Prince Rákóczi during a particularly turbulent political period against the German House of Habsburg. In the hopes of putting an end to this long and heated conflict, Sarkozy's interests took him down increasingly dark roads, up to the point where he started to physically bond himself with pages from various prohibited mystical works. I'm not sure what the rest of the Rákóczi family made of this, but after accruing enough forbidden secrets to cheat death, Sarkozy disappeared, along with the *Xenoglossia*. That was in 1709.'

Meadows cleared his throat and started to unlock a drawer in the desk. 'Once in a while, Avalon or the Covenant would hear rumblings of his activities, conspiring in this or that. But no one knew what he was really up to. If he had any loyalties or allies or if he was just in it for himself.' He removed a small filigreed box from the drawer, placing it on the table before the strip of paper. 'He was a ghost, figuratively. Evading each and all.' He pointed at the paper in the clamp. 'Until now.'

'All because Talbot dropped a scrap of paper?' Clyde asked. 'Seems reckless.'

'Seems fucking stupid,' Rose corrected. 'But then that asshole has fumbled a few times lately.'

'I'd call it fortuitous,' Meadows said. 'Actually, if anything, I'd call it straight-up arrogance. You see, having consulted the top authorities on mystical wards, I've been informed that the leaves of the *Xenoglossia* are protected by a cloaking spell—think of it like a stealth bomber deflecting radar signals.' He opened the lid of the box, staring approvingly at the contents therein. 'As it transpires, causing sufficient damage to the page revokes the protection. To carry on the analogy, this is similar to when a stealth bomber banks, exposing a flat surface for radar antenna to receive its return transmission. And so, when a page is damaged, it means the energy signature imbued in it can then be identified. Once that's established, the whole collection of pages within the book can then be tracked, and the last known whereabouts of Sarkozy can be located.'

'Sarkozy could be dead, relatively speaking,' Sarge posited. 'Talbot and those other vultures might have just pillaged his carcass at some point.'

'That's a possibility,' Meadows conceded. 'Otherwise, Talbot and his cohorts just tipped their hat to a very big fish in their ranks.'

'Talbot's the one who used the page, so he might still have the rest of it on him,' Darcy said, his large hands clasped beneath his exposed intestines. 'We can find him, kill him. And maybe find Bentley if he's still in one piece.'

Meadows fired a finger pistol at Darcy.

'How do we track him then? I'm guessing those aren't cigars in that box,' Clyde said.

'You will all be familiar with the contents of the box.' Meadows reached inside gingerly. 'Though the one you've all seen before was fully grown.'

It was a bookworm. A literal bookworm. A species of nematode from unknown dimensions with a partiality for the wisdom kept within mystical tomes. Indeed, the one Clyde remembered, a resident assistant at

Indigo Mesa, was a monstrous behemoth, a ropey spire of blind flesh with an array of dexterous tentacles and an uncanny mind equal to the greatest library filing system.

But this one was miniature enough to rest in Meadows' palm like a common earthworm.

'I must have missed a step.' Nat, who had never been to Indigo Mesa, leaned over the desk to get a better look.

Meadows held it towards her delicately, the small creature writhing sleepily in his callused palm. 'This species has the incredible ability to home-in on the written word. The more enchanted the text, the stronger the attraction.'

'Fresh out the box and straight to work, huh? Love the sweat-shop business model, Uncle M.' Nat leaned back, brushing ever so lightly against Clyde.

Clyde knew she'd done it intentionally, any flirtatious excuse to bump her body into his, but also because she had caught him glancing around for Kev.

'Well … shit, sir.' Rose appeared unconvinced by the bookworm's prospects. 'Do we have to wait for it to grow up first?'

Meadows brought out a sort of lidless petri dish from the same drawer, softly depositing the precocious creature onto the inky culture that glistened like a gasoline rainbow of mysterious energy.

'They mature with incredible speed. By tomorrow evening it'll be the size of a torpedo and ready to start tracking.'

Clyde thought about the implications of that little torn strip of paper, about a dead woman who had been a linchpin in Hourglass' combat efficacy, and imagined trying to fulfill his strike-team role without the help of two Sparks. He had thought this many times since joining the squad, and despite his newly evolving abilities, he still didn't think he'd last long without Ace and Nat.

'Tell me to back off if it's none of my business,' he said, 'but what will Hourglass do without the Astronomer? Will this create a reliance on alternative types of operatives like me and Rose, or is there a contingency plan for tracking Sparks? I only ask because, well, we've already faced down one enemy who killed your previous Spark-heavy team.' The Hangman held that honor.

Meadows pondered the question. 'We have a modest list of her projections securely backed up, but after that, we are in the dark. Estelle's own Spark ability was one of a kind, at least in our experience.'

'Not really the answer I was hoping for,' Clyde said.

'Sparks are big guns,' Sarge said. 'But as you just pointed out, the Hangman bagged and tagged three of them before we even started working here. It isn't always about who has the biggest arsenal as it is about using your resources wisely.'

'He's right,' Meadows said. 'Things can always be worse. For instance, Talbot stole the data conversion hard drive on his way out the door, but it'll be no use to Cairnwood; it will cook itself into a heap of plastic and junk circuitry the second an unauthorized user switches it on. Sunnyside up, we won't have to contend with a bunch of potentially radicalized Sparks too wet behind the ears to understand that Cairnwood are a problem and not a solution.'

'Speaking of, what do we do about David Bentley?' Rose asked. 'If he's still alive and with Talbot, do you want to keep him that way? His file says he has some anger issues. Bit of a loner too. I'm not one to make rash decisions about people, but this guy could already be a walking red flag; give him some real power and leave him with a group like Cairnwood, and one plus one equals a really bad day.'

Meadows had obviously already considered this negative scenario. 'I'm opting for capture. Once we have him in custody, he'll have a difficult life choice to make: informed, law-abiding civilian or fellow agent.' Clyde wasn't a Spark, but he knew that choice well. 'And I'd rather have another valuable asset at our disposal than a corpse. However, if he leaves you with little choice, eliminate him. It'll be a shame, but I'd rather lose him than one of you.'

Something suddenly occupied Meadows' attention. 'Send him in,' he said to thin air. Clyde then noticed Meadows' small earpiece. He continued addressing the team: 'Be back here tomorrow, nineteen-hundred hours. And we'll let the worm burrow.' He watched the miraculously wise organism sleepily roil about in the gelatin.

Clyde felt a gentle oscillation thrumming inside himself. Knowing it to be Kev's nearing presence, he turned to see him slinking towards them, Schulz having finally granted him access upon the boss' command.

Clyde admired Kev's restraint in not gawping at the looming bookcases as though they were pretty young things showing a lot of leg.

It went without saying that each shelf would be packed full of intrigue and shadowed histories, and insights into things daunting and beautiful throughout the universe, all of which Kev would pore over in his sleepless nights. Not that Schulz would ever allow him such an opportunity.

Kev stopped next to Clyde, receiving a supportive smile from Nat. But the atmosphere quickly became claustrophobic all the same. Rose adopted professional detachment; Barros wrinkled her nose as she waited for someone to break the awkward silence; Sarge and Darcy didn't seem to know where to look and so focused on the bookworm and the tiled floor, respectively; Ace seemed a hundred miles away from everything; and Meadows looked at Kev as though the troublesome agent had afflicted him with month-long constipation.

Clyde almost started talking just to break the tension, but Kev beat him to it.

'I know you probably don't give a shit what I think, but ... my condolences for your friend,' he said to Meadows. 'Best of luck to her on the other side.'

The subtext of Kev's sentiment hit Clyde squarely in the side of the head like one of the many heavy volumes creaking the stacks. If only Hourglass had chosen to act on their confirmed intel and decided to search for the Firmament Needle in the Null, they could have potentially orchestrated a new heaven already, and Estelle Page would be resting easy right now instead of wandering the tortured lands of the Null. He felt a storm brewing in the long, drawn-out seconds.

Mercifully, the storm never came.

'Dismissed,' Meadows told them. 'Except you, Kev.'

Kev waved Clyde on. They bumped fists, and Nat made Clyde lead them away with a playful kick to the ass. But as soon as he rounded a corner, Clyde stopped and leaned against one of the towering book stacks and listened in to the conversation between Kev and Meadows. Nat joined him. The conversation was as terse and sharp as was to be expected by now, Meadows having exhausted most of his scowls and bile during Kev's suspension proceedings. Still, the commander gave a parting shot that proved everything wasn't yet water under the bridge between the two of them.

'Clyde gave you a second chance, even if it was by accident,' Meadows said. Clyde glowered at such a tasteless and cheap shot, talking about Kev like his ghostly presence was a burden on him. 'Now I'm going to give you one too because, sadly, without you, Clyde's only a finger on a trigger. But if you ever try to pull this agency's pants down again, you'll wish your friend never dragged your sorry ass out of the Null.'

Clyde felt a spring coiling deep inside his abdomen, the sudden unexpected anger rearing to pop. He closed his eyes, expecting to hear Kev mouth off. Only nothing came. Not even a petulant expulsion of breath. It was so quiet that he could hear the turn of a page somewhere deeper in the library. The fact that Kev didn't rise to Meadows' challenge told Clyde exactly how much his friend wanted to be back here, working.

Nat placed a hand on his shoulder as if apologizing for Meadows' words. Clyde met her steadying gaze, letting her know it was alright.

Kev turned into the aisle, almost walking straight through Clyde and leaving his clothes piled up in an empty heap on the floor.

'It's good to be back,' Kev said, a pithy smile forming. He pulled his scarf up over his face again and returned the aviator shades to their rightful position, obscuring his eyes.

12

To say Dave was shocked would be underselling it. Admittedly, he had seen a few very unexplainable things of late, had even been the cause of one, but being tutored on a fragmented history lesson by something resembling a papier-mâché gimp wearing a giant book for a torso left him feeling sweaty and unwell.

Mercifully, the meet-and-greet didn't last too long, and Dave was led away from Soma Sarkozy and the council of mirror-trapped silhouettes to a quiet and peaceful study where he now sat with Talbot and Gabriel.

He was on his second cup of tea, this one going down much smoother than the last as he stared out the picture window that was almost the size of a cinema screen, admiring the ice crystals coating the trees and the hardy plants in the sweeping, snow-blanketed garden. The teapot came into view again without request, refilling his nearly empty cup.

'It's a nice garden,' Dave said, a throwaway compliment to allow his overworked mind time to try and process everything.

Talbot stared up from his pouring as though he'd never noticed the luxurious landscape before. 'It is, yes.' He withdrew the teapot. 'Do you have a green thumb?'

Dave was surprised at the question, still slightly detached from the moment. 'I've never even watered a plant. I thought...' What did he think? He was so scattered. 'I... err, I told my counselor'—he suddenly realized he had seen Annette only that afternoon!—'that I might look for a landscaping job. Some parks department thing. Seems like it might be a peaceful way to make a living.'

'If you pass me your CV, I could put in a word for you to be our new groundskeeper.'

Dave scarcely heard, his attention focused on the untrammeled, some-how-soothing snow of the countryside. 'You know,' he said, 'I never did the lottery. I always thought it was for desperate idiots clinging to a fantasy. But these Hourglass guys, they want me dead because I've hit some cosmic-powered jackpot. What are the odds? Maybe I could have been a millionaire by now.'

'Eloquently put,' Talbot said, returning the teapot to the tray and settling back into his comfortable wingback.

'Even with our vast archives and resources, we remain largely ignorant of the entirety of those historical events, this *great war* between paradise and hell.' Gabriel was sitting amongst them, his presence unnerving Dave with those bulging eyeballs of his and his sickly, frail form. But he moved as gracefully as a young athlete despite his appearance. He also lacked Talbot's sly wit and rapscallion charm, instead presenting a glowering intensity that was only exacerbated by the unblinking owl perched on his bony shoulder, which stared at Dave as though he was a rodent loose in the house.

'That's something we in the inner council wish to remedy, but there are limits to what even wealth and will can accomplish,' Gabriel said. He sipped from his cup, not partaking from the teapot but from a silver decanter beside the tray. Dave didn't like the rusty color of the liquid staining the rim of Gabriel's cup. It looked too much like blood.

'Hourglass views noble bloodlines such as yours as a threat to their ambitions. They manufacture their own shock troops with various methods and pacts in an ignorant attempt to prevent us from learning about the big picture. They enjoy controlling the light and shadows in the world, you see. Groups like theirs don't like what they can't control.' Gabriel pulled something small and grisly from a folded napkin beside his decanter and offered it to his unblinking killer pet, watching as it consumed it whole. 'That's why we need the shining might instilled within individuals such as yourself, to break the cogs of their machine.'

Dave checked with Talbot, who was nodding along.

'We seek the truth, and the betterment of mankind, enlightenment, and ways to better understand the mysteries kept hidden from us," Gabriel continued. 'Whilst Hourglass and their like-minded thugs merely want to prolong their militaristic stranglehold on occultist intelligence. But what else can you expect from cowards?'

The log fire was warming the room nicely, making Dave feel like he was trapped in some perverted Christmas card. He thought of Dickensian tales, and then punching his fist through a steel door, and of a big, tough-looking dude who created ice magic, a silver-haired strong gal who launched fully-grown unkillable men around like beanbags, and a hot Asian honey who'd gone to his apartment building to put a bag over his head, zip-tie his wrists and ankles, and drive him somewhere private to kill him.

'You've told me a lot,' he said, 'but it feels like you're still doing the cha-cha around the real question. What exactly do you want me for?'

'I think you know exactly what we want from you, Dave,' Talbot answered. 'These people want you dead because of something you've had inside you since birth. Something you didn't ask for. Does that seem fair to you?'

Dave couldn't deny the hot poke of anger he felt deep down. Targeted by assholes he didn't even know. He was a bartender with no aspirations beyond keeping to himself, watching movies, and keeping his sanity with the dream—or delusion, he thought sadly—that he might one day write a screenplay that opened the door to a new, better chapter in his life.

'Your very life is something they won't tolerate. I'm not one to put words in anyone's mouth, but if that was me, I'd feel extremely brassed off.'

'If this—'

'You have been blessed by a divine being,' Talbot pushed. 'One of many, but still too few. Are you prepared to let these authoritarian hate-mongers confine you? Kill you?'

Dave felt himself getting stirred up, Talbot's words mixing with his own personal feelings of outrage and victimization and renewed displacement and isolation. He was a genuine fucking freak, now fit to be punished by powers bigger than he. A hot coal was forming in the pit of his stomach. He breathed slowly, thinking about the moment, drinking in where he was—the cup of tea in his hands, the comfort of his chair, the warmth of the fire—anything to escape the nest of scorpions stinging his thoughts.

'Help us, David. You were meant for far more than serving swill to inebriated tossers. Your lineage is proof of this. Help us reject Hourglass and their lies, and their pathetic bully-boy need to control everything.'

Dave was literally caught in the middle, glancing between Talbot, to his right, and Gabriel, to the left. His heart was a war drum, beaten by a rhythm of lifelong ineptitude and a crushing sense of alienation from people. And now some fuckers actually wanted to harm him. For being different. He couldn't believe it. But they had already been to his home. He thought about the comfort of his shitty apartment in Buffalo, with his huge TV and thousands of movies that used to placate him after a difficult day. He thought about leaning back in the dark screenings of the Encore with a hot dog and a giant soda. He thought about all the dramas of the fictitious people he loved to get lost in. And he thought about how much he had become accustomed to being alone, watching the lives of others instead of living his own. Something had to change. He'd known this forever but had never had the courage to try. He thought of his future, of tending bar as an angry, lonely 70-year-old failed screenwriter.

'How do I help?' he asked.

13

NESTLED DEEP IN THE AMBER-LIT cove of some imploded industrial ruin, Kozlov kept a trained eye on the desolation outside, listening for sounds of movement over the soft, unpleasant chuckling that continued to carry across the vast wasteland like delirious white noise.

He cut off a strip of meat from his provisions and chewed the leathery morsel, imagining it was venison. The meat was tasteless, but it was sustaining, and his stomach and intestines found no quarrel with it. It had belonged to what seemed to be the Erebus equivalent of a small mammal, which he'd killed and dressed after finding it foraging for its own meal. His observations of local ecosystems was rudimentary at best. The thing he was chewing was some form of rabbit, in role if not physical appearance, that grazed on the bizarre vegetation or molds composed of ectoplasmic soul leavings, which was in turn feasted on by any number of the small to large horrors that stalked this realm, hungry for either flesh or any fugitive souls that leaked from Charon's infrastructure. It was one of many curiosities that continued to scratch away at Kozlov since his first jaunts over here with the Rising Path; for a dark world sustained and powered by death, there appeared to be as much biodiversity here as back on Earth.

Kozlov turned his head to check on Calkarion. The alien was resting deeper inside the collapsed structure, having backed its clamshell bulk in first. Quiet, reserved, it sat there like some fallen Egyptian god from an extraterrestrial landscape, the mechanical spider legs projecting from its waist producing small, motorized sounds as they irregularly twitched or flexed. LED glyphs glowed warmly within the confines of its clamshell wagon.

Kozlov regarded the stoic creature, watching as it demonstrated some painful-looking flexibility as one of its sinewy double-jointed arms slowly contorted backwards, reaching for the soft, glowing interior of its carriage, only to be met halfway by a mechanical arm extending out from the clamshell to meet its hand. A quiet motor whirred, and the deft metallic pincer placed something in Calkarion's palm before retreating back into the wagon.

Kozlov stopped chewing and strengthened his grip on his knife.

Calkarion brought the item into the amber wash of the collapsed shelter's strip lights. It was a rattle of some sort, beautifully crafted wood, its bright paintwork time-scoured, with a jester's grit-blasted face still smiling through the ages.

Kozlov's eye signaled the Arkhitektor to be at ease, the old spectral monk looking especially tired, a bone-thin apparition fading away through exhaustion.

Calkarion explained itself through more of its electronic vocals, the chest screen oscillating. 'This is my penance. The Imp King controls these lands from that terrible reality-crash of a fortress. I was an engineer on my world. A good one. I used to work at a facility that harnessed power from a very beautiful and valuable form of crystal. The company had the procedure down to a fine science, but there are always risks when handling such power.' Calkarion gently waved the jester rattle about the buckled walls of their shelter like a maudlin historian. 'It wasn't procedural incompetence or risk that destroyed this place. It was me. This thing'—holding up the rattle—'was a curse placed upon me by Kerzix. The Atheist's Marotte. He scattered countless of these things across the cosmos as a game. When some unfortunate soul accidentally makes physical contact with one, they become his game pieces. They lose themselves in a mad passion for chaos and destruction. But there's a catch. Kerzix's rival kings would react negatively if they believed he was skimming too many additional souls, and so not just anybody can activate the curse inside these marottes. They must also be faithless. Godless. I was only ever devoted to science, and so on the day I discovered this scepter, playing in the field with my children, my life was already over without my knowing it. The change came on quickly. That same night, I became one of Kerzix's fools, one of his Marotte Marauders. I traveled the several miles outside my town to this reactor, and I overloaded it to appease him. Two thousand, three hundred and fifty-six souls went into his pocket that day like little jeweled baubles … that's all they were to him. But to me they were my wife, my children, my friends, my neighbors. He brought this whole structure over as another one of his monuments of death. I wasn't even granted the peace of annihilation with my family, though I now know that such peace never existed. There is only this place. During the blast, Kerzix somehow spared my life, putting me to work here, hunting and hurting the souls of the faithful for security or entertainment.' He—for Kozlov now knew the creature was a former family man—slowly, thoughtfully rotated the marotte in his hand. 'Are you men of faith?'

Kozlov cleared his dry throat, the hacking sound derisive. He paused before answering, considering his beliefs and the hells he had walked through.

'There was only ever one true heaven, whose god we have no name for,' the Arkhitektor answered, slowly drifting along the chamber walls, his gaze occupied with introspection. 'But it was home to a race of guardians called the Luminaries. That's what we know for certain.'

'I wish that were true. I would do anything for my wife and children to find such peace,' Calkarion said. 'If you haven't yet realized, that place is nothing more than myth now.'

'Believe me, we know,' Kozlov said. 'This is all there is.' He pointed beyond their shelter to the blighted and hopeless wilds beyond.

'For me, faith is more than altars and old rituals,' Calkarion said. 'It's a handhold in a hurricane; not much, but a hope that chance or action might carry us through the storm.'

'I used to believe science and faith were contradictions of one another, but when you make it over here … ' Kozlov pondered. 'So many questions that neither science nor faith can provide answers for. Only action and experience.'

And just when Kozlov was starting to feel a pang of sympathy for this poor creature's plight, the Arkhitektor found a switch inside Calkarion's wagon, bringing the clamshell's interior to light. The sapphire glow revealed the mechanical crane arm and three curved wall racks of incomprehensible weaponry and mechanical tools. But most troubling were the several polished skulls, each one's shape resembling Calkarion's own species.

Kozlov sprang to his feet, pressing his blade to the onyx flesh of Calkarion's throat. 'I knew I couldn't trust you.'

'Those are my family.'

Kozlov flashed a glance at his companion, seeing the morbid interest in his eyes, then stared hard into those of the horseman.

'Kerzix allowed me to trawl through the irradiated ruins of my home to collect a memento before I started my royal service. He told me it was my reward.'

Those large equine eyes of Calkarion sank like stones beneath his grief, and Kozlov closely examined the clown paint matting the alien's long face. He didn't remove the blade from Calkarion's jugular.

'I was finally able to overcome Kerzix's decree. It wasn't easy, but I did it. That means I'm still alive, as you can tell.' He lifted his neck proudly, allowing the blade to scrape along the powerful cords of muscle. 'But I'll forever bear his brand. And I'm not the only one. But our resistance is minuscule compared to Kerzix's court of cackling savages. They are led by Sagillis, the ringleader who runs the Big Top, the living circus that crawls along these plains—originally from your human world I believe, a long time ago.'

That twisted human cannonball and the stilt-men dragged and loped through Kozlov's thoughts.

'It is powered by malignant forces and those corrupted souls of Sagillis and his entertainers. They patrol these lands, hunting for sport and security: refugee souls, escapees, immigrating nomads. You are both searching for something, yes?' Calkarion's eyes fluttered across Kozlov's necronaut armor, its brass mixed with the reddish tint of Zar-ptica root, an exotic plant foreign to the living realms. 'Your armor was forged with a species of fauna from Charon's former kingdom. I've seen it before.

That means you chose to come here. Why? Who in their right mind seeks out such a place before their time?'

The Arkhitektor spoke up: 'The Architect of the Empyrean. The Seeker of Light. These were lofty titles for my predecessors. It's with great regret that I say that Konstantin and I are the last of our movement.' The ghost of the arch-monk continued to examine Calkarion's various mechanical components for deceptions or devious threats. 'The founder of our sect first came here many centuries ago and discovered something beautiful in this barren waste of death and disease: Hope. A holy being, shimmering with the purest light, but trapped, half-drowned in the tidal waters near Charon's stead. We have no way of knowing how long he'd been there. Since the fall of heaven, presumably. But the angel saw our founder and handed him a desperate quest. The angel—*Luminary*—had an item near to hand but still out of reach.' The Arkhitektor closed his fist, grasping thin air in frustration.

'An item capable of undoing a great wrong: the Firmament Needle. The Luminary told our founder of how it could stitch a new heaven, restoring hope and light to the afterlife. Unfortunately, that's when Charon's chief demon, Vor Dushi, discovered our founder and the Luminary, wounded and half-submerged in those leaden waters; or perhaps the demon had known the Luminary was there all along and enjoyed his misery. But the demon took the Firmament Needle and the weakened Luminary from the tidewaters, carrying them away, and in doing so set a grand purpose at the feet of the first Arkhitektor.'

'We have not come all this way to be stopped by a fiefdom of giggling idiots,' Kozlov added, putting a little more emphasis on the knife's edge. 'We seek to find the Needle, and end all of this.'

Calkarion's large eyes angled from the Arkhitektor back to Kozlov.

'I have many weapons, as you can see. But I have no intention of wielding them against either of you. As for those skulls, they're penance, not trophies. Reminders of what I've lost, and what I will likely never retrieve. We can help each other. My allied resistance may be able to aid you in finding intelligence on where to search for the Firmament Needle. And in return, you can both help me dethrone a tyrant. What do you say?'

Kozlov's trembling sneer matched the shaky motion of the blade in his hand. Long-held fantasies of what he would do when he found the Needle promptly fired up.

'Unfit kings should be dragged from their thrones bloody and screaming.' He removed the blade from Calkarion's neck, and the Arkhitektor backed away from the revolutionary alien's devices. 'We'd like to meet your comrades.'

14

CLYDE KISSED NAT'S TATTOOED SHOULDER. They were both breathing heavily atop a quilt now in need of a good wash.

'I needed that,' he said, rolling over onto his back. The bedside lamp carved shadowed contours across his lean musculature and illuminated the multitude of tattoos flowing across Nat's athletic body.

'Me too. Not that the screen time wasn't fun, but it didn't scratch the itch the way that did.' Her face was rosy from their exertions, contented drowsiness swimming in her smoky eyes. She slid her smooth leg along his, her toes careful not to rub against the scarring about his ankle and shin.

Outside, a new snow was falling through the night, but Clyde had never felt so warm. He was staring at the ceiling of his bedroom. Nat was flat on her stomach, face on the pillow, turned towards him. Clyde felt her studious gaze on him and slowly turned to her.

'Why are you looking at me like a female praying mantis? You're not going to bite my head off, are you?' he asked with a lazy smile.

'Fuck no. If I did that, your dick wouldn't work anymore.'

'I'm just a piece of meat to you, aren't I?' He turned back to the ceiling. 'I feel so objectified.'

Nat slid her hand down his stomach to his wilting erection and fondled it a bit.

'I am a big fan of objects, though,' he added.

Nat giggled and released him, drawing a disappointed sigh from him. He reached over to the bedside cabinet and grabbed his sketch book, passing it to her.

'Oh yeah.' She seemed to remember a previous conversation, grabbing it from his hands and diving straight in. 'The royal tea party of snoozers.' She angled the book to get some better lamplight.

Clyde hooked a tangle of her long black hair behind her ear and watched her profile, savoring all the little nuances in her curiosity.

While she examined his art, he examined hers, his eye scrolling leisurely along the sensual curves of her supple shoulders and back, losing itself in the extensive mural of tattoos that, near enough, covered her whole body. He stared at the fearsome portraits of her ancient familial enemies, the Komodo Clan. Lethal warriors from various corners of East Asia, proficient practitioners of dark arts, and keepers of a dangerous secret: they knew Natalie's bloodline carried the fey energies of the Spark. He had never encountered them, but it bothered him, knowing how such a violent and obsessive cult was still operating in the world, hunting Sparks for their own ends, and it bothered him even more when he thought about Nat being that Spark. But it was some comfort knowing Meadows had history with her father, having helped him escape their clutches, and setting up a new life for him here in the U.S.; Clyde knew Meadows would employ any and all company resources to protect Nat. However, it was less comforting knowing that despite Meadows' best efforts, Sparks have previously died under his watch, people can't be protected every second of every day, and near enough anybody could be found these days. And to top it off, they would always have enough threats to contend with right here, even without such grudging familial enemies.

He was still staring at the fungi-capped samurai riding a giant Komodo across her back when Nat's voice stirred him.

'Oh, look at this dude!' She held up his impressive and bizarrely fearsome sketch of Dremel, posed like a demagogue mid-hate speech. 'This guy really one of the council or just part of your wet dreams?' Her finger tapped the caricature's head. 'I mean, what is going on here? They ... are they udders? Or dicks?'

'I think you have dicks on the brain.'

'Naw! *This* dude has dicks on the brain!' They fell in with each other's easy laughter.

After a peaceful lull, Nat's expression grew a little more serious. 'So this is Dremel?'

'That's him. I really get the feeling he doesn't like me.'

'You think it's a black thing?' Nat asked, her wit dry as desert heat.

'If you saw these things in person, you'd realize skin color probably doesn't enter the equation.'

She continued to slowly turn the pages, seeing exactly what Clyde meant, each leaf a new and wild oddity.

'I kind of wish I could see them,' she said. 'It's crazy to think that these things are always there, just waiting for you to close your eyes.'

Clyde's fingers restlessly played along her hip and lower back, tracing their way up and down her spine. His fingertip crossed off the Komodo Clan killer. 'Did you ever meet Estelle?'

Nat cradled her head on his shoulder. 'Nope. Whenever Uncle M. came to visit my mom and dad, he kept a pretty strict work/life balance, if you know what I mean.'

Clyde knew exactly what she meant. 'No shop talk. Would you say he's taking her death badly?'

'Even I have a hard time reading him, but … yeah, I don't think he's in a good place right now. And it isn't just the death of a friend. It's what she was and what she represented. Cairnwood have neutered the whole agency. No offense to you and all the other alternative talent out there, but me, Ace, Bentley, and whoever else are currently switched-on and operating, we're the last of the Sparks.'

'Not necessarily.'

'How do you mean?'

'Well, there will always be Sparks, right? We've just gotta find a new way of finding them.'

'You don't think anybody's tried that over the years?'

He gave her a noncommittal shrug. 'Doesn't mean it can't be done.'

'Look at you being the cheery optimist. Someone definitely got laid, huh?'

He laughed and leaned in for a quick kiss, then fell back onto his elbows. 'Optimist? I don't know, maybe. But it's kind of hard to know how to feel these days. It isn't just horror and existential dread on a daily basis anymore. And somewhere between you and knowing that there is a way to make a new heaven, things seem a bit brighter.'

Her laugh fluttered like butterflies in kindly amusement. 'You came, like, so close to being a total goof there.'

'Hey, maybe I meant it.' He folded his arms behind his head with a broad grin. 'Why are you with me?'

'All my other fuck buddies are busy tonight.'

Clyde winced. 'That's cold. But really?'

Nat contemplated this. 'My old boyfriends were always nuts. Drank too much, into this, into that, and we'd always bring out the worst in each other. You . . . You're the first nice guy I've been with. And I don't mean nice as in boring—fuck, quite the opposite. I mean nice as in stable. I feel safe with you.'

Clyde was floored. She, a Spark, felt safe with him? His heart fluttered, and he rolled back onto his side, wanting to gaze into her eyes. 'Man, our parents sure did fuck us, though, speaking as one dream-walking necromancer to a demi-deity. But hey, it's still better than being an intestine-feeding skavillid. *Optimism.*'

'It's a shame Kev can't siphon some of that cheery optimism from you.' Nat turned another page. 'I worry about that dude.'

Clyde stared quietly at the ceiling, thinking about his friend's unwavering fanaticism, but the truth was, despite his own mutual desire to find the Firmament Needle, time wasn't a driving factor for him. They all now officially knew the Needle existed, and it was somewhere in a vast, unmapped enemy territory. Today, tomorrow, fifty years from now, that objective would always be there; but the bigger complication was the fact that Clyde, like Rose and Ace—Nat he wasn't sure of—had previously ventured into the Null, an experience that—as per agency policy—required the ingestion of hoodoo granules to allow for agent tracking and exfiltration. This was a problem with no immediate solution. Clyde wasn't sure if the granules would be circulating in his bloodstream indefinitely, but it was an impediment that would have to be solved before he even considered heading over to the dead lands to search for the Needle.

But Kev was a man possessed.

'I'd hate to see him do anything stupid,' she said.

'Thanks for looking after him while I was away.'

'Don't mention it. He's kind of cool when he's not being so moody and distant.'

A bittersweet smile briefly settled across Clyde's face as he thought about the way Kev used to be, not just when he was alive but before he heard of that damn Needle.

'But hey, if I was stuck as a ghost who couldn't drink and bone, I'd be a bit cunty too.'

Clyde thought back on how excited Kev had been during that first morning, as Rose picked them up outside their old apartment to fly them out to Indigo Mesa for the first time. Kev's enthusiasm for the opportunity to do something had diluted his shock and fear at what he had become: a ghost with no place in the world. How quickly his golden opportunity had borne sour fruit. Clyde was worried his friend was slipping away from him again, because he knew there was certainly no way Kev would ever reclaim his enthusiasm for this job.

Nat held open the sketch book, revealing the rough drafts of the vertically conjoined pyramids, looking like an angular hourglass girded by a blur of multicolored light.

'What's this?'

Clyde glanced at the Gilded Hypnos and Obsidian Extremis and answered cryptically: 'The stuff dreams are made of.'

. . .

KEV INVITED CLYDE in with a distracted voice. The door locks slid open.

Clyde expected to find him watching something on the TV, or distracting himself with a video game, seeing as how Meadows had ordered the removal of anything so much as a pamphlet with the word abracadabra stenciled on it should it accidentally contain a smidge of arcane intel that Kev might put to forbidden use.

But it was worse than he feared. The scarcely furnished apartment was dark, and Kev was standing before the large window like an ethereal outline against the snow and lights. If he was lost in thought, Clyde would have to carefully steer him back towards sanity, or at least whatever passed for sanity in their lives. And so it was with some relief that he heard Kev humorously mumble:

'This asshole, here.'

Clyde crossed the room, stopping next to Kev, and stared through the swirling white snow to one of the buildings across the street.

It didn't take him long to see whom Kev was referring to. Even with the thick snowfall the agent was noticeable, sitting at the window of a rented apartment, not even bothering to hide.

'Even after reinstating me, Meadows still doesn't trust me.'

Clyde could have said any number of things to justify this continued level of scrutiny, but they were way past all of that now. The situation was what it was. 'This a new spotter?'

'There didn't used to be one over there. And believe me, I spent a lot of time staring out this window.'

'Doesn't mean he wasn't there before. They might have decided to stop sugarcoating the situation. I guess that's a sign of respect?'

'It's a sign that I'll never completely earn their trust back.'

Clyde suddenly became very conscious of possible listening devices, technological or thaumaturgical, that might have been installed on the premises. He typed a message onto his phone's notepad and showed it to Kev.

Do you want it back?

Kev gave it a few seconds' consideration, then shook his head. 'Fuck 'em.'

Clyde typed another: *Fancy a walk?*

. . .

'**THEY PROBABLY BUGGED** your place at some point,' Clyde said, knowing exactly what was coming next.

'No, you think … ?'

Clyde let Kev's sarcasm breeze past. 'I do. And that's why we're stretching our legs.'

They walked in easy silence along the snowy streets for a few minutes before Kev said: 'Not feeling the cold.'

'What?'

'Another perk of being dead.' Kev angled his big black shades at Clyde. 'You don't feel the cold.'

It had been a while since they played this dumb game. Shortly after Kev first came back from beyond, they'd both indulged in a macabre game of listing the pros and cons of being a tactile-deficient revenant compared to an incessantly needy living biological organism. Chalk it up to their collective shock.

Clyde offered a practiced smirk, but the sudden revival of the game only enhanced the sympathy and unease he felt for Kev's situation, as he had just come from a wild hour of sex with all the wonderful fatigue it brings, while Kev would never feel anything ever again, at least nothing sensual. But what could he say in response? He had no better alternatives of existence to offer his friend, and even if he could somehow unknot his friend's soul thread from his own, would depositing him back to the Null be better? Sadly, Clyde thought it might be. For an average person, the threat of a possible eternity in hell would be unbearable, but for a trained intelligence operative like Kev, who knew that, truly, the way out to paradise was indeed through, it was an opportunity for greatness and not just abject misery.

'Anywhere you want to go?' Clyde asked, knowing it was the lamest course correction.

'Not really.' A pause. 'You want to swing by our old apartment?'

That was unexpected. 'Okay. Why?'

'I don't know. Why do anything?'

'That your best answer?'

The snow was letting up a little as they walked through its threadbare skeins.

'Yeah, okay,' Clyde said. He'd been using every passing window and reflective surface to monitor their surroundings since leaving their building. His hand shot up to flag an approaching cab. 'Let's lose this asshole first.'

Kev didn't look behind them. He simply popped the hack's door open and slid inside.

*   *   *

THEIR OLD APARTMENT building on Myrtle Street hadn't changed; of course, it had only been six months, even if it felt longer than that. The overhead L-line provided them with some minor shelter from the snow's second coming, but the chill was starting to nip at Clyde's extremities.

'It wasn't a bad place, was it?' he asked. 'I mean, it sucks compared to the digs we have now, but it had a certain charm.'

Kev didn't say anything.

'So now what?'

They had let the cab go, and Clyde was beginning to think it might have been a tactical error. 'Please tell me you have something else in mind? Because if someone sees us standing here staring at a building like we're casing the place...' He pulled his hood aside, only then realizing that Kev wasn't even admiring the monument to their former lives but instead staring at the convenience store across the street. The place where he'd drawn his last breath, a bullet in his chest.

To Clyde's knowledge, Kev had never returned to the scene of his death before. He tried imagining what it must be like. Would it be like walking through a single moment frozen in time? Or a disorganized vignette of half-remembered senses?

'Dude... why didn't you just say?' Clyde said. 'You want me to go in there with you?'

Kev shifted from foot to foot, staring at the store like it was a mountain to be conquered. 'I'm not sure.'

'You've been thinking about this, though?'

Kev neither confirmed nor denied.

'For how long?'

'Since I first came back. But it always felt a little masochistic. And then all this happened. But when you went away with Spector, I didn't know what to do or who to talk to. Not like I had a lot of friends at the best of times, and then I pissed off our team.'

'There was Nat.'

'Yeah, she's been great. But she still had a life and job outside of running the Kevin Carpenter Sympathy Foundation.'

'It isn't just that place that's been on your mind, though, is it?' Clyde said. 'Maybe it's time you go visit your family. It'll freak them the fuck out at first, obviously, but don't you think they'd like to see you again? Talk to you?'

'What could we talk about?' Kev said, suddenly flustered. 'Where I came back from? What I do for a living? The things I've seen and know?'

'You could ask about them. You're a good listener.'

Kev seemed to mull it over, but Clyde could see no significant change in his friend's attitude.

'You're probably right,' he said at last. 'But I'm still worried about scaring them.'

'I'm not suggesting you sneak into their house and introduce yourself in the middle of the night,' Clyde said with an easy grin. 'I can do it for you. One day, broad daylight, I'll call them up and ask if I can stop by with some news.'

Kev seemed remarkably amenable to the idea. 'But maybe I should wait for New Year's. I don't want to pull some *Christmas Carol* Scrooge shit and spoil their holiday.'

'Kev, they lost you this year. Trust me when I say their year is already spoiled. Ruined. Same as next year, and all the ones after that.'

'They seemed pretty happy at the ice rink.'

'Being able to take your mind off your troubles doesn't mean your trouble's gone away. You being part of their lives again could give them some peace. And that goes both ways.' Hardly a day went by where Clyde didn't think about how it would feel if he were unexpectedly visited by the ghosts of his brother, Stephen, or his estranged dad. Most of the time it seemed like a wonderful prospect, but some days . . . It was complicated.

Kev mumbled something Clyde didn't hear, but it was a positive sound. 'Just make sure you leave out all that Null stuff, yeah?'

'Deal.'

Kev raised his fist for a knuckle bump. 'Thanks, man. I don't think I could handle any of this without you.'

Clyde felt like a fraud. 'It's my fault you're stuck here in the first place.'

'Actually, I think it's your dad's fault I'm stuck here.' Kev gave a deep and raspy guffaw. The feel-good humor pierced the leaden atmosphere. 'But I'm grateful for it, regardless. If it hadn't played out this way, I might never have learned that there's such a thing as a Firmament Needle.'

Clyde was shuffling his feet, his teeth beginning to chatter. He joined Kev in giving the convenience store one final glance. 'You still want to go in there?'

'No,' Kev said with some finality. 'Nothing to gain.' He started to drift along the sidewalk. 'It's getting late. Let's get back before my babysitter starts to worry.'

15

'**A**GAIN,' **TALBOT ORDERED, HIS VOICE** more supportive than his exasperated posture. 'Oliver can take it. Harder than coffin nails, these boys. That's what I call them.'

Dave flexed his hand and shook it. He wasn't sure why. His knuckles and wrist felt fine, but it seemed like a natural reaction, and he'd seen people do it in the movies. He stared at Oliver, the expressionless guard standing to attention before him: his nose already repaired, layers of smeared, colorless blood starting to dry, and the latest bruising around his eye socket quickly fading away beneath healed tissue.

'I'm sorry,' Dave said, feeling the itching creep of performance anxiety. He no longer knew if he was apologizing to the stoic guard he was pummeling or to Talbot and Gabriel, both of whom sat in red velvet chairs in the candlelit wine cellar. He felt small and foolish. A disappointment, waning under their pressuring stares.

'Come on, David. I know it's in you somewhere,' Talbot encouraged. 'Let's find it.'

Dave couldn't help but notice how Talbot's original swagger had diminished somewhat, giving him the whiff of a desperate gambler in sore need of a lucky hand. Ordinarily, Dave might have wondered if it was because he was so far failing to deliver the goods as expected, like some faulty divine product, but he'd first noticed this diminishment in Talbot when Gabriel had decided to tack himself onto their proceedings. Dave had a suspicion that Talbot and Gabriel were getting antsy about displeasing Soma, and that whether they did so or not was dependent on him.

Dave didn't want to disappoint them, but at the same time he didn't want to be here anymore. The blur of animal panic and heightened emotions of the afternoon had worn away, leaving him withdrawn and numb. His brain was fried from so much implausible stimuli: the sights and sounds of an unhinged mind. Except it was all real. But the quiet voice in his head was now asking a lot of questions about the motives of this lot— and Soma Sarkozy! But did he really want to go back to his empty life?

'David?' Talbot's voice, gentle, solicitous. 'You're stronger than you think.'

Dave returned a blank nod.

The guard standing before him displayed all the life of a brick wall but could certainly withstand a great deal more punishment. Flashes of the physical trauma those maniacs at his apartment building had done to some of these guards streaked through his head, and what they would do to him if they got hold of him. Oliver (if that was this guy's real name) and the other coffin nails were like fast-healing rubber men, but Dave wasn't sure if he himself could shake off a frozen shank or some paralyzing spinal trauma. And he didn't want to find out.

He closed his eyes, revisiting his big book of shame and humiliations, picking a few chapters at random: fourth grade, when his still-upbeat self was being polite and chatty to a female classmate, who proceeded to tell him to go away in front of the rest of the class; only a minor thing, but it had still left a mark, forever leaving him with an inability to engage in anything more than empty small talk with most people. He skipped ahead to his freshman high school days, the brutal time when his introversion really started to set in, twisting him into a hormonal antisocial shell. Even more damaging was the day his stress-induced IBS had caused him to shit his pants, an event the entire student body knew about before the final bell, and something that stayed with him for the remainder of his high school years. Shame burned through him like burning gasoline, the heat actually making him a little sweaty.

He tried to hold on to that feeling, and thought again of punching his fist deep into that steel door. His heart was now thumping with a sickly, moody beat. He thought specifically about what had angered him that night at work: the typical snarky disrespect from the other bartender, Cole; mopping up the piss in the "gents" restroom; being finger-snapped at by the rude, trashy bitch who had showed him nothing but contempt all night—Dave, eyes still shut tight, felt something happening now, a gentle thrum radiating deep along his radius and ulna bones like a struck tuning fork—he thought about Skimz, the local meth dealer who liked to humiliate him in front of his boys, the other bar staff, and anyone else within earshot.

'That's it, Dave.' Talbot's voice was a whisper, brimming with voyeuristic excitement.

Dave, jaw clenched, heart trying to outrace the insecurities coursing through him, opened his eyes and was shocked to see what was happening to his hand. Claret wavelets trembled the air, oscillating up and down his forearm.

He stared at Talbot and Gabriel as though he were holding a bomb, both of whom looked very invested in the destructive outcome.

Black anger bloomed behind Dave's eyes. He punched with everything he had. His knuckles ruptured Oliver's head like a 12-gauge shotgun blast at point-blank range.

Dave heard teeth scatter like dice across the stone floor of the wine cellar; he was still hearing them ten seconds later. At first he was afraid the teeth were reconstituting themselves along with the rest of Oliver's burst head, but then he realized it was just the sound of his own teeth chattering. Adrenaline had him shuddering; terror and revulsion had him horrified. A fine, colorless mist had spritzed his face and stricken eyes.

What had he done?

The guard's neck-stump gushed more of that strange plasma like a broken spigot. Dave needed to vomit.

He angled his broken stare to his partisan audience. 'I'm sorry. I didn't mean to ... *Oh God!*'

Talbot reacted like it was a tour-de-force theatrical spectacle, leaving his seat to start a vigorous round of applause. Gabriel was more subdued, but Dave saw a hungry look in the man's large eyes. He gracefully slipped away into the depths of the wine racks, returning shortly with a vintage Dave couldn't have guessed if his life had depended on it.

'I think we should have a toast.'

Talbot was very keen on the idea, no longer looking like a scolded child saddled with an admonishing parent.

Dave was too busy staring at the headless body, waiting for gravity to pull it down. He was sickened to the core at the damage he had wrought, but what troubled him the most was the tiny sense of glee dancing somewhere behind it. A depth of corruption hiding in the shadows of his morals.

The red tremors had left his hand, leaving the skin damp with Oliver's gluey ichor.

Finally, the body tumbled backwards as Gabriel popped the cork.

Dave noticed a tooth embedded deep between his knuckles but felt no pain. Must be the adrenaline. He pulled it out and watched as the ragged hole immediately began to heal over. *That's new.*

Talbot rang the small silver bell on the wall. An arched wooden door opened, and in walked two more coffin nails. Dave felt panicked. Excited. Appalled and powerful at what he had done and what he would likely be expected to do again.

The two newcomers dragged their headless cohort to one side without any semblance of feeling. They then came and stood before Dave like two more obedient targets.

'We are making progress here, young Bentley,' Gabriel said, passing the bottle of white to Talbot. Talbot guzzled it greedily straight from the neck. 'Once more with feeling.'

Dave tried to filter his scrambling thoughts, finding a grasp on that electrical prickling of anger and the dark joy of destruction. Tentatively, he found it. His tension bore outwards, banding his forearm in a furious red torsion.

With a nervous smile, courting his fear and the daring freedom of unleashed repression, Dave threw another punch.

16

IT WAS A DEN OF eyesores, but that was nothing new. Kozlov had followed Calkarion into the dark belly of some vast alien zephyr, broken-nosed and limp upon the ruins of what might have once been some exotic house of worship. The curious biological detritus of cryptic species lay scattered here and there, further grim decor for the local tyrant.

Calkarion led the way deeper inside, and Kozlov spotted a pair of oddities sitting around a glowing prism like a couple of desperados around a campfire. The first was a large iron body reminiscent of a spiky sea mine attached to stout arms and legs, with a wide, thick portal window showcasing several brains suspended in amber fluid and wired up to a gyroscope.

The second figure was more structurally complex by far, a robust humanoid body composed of a vivid bundle of yellow and white pollen, bound together within a densely intricate exoskeleton of copper-toned tubules. Its head, if it could be called that, was akin to a dandelion's seed head, a rudimentary face largely hidden within the quivering reeds.

Each of these two associates of Calkarion shared his brand of past ownership: a face-splitting red grin and a pair of arching cartoon eyes on a white-waxen face; the brand was painted across the dandelion head of the flora creature, and in the case of the walking sea mine, painted onto the window behind which its multiple brains floated.

Inhuman though they were, their suspicion of these new arrivals was plain to Kozlov. He respected it, knowing it to be a survivor's trait, and one that he shared. He gave his hidden companion a nod, at which the Arkhitektor appeared, phasing through a broken structure that could have been anything from a navigational machine to a piece of luxury seating. He raised his hand, revealing a bulging acid-leaking plant bulb floating above his palm.

'Are you familiar with these?' Kozlov asked Calkarion. 'We found a grove of them in the swamps along the outskirts of this principality. We watched as an animal took a bite, and how its jaws, throat, and stomach dissolved in under a minute. My comrade has already deposited a few more of them around the immediate area. Make that clear to your allies, should they decide to act on their suspicions.'

Calkarion looked vexed. 'I have already explained my motivations to you, and they are not untoward.'

'Trust is earned,' Kozlov told him. 'And if this pair are reliable enough for you to stake your life and mission on, I hope they are shrewd enough to be untrusting of the two strangers in their midst. At least for the moment.'

Calkarion quickly set to easing any miscommunications between his fellow ex-slaves and the human strangers he had led into their bunker. The plant-soldier glanced about the floor of the doomed airship, one of its extended finger tubules feeling about and finding one of the lethal bulbs near its heel. Without excitement or pending violence, it calmly withdrew its feeler.

Calkarion made some cursory introductions. The walking garden was called Quarmalls, and the brain tank Trillik.

It struck Kozlov how impossible a task this could prove to be if the party's universal translator should at some point perish. Maybe if he could take possession of Calkarion's soul at such a time … but would that help him communicate, or would Calkarion's soul be at a loss without the technological output of his vocal device?

'I understand you are both former serfs of Kerzix,' Kozlov said. 'I have no personal grudge against him, no more than the rest of the Order. But our goals are closely aligned. I believe we can be of use to each other.'

Calkarion translated.

A gentle reedy sound may or may not have whistled from Quarmalls, and Trillik offered a few electronic chirps.

'My comrade and I had a troubled history with a former regent of Charon,' Kozlov continued. 'I'm not sure how far word might have spread about our actions. I tell you this because, having slain that regent, my companion and I have made some very dangerous enemies here, so we all need to be doubly careful.'

Calkarion's big equine eyes challenged Kozlov. 'Charon has been gone for so long his House is in disarray. Even his great and terrible architecture is falling apart. Why do you think so many souls slip through the gaps of his pipeline network? Untold numbers leak out before reaching their designated Houses. That's why Kerzix makes a sport of hunting them down, to keep their numbers from ever growing large enough to rise up. As for the regent you killed, he was little more than a wild, unchained beast. A mindless knight, not a wise king.'

A bitter anger contorted the Arkhitektor's face, his tight seizure of the acidic bulb threatening to make it burst into a lethal mist. Kozlov exchanged a look with him, and after a moment, the high monk found his calm.

'That may be the case,' Kozlov said, 'but we both have a lot of pain invested in our dealings with that "mindless knight" and would appreciate it if you didn't diminish our suffering and our efforts. More importantly, it doesn't alter the fact that the slain regent carried off the holy item we seek, and one of the item's guardians. Presumably it took them both somewhere important for safekeeping, and that means it might have mentioned our repeated incursions to a higher command. The other Houses of the Order might be watching for us.'

Trillik beeped and booped.

'Charon's stand-in must have underestimated you,' Calkarion said. 'News of your conflict never made it beyond Charon's border. Neither of us have heard of you, and Trillik would have, if only from his former security position.'

'Then that's a good thing. We're clearly lacking a formidable force, so an assassin's approach is what we'll need.'

'Agreed. Now, we're all familiar with each other, so, Arkhitektor, do you mind?' Calkarion indicated the acidic fruit floating inches above the Arkhitektor's hand, on the verge of pulping.

The Arkhitektor lowered the bulb to the ground, letting it roll away into some far corner of the zephyr.

Trillik tapped its chest with a dense but dexterous finger, signaling Calkarion.

Calkarion opened a storage panel on the curved top of its spider frame, removing what looked to Kozlov like several pieces of scrap; however, they carried a slight luminosity. Calkarion handed one to Trillik, who swapped out a depleted power source for this new battery, inserting it into part of its complex machinery. Calkarion passed one to Quarmalls, who dug out a handheld-sized contraption from its organic innards and copied the process with clever filament fingers.

Calkarion, holding onto the third and final battery, saw Kozlov and the Arkhitektor's curiosity. 'I was gathering these when I met you.' With nimble fingers he replaced his own battery, slipping the new one into a belt around his waist.

An amber sheen rolled across Trillik's metal bulk and brain tank like a prophylactic force field. The same happened to Quarmalls, and then Calkarion. After several seconds, the amber sheaths blinked out.

'It produces a powerful neural buffer around our brains, nullifying Kerzix's psychological manipulation,' Calkarion explained. 'A technological breakthrough Trillik and I worked up while Kerzix wasn't paying close enough attention. It took a few prototypes before we were successful. Fortunately, Kerzix and his general, Sagillis, tend to let their violent appetites interfere with their better judgements, happy to celebrate after their sport rather than keep a close eye on their lieutenants—former lieutenants; those lapses in concentration allowed Trillik and me to regain our senses for a time.'

Kozlov's eyes moved from Calkarion's oscillating screen to his painted smile. His thumb and index finger parted up and away in a smile gesture. 'Do you still wear this for . . . motivation?'

'We took back our autonomy, our minds, but the branding remained. The mind and the soul are connected. Perhaps Kerzix's marottes have tainted us all the way to the core, or perhaps it's something else, something irreversible—some form of mystical searing. In any case, these shameful colors don't seem to run.' Calkarion tossed his used battery onto the floor. 'But it's a small price for free will.'

The crane arm extended out from Calkarion's armored wagon, holding a small metallic bucket. It was sealed, and something sloshed about within. Calkarion unsealed the latches on the container and passed it to his left. A drinking tubule jutted out from Quarmall's tufty head, and it took a long swig. Trillik and the Arkhitektor bypassed the sup, and Quarmalls passed it straight to Kozlov. It could have been a bucket of poison for all he knew, and his expression clearly stated this.

'It is harmless,' Calkarion said. 'Extract from a type of plant unique to a region called the Spinning Collapse. It's good for you. We drink in celebration of our unity and our cause.'

Kozlov sensed a cautious acceptance from the Arkhitektor.

'To trust.' He raised the container to his lips and took a small swallow. It was a little tangy, with a chalky mineral texture, but mostly tasteless. Still better than some of the food and drink that had lined his stomach since he got here. The life he'd led had long since wrung out any chance of a fussy palate: KGB operative, hermetic mountain monk, Erebian pilgrim, prisoner of Peklo, Erebian pilgrim once more.

Calkarion nodded, reclaimed the drink for himself, and drank deeply.

'We will cross the Madcap Flats to Lunacy Alley. That will lead us towards Kerzix's palace. It is heavily guarded, but we have knowledge of a secret tunnel and the Crown's security measures.'

'What about intelligence reports? Does a monarch who craves chaos have an orderly filing system, or does he keep everything in here?' Kozlov gestured to his head.

'He's a tricky one, but if you're referring to the Firmament Needle, anything he knows of it will be stored in the Rictus Folly.'

'What's that?'

The brain array whirred about within its ironclad body, emitting a series of low-frequency chirps that sounded to Kozlov like a very old computer slowly dying.

'A complex inter-world circuit channeling all of Kerzix's treasured memories, and those of his Marotte Marauders; their every rampage from across every world. Trillik used to help keep it organized when serving under the king. It makes sense that the capture and torture of a Luminary at the hands of the Order of Terminus would be a cherished memory. The Rictus Folly also helps to keep the power flowing through all of his marottes scattered throughout the cosmos.'

The Arkhitektor broke his silence. 'A place that important is surely a death trap. Will we be enough?'

'Are we ever enough?' Kozlov asked. 'We hold on tight to our convictions and hope the wind blows in our favor.'

More sharp atonal bleeps from Trillik, and a noise like a breeze through reeds from Quarmalls.

'It won't be easy, but Trillik knows how to disrupt the Folly's circuitry and the palace's power systems. We'll need to keep any enemy forces off him when the time comes,' Calkarion stated. 'I don't know if we can physically destroy Kerzix. Despite being former members of his court, we don't know the upper limits of his power. But breaking into the Folly will allow us to disseminate damning information across his whole network, including its links to the other monarchs.'

'What information?' Kozlov asked.

'Each of the Order's monarchs receives a percentage of all souls, but as I mentioned, Kerzix cheats by using his marottes. He hosts these big events, live-broadcasting any new Marauder rampages. But only his closest court members know that the Marauders are under his sway. Outsiders, including some of the Houses, think these bloodbaths are the work of religious zealots. If we can leak the truth of the Marauders, I don't see the other dead kings being too lenient. We can leave Kerzix ruined, and they should deal with him for us.' Calkarion paused, a sense of satisfaction about him. 'This will help us cripple him, and it will also allow Trillik to search the Folly for anything germane to the Firmament Needle.'

Kozlov nodded his gratitude, but there was something beyond logistics and threat assessments that concerned him. 'If we make it to the Folly, are you not concerned you might glimpse the memories of your time as a Marauder?'

Calkarion's large horse eyes swelled with a depth of humanity Kozlov had rarely ever seen in his own species, but it couldn't veil the bitter pain within. 'It troubles me every day. Troubles each of us. In doing this, we may finally put an end to Kerzix's cruelty. For that, we would each stare down our mistakes a hundredfold.'

17

N O MATTER HOW MUCH LUXURIOUS food Dave was presented with, all it did was sit heavy in his stomach, its taste unable to overpower the sensation of shame that ran through him like a hairline crack. The visceral imagery of exploding heads and his fists punching through chests remained frozen in his mind like a red-and-black fresco painted on the interior of his skull. Impressionistic violence.

Talbot and Gabriel had fussed over him a great deal, filling him with wine and gourmet food. Each corpse had been carried away by more of their own number, silent and passive. The coffin nails were remarkably durable, but even the hardest nails can be bent or even snapped in half. Talbot had said words to that effect with his hand on Dave's shoulder all chummy-like, pushing a champagne magnum into his hand still tacky with colorless gore. Talbot and Gabriel had said a lot of things, but Dave's roaring blood had made him partially deaf to a lot of it.

The violent revelry had concluded with Talbot and Gabriel retiring to unknown corners of the manse, leaving Dave alone to walk the building's many halls unimpeded. Instead, he sat by the picture window of his room, feeling warm and woozy from alcohol, tired from the banquet. His hands, now heavily soaped and scrubbed, lay like alien things in his lap. Two little monsters napping after their thuggery. And it was here for the first time that Dave realized it wasn't just shame that he felt: it was relief.

Annette Bancroft sat up in his mind, behind her desk with her certifications and self-help publishing deals, asking him how he was managing his temper. Dave almost sniggered drunkenly, a squall of clashing emotions and shock.

Not well, Anne. Not well.

He felt the first tear slip from his eye. What was he? A freak. A monster! Sparks. Spiritual wars between impossible forces that shouldn't exist outside of popcorn movies. Movies he loved and thought he wanted to live but now knew differently.

A sob broke his fragile state. Was he a killer? Could the coffin nails be described as anything less garish? Had he murdered them, or were they not even alive to begin with? They were not human, but that shouldn't matter. They were conscious beings. Snuffed out by the weight of his frustrations and rage.

He wiped his tired eyes and stared out the windows at the exquisite gardens. He hadn't moved in a while. He wasn't sure how long, but he'd watched the rising sun spread its Midas touch upon the deep snow, turning it from night silver to gold. What the fuck was he doing here? Okay, so he was a freak, but he'd always known that on some level; it just turned out that he was a bigger freak than he could ever have realized in his wildest power fantasy. Not just anti-social, but anti-human? But that didn't mean he belonged here. Talbot might have saved him from those Hourglass killers, but if he wanted him to be some Cairnwood leg-breaker, then Dave knew he would have to disappoint him.

What were his options? Thank Talbot for an interesting evening and call a cab? After what he'd done, what he'd seen and heard, would he be allowed to leave?

And if he could, did he really want to go back to his cold, empty life? No family. No friends. Deluding himself with silly notions of writing some screenplay that could get him an agent, maybe a meeting with a producer? He knew it was insensible, but when you have nothing else to hold on to, even the most outlandish possibility can become a life preserver.

He did have Salty's Tavern, however. A dead-end bar full of staff, all embittered at life, who thought he was quiet and weird, and clientele who hung onto society's fringes with dirty, broken nails.

Skimz popped into his thought bubble like he was about to experience an imminent mugging. Skimz, the meth dealer who frequented the bar the way a fly frequents dog shit. Skimz and his two fucking two-bit asshole hangers-on, Grizz and Tags.

Dave silently dwelled on the choices and circumstances that had built his poorly constructed life. Then he thought about the three types of anger: passive, direct, assertive.

A thread of something ugly sprouted through Dave's wallowing. Skimz, Grizz, and Tags all staring at him like he was a piece of meat whenever he served them, their eyes empty of anything but contempt and mockery for his bumbling personality. He was nothing to them. His life as ephemeral as cigarette smoke.

But it wasn't just those three bottom-feeding drug pushers. It was all the other broken-down assholes he served beer and shots to, and his loud, obnoxious co-workers. All the people he passed every day on the street who had that little microsecond glance of distaste in their eyes when taking note of him. The way they all made him feel.

Passive anger.

That cunt with the ice shank and that little bitch who chased him through his own building like she expected him to just roll over and die.

Passive anger.

Weak all his life.

A sad, pathetic fuck who couldn't even manage basic human interaction to anything above bare-bones pleasantries and a forced smile.

Why me? he thought. *Why can't I just feel normal in my skin?*

Lifelong questions he'd never figured out an answer for. And neither could the illustrious Annette Bancroft.

But I'm not normal. Am I.

Dave tensed his knuckles. It felt nice. The hard bones knowing their purpose innately. He pictured red, twisting devils whirling along his arms, red pennants of absolute wrath ripping into jeering faces.

The anger was a passive shield. And a big fucking direct sword.

He relaxed his hand, suddenly scared, and chewed a nail. Escape. That's what he needed right now. He pulled out his phone. Talbot had provided him with the Wi-Fi, thank God.

He streamed a movie to ease his pounding thoughts. A secondhand story and people he could understand from a distance. Vicarious living through archetypal characters, bound by script and viewer expectations.

A welcome relief.

18

'**S**o how are things going with you two?' Kev asked.

Clyde thought about Nat and tried to suppress a smile. 'Good. It's easy being with her. No pretense or anything.'

'Cool. I like her,' Kev admitted out loud for the first time. 'I hate her music, but I like her.'

That was one smile Clyde didn't suppress. He wasn't a big fan of punk rock either, but he'd be lying if he said some of it wasn't rubbing off on him.

They sat at the empty dining-room table, the cold wintry light of morning bathing the apartment in a clean hue.

Kev was moving a couple of broken listening devices about the dining table like he was a con man running a shell game. After getting back from his walk with Clyde the night before, he'd performed a thorough check for bugs in his apartment, and since his apartment was little more than an empty placeholder, it must have been difficult for the agency to plant them inconspicuously. It wasn't for lack of trying on their behalf, but Kev managed to find them without too much hassle: one on the lintel above the large lounge window—the one facing the agent in the building opposite—and one closer to the kitchen, on the underside of a cupboard. Despite turning them into micro junk, nobody at the agency had bothered him about it yet.

'She helped me more than I let on,' Kev said. 'Nobody else seemed to give a shit, but she was there to talk to me.' He glanced around his empty apartment. 'I'm happy for you, man. You deserve whatever happiness you can get in this life.' Before the scene became too poignant, Kev was quick to add, 'Are you going to meet the parents anytime soon?'

'Neither of us have mentioned it, but ... I don't know. It'll happen when it happens.'

Clyde had a sudden chilling thought that if this situation stuck to its traditional course, he might end up with Meadows as a surrogate uncle-in-law instead of just a grumpy boss.

'About last night, you haven't changed your mind?' Clyde held up his phone like it was a prop, intimating calling Kev's family.

Kev was slow to answer. 'No. Maybe I do need to do this. I'm just scared.' He seemed very small all of a sudden.

'I know. Everything's happened so fast, but I think you might still be in shock. I know I am,' Clyde said with a weary head-shake. 'Think about it: you died, came back, and then before you had any real time to process it all, we were training at Indigo. Right out the gate, you're on your first assignment. And it was work and horror right up until your suspension. I don't think it's been healthy to be so reliant on a job. You're disconnected.' Clyde watched all this sink into Kev's expression, but it was very nuanced.

'And I'll just come out and say it,' he went on. 'I think Meadows handled this badly. I do think you gave him a real reason to come down hard on you—'

Kev was about to interject, but Clyde stopped him. 'But I still agree with why you did it. But of course he's not going to see it that way. Still, I think he should realize the shit you've been through in a very short space of time.'

Kev was silent for a beat. 'You think I should complain to Human Resources?'

Clyde smiled. 'I think it would do you good to have your family back. Some stability outside of work ... ' Clyde felt a trickle of shame flush through him at the words thought but left unsaid: *Outside of me.*

'It wouldn't be selfish?' Kev asked, giving the broken bugs a quick tight spin about the table. 'Because I'm struggling to know what's selfish and what isn't. Am I selfish for hiding the truth from them, or selfish for burdening them with it?'

'You're their son, and Rhi's older brother. That's a bond too big to be simplified like that. I think they'll want to see you.'

Kev was losing the ability to sit still. 'Okay, do it.'

Clyde took a breath, cleared his throat, and pushed dial on the number for Aaron, Kev's dad. With his mom being a high school teacher, she'd still be busy winding up for Christmas break, but Aaron was a software engineer whose work schedule was much more flexible.

'Put it on speaker,' Kev said.

Clyde did, and watched as Kev squirmed with each lonely ring.

Finally, it was picked up on the sixth. 'Clyde?'

Kev's chest hitched when he heard the voice.

'Hi, Aaron. I'm sorry to bother you—'

'Don't be ridiculous, it's good to hear from you.'

'You too.' They both bumbled along, the gradual slip of time having stolen away the easy rapport they once shared. Clyde felt exposed and was quickly beginning to doubt his own advice. 'Erm, how are you doing?'

'I'm getting there,' Aaron answered, and the raw hurt in his voice that Clyde remembered from their last talk had softened a little with time. 'We all are, but it's tough. It's just…each day does make it a little easier, but then every now and then some random little thing will open up a hole. But all we can do is keep on, right? Pray he's in a better place.'

Kev was staring at the phone as though he was scared to blink, ethereal fingers around the edge of the table.

'Are you holding up okay?' Aaron asked.

Clyde looked at Kev, seeing the doubt on his face and feeling it slowly flow over him like a rising tide. How to answer that?

'I have some news I think you'll want to hear, but I would prefer to do it in person.'

'Okay…' Aaron's voice became hollow.

'And I would prefer it if Sandy and Rhi were there too. Would that be okay?'

'What's this about?' Aaron sounded dubious.

'Kev. And I think you'll be very happy to hear it.'

With some trepidation Aaron agreed, but he still sounded confused.

'Is there a day that works best for you?' Clyde asked.

Aaron *ummed* and *arred* before: 'Sunday, twelve o'clock okay?'

Clyde nodded at Kev, trying to drum up some positive response from him.

'That's great, yeah. Your place okay?'

Aaron still sounded flummoxed. 'Sure.' And then: 'Can I ask what this is about?'

'It'll make sense, trust me . . . ?' Clyde didn't know why he phrased it as a question. It wasn't meant to be.

'I do. Thanks for calling, Clyde. I look forward to seeing you.'

'Me too. Bye.'

The line went dead, and the room seemed as empty as a vacuum. A distant car horn beeped somewhere outside, city noises slowly filling the quiet.

'You okay?' Clyde asked.

Kev dissipated through the back of his chair, walking a little groove into the wood. He made a positive noise, something like *umm-hum*. But it was impossible to miss how fraught he had become.

'You'll need to cover that up when you meet them,' Clyde said, nodding towards the gunshot wound in Kev's chest.

Kev nodded, pacing back and forth. He took his seat again. 'Yeah, I'd hate to freak them out,' he said without humor.

There was a knock at the door, or rather an impatient light kicking.

Kev slid the bolt back and opened it without leaving his seat. Nat entered with a cardboard holder of two takeout coffee cups and a bag of pastries. Her long, dark hair and leather jacket were dusted with snow. She heeled the door shut behind her. Clyde took his latte from her, and she dropped the bag in the middle of the table before straddling a free chair, grabbing a croissant and tearing into it.

'Dude, I'd fucking hate to be a barista this time of year. Customers suck.' She carried on chewing, then took a slurp of her vanilla latte. 'Here you go, K-pop.' She reached into the paper takeout bag. 'Hot off the mess.' She brought out a copy of *Through the Veil*, a locally produced journalistic dead end, a waste of pulp focusing on the whackiest stories from the dimmest minds. The lurid-colored eye-grabber catered to a small but loyal demographic of people who hungrily sought out accounts of mind-controlling broccoli or Nessie actually being some cursed Scottish king.

She dropped it in front of Kev, on top of the broken bugs. The front page was an article concerning an individual who claimed to have had dream visions of a murderous circus tent.

'All reliable sources, I'm sure.' Clyde took the lid off his coffee to let it cool and grabbed a blueberry muffin.

'Set your minds to dumb.' Kev rested his chin on his hand and started perusing.

Clyde knew Nat had been bringing Kev the periodical fluff each week as a goof. If his suspension had barred him from reading and re-searching legitimate weird tales, then at least he had this crap to enter-tain himself with.

Clyde noticed how Nat was watching Kev over the rim of her cup with an amused twinkle in her eye and felt a deep surge of warmth for her, content with the jovial bond she and Kev had struck up in his absence.

'So why were you two looking so shady when I came in? High jinks? How about we fuck with the agent across the street?' She continued to scarf down her croissant. 'I have no evidence, but I'm blaming him for planting those bugs.'

'Clyde's talked me round on seeing my family,' Kev said, gaze unwa-vering from the magazine.

Clyde swallowed some muffin.

'Oh,' Nat said. 'You don't sound pumped?'

Kev still didn't look up.

Before an answer was forthcoming, Nat's phone rang: "If the Gov't Could Read My Mind" by The Vandals.

Meadows.

Clyde checked his phone, thinking he must have accidentally switched it to silent and missed a team-wide message, but no, he had vol-ume. Either Meadows' little sub-network of spies was keeping close tabs on Nat as well as Kev, or he was assuming Clyde and Nat were ostensibly joined at the hip.

The call was brief and one-sided.

'The worm has girth,' she said, sliding the phone back into her jacket. 'Let's go, boys.'

19

 LYDE WAS GOING THROUGH SOME loose warm-ups with Kev. Neither had seen any action in a few weeks, so it was good to fine-tune the muscle memory and instincts before getting into some potential deep shit.

As lumpy, oil-black sludge men go, each of the attackers was perfectly symmetrical on either side. This wasn't a sign of beauty and physical perfection, but the result of Schulz's training room: the Rorschach. Being a current and former psychiatrist, the ink-blot medium was something he had employed on occasion during his clinical years.

That and electroshock therapy.

Both modes of treatment now, and possibly forever, a part of the doctor's existence.

The rogues he conjured up in this room, however, lacked ambiguity and were not for a patient's personal interpretation. These oily horrors were very understandable to all agency combatants; they were imminent physical threats, and nothing more.

Clyde had decided to forgo firearms for this session. Having fired off a few rounds in the range at Indigo between Spector's sessions, he was using this time to briefly reacquaint himself with his and Kev's shared power over physical matter. Drawing on some of his friend's ability, Clyde used telekinesis to cheat gravity a little, fire off some percussive shocks, push, pull, fling, hurl, and even crush.

It was all very rote by now, with too little time spent apart to develop ring rust. But Clyde had sure missed these borrowed abilities in his absence, and what made it all the more satisfying was the lack of guilt he felt in dispatching these lifeless attackers.

'On your six,' Kev called out casually.

Clyde found a tar-man lurching over his shoulder and spun around the clock; it had one sloppy fist poised to smother his face and head. Clyde swept him into the air as though a bracing wind had suddenly howled up through the ground. The loose-limbed thing was twisting at the apex when Clyde condensed its whole form into a jet-black basketball. Controlling it with precision, he tested its bounciness with a few dribbles and passed it to Kev, who buried it through the chest of two more slithering tar-men before passing it back.

Nat didn't need the practice and was content to offer moral support. She was relaxing in the corner of the large white room with her bucket headphones on, back to the wall, legs V-spread, thumping along to one punk track or another on her mystical bass guitar.

Clyde spun the tar ball on his finger and signaled Kev with a prankster's smirk. Going for a 3-pointer, he guided his arcing shot with smooth manipulation. It was ten feet above Nat's head when she casually tilted her instrument's headstock and disintegrated the black orb with a pulverizing tunnel of sound.

She wagged her tongue and flipped him the finger. Her offending digit went right back to picking up the breakneck rhythm of her index finger, galloping across the violet-tinted strings.

Clyde suspected he was falling for her in a pretty big way.

'Should we switch this up?' he asked Kev. 'When I said warm-up, I didn't mean novice level. This is baby shit, man.'

Kev shrugged, a dearth of enthusiasm in face and body. He stared at the observation window of the training room. Schulz was in there, or at least part of him was, some fragment of consciousness at their beck and call to regulate their training requirements; the variety of opponents was a matter of personal request, or one of the memorized beasts dredged up from Schulz's years of experience with Meadows' shop.

'Let's save our energy for when we throw Talbot his surprise house party,' Kev said.

Only a few tar-men remained, circling them like they had just woke up on the wrong side of the inkwell. Clyde turned towards Schulz, thumb down like a Roman emperor at the Coliseum. Schulz obliged, and the lumbering ink-men vanished without a trace, leaving not so much as a black spot on the pristine white surfaces.

Nat, halfway through the chorus of a Misfits song Clyde could almost recognize, vanished her bass into thin air and removed her headphones.

'Careful, guys, you almost broke a sweat.'

'We're just getting limber,' Clyde said, pulling her up by her outstretched hand.

'I need some sugar,' she said.

He leaned in for a quick kiss, but she played her game of pretending not to notice him and sliding away. He smiled at her innocent ball-busting tactics, knowing exactly how little innocence there was in her. She enjoyed the teasing and the control.

'The one cool thing about Christmas apart from the lights?' she asked. 'Gingerbread lattes.'

'You had one before we got here,' Clyde said.

'That was vanilla. Check your facts. But that was my fuck-up. I should have gone for gingerbread. You think if I asked Uncle Meads about opening a coffee shop on site he'd be down?'

'Probably would if he could plant tracking chips in the muffins and kill switches in the cookies,' Kev muttered.

'Maybe I'll just buy you the syrup for Christmas,' Clyde said. ''Tis the season.'

Schulz's voice crackled over the speakers. 'Deputy Director Meadows is ready for you in the library.'

'Alright, bookworm must be in his teens by now,' Nat said, sounding pumped. 'Let's go see if Talbot has any overdue library books.'

■ ■ ■

THE BOOKWORM WAS no longer a mere smidge of a thing but a 12-foot-long fresh-leathery thing, slowly, almost luxuriously writhing about on the library's tile floor. Several of its shoots were binding themselves about the torn page of the *Xenoglossia* like a swooning romantic clutching a love letter to their chest.

Meadows, jacket off, tie loosened a little, wasn't alone. Next to him was a plump and unfamiliar member of staff: a middle-aged Indian woman, her self-serious posture offset by a lighted Christmas sweater, Rudolph's red LED nose flashing all the way. Shriya Haasan was the head librarian of this collection of arcana, and an authority on bookworms.

'I can see on your faces that none of you are sure what to do with this darling creature,' she said. 'Rest assured, just like most living things, it's all instinct. Right now he's got a very good sense of the unique energy trapped within the page, and upon request he'll follow the trail to the current source.'

'There's a tracker placed on him so we can follow his subterranean route,' Meadows added. Clyde thought he looked tired and imagined him up all night, pacing about the building with his quiet anger and pain, making calls or combing through reams of intel for anything strategically devastating to be unloaded upon their powerfully insulated enemies in Cairnwood.

As for Ace, he was as pale as snow in moonlight, and as quiet and ominously threatening as black ice.

'That trail could lead anywhere,' Clyde said. 'What if he surfaces on a tangent? He could put us in a place we really don't want to be.'

Rose and Sarge nodded along slowly in agreement.

'He'll remain underground unless told otherwise, so he'll be safe,' Shriya said. Her coal-dark gaze sparkled behind the hooded wrinkles of her eyes, expressing a deep fondness for the clever creature.

'I think he's more concerned about our safety than the worm's,' Ace said.

'In all likelihood, the trail will lead to a significant Cairnwood location,' Meadows said. 'Somebody like Sarkozy wouldn't have stepped out of the shadows after all this time for a Red Roof Inn. If he is involved with Cairnwood, it'll be a Cairnwood property, and somewhere local, at least within the state lines. We're on a tight clock, with no chance of prolonged aerial recon, so in case they're holding Bentley at that same location, I'm authorizing a full-scale assault to ensure you are all equipped enough to succeed in bringing Bentley into our custody and putting down anybody who gets in your way.'

'We might get lucky,' Nat said. 'If Bentley doesn't know what his power is or how to control it, maybe he'll fuck up and take Talbot and the whole lot of 'em with him.'

'I lost most of my optimism with my youth, but that is a possibility,' Meadows said.

It took Clyde a second longer than he would have liked to pick up on the darker meaning hidden in Nat's flippant remark, thinking about the story she'd told him of the devastating emergence of her powers. He pictured her, drunk and partying in an old warehouse where her old buddies and bandmates used to hang out. Her power unexpectedly blooming beyond her control, all the noise and brash music like an air current through soapy water, building and building an increasingly gigantic sonic bubble. Until it burst. Nat was the only survivor. Could Dave survive a possible power malfunction?

Clyde glanced at Kev from the corner of his eye. There was no attitude from him, no further remarks about fighting a pointless fight. Nothing. In fact, Kev seemed to be paying very little attention to Meadows at all, being more focused on Rose—no, not Rose. Barros, floating beside her old combat unit.

The young worm started to get excited, much in the way of a dog eager for walkies.

'He ain't going to piss, is he?' Ace asked, wrinkling his nose.

Shriya avoided the question and, through some form of unknown communication, cajoled the worm across the floor to a large golden disc engraved with symbols. With the flick of a switch, Shriya dropped the disc into two hinged flanges, revealing a deep, dark hole. A cold draft moaned its way up to dampen the warmth.

'Saves on floor repair and lawn maintenance,' she said.

The worm slid down it as though it was what it was born to do. The two half-circles clunked back into place.

Meadows tossed a small device to Rose. 'Transponder.'

The screen displayed the steady ping of the bookworm's cavernous route. It was avoiding the seabed and heading in a northwesterly direction.

'The two assault teams are on standby,' Meadows said. 'Bring Bentley in alive unless you have absolutely no other choice. I still want to give him options before ruling him out as an ally.'

'And if Talbot's there?' Clyde asked.

Meadows reflected on the question. 'Hurt him to the point of death, but bring him in too. We can always use inside information.'

Rose elbowed Ace, who in turn gave Clyde a nod, who finished with a gentle caress of Nat's hand. He saw Kev still resembling a man trying and failing miserably to fit in. They set off for the armory.

20

DAVE AWOKE TO A LIFE he didn't recognize, in a room utterly incomparable to his apartment. And then it all came rushing back to him. Shame, horror, depression, but then, the tiniest glint of...*purpose?* His life felt curiously like the beginning of a crazed power fantasy, which he couldn't deny held a certain despairing charm, like some past-her-prime bar skank who seemed doable after five or six beers. He checked his phone, seeing it was still before noon. He'd only had a few hours of sleep and felt rough. Not wanting to lie there with his thoughts, he slid off the most comfortable bed he'd ever slept in and decided he should seek out his hosts. He was met at the door by one of those loquacious coffin nails holding a tray of scrambled eggs, juice, fruit, and coffee, all of which set his stomach into fits of unbridled need. He politely accepted the food without further comment and retreated back into his room, closing the door behind him.

He wondered if the coffin nails knew about what he'd done to their fellows the night before, and briefly considered the chances that they might have poisoned his breakfast. But then hunger won out.

Hours passed with him undisturbed in his room. He checked several times to see if a coffin nail was posted outside his room but found the long hallway completely empty apart from more owl statuary. Strangely, despite the hospitality, he was hesitant to venture out, worried about what or who he might stumble upon.

So he spent most of the day distractedly jotting his thoughts and moods down into the notepad Annette Bancroft suggested he carry around, and making half-hearted notes for his screenplay, all the while trying not to dwell on the skewed reality of his situation. He was beginning to feel like some exotic pet kept in a plush cage when there came a soft rapping upon his door.

'Yeah?'

Talbot poked his head in. 'Good afternoon, Dave. My apologies for keeping you cooped up in here. I know it's utterly redundant now, but you were free to walk around. I should have stated that last night. You are a guest here. How was your breakfast?'

Dave gestured to the empty dishes he had piled neatly on the bureau.

'I figured you would be quite ravenous, and we have a terrific chef. I presume it was up to scratch?'

Dave mumbled his agreement. 'Actually, I was a little worried about eating it at first.'

'Oh?'

'Don't take this the wrong way, but none of you are human. I don't know what you all eat or drink, but I'm pretty sure Gabriel was drinking blood from a teacup yesterday.'

Talbot made no attempt to deny this. 'But you had no trouble eating last night.'

'I was starving.' Dave thought about the energy he must have spent putting his body through such impossible feats. 'Wait, there wasn't anything weird—'

'It was all food fit for human consumption, Dave. Even though you are already something above and beyond humanity. Still, we have no need, nor want to make you into something else, so don't fret about your food being spiked with eye of newt or any such nonsense. We only want you to be you.'

There was a clear resurgence in Talbot's boldness now that Gabriel was absent.

Talbot crossed over to a high-backed chair draped with Dave's coat. Dave expected him to fuss over it and correct him on some matter of proper housekeeping, but he simply ignored it and sat down.

'Tell me about yourself, Dave.'

'Isn't this whole thing more of a show than tell? I'm here because I'm a Spark, not because of my past.'

'Correct. But don't diminish yourself. You're a person too. You had a life prior to the hard left turn you have taken. Did you have a family?'

Dave didn't really want to dredge up his upbringing, but Talbot seemed sincerely curious about him. Sitting awkwardly on the edge of the bed, he sighed deeply, as if about to lift something heavy.

'I had a mom and dad, but I was an only child. My dad took off when I was five. I think he was cheating on my mom. I didn't see him again after that. No calls or annual drop-ins, not even a birthday card.'

Talbot crossed a leg, face solemn and attentive.

Dave picked his way through his history as though there could be tripwires hidden amidst the words.

'My mom, she, uh—she died when I was nineteen. Aneurysm at work. She was a florist. The house always had the most colorful plants. I think she thought of them as her other children,' he said with a wistful smirk. 'She was incredible, you know. Did everything she could for me. But I always had this dad-shaped void in my life that I was trying to fill. And I think she knew that. I never pushed her away. I think I was just, I don't know... emotionally absent, I guess. I never did learn how to act around people. I always felt like the worst actor on stage whenever I was trying to be social. After a while I just stopped trying. But my mom was awesome. She deserved better.'

'I'm sorry to hear that,' Talbot said, empathy coating his words.

Dave bobbed his head, thinking it was over, but Talbot still seemed to be waiting for more. He could give Annette Bancroft a run for her money in the listening department.

'I've been alone since then.' He clasped his hands together.

'Tragedy reshapes a person. Sometimes that person crumbles in the process, and sometimes they become something so much more. You already know that you are so much more, David. It's in your blood. But here,' Talbot lightly tapped his own forehead, 'this is where you need to reshape yourself. I can tell you are still a little confused, conflicted even, about using your gods-given power. But lions don't feel remorse for eating gazelle. I won't pretend that your life is going to get any easier, because in truth it will likely get harder, but this is your opportunity to become something more. Something you were meant to be. *Greater.*' Talbot slowly got to his feet. 'Think on this. Don't shy away from it. Think.'

Dave felt the troubled expression screw up his face as he thought about being forced to use his innate knack for destruction on another person: a soldier, a Spark, agents plotting his demise. He shouldn't feel bad about self-defense. His direct aggression could be a tool under the correct circumstances. He peered up at Talbot, a meek and gracious smile forming. 'I will.'

Talbot offered a near-paternal look of pride and warmth. And then, like a cold-blooded reptile, his eyes shone like sequins before he turned away.

'Am I the first? The first Spark you have taken in?'

Talbot turned back slowly. 'Yes.'

'Why now? Why me?'

'This is a zero-sum game we play with Hourglass and their cohorts, and the manner in which we found you was quite extreme. But I suppose it was a long time coming. Sparks can be powerful guns with hair triggers, and whilst I have faith in your potential, Hourglass still has more guns. To further the tired metaphor, when the time comes, we will need you to pull that trigger of yours.'

Dave felt his heart fluttering, his nerves amped up to a bustling hive of wasps. He didn't speak. All he could do was offer a contrite and modest smile.

'If you'll excuse me,' Talbot said, 'I have a small matter to attend to, but I promise I'll be back shortly. And we'll go for a drive; it can get awfully stuffy in here. You're not alone now, David.'

Dave stared at the closed door after Talbot's departure, sinking into the silence of the room. After ten minutes or so, he picked up his phone and unpaused the movie, the first *Scions of Saturn* movie, a favored comfort watch of his. It was twenty minutes in, and the unlikely hero, having found himself lumped with some equally unlikely new allies, was stumbling over the first explosive obstacles of what some screenwriters called the Hero's Journey, but a glimpse of his deep-seated mettle assured audiences he was primed for greatness. Dave watched the movie and wondered why real life had to be so complicated.

21

 LYDE CHOSE HIS USUAL ARSENAL of two semi-automatic pistols and an assault rifle, keeping it relatively light. It was a tactic he had trained for early on at Indigo Mesa, and fitted well for his and Kev's methods.

Rose went for her typical more-is-more approach, signing a multi-barrel grenade launcher out of the inventory. She was strapping it over her shoulder when Kev finally broke his quiet brooding, asking her, 'Can we put all this behind us before we head out there? In case one of us doesn't make it back.'

Kev had been an apt pupil of Rose and the ISU back at Indigo, soaking up everything he could about strengthening and honing his power. Perhaps it was this that led to Sarge giving Kev a solemn nod. As Rose's former commanding officer, Sarge always was more of an experienced and level-headed sort compared to Rose's aggressive-terrier mindset. Perhaps sensing this unspoken detente, Darcy exchanged a wordless high-five with Kev, a small glimmer of relief on his blue, bloodied lips. And of course, Barros held no grudge whatsoever, looking pleased to see the prickly tension smooth out between them. And all it took was one of the two stubborn parties to use words instead of scowls and silence.

Clyde felt a pressure lift from his chest, and Nat, with her fingers casually hooked in her body armor, shared a reserved smirk of victory with Clyde.

'Focus on the mission, and you'll stand a better chance at not dying' was Rose's contribution, delivered with barely a trace of interest. And that's how easy it was to undo an almost touching moment.

Kev made a derisive sniffing sound and slowly backed away. Clyde tried to catch his eye, but it was no good. Kev went back to staring about the room like none of it really mattered to him.

'Wrong call,' Sarge said to Rose from under his breath.

Clyde was preparing to have a word with Kev, but he saw Barros give Rose an insolent glance before drifting over to where Kev stood.

'Where you going, Barros?' Rose snapped.

'We're not in the Army anymore, Hadfield. Feel free to think for yourself once in a while,' Barros snapped over her shoulder.

Sarge must have seen Rose readying to fire back and took her aside to calm her. This was a time for focus, not in-squabbling.

Clyde decided to let Barros handle this for the moment, since she held equal share of the blame with Kev for denting the team morale. It made sense to let them pull each other through this. They spoke quietly, and Clyde couldn't make out what either of them was saying. He planned to ask Kev about it later, if they survived.

Out on the airfield, Ace was already waiting for them, his typical number 9 hockey jersey pulled taut over his armor. Snow flurries skirted about him and the two teams of ten agents, all of whom were equipped to take on the hordes of hell itself. Both teams were comprised of ex-members from various military and federal departments: all highly trained and experienced, and all hand-picked. But even those with the most combat experience carried themselves with a cautious readiness, knowing full well the dangers they'd soon be tackling. Clyde couldn't help but admire their courage, battling the things they did each day without the benefit of any paranormal enhancements. Nothing but heart and, yes, admittedly top-tier weapons and resources, but to wield them against the caliber of threats capable of psychologically ruining a person drastically evened the playing field.

Kev looked more focused, as if less bothered by Rose's attitude than aggravated and ready to do something. Clyde wondered if that might have been Rose's plan: to piss Kev off enough to ensure he was not stuck inside his head but ready to turn his pent-up frustrations outward.

'You with me, bro?' Clyde asked Kev.

Kev, devoid of disguises for the operation, only squinted and clenched his jaw in response.

Clyde caught Ace watching him as he and the team approached. There was something of a caged-beast aura about him. A hungry lion waiting for the bars to be removed. He wondered if Ace was fantasizing about all the things he would do to Talbot if he got his hands on him. The two teams of pure human agents—Clyde didn't know if he still classed himself and Rose as pure human anymore—began to split up, piling into the four waiting attack choppers. Ace started up the ramp of the large V-22 Osprey, the vertical take-off plane set to lead the aerial arrow formation. Clyde followed in Ace's chilly wake.

22

DAVE'S MOVIE HAD FINISHED, BUT during the whole of the third act, all he felt was restless and a growing lack of interest; and it wasn't because he had watched *Scions of Saturn* over a dozen times. It was his head, so full of reeling thoughts it was darkening his mood. He simply couldn't shun Talbot's words about his "gods-given talent." It was kind of funny, really. He now knew that beings of tremendous power really existed, yet he couldn't help but shake his head ponderously at the knowledge that he was one of them. It was odd, really, that despite such revelations, he still found his own faith in anything even remotely quasi-religious in very short supply. But then, why wouldn't it be? According to what he'd heard, Heaven was over! What did that leave? Uber-freaks vying for control. That did little to inspire any reforms in the gosh-golly department of religious enthusiasm. It all just sounded like chaos. Like everything else in life. But if nothing else, at least he was one of those with a little bit of power. The world had become so much bigger and scarier, and he didn't like the idea of being helpless in it.

It was now a little after four p.m., and sitting alone with his thoughts was slowly driving him nuts. He decided to go for a wander. Talbot or even Gabriel must be around here someplace. A chilling thought almost froze him before he reached the door: *What if I bump into that fucked-up book guy Sarkozy?* He had disappeared through that mirror of his, but what did that really mean? Fuck-all, that's what. This was now a world where things like him and those other shadowy, faceless mirror people could hop in and out of this world the way Dave hailed a cab. On a whim, he grabbed his long winter coat and slipped it on, deciding that if he couldn't find Talbot, he would see if he could walk the snowy gardens.

Plucking up his guts, he gripped the doorknob firmly. The hallway was quiet, still as a tomb, and the silence only enhanced the unsettling owl statuary perched on the walls and ornamental cabinets. But the silence allowed for something else too: a deep, mechanical drone, just barely audible. The sound of a distant engine maybe? Vintage cars in the manse's undoubtedly massive garage? Maybe it was a passing plane. A flicker of queasiness went through Dave, as visions of Talbot hopping aboard a helicopter and deserting him in this crazed fortress of billionaires and whackos assailed him. A silly thought, surely. Dave, careful to not sound too big-headed, knew he had some value to these people. Which meant the distant engine noise could be a visitor.

He reached the end of the hall when the throaty roar of commands started up from somewhere outside on the building's grounds. Running to the large balcony window, he stood in dumbfounded stillness at what he saw: a fleet of black choppers of the sort he'd seen in a dozen war movies angling in from the furnace-cast sky like pissed-off wasps. He thought of *Apocalypse Now* but felt like he belonged more in *John Carter*, a superhuman fish-out-of-water transplanted to a world he didn't fully understand. But Dave didn't view himself as a damn hero, and there was certainly no princess in need of rescuing here. He was just an angry guy with an above-average temper looking for a place to fit in.

The muted coffin nails—who, as it transpired, actually could talk if necessary—spat commands to one another and commenced spraying the airborne attackers with machine-gun fire.

It could only be Hourglass.

Dave thought of that ice-cold son of a bitch coming at him with a cold shank. Outrage slowly seeped into his terror like oil onto water, and the burning oil soon won out. What right did they have? He hadn't hurt anyone. Memories flashed like sun dogs of his hands rending those coffin nails in the wine cellar. But that was different, wasn't it? They weren't human.

And neither am I! he thought.

A rocket left one of the choppers' pods in a screaming trail of smoke, blasting the lawn and three coffin nails into a shower of soil, torn limbs, and viscous fluids.

Dave saw a central vehicle amidst the helicopter squadron. One of those weird aircraft with two vertical arms, each one spinning its own propeller. He'd seen enough and sprinted for the grand staircase, launching himself down the wide steps two and three at a time. Talbot or Gabriel had to be here somewhere. They'd know what to do.

. . .

CLYDE BREATHED SLOWLY and deeply, keeping his hands busy with the twine. He certainly wasn't trying to fall asleep, but even flying into a combat situation, Spector's trick had its use, the simple activity helping him achieve a meditative calm. Outside was hell and hot, screeching metal, but inside his head it was becoming a distant thunderstorm, heard only through a warm daydream.

Nat was sitting opposite, headphones on, leg bouncing, charging up her sonic reserves. She looked as calm as Clyde felt, but Clyde thought he saw something twitch beneath her expression. Something he had seen a few times since slaying Charon. What could initially be mistaken for apprehension by somebody who didn't know her as well was actually mild discomfort. Even under the red lights of the aircraft's interior, he noticed how her eyes started to crackle with violet skeins. She winked at him, closed her eyes, opened them. The violet surges were now humming with a steady control. She removed her headphones and gave him a soft smile. He now hated the idea of going into battle with her. There was a pressure in his chest that he attributed to the fear of losing her. He smiled back.

Their V-22 Osprey started its descent. Rose stood up as the rear cargo door lowered, positioning herself behind the mounted mini-gun. The tiltrotor aircraft gently turned 180 degrees while continuing its descent. Framed before the open cargo door, Rose was colored by the falling sun in molten reds and blacks. Her stout frame barely moved as she raked devastating fire over the enemy charging across the snowy lawn to meet the invading force. With a few gentle hip pivots she shredded lanes of gunfire across the shooters taking cover behind the portico columns, and blasted apart others positioned at bay windows.

Ace came up beside Rose, his skin pouring off wisps of frigid vapor, his body armor and hockey jersey growing a layer of rime. He stared emotionlessly at the havoc Rose was throwing down.

Nat turned her attention from Rose's slaughter to Clyde. 'I don't believe in jinxes, so I'm just going to come right out and say it: Does this feel too easy?'

Clyde wasn't sure what he thought about jinxes personally. But performing a siege on a Cairnwood property, only to be met with standard-issue resistance, did feel a little safe.

A dark shadow erupted from the dense treetops. No, not a shadow— a black cloud. A suicidal onslaught of owls. They engaged the Osprey and the heli battalion as though they were attacking nothing more formidable than a gallivanting mischief of mice. Even over the shrilly throb of engines and rotors, Clyde could hear the screech of impossibly sharp talons and the percussion of beaks going to work on the Osprey like power tools. The pilots yelled in shock as the cockpit window was besieged by the frenzied hunters, each one with a wingspan almost large enough to blot out their view. Beaks chiseled the glass into a pane of frost. In moments, the first beaks were inside the cockpit. Wide eyes and dark-tufted heads followed.

Over the din came the unmistakable sound of a helicopter nosediving somewhere into the snow-blanketed grounds.

The V-22 banked sharply, the open door displaying more bedlam: a second helicopter twirling in a mad, smoking descent; a third still airborne, its main prop stalled by gouts of feathery gore.

Rose was no longer taking aim at the ground forces; she was trying to snatch several of the owls swooping into the belly of the open aircraft. All at once, the bold predators ruptured under some invisible force, reduced into blood-filled bubbles. The gory baubles were cast back out into the rushing air, releasing their red pulp. Kev lowered his hand, nonchalance personified. Rose threw him a look, and somewhere inside of it there might have been a glint of gratitude.

Clyde felt his buttocks leave the bench seat as the V-22 suddenly dropped the last ten feet with a brain-rattling smash into deep snow and frozen turf.

The engine whined to a death keen, but the gunfire and the cries of the owl swarm remained deafening.

'Let's go!' Rose cried, grabbing her six-chambered grenade launcher from the wall rack and leaping into the fray.

Ace pulled down his hockey mask and silently followed her.

Clyde jumped up and, unable to resist, he pulled Nat in close and gave her a quick kiss on the lips, feeling a tremor of vibrato shuddering her whole body, not out of fear, but a gut-wrenching rumble of bass frequencies ready to tear something apart.

'Be careful,' she told him. Her eyes flared violet, and she hurried out of the crashed plane, her bass rifle materializing in her hands.

Clyde was ready to chase after her into the fire but paused to check on Kev. 'Is your head in this?'

Kev, emotionless, raised his fist for Clyde to bump. 'Every single day.'

Clyde bumped it, taking on a surge of telekinetic power.

．　．　．

DAVE TREMBLED WITH fright as he sprinted around the sparsely populated mansion in search of help but finding only abandonment. He was alone, left to die in a war that had drafted him without consent. And somewhere deep inside, the old coal pile of simmering anger was being stoked again.

The cloistered window before him exploded inwards in a hail of glass, bringing with it a black-suited body tripping over its own dancing, spasmodic feet. Dave was about to leap over the prone figure leaking its colorless blood until it twitched back to life. The coffin nail was up swiftly, exposed wounds glistening through its shredded suit. It raced back out into the battlegrounds. Dave didn't dare stick his head out to check on the situation. He already knew what it was: fucked.

His nose twitched with a cornered dog's snarl while he sprinted down a never-ending hall of large windows, finally coming upon the old treasury. For a heart-faltering second, he imagined the double doors would be locked tight, until he remembered what his hands were capable of. But he tried the door handle first. It opened easily.

'Ed?' he yelled into the vast room, eyes criss-crossing the exhaustive display cases and robust pillars in search of Talbot. He slammed the door shut behind him, hoping the garage was somewhere near this end of the building. They had to park the limo and those armored cars around here somewhere.

'Eddie?'

No answer. Only the continued rattle and spray of gunfire and rockets outside.

'Gabriel?'

Something exploded, shaking the entire house.

The bookshelf enclosure caught his eye. Could Talbot or Gabriel be in there? Dave had an idea to sprint over and check it out, but ideas of being dragged through portal mirrors stymied him. He spotted another set of doors at the far side of the room. He just hoped there wasn't a load of gun-packing psychos on the other side of the doors.

He quick-stepped through the rows of artefacts, not knowing which were weapons and which were items of a more esoteric magic. He didn't want to accidentally brush against some object and find himself turned into a fly or his ears sprouting spider legs or some other such craziness.

Besides, if it came down to it, he wouldn't need weapons. Edward had shown him what he was capable of. All this time, all the years of eating shit and politely swallowing it, he'd had the power to do something about it. And it didn't require the use of some bizarre relic.

Edward's advice came back to him: *Anger is a tool.*

He was halfway through the huge room when the doors before him swung open. Dave almost skidded to a stop, a single ribbon of crimson girding his hand and wrist. It was Talbot, who appeared almost happy to see him.

'David? A bit more time would have been nice, but this is one of those run-before-you-walk scenarios.'

Dave noticed a large black canvas bag slung over Talbot's shoulder. 'Where's Gabriel?' he asked.

Talbot wore a look of harried concern. 'Feeding his birds.' He quickly unzipped the bag and, to Dave's surprise, commenced shattering display cases with his bare hands and ransacking the various artefacts.

'Are we helping him?' Dave asked, wondering if Talbot was stocking up on magical items to fight the intruders. But the man seemed more thief than gallant defender. He was breaking into the third glass-topped pedestal to scoop out its wares when the ground shook again. Chandeliers shook, several more glass cases shattered, and the tile floor cracked open with a deafening rumble.

Dave watched the ringed shelter of bookshelves in the heart of the room wobble this way and that, and through the apertures of the bookcases he could have sworn he saw a large, slithering worm retreating back into the earth before a couple of bookshelves lost out to gravity, spilling their many volumes like dry guts before toppling over and smashing the council of mirrors into a thousand glass shards.

'How did they find us?' Dave demanded.

Talbot looked disagreeable. 'Hourglass finds a way. They always bloody do.'

'We need to get out of here. Can we grab a car?'

Talbot hefted the bag as though it was weightless and gave Dave's shoulder a friendly squeeze. 'This is your moment, David. The forces of corruption and greed and sheer amoral evil are kicking down our door. You're blessed. A Spark. A damn holy warrior.'

The doors exploded inwards behind them. Talbot stepped aside, elbowed open another glass case, and seized an ornate pearlescent candelabra. He brandished it before him, each candle holder igniting like a slimline jet engine, streaming liquid fire thirty yards towards the jacked-up blonde woman and the ice-man in a hockey mask. The ice-man dragged the woman behind a heavy riot shield of ice before the burning streams touched them. The doorway was not so fortunate, catching fire and burning while Talbot dropped the smoking candelabra into his bag.

'I suggest making a fist or grabbing a weapon, young David.' Talbot slipped behind a wooden pedestal as a barrage of frozen crystal shards whistled inches from his face.

Dave stared at the icicle clusters embedded in the hardwood pedestals sheltering Talbot. The thought of facing down the big cold motherfucker had him shaking. Even with his power—a thing that he had hardly grasped—it felt like too much too soon.

'Bentley? David Bentley?' the iceman bellowed. 'We're here to rescue you. These guys are maniacs, don't trust 'em!'

'They really sell it, don't they?' Talbot grinned at Dave.

Dave witnessed Talbot reach into his bag, rummage around for a moment, and, with a courage Dave couldn't understand, step out into full view of the Hourglass agents, a silver whistle in his hand. He raised it to his lips and blew. At the shrill, sustained tone, an inky, deep-blue pigment started to form out of thin air, slithering and drifting towards the agents. It quickly gained substance and mass, coalescing into a mob of faceless Victorian-era policemen. Dave was dumbfounded. He didn't know whether to laugh or scream as the cops charged forward, swinging their truncheons. But the rhino-strong woman and the ice-man dispatched them back into the ether without seeming to break a sweat.

Dave couldn't leave Talbot alone in this fight. He tensed his fists and felt his heart launching into overdrive.

Stepping out from behind his cover, he caught the bulky hockey enthusiast off guard, putting everything he had into his punch, but hesitated at the last possible second. Still, it packed a wallop. The impact of Dave's knuckles broke the thick ice shield and bowled the ice-man backwards until he slid to a dead stop against a marble column. Dave ducked out of sight again as the muscle-woman swung the business end of some mean gun in his direction.

Talbot chuckled and gave him an approving nod. 'That's the mettle I like to see.' He smashed, grabbed, fired, and bagged, smashed, grabbed, fired, and bagged, looting as many pieces of strange arcana as he could in his retreat. Dave noticed how Talbot's bag full of purloined inventory didn't seem to be getting any bulkier, just swallowing them up as if the occult items were nothing more than air.

Talbot tossed an old, desiccated hoof to Dave, who caught it, glancing at it quizzically. Holding it by the remnants of the foreleg like a hideous magic wand, he somehow managed to fire off a jolt of energy that took form as a muscular stampede of bison, charging straight towards the platinum-blonde barbarian; but she was a hard target, dashing out of the way, leaving the plane beasts to demolish a path behind her.

Dave ran after Talbot, not wanting to stay behind and slug it out. Talbot looked like he had an exit plan, and Dave meant to go with him, one way or another. He had just about caught up with the man when everything went wrong. Somehow the air left his lungs, painfully. Gravity released him temporarily. There was light, there was heat—a terrible, scorching heat—that would have blistered his skin if not for his heavy coat. And then there was a silence like he had never known before. Sailing through the air but coming down fast, Dave saw a jester-headed staff, locked away in its glass case, grinning malevolently as he approached. And somehow, in the jumble of centrifugal nonsense his brain had become, he remembered what Talbot had called it.

A marotte.

Everything speeded up quickly after that as Dave's limp body crashed through the display case. There was a sickening snap, either his own bones or the staff in the case. It must have been the latter because the last thing he saw before consciousness left him was the severed jester head lying inches from his own head amidst shattered glass and blood, and it seemed to him that he could hear its maniacal laughter

. . .

CLYDE TRAIPSED THROUGH the dark wood ensnaring the mansion grounds. It was a deep and wintry living thing that seemed to exist purely to lose men and feed them to its crafty denizens. He stared up through its thatch of knotted branches and dark leaves—the boughs so dense that nary a flake of snow had penetrated to dampen the soil or roots— watchful for more of the ravenous owls.

Nat was a few paces behind him, and behind her, a few of the surviving agents brought in to help with bird control. Kev and a ragged number of agents had stayed out in the open, suppressing the remaining ground forces, while Ace, Rose, and the ISU investigated the house.

The forest opened into a large grove, a perennial emerald hollow for what was a tremendous and disturbingly folkloric wooden owl sanctuary. At its center stood a gaunt figure in a heavy coat, slightly stooped, with hands and scalp moonlight pale. He straightened and flung his arms out in a scarecrow posture, and bursting from the dark wooden house behind him came a rush of owls, yellow-eyed demons that formed a feathery whirlwind of beaks and talons around their summoner. Clyde, dispensing with his assault rifle, went straight for the heavy artillery. He reached out with his loaned spectral kinetic energy and tried to take invisible hold of the figure's outcropped arms. Nat's bass was quivering like a stack of bass cabinets ready to blow.

The owl-master's head slowly rotated until his chin and hooked nose hung over his shoulder blades. His eyes were frightfully large, with pupils the size of dimes. Clyde didn't get a good feeling from the smile slowly curling its way up the angular face. The owl wrangler drew in his outstretched arms with one sharp motion, slipping Clyde's grip, and with a single bound he was up amongst his subjects, hidden in a barrier of circling owls.

They launched their attack.

Nat fired a rhythmic pulse into the wave of raptors. They fell in clumps, the throbbing vibrations devastating to their hollow bones. Clyde was attempting to corral the owls into a transparent prison of energy when he glimpsed a spry pair of legs leaping and gliding high across the ceiling of branches. Two of the easier pickings, agents with nothing more than firearms and courage, were dragged up into the canopy by the owl-man. Hearing their screams, Clyde turned just in time to see a pair of inhumanly large yellow eyes, gleeful and cruel, before the owl-man was gone once more, talons clamped around the helpless, screaming agents.

'Nat!' Clyde screamed over her racket, pointing at the owl sanctuary. 'Level that place!'

He aimed up at the canopy, firing an invisible mushroom cloud of kinetic energy. Heavy boughs snapped like bones, scattering the surrounding woodland with fresh timber and a storm of evergreen leaves.

Nat's fingers sprinted across her glowing bass strings, her left hand locked into a punk rock standard. She traded owl-swatting for building demolition, aiming the glowing headstock towards the massive wooden shelter. She watched with burning violet eyes as the home fell to toothpicks. The remaining owls took flight, leaving their home, their slain kin, and, presumably, their master to their fates. Nat's beautiful deadly gaze faded slowly, the violet veins cooling, her eyes returning to their normal color. She slung her bass into a dazzle of vanishing violet particles. Prying her eyes up from the carpet of feathers and pulverized owl viscera, she said, 'Where did the bird-man go?'

Clyde gestured out of the grove towards the battleground and the mansion beyond. Holding up a long spectral shield, he led the way forward.

▪ ▪ ▪

ROSE LEFT THE guard's broken corpse where it landed. She had inflicted more damage than a speeding truck, and even for these tough bastards, if it did manage to survive, it wouldn't be in fighting shape for a while. She took the short flight of steps down into a parking garage that was bigger than a car showroom. Slim windows near the ceiling shone slants of evening light onto a sleek limousine, a fleet of armored cars, and even a not-so-modest collection of genuine classics. It would sure be a shame to waste these beauties. She lowered her combat shotgun, once again opting for her grenade launcher.

Thunk. The first grenade sailed across the large room, and a Rolls Royce Phantom became a burning skeleton in less time than it took her to choose a second target; a pre-WWII Vauxhall 30/98 that reminded her of Chitty Chitty Bang Bang.

Thunk. Another wipe-out.

'I bet that was expensive,' she called out, goading Talbot.

Extractor fans started to automatically siphon out the black smoke. The sprinkler system kicked in, dowsing the whole car museum. The cold rain quickly soaked her through.

'I know you're in here, you rat bastard.' She lowered the empty grenade launcher, falling back on her shotgun, and moved quietly for one with such muscle and power. 'I thought you would have loved an opportunity to get your hands on me after I crashed your little Manhattan gala.'

Nothing moved. The only sound was the sprinkler rain puddling on the smooth cement floor.

She sent a mental signal to her internal bunker, signaling the ISU to fan out and sweep for Talbot. Sarge and Darcy appeared stone-faced between the raindrops, splitting off like Rose's pincers. She walked straight down the center of the garage with Barros watching her back.

'That was supposed to be a big moment for you, wasn't it? Greasing the palms of all those tacky bigwigs, all ready to hear about the exciting future of energy: souls! A new market you and Cairnwood could corner.' The floor was slick with water. 'It sure was fun fucking that up. I bet it set you back a bit. What's the matter, Eddie? You got nothing to say to me?' She stalked down the aisle, trying to catch glimpses of movement through the rain sheeting the windows of the cars. 'You really are the gutless type, aren't you? Shit, at that party, one second you were right there, then the next you and your chopper were nowhere to be seen.' She swung between two cars, shotgun poised.

Clear. She continued down the aisle.

'Then there was all that business with Charon and Sharp. No one even caught a glimpse of your chicken-shit ass during any of that.'

Slide.

Aim.

Clear.

Move.

'But you must have been hiding your balls somewhere in those fancy pants of yours. Attacking the Syrup Farm?' Rose exhaled slowly, hitting an ominous note in awe of how much trouble he was in. 'Killing the Astronomer, trying to recruit Sparks? Is this the same Edward Talbot? Because from here it seems like you're back to being a fucking chicken-shi—'

Talbot lunged out from between two cars with a reptilian killer instinct. Batting her shotgun away, his damp manacle of a hand latched around her corded neck, choking her. Rose saw his true face up close. No nose, only nostril slits. Hairless, rough leathery scalp. A wide and exaggeratedly long philtrum gave him the look of a devolved snake-man. His perfect teeth were now perfectly lethal white hooks, glistening with spit or venom. And his eyes shimmered with a swamp-gas tint, drinking in all of her choking struggles.

Lifted from the ground, Rose's boots couldn't even scrape the floor. Digging her industrial presser-strong hands into his wrist, she squeezed with enough pressure to bend steel. Only nothing bent except his cufflink. The ISU closed in, swinging their own haymakers. Each fist phased through Talbot without effect.

Consternation froze Darcy's wide, plain features. 'He's got no soul.'

Still squeezing Rose until her face was red as a polished apple, Talbot chuckled, a wet contemptible sound. 'Who said I don't have a soul, you silly git?'

The ISU traded looks. Whether or not Talbot was bluffing about having a soul, something was barring them from bludgeoning it, hence *him,* into submission. They watched Rose frantically. Powerless to help.

Rose, her throat a hot, raw space, continued her own crushing attempt on Talbot's wrist, then his fingers. She watched through choking tears as Sarge, Darcy, Barros—her family—slowly began to fade back to the Null.

Rose swung her legs up, using Talbot's outstretched arm for leverage, and stamped her boot heel into his face. His sodden grip slipped from her throat, just long enough for her to get into position for an arm bar attempt. Yet somehow his hand quickly slipped around her throat again, and she realized that Talbot was more powerful than she had imagined.

'How's this for gutless?' he rasped, his voice smooth and dry as snakeskin.

He wasn't trying to choke her this time. Rose felt her body becoming run down, as if it was fighting the sudden onset of a devastating infection. Her head started to swim. Her muscles and limbs started to ache. She stared into those lifeless green eyes of his and heard her old combat buddies raging at their ineffectuality.

Talbot gave a hacking cough, a sudden surprised expression of pain on his ghastly face. Rose stared at him in matching confusion, watching as his arm seemed to bend back and break at the elbow of its own accord, dropping Rose. The next thing she knew, Talbot was being used like a sledgehammer to pound dents into various cars.

'Kev!' Barros cried out in relief.

Rose rolled over, coughing, got to her feet, and sure enough, Kev was standing there, sprinkler wash pouring through him, and using his hand to guide Talbot's destruction. She wanted to say thanks. Wanted to perhaps say a little more than that. But her throat felt like it had been fused shut. She turned around, eyes blazing, and wanted very much to test her strength again. But this time, it would be her knuckles against the structure of Talbot's facial bones.

Talbot wriggled and writhed in mid-air like a snake in a sack. He reset his broken arm with an angry hiss, wrenching the hyperextended elbow back into place, allowing his remarkable regenerative ability to quickly begin reknitting the bone. His other hand slid into his trouser pocket, but Rose didn't see what it was that he clutched: a rabbit's foot. Slipping it into his scaly left palm, he smiled as if in anticipation. Just then, Kev inexplicably lost his grip, allowing Talbot to recover and run. But that wasn't all: several of the light fixtures above Rose unexpectedly blew, adding a shower of sparks to the sprinklers. The power surge stole a reaction from the team, but not as much as when, against further odds, some of the smoldering cars openly defied the sprinklers, their extant flames growing new hot tongues, lapping and leaping to neighboring models to create an impossible conflagration.

Skittering to his feet, the snake-man in leather shoes hauled up his bag of stolen talismans and weapons, and using the fiery distraction, hobbled over to his Jaguar F-Type. Rose recognized the car from surveillance and intel, including the fact that it had been previously blown-up outside Elzinga Asylum. But this model was the same right down to the same shade of green, only this one briefly shimmered with a coating of protective runes: bomb-proof? Thumbing the fob to open the garage door, he stamped on the gas, roared out of the garage, and skidded around the salted driveway and out of sight with a mad, joyous cackle. Rose hobbled after for several yards, knowing it was useless. The car was already speeding away into an inky blot.

The ISU rallied around her, but Kev stayed back a few paces.

Rose waved off the concern of her close-knit spirits and found the courage to lock eyes with Kev. 'You saved my ass.' The moment felt more painful and difficult than the life-and-death struggle she had just endured. 'Thanks.'

Kev nodded. 'I've seen you bounce truck tires like medicine balls. Is he really that strong, or is something else going on with you?'

Rose knew exactly what he meant. Talbot was strong, incredibly so, but she knew her own strength had been a little unreliable these past weeks; nothing major or overtly noticeable, at least until now. She glanced at Barros without intending for it to signify anything, but she also knew Kev was sharp enough to notice. The little rift in the ISU's camaraderie was weakening more than their morale.

■　■　■

THE OWL MASTER was waiting when Clyde exited the woods, standing amidst a hell-begotten garden of burning helicopters, crimson slush, and sundered corpses. Huddled, wounded, and gasping at his feet was one of the agents he had abducted in the woods; one hand forcefully held the man's head back as the talon of the other scraped micro hairs from his exposed throat.

Clyde made a careful visual sweep of the surroundings but couldn't see Kev anywhere; he could, however, feel his presence off somewhere in the direction of the mansion. He sure would have liked his assistance right about now.

'You murdered my companions.' The owl-man's cultured voice held a quaver of emotion, but there was also a slight trill that was unsettlingly avian. He had also taken on more characteristics of his cherished species: his hooked nose had hardened into a sharp, cutting beak, the razor talons had grown longer, perfect for blinding and opening, and even his feathered collar seemed to have developed into a fuller, warmer cushion.

Clyde knew the agent was most likely beyond help. Words would never spare his life. He thought about dragging the agent to safety but feared he'd inadvertently pull him into a neck-breaking tug of war with the owl-man.

But he had to try something.

Nat's bass appeared at port arms.

Clyde let his invisible grip cinch gently around the agent's ankle. If the wounded man felt it, he was too out of it or too smart to acknowledge it. Clyde pulled with his right hand and pushed with his left: the agent slid through the deep snow out of harm's way as the owl-man was simultaneously blasted back several feet by a blast from Nat. He flipped in the air with majestic grace. Nat took aim again, but the bark and growl of a finely-tuned engine snatched her attention. A Jaguar came flying around the rear of the mansion, expertly controlling a fishtail skid.

Nat unloaded, her blurry fingers firing an endless series of rapid sixteenth notes, only managing to pummel the air, the snow, and the charred black cover of a chopper the owl man ducked behind.

Without slowing down, the Jaguar convertible whipped along the winding driveway and veered towards the edge of the lawn, rolling its roof back. Clyde saw a grotesque slithering creature in a suit at the wheel. Talbot? The owl-man sprung into the air and dropped neatly into the passing convertible. Nat sent a bass wave at the speeding car but succeeded only in devastating the road in its wake. When Clyde tried to pull the car back like an invisible tow-truck, his grip slid like Teflon from the vehicle as symbols flared to life around the chassis.

A charm? Some runic ward?

He watched, bewildered and frustrated, as the car sped off, rapidly shrinking to a distant speck.

'Would you think less of me if I ask *who* that was?' Nat asked, her eyes staring hard at the car's wake, its engine noise fading fast.

Clyde barely registered the owl witticism. 'We can add him to our files,' he said in a huff. He called Meadows, who was heading operation control; their local aerial transports were finished, but HQ could still track Talbot's car by satellite and then traffic cams when it reached public roads.

Meadows responded with the runner-up prize in good news: there was no immediate air support in the area, with all remaining helicopters already out on assignment, but an armed ground transport complete with medical assistance had already been dispatched to their location from a satellite office.

With nothing to do but wait, Clyde searched about the scattered bodies, finding no noticeable signs of life, while Nat tried to offer what limited assistance she could to the wounded agent who had a near miss with the owl-man.

Clyde called across the team channel, praying there were no further fatalities. Ace reported back. As it turned out, there were quite a few more, including David Bentley.

23

Y THE TIME THE HOURGLASS clean-up and medical crews arrived, the mansion's courtyard and perimeter lights were doing a severe job of highlighting the destructive tableau. Deceased agents were zipped up in bags as the remains of Cairnwood's operatives—some in pieces and still twitching—were placed in a specialized Perspex hold in the back of a large black juggernaut, en route to be incinerated. The clean-up crews, clad in dark specialized beekeeper suits, were hosing down the burning helicopters while others scooped up splattered owls and investigated the collapsed owl sanctuary.

'What a waste.' Clyde sat on the top step of the portico, watching one of the company meat wagons trail off with a cargo of corpses. The medics were in the middle of depositing David Bentley's body into a second truck crowding the gravel driveway.

Ace was over there too, having decided to ride back to the Madhouse with Bentley's body. Clyde wasn't sure why Ace had decided to do this, but Ace hadn't said much and had seemed a little taut around Rose.

'He had an ordinary life yesterday,' Clyde said of Bentley. 'And in less than forty-eight hours, he was caught up in all this, and now off he goes.'

'Another notch for the Null,' Kev said.

'Another notch for Cairnwood,' Clyde corrected. 'They might have wanted him for their own uses, but him being dead also keeps him off our team.'

Rose sat on one of the portico's steps near Clyde, a medic examining her bruised throat with a tender hand. The medic asked a few questions and made a few comments that Clyde didn't hear before hurrying off to see the next triaged agent.

Clyde watched Ace climb into the back with Bentley's body.

'He made his decision,' Rose said, swallowing a small vial of the EMT's medicine with a wince. 'He sided with them,' she rationalized, her voice hoarse.

'What did he really know?' Clyde asked. 'He got picked up by money and surface-level charm, brought to a place like this. We have no idea what they were filling his head with. Then we come flying in and turn the place into a war zone.'

'It's a bitter pill to swallow, but that's war, Clyde. I know your feelings on the matter, so I'll respect them, but I'll also get to the heart of it: when somebody's trying to kill you, it doesn't matter what propaganda they've been fed. They're an enemy hostile and have to be treated accordingly.'

Clyde had seen the damage to Bentley's body. He was hit with a grenade blast, but while his limbs had remained intact, the shockwave and brutal landing had proven too much to withstand. 'And there was absolutely no other way to deal with him than taking him out with a grenade launcher?'

'He wasn't armed with a penknife. He was a fucking Spark. A Spark playing around with Talbot in a room full of some very fucking scary and unknown weaponry.'

'If I'd gotten there sooner—' Kev started to say.

Rose stopped him. 'This one isn't on you, Kev. We all had our hands full. We didn't know what the situation was, and by the time we did, it was practically over.'

Clyde was surprised to see Rose jumping to Kev's defense, but if Kev shared the surprise he didn't show it, switching his attention to some of the surviving agents still being patched-up, doped-up, and taken into all-black ambulances.

'We were unable to save Bentley, but you saved some of ours tonight,' Rose finished. 'That shit matters. Don't forget that.'

'No one here can hog all the self-pity to themselves,' Nat said. 'We all failed Bentley. Maybe if we had been able to get to him before Talbot, things would have turned out different. Then again, maybe not. For all we know the guy might have been a lost cause from the jump.' The driver of the meat wagon closed the doors, sealing Ace from view. 'I never would have guessed it when I first met the dude, but the snowman actually does have a heart somewhere under that hockey jersey.'

Clyde watched the van as it started to roll away. 'He's trying to hide it, but this thing with Estelle Page seems to be eating away at him. He's not the most open book, but maybe he feels guilty for her too. If he wasn't working this side of the border, he might have been there to save her.'

Nat didn't look too convinced. 'He didn't have much say in the matter. And it's not like he can cover all of Canada.'

An arcane acquisitions team paraded past them down the steps, carting off various items and trinkets in heavily sealed cases.

Rose watched them go, cocking an eyebrow. 'Talbot was grabbing anything that wasn't nailed down, so either the rest of this stuff is junk, or he had a shopping list.'

'Like a lucky rabbit's foot, or *unlucky* rabbit's foot?' Darcy posited. The big, wide farm boy still appeared rankled by Talbot's knack for slipping away.

'Is that definitely what you saw?' Sarge asked him.

'A fuzzy white thing with nails on? It was quick, but I definitely saw it in his hand when he jumped into the car. I spent enough time dealing with the pests on the farm.' He glanced at their faces. 'Humanely. Besides, how else do you explain violently random electrical faults and fires?'

'I don't know if I'd trust my life to a rabbit's paw if that's the sort of help it offers,' Sarge said. He turned to Clyde. 'But speaking of mixed luck, it turns out Talbot has a soul, but we can't touch it. Think you could you do anything with that?'

Clyde was taken aback, both by Darcy's insinuation about attacking Talbot through the Median, and also the dangers such a potential strategy might pose. Could he even harm a soul thread in that place?

He didn't consider what he'd done to the Hangman as harming, but more of a cold bucket of water to the face, waking him from Charon's mental influence. But *severing* Talbot's thread, or anybody's for that matter? He didn't know. He thought about the white fire engulfing his dreamer's hands. Maybe that could do the trick, if he knew how. But it wasn't like he could ask Dremel and his council. Tantamount to suicide. But Spector...?

'It's not much for me to work with,' Clyde said. 'And I don't want to start angering the powers-that-be, you know?'

Sarge winced in disappointment, his face shrapnel mangling his countenance further. 'Damn shame.'

Something, a *large* something, reared up out of the snowy lawn, deep in the shadows. Clyde's pulse kicked up until he realized it was the young bookworm, desultory in its chief task but still aroused by the transient mystical energy traces belonging to any number of the grimoires that had come and gone from the premises.

Seeing the worm raised an entirely unrelated question. 'Was there any sign of what's-his-name, Soma Sarkozy?'

Darcy shook his head.

'Judging from all this shit they collected,' Rose gestured to the procession of agents carting off curios and curses, 'they probably got hold of that book some other way. Meadows might have been off on this one. Sarkozy's probably nothing more than a chapter in a history book.'

'What about this owl guy who fled with Talbot?' Darcy asked. 'You think he was the shot-caller here? We haven't seen him before, and the juicier bugs tend to dig deepest.'

'We'll run the footage by Meadows, see if he's somewhere in the database,' Rose said. The pinhead camera on their body armor would have recorded the encounter. 'One thing's for sure: if he didn't have a good enough reason to hate us already, he's fucking vexed that we deep-sixed his birdies now. I think there's a chance we might get a more personal visit from him before too long.'

They loaded up into the back of a waiting van but hadn't even managed to vacate the premises before Meadows spoke over their comms to deliver more frustrating news. 'Talbot's car is somehow evading satellite detection. And the southbound interstate traffic cams have started to scramble and black out.'

'He had wards all over his car,' Kev said.

'A whole cloak of them from what we saw,' Barros added.

'That's why I couldn't grab hold of it,' Clyde grumbled. 'Guy's got a charmed car and a charmed life. At least we know what direction they're headed in. Southbound. You think he's heading back for NYC?'

Meadows didn't rule it out nor confirm, unsure of what other boltholes Cairnwood had set up in the state.

'Shouldn't be too big a problem, though. The surveillance teams can follow the blackout cams like breadcrumbs,' Barros pitched with some much-needed optimism.

Meadows was quick in letting the air out. 'The cameras haven't come back online yet. It won't matter if the surveillance teams followed his blackout wave if his final destination is a piece of enclosed private property.'

'Anybody else starting to think this whole op was total FUBAR?' Rose asked. Nobody disagreed with her. 'Talbot's like the fucking Road Runner.'

'And we just lost what might be the last Spark the agency ever finds.' Nat's knee bumped into Clyde's and lingered there.

'Then let's make sure we don't lose any more,' Clyde said to her, leaning a little closer.

24

L AUGHTER WAS ALL HE COULD hear, floating in darkness. A distant wet chuckle. Borderline mindless. Delirious. Insufferable. It came from a far-off place, reaching him through this infinite abyss. Confusion was all he knew, but slowly things started to piece together.

And Dave remembered himself. No, wait ... that wasn't right. He remembered the cold, empty facts of his life: his name, his family—deceased and/or as good as—where he lived, where he worked. But they might as well have been fragments of a stranger's life, as he felt absolutely nothing.

Nothing but a keen, fiery slash of rage cutting through the darkness, the red line splitting the black sheet in his mind like a knife parting a cinema screen. The black flaps peeled apart, and the laughter became a deafening crescendo. And Dave saw sights he couldn't believe. It was a deranged world, part macabre Disneyland, part multicultural/multi-disaster zone, with fire-gutted buildings and vehicles—most of them of stunning alien design—all shaken together and left to lie where they fell.

The hallucinogenic cartoon world started to fade away, and the next thing Dave knew he was in a large room that resembled an abandoned TV studio, staring at a giant mechanical mouth, so artfully crafted in its gaping humor it could pass for an animatronic greeting the new visitors of this bizarre theme park. Its lips must have been some type of fiberglass, lighting up the large chamber in a constant wash of snowy TV static.

The gentle jingling of bells caught Dave's attention, the rhythm of the soft tinkling indicative of approaching footfalls. Dave couldn't move his body, but he could turn his head about, his eyes finding a slim figure emerging from the static-washed gloom, entering the TV glow of the gargantuan laughing mouth. It cut a chilling figure, like something from a child's nightmare. Color started to bleed into its monochromatic form as it neared, its lean and sharp-boned figure almost lost in a puffy, purple-and-orange court jester costume, with flared wrist cuffs and a tingling bell on the end of each curled boot. But there were other bells that held Dave's gaze. The cap and bells didn't look synthetic but organic, with several thickly muscled tentacles writhing from their perch atop his head, each one ending in a shrunken skull whose jaws were clamped around a small bell. But it was the creature's face that was the worst, a grotesque parody of humor, with a mouth so painfully contorted that fishhooks couldn't have peeled a wider, more violent smile, with flesh a pocked and dry ochre like hard, sunbaked clay.

He bent at the waist, not to bow politely but to take a better inspection of Dave's kneeling posture. The jester's eyes were permanently frozen in a fashion not unlike his mouth, the upper lids pinned to its brow like narrow archways, fully exposing two manic, gleaming eyes. He took a few more jingling half-steps towards him, stopping almost nose to nose with Dave, who still couldn't budge a muscle.

The smiling captor slapped a hand to the top of Dave's head, turning it this way and that, examining him closely, and after a few seconds, disbelief and merriment enlivened his eyes.

Killing a snide chuckle, the jester ran a hand over Dave's head as though reading braille. 'By all the spatchcocked angels, what have we here! Your soul … it's … is that? You just died, but … You're hard to kill! What are you—are you … It is! You are! Luminary energy!' He shrieked a demented laugh. 'Those shiny idiots. Poor losers. But you're a Spark. An *exceptionally* tough one. I can feel it in your soul—tougher than those cockroach things on your world. Good for you. That's great!' He did a giddy little dance, skipping and back-flipping about in a circle, all the bells sounding like a couple of tambourines being battered together, before finally calming himself.

'Welcome to my house, David Bentley of Earth. The House of Strange Fates. Fit for those strange, silly sorts who pledge their souls to fictitious saviors. As for your strange fate, it has granted you the tremendous pleasure, the wild misfortune, the bloodletting, fire-starting servitude of my royal court.'

Behind the ugly creature, the lips of the giant mouth stretched open in ecstasy, the static-fizzing lips parting to reveal a streaming gullet of mesmerizing color. 'I am Kerzix the Imp King! Presider over false pantheons and delusional theology.' He raised a finger as long and slim as a flute.

'But since you're here, personally honored by my presence, I know you're not one of the countless scared flocks whispering prayers to empty air. You renounced the false gods of your world's cultures, but sadly for you—but happily for me—there *are* deities,' he leaned in, all teeth and bulging eyes, 'and I'm the closest thing you'll ever get to meeting one.' Kerzix straightened, snapping to attention.

'My entitlement is the souls of religious flocks, but I take it upon myself to make sure the occasional atheist doesn't slip away all smug and righteous. You broke one of my Atheist Marottes in your hilarious, calamitous conclusion to life. Those scepters are finely tuned for faithless souls such as yours. Let's call it an affinity. That means you're now mine. And you are going to break much, much more for me. You owe me a tribute, tithings of souls, regardless of creed. I must explain. Whilst I have specific appetites, there can be lean seasons in this place. Devout belief systems move like the tides, ebbing and flowing, influenced by the hardships of each world and society. A king must provide for his loyalists, and I'm not above taking in a few additional souls here and there, regardless of their faith or lack of. So you will be tasked, David Bentley of Earth, in stirring some big, *BIG* chaos. Panic on the streets, and souls in my pantry.' Those long fingers waggled towards the giant mouth. 'You are the newest of my Marotte Marauders. Any questions?'

Dave had plenty of questions but found that speech was currently beyond him. Was his mouth sealed? Tongue numb?

'That's what I like to see, nothing to hear.' The Imp King rubbed his palms together, then patted him on the head like an obedient dog.

'Go forth and gather me my bonuses. The bigger the better, but don't exceed 999 souls in one sitting; I have a rule in place not to cull too many at once, in honor of the other Houses. Some of my happy little collectors have been overambitious in the past, and with you being a Spark, I can only dream of the harvest you could bring me if you set your mind to it. But this is all a game, you see, and if you were to somehow claim all of a world's game pieces in my name, it takes away a whole arena for the other kings, and, well, they can be no fun sometimes.' A beleaguered sigh, sudden as a sugar crash, seemed to pull the mad king down. 'And these games of chance and death do grow dull over the eons. Variety is essential.' Akin to a quick slap across the face, the imp shook off his jaded attitude, and Dave suddenly found his eyeballs inches away from two rows of flat teeth. The jester finished leering and rubbed a glove across Dave's face, smooth and gentle. Moments later, Dave felt his face starting to itch, like a full colony of ants in a sugar frenzy, but the sensation didn't last too long. Yet something still felt a little off. A little numb.

'You know what the irony of all this is?' the Imp King asked. 'You yourself are a descendant of an *actual* god race—a weak-blooded bastard, but still . . . And now you're all mine. Now, in my name, and the name of this House, rise.' A phantom tingling started in Dave's extremities, and then his limbs. 'Awaken. And go forth, my faithless, killer fool.'

Dave's world faded to black again, and he felt all those distant aspects of himself, mind and soul and history, fall away, leaving only his anger to fill the void.

■   ■   ■

DAVE AWOKE TO absolute darkness. He could wriggle his hands and feet, but he was confined in something, a cool and slick material brushing his face. A vinyl sack? Then he remembered his last moments. Helping Talbot fend off those Hourglass assassins. Knocking that big cold motherfucker with the hockey mask into a pillar. And then that chick with all the muscles and a damn grenade launcher. The blast. The heat. Crashing into that display . . . with the jester's marotte.

The Imp King. It wasn't some lurid dream. The imp was real! Dave tried to sit up, struggling against the fabric, trapped in darkness. He heard gasps and startled chatter, muffled through the bag.

The darkness split open with a zip. Bright lights blinded him, cold and blue, eclipsed by the large icebox-sized figure looming over him. Dave recognized him instantly. The ice-man.

And he felt a fury race through him surer than the tip of any spear. Thrashing loose of the body bag, he swatted away numerous seizing hands and turned to see Ace and several others all dressed up and ready to kill.

It wasn't simply the surprise of his resurrection showing on their faces, but a startled acknowledgement of his face. Dave didn't know if he was hideously scarred or burned, but he wasn't in any pain, which was surprising.

He couldn't help but notice the shelves of other corpse bags stacked either side of him. It was a large vehicle, a truck, and it was in motion.

Some scrap of himself that he hardly recognized tried to fight through his confusion, struggling to master the blind fury pumping through his veins, but it steadily sank under a pitch-dark oppression. His forearms started to throb, his hands too, as the muscles tensed and became girded in miniature red tornados, seeking maximum devastation.

'*BENTLEY!*' the cold one shouted, raising a palm up. 'We're not trying to hurt you.'

Dave could still smell the burnt scent of his own skin, and saw the singed ends of his trench coat. Vignettes of aerial assaults, armored troopers, and an attempted abduction at his own apartment streamed through his head like a badly edited movie reel. The movie continued: choice cuts of his lifelong inadequacy and awkwardness, and the coup de grace, his first-person POV of smashing through a glass case and breaking a jester's staff.

Kerzix's marotte.

Atheist Marotte.

Marotte Marauder.

Sick laughter trickled through his deepest thoughts, tickling his reptilian brain. What occurred next was reactionary.

Dave tore through several of the armored agents trying to defuse the situation. Dave wasn't falling for it. They were only trying to lull him into a false sense of security, make him complacent so they could more successfully kill him this time. Unlike the coffin nails, these attackers bled crimson by the bucket. Heads burst like spoiled tomatoes hurled at a court jester, and those still in tactical helmets found their cranial protection wanting.

'We're not your enemy!' the ice-man roared, his already large hands growing with a thick layer of ice.

Dave wasn't listening. He was fed up with being everybody's punchline. These people, this ice-man, didn't want to lose their status quo. They wanted to take his power from him. To kill him.

Dave launched himself past the splattered suppressors, hitting Ace like a riled-up attack dog.

Ace, the bigger, much heavier man of the pair, was able to twist him away, slamming him from wall to shelf to wall again, but the smaller man's tenacity was exceptional.

Dave stared deep into the twin blizzards of Ace's eyes, watching his skin paling under a new frost.

'This is the fork in the road, Bentley!' Ace grumbled, head-to-head with Dave. 'Whatever Talbot told you is a lie. We want to help you. You can still come back from this. You're one of us.'

Dave's thoughts were an epileptic mist of confusion and doubt and blind anger.

'Funny,' he said, barking a laugh that sounded more like a kicked dog. 'He told me you guys are liars too.'

Dave released his grip on Ace's hockey jersey and pulled back for a big, sloppy punch, one still capable of awful things with his new devastating potency. Ace slipped the shot, the red cyclonic fist tearing through the steel-lined side of the meat-locker truck.

Ace spun away from Dave, sliding his armored hockey mask into place, and started to seal the rear doors shut with a wall of ice. 'Skinner! Pull the truck over,' he bellowed into the front cab.

He was about to call in for back-up over the comm-channel when Dave charged again, his lack of fighting skills compensated by sheer force, crashing into Ace and sending the pair of them smashing out of the frozen-shut rear doors. One of the doors came off the hinges, which they rode down the interstate like an ice floe on a hot sea of orange sparks. Car headlights sliced wildly this way and that across the lanes, their horns blaring.

Up ahead, the truck came to a skidding and hissing halt, spraying slush and salt. The door ride came to lurching stop, dislodging the combatants. Dave was up, stalking towards Ace, when on impulse he lunged across the lane to stamp-kick the flank of a passing car. The passenger door crumpled inwards, spooking the driver into swerving through the guardrail. A nasty little chuckle leaked out of Dave's mouth.

He continued towards Ace, watching him building a suit of glacial armor, the fresh-falling snow blessing him.

They clashed in the road as cars skidded and swerved away from the two maniacs. Dave could tell Ace was doing what he could to drag the fight away from the interstate. But Dave didn't want that. He was happy right here, hearing the distant delight of the Imp King somewhere in the far reaches of his mind. Was it an echo? He didn't think so; part of him felt like Kerzix was viewing this through his eyes like some type of snuff-action movie.

A fist like a junior iceberg slammed down onto the tarmac, right where Dave had just been standing. Dave had scrambled to the side but still felt the tremor in his feet. He flung himself towards the giant frozen fist, battering at it, hammering chunks of ice across the lanes like diamonds. Breaking enough of it down, he found Ace's arm poking out of it. That was much easier to break. The ice-man's roar of pain could be heard over the rush of cars. A spiky gauntlet of purest white ice sliced across Dave's abdomen, but he was bouncy and awkward enough to skip away from most of the damage. It still hurt, though. It hurt terribly. The heat of his blood spilling down his legs felt magnified by the sub-zero weather. The gimped ice-golem struck out again, several icicles whooshing through nothing but cold air. Dave clung on to the passing spear-arm like a drunk cat, finding the whole thing unexpectedly amusing. The frozen arm whirled about in an attempt to dislodge him. Sure enough, Dave lost his grip on the slick ice, along with the skin of his palms and fingers. He bounced along the hard blacktop, right into the path of a skidding car. The bumper stopped at an angle, inches from his face. Dave laughed again, but it carried a pang of confused sadness. Up on his feet again, he lashed out, his fist going through the hood and the engine like they were made of Styrofoam.

All around him cars had slalomed into a multi-lane bottleneck, choking the interstate. Behind the criss-crossing high beams, silhouettes ran in terror or stared in muted disbelief at the fight, filming what they could on their phones.

It sent a hot, liquid tingle of satisfaction through Dave. To be noticed. To be feared. To be respected.

It felt wrong.

It felt terrible.

It felt incredible.

Patting his slashed abdomen, he noticed that the wound had already closed over.

The big bad ice-man was on his feet, the crossing headlights making him shine in gold and sapphire. His broken left arm had retreated into a dense protective shell of ice. His right gauntlet now held a gleaming sword. Dave sprinted towards him with joy in his heart, then threw himself with abandon away from the sword's whistling arc. The messy landing would have hurt an ordinary man, but any bumps and scrapes were already gone by the time he was up and running again.

In close, fists swiping red, he dismantled Ace's armor, taking away every weapon raised against him. He was a typhoon of destruction. With ragged breaths, relishing the hot pump of rage in his heart, Dave stared down at the beaten man. A Spark like him. A powerful weapon.

And look at him now. Wounded and on his knees, surrounded by the detritus of his shattered armor. The hockey mask stared up at him, and Dave could see—no, he could *feel* the anathema radiating from the man's eyes. Dave grabbed him by the back of his black mullet, and with a single perfect, piston-precision shot, cracked the hockey mask in two, bludgeoning the face beneath. Ace fell to his back, spitting up blood from a savagely split lip, and another missing tooth, his bottom jaw's left lateral incisor.

Dave dropped to his knees. And after what might have been a moment of reluctance, straddled Ace's chest, pinning him.

'Your face . . .' Ace muttered. 'Something's happened to you. My guys— Hourglass . . . can help you. You should be . . . on our team.'

Dave found that he couldn't talk. Only capable of staring down at the bloodied face beneath half a hockey mask. An acceptance of the inevitable steeled Ace's features.

'Go on then, pussy. Finish—finish what you started. Just know . . . you do this, there's no coming back. You know that, right?'

Dave's fist came down with a mind of its own. He climbed off the frozen warrior and marched towards the still-waiting truck. The driver did what he could with the meager weapons he had available to him. It wasn't enough. Climbing behind the wheel, Dave threw the truck in gear with thoughts of fire and screaming. He thought about going back to Buffalo. About stepping on people like cockroaches in his glorious homecoming.

He was twenty miles over the speed limit and had already sideswiped a number of too-slow vehicles when he caught his reflection in the rear-view mirror: his entire face and neck was wax white, a big blood-red circus grin climbed up his cheeks, and his dark eyes were inside two black-lined arches rising up to his forehead like some cartoon character.

Tugging down his singed and tattered beanie, he found that his hair was gone, his entire head also painted white. His mouth split into a grin. A smile inside a smile. Sincerity inside a simulacrum. But inside his head, the cavorting carnival of pain played on.

Changing lanes for the upcoming turn-off, he left the roads behind him resembling a demolition derby.

25

K OZLOV PERCHED ON A MAKESHIFT running board behind Calkarion. 'They're closing in!' he yelled over a drilling hum that rattled the very depths of his ear canals. The swarm banked in, solidifying like a huge closing fist. They were small as mayflies, but through squinted eyes he saw that they were actually tiny bubbles holding an electrical current. A bad thought. A bad idea. A literal swarm of negative thinking.

Kozlov rubbed at his throbbing skull, feeling the itching desires of murder and suicide continue to take hold. With a feral snarl, he glanced at Trillik, behind him in the wagon, and entertained the outlandish thought of trying to smash open its nutrient tank and bludgeoning the brains within; then maybe he could throw himself below the iron wheels of this rolling armored shell.

The Arkhitektor struggled to reattach a dangling wire to a small boxy power supply within Calkarion's shell: the piece of tech was a repellent device capable of emitting a unique subsonic frequency. The rutted terrain had rattled loose the wire at the worst possible time.

Quarmalls rode atop the shell's roof, shedding another wave of pollen into the air; it had only proved to be a mild deterrent to the swarming threat thus far, but little help was still better than none at all. The pollen dispersed upwards into the swarm, confusing the swaths for a short reprieve, causing them to pull back.

Kozlov had seen enough of the local fauna on the far edges of this flat landscape, slamming their skulls against the ground until they cracked, herds of other creatures suddenly turning feral on one another in the presence of these terrible pests. This region more than earned its title of Madcap Flats.

The Arkhitektor was likely immune to their effects, being a spirit, but Kozlov was still feeling that black aura of depressive symptoms trying to insidiously creep into his head proper. The Arkhitektor slid the power cable back into the transmitter, and immediately a hum beyond Kozlov's hearing spread anarchy amongst the plague of depressive parasites, dispersing them in every direction except for that of Calkarion's trail.

'Well done!' Calkarion said, his digital voice unaffected by the bumpy road.

Kozlov nodded his relieved gratitude to his old mentor. Rubbing his forehead, he allowed himself a few moments to close his eyes and find his calm.

The Arkhitektor passed through the carriage's ceiling to assist Quarmalls in gathering up some of the trailing pollen, helping to pack it back into the organic mesh-work of its body; it could produce more, but there was no sense in wasting any in case the transmitter jerked another wire free or broke down completely. The flora-humanoid acknowledged the monk's help with all the warmth and gratitude one could expect from a being with a faceless seed head; the painted clown smile would have to suffice. Quarmalls crouched low, clinging onto the roof, its coppery tendrils, strong as steel wire, cinching about a number of handholds.

The Arkhitektor sank through the roof, settling beside Kozlov on the bench. 'The one upstairs,' he said in Russian. 'He reminds me of you.'

Kozlov stared at him in confusion. 'I don't see the resemblance.'

'The way he cares for the pollen he carries. It's similar to how you carried the souls of our sect—may they rest in true death, and not here. The way you still carry me.'

Kozlov grunted. 'If he's fortunate, he'll keep better care of his loved ones.'

His mentor placed a hand on his shoulder. 'We could not have asked for a better caretaker than you, Konstantin. Their losses were not your failure.' A stern glower briefly swept across his face. Kozlov knew it well: guilt. It was one of his own most prevalent expressions.

'And it wasn't yours either,' he said. 'None of them blamed you, and neither did I. They lived and died honorably. True to the oaths and duties of the Rising Path. It's a terrible shame they won't get to see our paradise.' He leaned over, making sure his mentor could see the sincerity in his eyes. 'They died heroically, at the hands of men full of hate and no honor. This place, this bane...' He unfurled his hand outwards to the land around them. 'At least they're not stuck in here with us old mules.'

'Oblivion.' The Arkhitektor seemed to ponder his next words carefully. 'Do you think that is what greets those who face true death?'

Kozlov scratched at his ashen beard, feeling very old and tired. 'Are you losing faith in our mission?'

The Arkhitektor's answer was immediate. 'Never. I just hope that heaven is what we expect it to be.'

Kozlov smiled softly. 'It can be whatever we want it to be.'

'But that won't please everybody.'

Kozlov's eyes narrowed at the road ahead. He was about to challenge his mentor's wavering opinion on their sect's foundational tenet—the eschatological salvation of all things from the cruel tyrannies of the Order—when Trillik interrupted him with a sequence of blipping noises, their community of brains relaying messages as they cycled around on their centrifuge. One large industrial hand extended outwards towards the horizon.

'The sky,' Calkarion said. 'The royal watch.'

Kozlov glanced up and saw the large moon-skull slowly fading into the toxic green sky like a cackling death-head peering through a chemical fog. It had been a long while since Kozlov had seen any of these celestial observers, and Calkarion's declaration confirmed his old suspicion that these were, in fact, a form of intelligence-gathering: *the royal watch*. A more macabre and chilling version of the watchful satellites that girded Earth's atmosphere like a constricting belt. He hadn't seen this particular moon before, but it wasn't subtle in its allegiance: trailing from the crown of the deathly visage was a droopy jester's hat of asteroids molded together by a shimmering gas cloud.

'Does it know who we are?' Kozlov asked. The idea was to cross these cursed provinces in secret, avoiding any and all security checkpoints and countermeasures—should a domain like this possess such meticulous organization. But if that sky-bound observer had become suspicious, there was little any of them could do to hide out here in the open.

Trillik beeped and chirped. One of the brains acted as a spokesman, its thoughts quickly translated by Calkarion.

'We are safe. It's a routine check. Trillik has an understanding of such procedures.'

'He—*they* commanded that thing?' Kozlov asked, his gaze strafing from Trillik to the giant skull hanging in space.

'They performed some regulatory security functions,' Calkarion said. 'Mostly they operated on the Rictus Folly, which granted them certain security clearances within the palace. Collectively they were one of Kerzix's most trusted aides.'

'Empires tend to fall from within.' Kozlov admired the brain tank. 'I dare say this mission would be a significantly more risky undertaking without your alliance. We are grateful.'

'Believe me,' Calkarion said, 'the honor is all ours.'

They carried on for the best part of five miles, watching the lunatic landscape and taking comfort in each other's presence. A mile or so off to their left lay another of those giant smiling mouths, entombed in the earth like a titanic clown buried alive. It was cackling in such a frenzied manner that Kozlov thought it must somehow be in pain. It was a deeply troubling sound. The laughter of a broken and bereft mind.

They crossed a rivet in the earth and found themselves drawing the attention of some of the more ghastly local wildlife.

'Madcaps,' was all Calkarion said.

The reasoning behind their name was quickly apparent. Built like some doomed offshoot from the Triassic period, these nascent-armed saurians were in the middle of a jibbering battle. Silver-skinned with red polka dots, they were clashing their blind, domed heads together with yips and whoops. Even without eyes, they somehow became collectively aware of the fresh game entering their vicinity, angling their heads around, staring up the declivity at the passing travelers.

Calkarion's vehicle suddenly jolted as though it had been rocked from behind by a bulldozer, the hit practically tossing the horseman five feet vertically, dislodging him from his platform behind the spider. Kozlov just about managed to grip hold of his bench seat, preventing him from being launched into the back of the horseman.

The Arkhitektor shot up through the shell's roof to see what happened. 'Madcap.' He fended off the beast's second attack with a mighty shove, rolling it bodily along the hard ground.

Kozlov glanced down the declivity to their right, seeing the rest of the madcaps break into a sprint, taking the incline with gusto, sensing an easy kill.

The sound of jarring metal coming from the shell's wheels was worrying, and Kozlov wondered how they would all fare stranded on foot against the gathering clan of heavy-skulled reptiles.

Quarmalls discharged another cloud of pollen. There was no downwind to direct the swarm, but it didn't seem to need one. The pollen cloud enveloped the stampeding beasts in sneezing, yipping confusion, the leader of the pack accidentally stumbling the last several feet, threatening to blunder straight into the side of the shell, likely flattening Kozlov in the process. Instead, Trillik's open manacles shot out, seizing the madcap's muscular neck. The brains whizzed around their solution tank, and the crushing clamps pumped a lethal electrical current into the madcap before throwing its frothing, seizing carcass to the ground. Kozlov clambered up to the scalloped roof of the shell, jumping behind the embedded gun turret. He was about to strafe a bloody path through them when Calkarion regained his balance, resuming control of the spider, gathering speed and rhythm, and speeding them away from the gang of confused madcaps still determined to close in and break some bones.

'Hold tight.' Calkarion knocked it up a gear, the metallic spider chassis scrabbling across the lumpy miles.

Kozlov continued to man the roof turret just in case, but they managed to lose the madcaps easily enough, though the hinges of the spider legs had started to make an unwelcome grinding cacophony. They would need to find a quiet place to rest and allow Calkarion to assess the damage. Before too long, the topography of the flats started to crest steadily upwards into steep edifices and warped corridors of distorting mirrors. That's when another sound took precedence over the grinding hinges. Carnival sounds? Distant, off-key organ music, borderline atonal, mixed with the orgiastic moans of pain and dementia.

Kozlov's nerves ran cool. What had Calkarion mentioned after their first meeting? The Big Top. The Imp King's mobile security division. If the Big Top was only a couple of miles from this position and moving back towards the palace, then timing and opportunity might have worked against Kozlov and his allies.

Calkarion slowed his pace and quietly carried them forth into the Alley of Doomed Prophets.

26

CLYDE STOOD AT ACE'S BEDSIDE, staring down at the man he had started to believe couldn't be stopped. Hurt? Sure. Hurt badly? Under the right circumstances. But this? A coma?

The wait had been unbearable, but after hearing the doctor's news, Clyde would have preferred to have still been stressing and waiting outside in the hall.

Now he couldn't stop looking at the purple-and-red hamburger that used to be Ace's face. Eyes swollen shut, lips having practically burst under the power of his attacker's knuckles. David Bentley's knuckles. He had even broken Ace's left arm, which was currently set in a large cast. But these wounds would certainly mend in time, unlike the uncertainty of him ever waking up.

The Madhouse medical team had said, in no uncertain terms, that waking from comas such as this was up to chance and the gods; an answer that displeased Clyde to no end. It seemed that for all of the magic and advanced tech at their disposal, there were some things that couldn't be waved away, and the brain remained a fragile and incomprehensible mystery.

Clyde was no god, but he did have a way—or he at least thought he might have a way—to alter Ace's chances of waking up. It was Sarge's earlier question that had stirred it: could he significantly affect other souls from inside the Median? He might be limited in binding their threads to his own, but what if there were other ways to provoke a response here in the land of the living?

He was thinking about asking Spector, and whether it was a really good or a really bad idea. Dremel and his council would be looking for a reason to expel him permanently on the grounds of his innate association with the Coma Weaver, but now that the idea had taken root, it was receiving nourishment from a stream of theories.

'He looks chipper for a dead guy,' Nat said, her voice flat. She sat in a chair in the corner of the room, staring expressionlessly at the TV on the wall depicting shaky footage of Bentley brawling with Ace. 'They declared him dead, right?'

Several news stations had pounced on the uploaded camera footage of the snowy interstate battle. Despite the naysayers and the scoffers dismissing it as some sort of prank—they can do anything with computer effects these days!—multiple videos from multiple witnesses, complete with their corroborating statements, proved that this incredible event had actually occurred. The number of fatalities amongst the sea of wrecked vehicles was still being tallied by the authorities but was certainly in the dozens.

'What's this painted-face bullshit?' she asked.

'I doubt our EMTs were practicing their make-over techniques on his corpse, so ... Spark related?' Darcy asked.

'I think Occam's razor would tell us that it's probably tied to Cairnwood,' Barros stated. 'I mean, were the Luminaries big on clowns?'

'You saying Talbot placed some sort of clown-themed time bomb on Bentley?' Nat asked.

'It sounds silly when you say it.' Barros looked at Rose askance, as though weighing the importance of asking her the following question: 'When you blasted Bentley, did he have any artefacts on his person?'

'You were there,' Rose answered, crossing her arms defensively.

'Maybe you saw something the rest of us didn't,' Barros said, glancing at Sarge and Darcy.

'I saw a herd of huge fucking cows and various shades of fireball,' Rose said. 'There was a lot of strange shit being passed around. You're asking the wrong person.'

The talking heads were replaced by live news-chopper footage follow-ing the unknown perpetrator as he continued to cause bedlam on the highway, his smoking and battered truck carving a path west along US-6.

'Buffalo,' Nat said. 'You think he's going home?'

'Then that's where we'll bury him,' Rose said. She stood opposite Clyde on the other side of the bed, the ISU flanking her, watching Ace's body continue to live while his mind and everything that made Ace *Ace* was stranded on a different plane, possibly never to return.

'You want to kill him?' Nat asked, uncertainty in her voice.

'Look at that fucking psycho,' Rose burst out, pointing at the news. 'It wasn't my first choice, but fuck yeah, I want to kill him. We've killed for less. Look, we tried to help him, but Talbot beat us to it. Either Bentley was a fucking head case to begin with, or they did something to him. Doesn't matter now. We're a soldier down. And with the way my strength has been on the fritz, our force is diminished further. We can't have some-body as dangerous as him running around. We need to put him down, quickly and permanently.'

Kev had remained quiet on the trip back, but now he found his voice. 'Whether we bring Bentley in dead or alive, I think the real question now is,' his thoughtful eyes cut back and forth between Rose and Barros, 'are you two going to try and bury all this negativity between you? I hold my hand up and accept responsibility for the rocky patch between us. But you both need to move past it. You have too much history together to allow one mistake to derail your friendship, and this team. If it's a lack of trust creating the weak link in your chain, and affecting your abilities as a unit, then for the sake of the team, for the sake of Ace, and for anybody else out there who might fall victim to this maniac's rampage, get over it.'

Sarge offered a lukewarm smirk. 'Curly's got a point,' he said to Rose, which earned him a small look of gratitude from Barros. 'What's the ex-pression: "To err is human." You're stubborn to a fault, Rosie. And last time I checked, I'm still your ranking officer. I'm dog tired of the tension between you and Barros.'

'Not in the Army anymore, Sarge,' Rose said after a moment. 'But you're right.' She singled Barros out. 'We've been through too much shit together, and that was back when our lives were conventional. I don't want to be mad at you. And I need my strength back. We good?'

Barros nodded, relief in her eyes. 'Always.'

'Sorry to interrupt this tender tearjerker of a scene, but we have another problem to consider,' Sarge said. 'Take a look at that.'

Clyde raised his eyes to the television screen. The stolen Madhouse truck lay on its roof. A number of corpses in vinyl bags had been flung from the rear of the truck, wrecked State Trooper cars were scattered around. The cab of the truck was empty. That meant Bentley was on foot, somewhere in the woods surrounding the highway.

'Bentley's off the radar,' Sarge continued. 'We'll have to wait for him to resurface. When he does, I'm betting there's going to be a lot more bodies dropping.'

'When he does pop up, how do we handle it?' Nat asked.

'Something Sarge said earlier got me thinking,' Clyde said. 'I'm an outcast in the Median. There's still a lot of stuff I don't know about the place. But hypothetically, what if I could interact with soul threads in other ways?' Clyde gently patted Ace on the upper arm. 'At first I was thinking: What if there's a way I could wake Ace up from inside there? Maybe, maybe not, I mean… the thing inside me isn't called the Coma *un*-Weaver. But who knows?' Clyde took a breath for what he was about to say next. 'But what if there's a way for me to destroy a thread instead of saving one? The Weaver can definitely do that.'

Kev and Nat shared a glance and then gave Clyde a concerned look.

'Okay, pal, this sounds dangerously like a dream demon getting its training wheels,' Kev said, his brow furrowed.

'No, it's all me.' Clyde returned a dead-eyed expression. 'Look what Bentley did to Ace. Such power. And this.' He pointed at the highway slaughter on the TV. 'We don't know the full extent of his ability. The ISU can't just pull the soul from his body; he's a Spark, too powerful. And I don't like the thought of either of you,' he glanced from Nat to Rose and back again, 'lying here in a bed next to Ace. Not if there's a safer solution. Not if there's a chance that I could quietly stop him.'

Barros asked, 'When you say quietly stop him, you mean—'

'I'm with Rose. Kill the motherfucker.'

'What might that look like?' Kev asked. 'You call Spector up, run it by him, and then the pair of you sneak behind the Reel's judicatory like a couple of midnight grave robbers?'

'I'd say like a couple of assassins, but yeah.' Not for the first time, Clyde felt detached from himself. He didn't recognize the person he had become or believe the words he was speaking. Is this who he was now? A cold-blooded hitman?

He had expected some pushback from Rose. What he had proposed was a politically risky act, interfering with company policy by way of becoming more deeply engaged in House rules. But it was Nat who showed some reluctance.

'That could be dangerous.' She took a step towards him, hands deep in the pockets of her leather jacket. 'You already got what you needed from Dremel. You said yourself, they're not the types who appreciate unscheduled social visits. And being tainted by that demon?' Her eyes flashed with a split-second violet storm of concern. 'That probably puts you one rung below a leper in their opinion. What happens if they catch you?'

'Can't be the craziest thing I've done,' he answered. It clearly wasn't a good enough answer for her, so he gave it a little more thought. 'It's just hypothetical, remember. For all I know, it might not even be possible. But I can at least run it by Spector, get a professional opinion.'

'You said you want to do this because you're scared of me being outmatched, one Spark to another,' Nat said. 'Why am I the one who has to be scared for you?'

Clyde stepped in closer, his hands lightly brushing her hips, pulling her hands from her pockets, his fingers entwining with hers. 'If I do this, if I *can* do this, I'll make sure there's no risk. No collateral.' He shot a look at Rose. 'Can we just keep this idea between us for now? Until I talk to Spector.'

Kev, naturally, was a lock. And so, too, was Barros. Sarge and Darcy, professional and trusting, hadn't made too much of a stink over Kev and Barros' former disciplinary action. They seemed begrudgingly accepting of the proposal. But then there was Rose. For a second or two it looked like she wanted to argue the idea, a swift return to her obstinate obedience to chain-of-command. A new tension filled the room, her eyes crashing against Clyde's in a battle of wills. Any urge she might have had to do the company-thing flickered and died, and she quietly rested a hand on Ace's shoulder, almost sisterly.

Nat still seemed a little uneasy with Clyde's idea. He read it in her expression and her body and knew another conversation about it would be forthcoming at a more private time and place.

'Trust me, if Spector says no—and I'm certain he will—I'll drop it,' he said, hoping to convince her. He didn't like lying to her, and kissed her lightly on the lips as if to punctuate the conversation.

Their phones beeped. Meadows. Rose grabbed the TV remote and switched from the news to sports, finding a hockey game for Ace to maybe hear. Clyde led them solemnly out of the medical wing.

27

B Y THE TIME THE JAG rolled into the private parking garage of the members' club on 57th Street, Talbot and Gabriel had long since reverted to a semblance of humanity.

The members' club was all old timber, stone, and brass. It was also Cairnwood founded, and as such, only clientele of a particular breed was eligible for membership; whether they be blue blood or hell-skinned, it was not a place for sentiment. And yet...

'They were my darlings, Edward. My beautiful creatures. All of them... gone. Butchered.' Gabriel's huge eyes seemed to be blind to the austere appeal of the lounge, witnessing nothing but owl corpses.

Talbot could only feign heartache as he sipped liquidized soul essence from a vintage slave lineage. The cask had preserved it beautifully, and he could really savor the harrowing grief.

'We have been trading atrocities with Hourglass for around seventy years. They have cost us more money and opportunities than there are worms in a graveyard. Before we had put down our foundations on this continent, it was Avalon and Soteria drawing our blood in Britain and Europe. We have each sunk to the depths necessary to survive, to succeed. But it's been one hundred seventy-three years since anyone had the effrontery to murder my darlings.' Gabriel gave him a calculating look, reminding Talbot that he hadn't forgotten about his one murderous act against one of his beloved owls.

Talbot had the decency to appear briefly remorseful and continued to nod along to the pity party, grateful that he had at least been spared a full car journey's worth of moping. He simply had to take Gabriel's mind off the dead feathery little shits and get it back on to the business at hand. 'Hourglass will now have their hands full of some very choice artefacts in seizing that property,' he observed.

Gabriel's bulging eyes glistened. A sharp tooth unsheathed from his curling lip. 'An exquisite collection. Centuries worth of acquisition.'

Talbot didn't feel like disclosing the bottomless bag of stolen arcana currently residing in the boot of his car. 'How will Sarkozy react to this? This loss, well, it's certainly a step above some of our recent failings. The last couple—'

'You mean *your* recent failings.'

Talbot bit his lip, humbled. Smiled. 'Of course. They were purely fiscal. Matters of industry. And it was always inevitable that new markets like the soul pipeline and enhanced assassins would be met by one saboteur or another: a competitor or legal. But your curation? It wasn't even a target, but it's now a bonus in our enemy's hands. And it was bringing the Bentley chap to your home that brought the wolves to your door. A glaring oversight on your behalf, with all due respect.'

'But how did the wolves get his scent?' Gabriel asked. 'How did they know to find him there?'

'We may never know. And at this point it's redundant. We must deal with the now.'

'The reliquary was largely an enthusiasm of mine. Nothing was lost that cannot be replaced. This doesn't impact Cairnwood's future.'

'I sincerely hope you're right.' Talbot quaffed the quietly screaming dregs of his drink. 'You've proven to be a stalwart member of the inner circle. It would be a crime to lose your seat. Cold comfort, I'm sure, but at least the mirrors were shattered. Even Hourglass won't be able to piece those back together. The identities and whereabouts of Sarkozy and the rest of the circle will remain hidden.'

Talbot signaled the waiter, a long-limbed and longer-skulled servant in a royal-blue silk vest, adorned with a small emblematic gold pin of a cairn.

If Talbot recalled correctly, the waiter's name was Hammond. Another one-time human. He had been part of the doomed construction crew that had ventured over to mine the Eidolon Trench before succumbing to wounds from a creature given the nomenclature of bodybag. Infected, he had been shipped back and handed off to certain Cairnwood interests for study. Sadly, despite morphing into the chilling, emaciated creature that was diligently serving the patrons, Hammond had thus far proven to be fit for little more than mixing drinks.

Hammond rolled over a gilded drinks trolley, decanting glassware misted with a slight veil of weeping tears. The grief flowed richly into Talbot's tumbler.

'If we may switch up long-term prospects for short-term,' Talbot said, 'what do you make of the news eating up the airwaves?'

'You mean our Spark?'

'I do. Bentley survived.' Talbot tapped away on his phone, bringing up news hits of the recorded highway fight. 'And he did a number on one of those Hourglass rats. We could find him. He remains highly valuable.'

Gabriel leaned forward, engrossed in the shaky camera recording of the fight between Ace and Bentley. 'Hold on a moment … his face. Is that—'

'Yes. I believe our plucky chum inadvertently broke the marotte in your collection.'

Gabriel's curiosity was a brief flight and a crash. 'Then he's no longer any use to us. What good is a man we can't control?'

'Maybe we can, maybe we can't. At the very least, perhaps we can point him in the right direction. For the owls.'

Gabriel perked up. 'Perhaps it would be making the best of a bad situation.'

'Exactly.'

Hammond rolled off to dispense more misery to the inhuman and abhuman members sitting quietly in the lounge. Gabriel took his glass. 'But first I must head upstairs to consult the mirrors. Sarkozy must be apprised of our losses. Then we find Bentley.'

'To Cairnwood's silver future.' Talbot raised a fresh glass, the elbow of his shirt and suit jacket still tacky from the dried ichor of his previously broken arm.

Gabriel, forlorn but recovering swiftly, raised his own. 'To *our* future, though I presume it to be one of a gloomier shade than silver.'

28

'**H**E'S ONE OF THE ORDER?' Clyde said, barely able to believe what he was hearing. 'Kerzix the Imp King?' The tablet in his hands contained a frozen image of David Bentley taken during his fight with Ace, zoomed in and fuzzy, a sharp contrast of shadow and high-beam headlights. It was a disturbing face, mockery painted over violent determination.

'Yes,' Meadows answered gravely. 'Of the House of the Strange Fates.'

'You're shitting me,' Nat muttered, sounding as incredulous as Clyde. 'First Cairnwood drops Charon in our path, now this guy. What do you get the asshole who has everything?'

'Cairnwood's local proprietor, presumably this owl individual, had an extensive reach for exotic antiques, but where Charon's eye would have been equivalent to a Fabergé egg, one of these marottes would be more like some mass-produced kitsch, though admittedly extremely dangerous kitsch,' Meadows said, gazing at the broken marotte placed before them.

They had reconvened in one of the forensic suites of the R&D department.

Meadows had divulged some top-secret history on an unexpected enemy. Various paper extracts, though brief, filled in some blanks. And while the agency clean-up crews had come away from Gabriel's mansion relatively light-handed due to the number of empty or broken display cases in the reliquary, they did find a lot of books of various editions and dangers, and, of most pertinence, the broken halves of the jester's scepter, a thing both ancient and hideous.

'Imps are mistakenly believed to originate from Germanic folklore, vicious prankster demons who enjoy forming destructive friendships that have a tendency to end very badly. The truth, however, is that our entire accumulated mythology of these creatures stems from this one monarch. Being one of the Order's kings, Kerzix isn't some run-of-the-mill jackass trying to get a few chuckles by ruining some schmuck's life. He's more broad-minded, with an acquired taste for punishing souls whose faith has been misplaced in their cultural and societal gods. Kerzix views such people as foolish, and so in death, they all come to fear him instead of some fictitious authority.'

'What's the policy on this thing?' Kev asked of the marotte. 'Ship them off to Indigo, have the hoodoo send a few agents over to drop it off in the Imp King's backyard?'

'If we had found it intact, we would have locked it away where nobody could get to it. But this one is now nothing more than kindling. Kerzix enjoys playing a nasty game of distributing these things across populated living worlds, creating anarchistic terrorists out of whoever encounters them.' Using a small steel implement, Meadows pressed down on one jagged half of the scepter with only the minimum of force, creating a series of large splinters.

'Why didn't it turn the owl guy or Talbot into a murderous jack-in-a-box?' Barros asked.

Meadows considered it. 'I don't really want to know what gods they pray to. But the catch with these marottes is that they only work once, and it must be a faithless soul. According to Trujillo, Kerzix hedges his bets in the soul stakes. It isn't enough that he rakes in the souls of the faithful, so he uses these little dirty tricks,' he jabbed the scepter with the steel prod again, 'to net some more.'

'I never thought I'd say it, but I'm sorry Bentley never accepted Jesus Christ as his Lord and Savior,' Sarge said.

'Or L. Ron Hubbard,' Darcy added.

'So now we have a Order-sponsored lunatic with the power of a Spark.' Rose shook her head in exasperation and crossed her arms.

'Bentley isn't the Imp King's first subject on our plane, but he is the first on U.S. soil since Hourglass started operating. We have, however, corroborated this scepter with reports from Avalon and Soteria, who have shared their records on several other documented encounters with similar transmutative items, with particular emphasis on two cases involving very destructive individuals: one a comic from the Roman Empire, the other a court jester from Renaissance-era Germany. Both of whom stirred up a mass panic of bloodshed and hysteria before being dispatched.'

Illustrations of several different scepters were adjoined by a brief paragraph explaining that the archetypal medieval minstrel copied their image from the hellish clown who tried to assassinate a Roman senator before hacking down a number of guards and setting fire to a consulate chamber.

'How did they stop them?' Clyde asked.

'They died as easily as any man,' Meadows answered.

'So Bentley coming back from the dead, that's…?'

'Might be part of his Spark skill-set.'

'Fuck,' Nat muttered.

Meadows concurred with a morose expression.

'Has Bentley turned up yet?' Clyde asked.

'Aerial recon and all traffic and street cams are still being monitored. He can't hide forever and very likely won't want to. In case the working theory is correct and he is returning to Buffalo, we have eyes on his apartment, place of work, and all known locales.'

'What about Talbot?'

'With those protective runes on his vehicle, not a whole lot. We followed the chain of scrambled traffic cams, the last one being in Manhattan on 57th Street. But we don't know where it went from there. There's a lot of private property on that street. Chances are it's squirreled away into some parking spot.'

'Billionaires Row,' Nat said. 'Probably a whole lot of secret places in those buildings.'

'And by the time we secure warrants to search every building, he'll be long gone.'

'So once again the rat found himself a hole. I guess Bentley's the bigger issue right now, though,' Barros said.

'I'd say that's a fair assumption. The other two flash-in-the-pan lunatics were short-lived, committing their wave of destruction before the afflicted individual was either killed or died at their own hands in some reckless attack.'

'Killing him is fine in theory,' Rose said. 'But how? He isn't some regular guy. Even by Spark standards, he's a major threat. The footage showed him walking off some serious trauma from Ace. And I hit him with a grenade before he—' She broke off, and an expression of sudden understanding spread over her features. 'It was my fault. All of this is my fucking fault. I blasted him into that fucking laughing stick.'

'There's no value in focusing on that now,' Meadows said. 'Deal with it in your own time, Agent. Preferably with a bottle of something strong.'

Clyde had slowly tuned out of the briefing, the facts of another monarch having entered the equation already complicating his rough strategy for stopping Bentley. It was his repeated exposure to Charon's dark energies, exuded through his physically and psychically altered pawns, that had stirred the Coma Weaver awake in the first place, putting Clyde in the sights of Dremel and his council. Would tangling with Bentley's soul—or was it Kerzix's property now?—further nudge the Coma Weaver into waking? If nothing else, it would undoubtedly give Dremel cause to kill him.

But would he rather risk Nat's life by having her face Bentley? The answer was immediate and obvious.

'What if I try and undo Bentley's curse from inside the Median?' Clyde asked. 'It might not be possible. I might not even know how. But if I can get Spector to help me, he could ask the council to run it up the ladder to show us where Bentley's thread is. Get a look at it, see if this jester's curse can be removed.'

Clyde was actually amazed Meadows allowed him to finish his whole thought, because if his expression was anything to go by, it was crystal clear that his answer was an emphatic no.

'We are already dealing, albeit indirectly, with a House of the Order,' Meadows said. 'Doubling down on this mess by asking another—one of only two Houses on our side, might I add—to engage in subterfuge is not a stable solution. We can't risk triggering a series of diplomatic hostilities between ourselves and the less lenient monarchs who are itching for conquest.'

'Hate to sound like a kid on the schoolyard, but the Imp King started this,' Nat said. 'We're just trying to stop his cross-state joyride.'

Meadows gave her a funny look. It was faint, but Clyde still saw it. Disappointment? Maybe. No, wait... betrayal.

'Then do the files mention if there's another way of reprogramming these psychos without relying on direct force?' Sarge asked, giving Clyde a partisan glance. 'Because if not, and Bentley's got his mind set on causing as much collateral damage as possible, it won't do any of us much good to add fuel to his fire by getting involved in a public engagement.'

'I'm not in disagreement,' Meadows said, 'but conspiring with the Glowing Reel, a House that is supposed to remain impartial, could cause significantly more collateral damage if it provokes the other heads of the Order into reneging on our long-standing detente.'

'If I may say something,' Kev said, receiving a mildly hostile look from Meadows. 'I have to point out that it seems like Kerzix has no issue with bending the rules we're striving to protect. And wouldn't any strategy we use to stop Bentley, either directly or covertly, be viewed as a hostile act against Kerzix's crown, thereby risking the treaty?'

'Excuse the trite analogy, but the Imp King has always been a wild card, more liberal in flouting the rules that hold our balance together,' Meadows said. 'But the removal of one of his chaos agents can't be considered an act of war, since such activity is already viewed as an illegality within the Order. However, if we conspire with the Glowing Reel to clean up one of his problems, then it's a different matter entirely. The Reel are ostensibly on our side, but only because a war would be costly to them in souls and dreams, and so they're supposed to remain clear of any hostile actions between us and the rest of the Order's forces.'

'Great. So, we have a super-powered suicide bomber out there waiting to go off, and he's already got a highway death toll of sixty-seven.' Rose's brow crumpled as if beneath the weight of guilt and frustration.

'This isn't on you,' Barros said. 'How could you have known this would happen?'

'Sometimes you're okay, Barros,' Rose said. 'But don't bullshit me. My shock and awe caused this.'

'What about Ace?' Clyde asked Meadows. 'With permission, I'd still like to run my last idea by Spector. Maybe there's a way to wake him from inside the Median.'

'Out of the question,' Meadows said. 'Your work with Spector was to parley with the Reel so they wouldn't view you as an enemy and kill you on sight. It wasn't so you can make a habit of dropping in and out of the Median like it's a damn flophouse. Especially in your precarious condition. Speaking of which, it might be safer if you take a back seat on this one. We don't know if exposure to Bentley might stimulate the Coma Weaver in the same way Charon did.'

'But what if Ace doesn't wake up?' Clyde asked. 'We can't just leave him there like a vegetable.'

'Must I remind you of the risks of your job?'

'I'm okay with the risks. You're the one who seems scared of taking one,' Clyde said, holding Meadows' stare.

'Choose your next words very carefully, Agent Williams. I would hate for you to spoil the good work you have done for us here.'

'Ace deserves more than to waste away in a damn bed,' Clyde said bitterly. 'He'd rather be cut loose into the Null.'

With the utmost of professional calm and detachment, Kev said, 'If not for the merits of the man himself, think of the waste of talent it would be to leave him in a coma.'

Meadows went to say something, paused, and chose something else. 'You think I'm being heartless? That I don't care about the health and safety of my agents?' He gave a bullish exhalation through his nose. 'I've just been on a call about burying an agent—a *friend* I've known for longer than most of you have been alive. I have a lot of fond memories of Estelle. Starting out in the agency, finding our ways in this terrifying world.' His wall of professional detachment eroded a little. 'It doesn't matter how long you spend in this life, you always think you'll have another chance to see the ones you love before they go. I'll miss her. I've buried too many friends. I'm not happy leaving Ace like that. But he still has a chance to wake up of his own accord.'

'The doctors didn't sound hopeful,' Clyde interjected.

'Doctors are pragmatic by nature. They don't traffic in wishful thinking. But people can wake from comas, and if anybody is tenacious enough to do so, it's Ace. He's tough as old leather.'

'So's the guy who put him in a coma,' Clyde said. 'And he might put more of us in one too if we have to engage him head-on.'

'It's becoming very clear that this team has a limited shelf life. There's some top talent standing before me, but all the talent in the world doesn't mean shit if they can't work towards specific objectives. In case some of you are forgetful, I'm the one in charge here. You're not my advisors, you're my soldiers. And as such, you don't understand the intricacies of steering a ship through diplomatic waters. Now, we have an incredibly dangerous individual running loose out there. For Ace's sake, I want you all on standby for when Bentley resurfaces. In the meantime, I'll be considering a more hands-off solution to dealing with him. Once he's been dealt with, those of you who continue to find problems with my management style are free to resign.' Without another word, Meadows exited the room.

29

C LYDE NEEDED SOME FRESH AIR and space away from the bureaucratic clutches of officialdom. He also needed to find a Christmas gift for his mom and so decided to head all the way back into the city, asking Nat and Kev to accompany him in some shopping. Nat agreed that it was a better idea than sitting around waiting for the bell to ring, and she could try and find something for her parents too. Clyde found the sights, the lights, and the overall seasonal festivities a pleasing distraction, but he knew they were as hokey and cheap as his sense of calm. It didn't take long before he spotted a suspicious man tailing them through the crowds of a Brooklyn holiday market.

There was always a chance it was just some average Joe grumbling his way through this stressful season, but Clyde had sighted him in their vicinity three times already and knew it was another spook tasked with keeping an eye on Kev; or, Clyde wondered, was he the one now being observed?

He sipped his mocha, pretending he wasn't looking. 'Have you noticed—'

'The sketchy dude following us?' Kev was feigning interest in the stalls of seasonal knickknacks across the street. 'It's Del. One of my favorite babysitters. I haven't seen any of the other regulars, though.'

'Bit lax using one of the guys you've already made,' Nat said. 'I guess nobody else wants your sloppy seconds, Kev.'

'I don't think they care about blending in anymore,' Clyde said, moving them calmly along the bustling streets. 'And I don't think they're just watching Kev.'

'Your big idea to stop Bentley and save Ace?' Kev asked.

Clyde faked a smile, lifting his shopping bag to point out the glitzy decor of another display. 'I think so,' he mumbled, suddenly wondering if any of these spooks could lip-read. 'Meadows might be worried I'll go behind his back and talk to Spector, try and rope him into helping me.'

Nat exhaled, the steam of her breath vanishing in the cold air. 'You wouldn't be that dumb, would you? Even if you asked, how do you know Spector wouldn't call Meadows as soon as you hang up?'

'I think I can trust him.'

'The ex-professional thief?' Kev asked.

Clyde's brow furrowed. 'I thought you were into the idea?'

'I am.' Kev's emotional detachment was starting to become borderline pathological. 'I think it's a good idea. Doesn't mean I trust Spector. Still worth a try, though. Maybe he'll be into it, helps, then feels an itch to blab about it. Maybe he doesn't. Still, worth a try.'

'Against all odds, I've grown to like Ace. He's a stand-up dude. My kind of creep. But what you're talking about could put you in needless danger.' Nat's eyes withheld any flickering of power; Clyde saw only concern there. 'Dremel and his sleepover buddies don't sound like the sort to be throwing around favors. Definitely not for you with your situation, and multiply that by ten since we're also dealing with another House of the Order. Maybe we should wait a little, just until we clear up this shit with Bentley and the imp. Who knows, Ace might wake himself up.'

Clyde held her with his stare, and the rest of the world melted away for a moment. 'I'd do the same thing for you.'

'You too,' he added to Kev, not wanting him to feel any more detached from this world than he already did.

Kev shirked the sentiment, too engrossed in scanning about the crowds for any of Del's little helpers. 'I'm secure in your love of me,' he quipped.

Nat gave Clyde a quick peck on the lips, if only to enhance the lie that they were oblivious of being tailed. 'I know you would.'

Clyde knew deep down that helping Ace was only part of it—it was a huge part, the bulk of the iceberg, as it were—but it was also a need to see how far he could go before Dremel or the others got wise to his presence. It was dangerous, stupid even, and against agency policy, but he had to know more about what sort of change, if any, was capable of being made from within the Median. Especially if he was going to one day help Kev and Konstantin shake up the Order's establishment and perhaps, one day, find his brother and dad.

'I want to do this, Nat. I need to. In a way, I'm doing this for everyone.' He felt absurd saying such a thing, but that didn't make it any less true. 'I don't know what that means yet, but I'm hoping that if I can help Ace or stop Bentley, find a way to operate without waking the Coma Weaver, then it could be the start of something bigger.'

Nat chewed her lip for a second, wrestling with something behind troubled eyes. 'Fuck! I can't do this . . . '

Clyde's heart thudded, heavy and slow. He anticipated the worst. 'What?'

'I can't keep this locked up, pretending it's . . . ' She huffed. 'I'm not a spy. This isn't my type of gig.' She composed herself, started again with a new firmness. 'Meadows asked me to watch you. Wants me to discourage you from doing anything dumb or getting influenced by—' Her hand jerked towards Kev.

Clyde paused, letting the reverberations from her revelation settle over him, thinking over their true implications. Meadows was controlling, it was a prerequisite for his job, and so what surprised him most was how it didn't surprise him, nor did it overtly bother him. What bothered Clyde was how easily Meadows had lost faith in him, coming to view him as a liability. Viewed him and Kev as a pair of untrustworthy fuck-ups more concerned with wanting to tackle real, meaningful change instead of upholding the lame status quo of a shortsighted and submissive charter. But all of it paled compared to the idea that Nat had been taking notes on him.

'How long have you been doing this?' he asked, trying to sound reasonable.

'Since the day you went back to Indigo. He took me out for something to eat, and we talked. He was concerned about what Kev and Barros did.' She keyed Kev into the conversation with an apologetic look. 'Wanted to make sure nothing else like it happened again. And that's another thing that has me worried. If you do become an unwanted house mouse for the Reel, it won't just be Dremel you'll be provoking. Meadows won't be as lenient next time, and I'm not talking ankle monitors and a shittier-than-normal attitude. You'll be arrested. Thrown in the Fish Tank, and from what he hinted at,' her eyes widened as if taking in some awesome or awesomely terrible sight, 'that place sucks.'

'Well, that won't mean much if Dremel cuts my cord. My ass will be in the Null, and Meadows will be arresting a corpse,' Clyde said. He had almost forgotten about their watcher, Del, until, with a flustered glance, he very nearly made eye contact with him. He fumbled about with his shopping bag and mocha, not knowing what to say next. 'So is that it, then, between us? Is that why you got so close to me when I went to Indigo? Talking every night. Hanging out with Kev.'

Nat almost looked offended but seemed to realize how it must look from Clyde's point of view. 'No, of course not.'

'Before I went, we fooled around a little, but it felt casual,' Clyde said, tone accusing. 'You were tricky to get a bead on emotionally. But then—'

'I told you it wasn't just Meadows. That was shit timing, that's all. Despite my best intentions, I've got feelings for you, and that's something I usually try to avoid. I spent so many years getting drunk and fucked up and pretending that I didn't care until . . .'

Until her Spark ignited and accidentally exploded her band and her friends at a warehouse party.

'You're stable, dependable, and I don't want to throw that away. Why do you think I just told you about Meadows asking me to be double-agent mole patrol?'

'Could be another trick,' Kev suggested, still a master of nonchalance.

Nat frowned at him, accepted his distrust, then locked eyes with Clyde. 'I love Meadows. That grumpy old bastard is as good as family, but I can't keep doing this sneaky shit. That's why I told you.'

Clyde didn't know what to say.

'That fucking sucks, Nat,' Kev said, his voice flat, but the lack of feeling made it hit as hard as a tirade. 'I actually thought you gave a shit for a minute there. Guess you're just another one of them. Another Rosie the Robot blindly following Hourglass policy.'

'That's not me at all, Kev. I'm not that good of an actress. I liked hanging out with you, I really did. And no shade on Rose, but don't call me a fucking robot. I don't get swept up by no Pied Piper. It was my stubbornness that kept me from accepting Meadows' training sooner—if I had, a lot of my friends would still be alive. I'm indebted to Meadows and didn't want to let him down. But . . . I guess I just did exactly that.'

'If I talk to Spector,' Clyde said, 'I guess that means your conscience will need to report that too?'

Nat tilted her head back, exasperated. 'Not when I think you're doing the right thing. Even when the right thing scares the piss out of me.'

A swell of emotion coursed through Clyde: a warring mix of doubt, frustration, but also love, the latter of which felt all the sweeter because of its precipitous risk and uncertainty. He didn't want to lose that feeling, the way she had made him float these past weeks. Did he trust her now, in this moment? He wanted to. That was a given. He knew she'd risk a world of trouble for him, something she had already done, the pair of them having stared down death together. Was that not a good enough cause to put a little faith in her allegiances?

His lopsided smirk brokered the peace between them. 'I told you, I'm not going to be taking stupid chances with Dremel or the Weaver. If it's doable but too risky, I'll call it off.'

Nat returned the smile, slowly at first, wary of Kev's silence.

'If he trusts you, I trust you,' Kev placated her. 'Just remember, if you screw us in a less favorable way than how you're already screwing him, I can hurt you, and you can't even touch me.'

Clyde flicked a wary glance at Kev.

'The only screwing that will be going on will be mostly consensual between me and him,' Nat retorted. 'So what now? Do you take a nap and have a quiet word with Spector?'

'I don't know how to contact him from inside the Median,' Clyde answered. 'I'll have to contact him from this side of the pillow first.'

'They're probably already keeping track of our phones,' Kev said. 'And these idiots,' he said of Del and his presumed assistants seeded about the crowds, 'will be expecting you to make the call to Spec. So I'll break off, go buy a burner, and ask him for you.'

It sounded good to Clyde.

'But if Spector blows me up to Meadows,' he said to Nat, 'you make sure to spring us both out of the clink.'

Nat gave him a wry smile with a side of doubt. 'You're probably over-estimating my talents, but maybe I'll smuggle you in some cigarettes.'

'Not my first choice, but I'll take it.' Kev broke away from them, and Clyde noticed how Del scratched the corner of his mouth, likely muttering orders to another spook.

'Are you coming back?' Clyde asked him. 'We should probably buy something for tomorrow.' For a few seconds Clyde thought Kev had forgotten about their date with his family, but seeing how Kev seemed to briefly seize up, he knew that wasn't the case. Kev remembered, alright, and was clearly still nervous about it.

'No, I'm going to take off. A little Christmas goes a long way. If anything goes sideways while I'm gone, I'll take the heat.'

'Don't be stupid, man. It's my idea, I'll be taking the rap,' Clyde said, feeling a flutter of panic now that the plan was in motion. He was putting a lot of faith in Spector siding with him.

'You two have fun.' Kev merged with the shoppers and was quickly gone.

'I'm sorry about all of this,' Nat said. Now that Kev was gone, a seldom-seen vulnerability hung itself around her like a ripped cloak. 'Meadows has done a lot for my family, and I felt trapped.'

'It's okay. But if you ask me, it was a pretty fucked-up position he put you in.'

She took it on the chin. 'It was necessity. He believes in what he's doing. I mean he must do, right? His isn't the sort of job you accidentally fall into.' She loosely grabbed Clyde's hand, the shopping bag twirling gently from his fingers. 'But I haven't told him about our hooking up; that all happened so quickly.'

He smiled flirtatiously. 'It's nice to feel something besides 24/7 anxiety.'

Her dark and starry bedroom eyes flickered with a faint violet sheen. 'So what do you want to do?'

'I was thinking pizza, then find ourselves a nice private place.'

'Get out of my head!' She hit him playfully on the chest. 'Since we're waiting for Bentley to do something horrible, we could hang around a safe house.'

He laughed. 'Man, we're just totally sticking it to agency policy tonight, aren't we?'

'Breaking rules can be fun.'

30

Talbot knew Gabriel's meeting with the inner circle could have gone better from his dour expression. Whatever had been said in there, it had taken them long enough to say it. In Gabriel's absence, Talbot had slipped unexpectedly into a drinking mood, tackling glass after glass of gin as the hours fell away to usher in a new dawn, and his thoughts bobbed from excited to somber until, finally, Gabriel returned. As it transpired, the kingmakers didn't give much of a toss about some lost trinkets and seized books. What they couldn't wrap their heads around was the continued run of bad luck that continued to stain Gabriel's once-sterling reputation.

'They hold no grudge against you, Eddie. I explained how your slip-ups are really my own, since it was I who vouched to take you under my wing, as it were.'

'I'm overcome with relief.' Talbot ran his finger along the rim of his glass, distracted. He silently marveled at Gabriel giving himself credit for magnanimously heaping the blame onto his underling, doing what he could to stay a shoo-in with his time-honored partners.

'You started off so well. For years, *years*, you were a resounding success. A rising star. Sharp, tough, with remarkable judgement. You were hungry.' Gabriel loosened his tie. 'I don't know if you've been distracted lately or if your heart just isn't in this anymore.'

Talbot had a sudden urge to bite his tongue. He murmured, 'And is that what you told the old boys? That I'm distracted? Some bumbling, fucking oaf?'

Gabriel gave him an admonishing look, not appreciating his tone.

Talbot cut him off before he could be interrupted. 'I might not have a club ring, but I'm not some stooped warehouse laborer.' A flash of memory of him scrambling for pennies on the cobbles rose up like indigestion. 'I'm still a reputable member with something to lose. How long before they decide that your gracious tolerance of my incompetence is no longer acceptable? That I should be cut loose? And you're sitting there, in the spectacular ruins of a plot you're as much responsible for as I am, expecting me to be grateful for your honesty in painting me as the whipping boy in all of this? And for what...? So you'll get a cushy position somewhere else whilst I get to continue polishing your shoes.'

'This conversation is taking a very hostile turn. You should be grateful your head is still attached to your neck. As it stands, we can pull ourselves up by our bootstraps and try again. We still have our positions, which we should both be grateful for. And yes, now that you've mentioned it, I've been granted a new seat at the table for operations in Chicago. And unless you would prefer to continue this little tantrum of yours, I would like you to assist me there. This local Hourglass office can be my successor's problem when they establish a new stronghold here. Personally, I'm happy to see what business we can tap into in the Windy City. The change of scenery might do us both some good.'

Talbot stared at his gin as if he were scrying their future. 'You really think running away to—'

'I'm not running,' Gabriel cut in with a threatening glare, and Talbot saw his reflection being devoured in those obsidian eyes.

'Hourglass have offices in every major U.S. city,' Talbot continued. 'They're a national concern for all of our North American and Canadian industries, but more to the point, this current crop of arseholes have it in for me. I'm no longer a blurry face on a photograph or a mysterious name to this bunch. I've become familiar to them—which, I must admit, I'm not greatly fond of—but having said that, I've started to realize how much I've missed the dirty work. The phone calls, the delegating, the meetings and the signatures... Gabriel, I didn't realize how much it all bored me until you punished me by sending me off to attack the Syrup Farm. Being the point of the spear, it's *exhilarating.* I used to fight for everything I had. I killed for a scrap of rock-hard stale bread. And somewhere along the way, I got too caught up in all of,' he glanced about the appalling Old World decadence of the club, 'this.'

Gabriel sat very still, giving Talbot his five minutes to come back to his senses.

'So if you think hiding in Chicago will bring you joy, you go right ahead. Sooner or later our local problems will get a sniff of the owl man they witnessed in upstate New York, the one they've undoubtedly already linked to the grooming of a Spark and the attack on their Canadian facility, and they'll join their Illinois compatriots in dealing with you personally. As for me? I've grown attached to this city. It's lost a lot of its old class since the 1920s, but I still call it home. And I'd sooner build something new here than flee to some fresh start with the same old stale problems. I think what I'm saying is,' Talbot felt his heart beating a delirious rhythm of liberty as he knocked back his gin, 'I'm tired of working under you, *sir.* This issue with Bentley is as much on you as it is on me. Other than that, I count my two losses against a hundred-plus years of hard work and success. I'm due a promotion.'

'Well, I'd be very happy to relay this little outburst of yours to the circle.'

Talbot motioned to the waiter for another gin.

Gabriel's eyes locked onto the ring on Talbot's finger. 'I see you helped yourself to one of my pieces.'

Talbot pretended to have forgotten all about the ring. 'Oh? Oh yes, Leberecht's Maquette. I never got the opportunity to use it in Canada, but I'm curious about it.'

The dapper barman whisked over with a new glass of gin on a tray. That's when Gabriel spotted the canvas bag under their table.

'I recognize the luggage too. So you found the time to steal anything that wasn't nailed down as our enemies were at the gate.'

'Investing in my future.' Talbot took the gin with a smile. 'And you know, something else has occurred to me. I'm sure our Chicago associates will have a very nice, very extensive collection of rare items too, same for every single power base Cairnwood has dug for itself across all territories. But it's the same as with your dead birds. All you do is collect these amazing items, hoarding them for some rainy day without ever realizing that we can never leave the house without an umbrella.'

Gabriel's voice dropped to a quiet tone that demanded attention. 'I'm the curator, and whilst not the only one in Cairnwood, I pride myself on being the best. Now you listen, you insolent little shit, we gather such items—'

'Blah-blah-blah.' Talbot scowled, his patience burned out. 'For profit. For security. For some war the circle thinks is coming tomorrow or ten years or a millennia from now. Whenever they pull out their big scheme—which, for the record, is as fucking preposterous as it is insane—I, for one, will be drinking to their eventual failure.' Which he did, with a deep swallow. 'I enjoy a good Faustian bargain as much as the next man, but not that. I think Sarkozy and all the rest of the upper management are in need of a good culling, because it seems as though you're all steering this ship towards the rocks.'

'You're a dead man for even thinking that.' For Gabriel, the presence of the waiting bar host must have been akin to a fly in his ointment. 'What are you standing there for? Go fetch somebody a drink!'

'He's here for this.' Talbot activated the tiny pin switch on Leberecht's Maquette and tipped the ring's dull stone towards Gabriel.

The ring was a playful piece from ancient Europe, once belonging to the eponymous Leberecht, a renowned black-magic strategist who viewed genocide as nothing more than the removal of a lot of stratagem pieces from a tactical map.

The stone became a concentrated typhoon of liquid clay. Gabriel's mouth unhinged in shock, as though trying to catch a breath. He tried to move, but the most he could manage was some strained twitching of his smaller joints and muscles while his body started to seize up in its sitting position. Talbot almost forgot and lurched from his seat to wrench Gabriel's club ring from his finger, and not a moment too soon, as Gabriel's body started to shrink down smaller and smaller, his flesh and clothing lightening to a pigment not unlike setting clay, and when the process had finished, Gabriel was nothing more than a small, thumb-sized figurine.

'I thought you might have appreciated this,' Talbot told the lifeless figure, reaching over to pinch him up from the now huge amphitheater of the armchair. 'The irony of it. Though it's a shame I didn't get you in a more dramatic pose.' He placed miniature Gabriel precariously on the rim of the bar manager's tray, then removed a few choice volumes from the void of his luggage.

'As agreed, this is our little secret.'

The barman braced the grimoires under one arm, his eyes fluttering furtively to the fair number of witnesses in the lounge: witnesses of all forms and caste.

'Don't mind any of them. It's only business.' Talbot finished his gin and settled the glass next to Gabriel. 'Find a nice little spot behind the bar for him. He might make a nice conversation piece. And so...' He bent down to haul up the bag, thinking about whether or not David Bentley would be predictable in his wrath's journey, but more curiously, he found himself thinking about why he cared about the loose cannon at all. 'I best get going. I'm a busy man. You have a pleasant night and enjoy those books. Some first editions in there, very valuable.'

THE BRICK HOUSE ON SHEPHERD Avenue was tastefully dressed for Christmas: warm and inviting with white and blue lights trailing the window frames and front door, more coiling around the small, potted cypress trees on the porch. Kev was hunkered down on the snowy roof of the house opposite, hidden behind a large, ostentatious display of Santa and his reindeer.

He was thinking about what it was like inside the house: his mum Sandy's typically infectious seasonal glee as she went overboard with the cooking, elated to be putting all her focus on something other than grading high school IT assignments; his sister, Rhianne, was probably still watching one of the traditional Christmas movies they used to enjoy—or perhaps she was with that new boyfriend; and his dad, Aaron, would be smiling and humoring Sandy while pretending to enjoy the holiday as much as she did. Kev and his dad used to tease her as they sipped beer and watched crap on the TV before being guilt-tripped into helping her with the decorating or extra shopping or signing endless greetings cards for neighbors, friends, and family, but never the cooking! Both Kev and his dad maxed-out their culinary skills when pouring milk on their cereal. It all seemed so typical. It was like he hadn't been shot dead. It was dumb, and he hated thinking it because it was so pitiful, but he couldn't help thinking about how easy or difficult it might have been for his family to move on. It was a morose topic to brood on, and after a few minutes—or maybe thirty—he reasoned that it was the human condition to push forward. It was survival, for the soul if not the body. He felt no sense of betrayal on their part. This was him digging into the wound—literally, his fingertip circled his bullet hole—and he hoped they were putting things back together and moving on with their lives. It had certainly looked that way at the ice rink the other day.

A tired, wistful smile gave a spirited effort to shape his mouth, but failed.

Kev couldn't do it. He couldn't see them tomorrow, or any other day. It wouldn't be fair. Life goes on, and they were forging forth with theirs. He didn't want to open up their wounds again, or field questions to which he could only offer lies or depressing truths.

He glanced down the frozen street, warm lights in all the neighbors' windows, knowing where to look, spotting the agents parked-up and keeping vigil on his family.

Hourglass insulated an agent's relatives and loved ones from their dangerous work and even had other agents shadow them during heightened circumstances, just in case. But right now, Kev assumed the watching agents were really only keeping an eye out for him. Maybe he hadn't been careful enough in buying the burner phone from the corner store, an act that would inevitably look suspicious. Did Meadows now suspect something?

Kev set up the burner and texted Spector. Giving his familial home one final look, he slipped the phone into his pocket and quietly dropped off the roof into the neighbor's backyard. He didn't want to go back to his apartment right now, knowing that Clyde and Nat were probably banging each other's brains out in the apartment opposite while he sat in a dark room, being observed by more agents across the street. Without knowing what else to do for the rest of the night, he headed back to the subway, deciding that riding the A train for an hour or two wasn't the worst idea in the world. But halfway there he changed his mind.

. . .

HE DIDN'T KNOW why he decided to take several trains and a very long, brooding walk to the Madhouse, but it was an urge he was compelled to follow. And with nothing else to do besides sleep, it felt like the better of the two options.

Halfway through the spacious lobby—quiet at this hour—the air began to lightly crackle and charge for several seconds, and when the popping subsided, Schulz was standing there.

'Hey, Doc,' Kev greeted, his hands in his pockets.

'Good morning, Kevin. Have you come to check on Ace?'

Kev glanced about the lobby as if searching for his answer. 'No. But are there any updates?'

'He remains stable.' Schulz watched Kev like he was a burglar snooping about his house. 'You looking to do some research? Training, perhaps?'

'Actually, I think it just dawned on me why I came here.'

'Oh?'

'Can I just talk to you? Like a patient?'

Schulz tilted his head back a few degrees, his eyes narrowing. 'You're afraid.'

'What?'

'Of course you can talk to me. But I already know why you're wandering around here at this inhospitable hour. It's the same reason many people go on such aimless rambles, the quick and the not-so-dead. It's because you're afraid of the things knocking about your head.'

Kev didn't repudiate the rash analysis because, to his surprise, he felt its accuracy penetrate straight through to the heart of the matter. But he wasn't going to make it that easy for Schulz. 'What makes you think I'm afraid? Maybe I just think sleep is wasted on the dead.'

'Maybe you do. But you came here to talk patient to doctor. In my … *unorthodox* career,' Schulz made a passing glance at his electrical hand, gently making a fist, 'one thing I quickly learned was that people don't decide to talk to psychiatrists because their lives are going so well. Even if it's only something minor—mild concern, a niggling worry—all of them always come down to fear. It's the greatest motivator. Am I strong enough? Am I smart enough? Attractive, secure, healthy, rich. If you will excuse my vulgar language, life is fucking exhausting.'

Kev rolled his eyes in agreement. 'And then there's people like us. So tell me, since I'm not alive, what makes you think I'm afraid?'

'Security, or lack of,' Schulz answered.

'Go on.'

'It might seem on the contrary, with your steadfast determination to risk everything by entering Erebus to shake every haystack until you find the Firmament Needle, but it's this very pursuit that underlies your fear. You are so desperate to find your own sense of peace that you will rush headlong into disaster, feckless of the larger consequences.'

Kev thought on that for a moment. 'Maybe it is out of fear, but that doesn't necessarily mean it's a selfish act. Not when I still firmly believe it would be for the greater good.'

Schulz sighed lightly, something that sounded almost like electronic whirring. 'Is there anything else you would like to get off of your chest? Because technically I'm no longer a licensed psychiatrist, and I don't want to beat my head against the wall by rehashing this debate.'

'No, you're right. And I'm not here to try and argue my case about it. But I will say I'm sorry for snooping about the files. I didn't mean to get you in any hot water with Meadows.'

Schulz waved it off. 'Bygones.'

'Okay, cool.' Kev's eyes wandered a little aimlessly, driven by vague thoughts. 'Probably a long shot, but is Meadows still here?'

Kev fell under Schulz's scrutiny and wondered what sorts of PLE security measures the shrink/defense system was mulling over.

'Might I ask why?'

Kev didn't like the look he was getting. 'I thought I was off the naughty list.'

'Officially, yes. But I still sense a significant dislocation about your person. And I'm privy to the reports of Agent Del Hargreaves and his team; you have been enjoying playing games with them, running them in circles.'

'I think the fact that I'm still being observed by them is evidence I'm still untrusted.'

'As I said, your attitude towards the agency remains derisive, or worse, indifferent. You can't blame me for being curious about your interest in seeing Deputy Director Meadows at one-thirty in the morning.'

Kev thought about mentioning Nat's confession. The double standards of their trust. 'I'm not going to hurt the guy.'

'I'm fully aware of that,' Schulz said, puffing his chest out a little.

'I thought I'd try and see how he's doing.'

'It's okay, Doctor.' The third voice flowed smoothly through the lobby with gravitas and authority. Meadows stood at the T of a corridor, tie loose, shirt sleeves rolled to the elbow, and looking very tired and yet too keyed-up to sleep. 'I could do with the company.'

Schulz obliged, but before crackling into the ether, he bid Kev a good night and good morning.

. . .

KEV HADN'T BEEN in Meadows' office before. It felt overwhelmingly ominous that he, of all the new team, was the one witnessing the inner sanctum. It was also overwhelmingly sterile, to the point of resembling Kev's utilitarian apartment: a sleek black-glass desk with ergonomic chair, laptop, a phone, and a few filing cabinets. A flat screen for conference calls took up most of one wall. Right now it was showing a soothing video loop of a serene island sunset; from what could be seen of the island, it was wild and beautiful, the steady liquid-gold surf almost stroking the beach into a gentle slumber.

The sparse furnishings only made it easier for Kev to notice the Syrup Farm report lying neatly open on the desk.

Meadows reclaimed his chair, leaning back in it and exhaling softly. But the repose was cut short, with Meadows bringing himself to lean over his desk, one hand lightly brushing the report aside.

Kev noticed there was a guest chair against the wall, but he decided to simply float cross-legged in the air.

For an anxious few seconds Kev thought they would both just sit there in tense silence, both regretting how they each got here.

'You want me to pull Hargreaves and his team from observing you? That why you're here?'

Again Kev found himself thinking about disclosing Nat's admission of keeping tabs on him and Clyde but decided to see where this went first.

'I don't know why I'm here, if I'm honest. But sure, give them something that isn't a complete waste of time and resources.' Kev gazed at the exotic paradise filling the wall, feeling very much a strong kinship with its secluded nature and isolation. 'Nice view.'

'Borneo. I haven't been there in a while. I keep telling myself I'll make time to visit it again but ... work. Life. *Death*. Something always gets in the way.'

'Looks nice from here.'

'I got around a lot of Asia back then. Those archipelagos are like a whole new world.'

'Was this back when you were doing ops there?' Kev anticipated a muted response, maybe a change of topic from Meadows. He was surprised.

'That's right. It wasn't always work. I got downtime too. The deep-sea fishing is great.'

'I'm betting Nat was the catch of the day, though, huh?' Kev was stalling, circling the real reason he came here, and he suspected Meadows knew it too.

'She was nothing but a twinkle in her father's eye back then. But I'm happy I was able to help her father escape his troubles there.' Meadows allowed himself a few more contented seconds to watch the South China Sea before turning his attention to Kev.

Kev decided to get it over with. 'I think I'm tired of being apathetic. We don't know each other too well—how could we in such a short span of time? But for a short while there, this job meant everything to me. It was a place I could belong. And I believed I could do some good. And then all that shit happened with the secrets and the omissions.' He saw Meadows' eyes beginning to verge into hostile territory and quickly shifted the subject. 'But I'm not here for that. I don't care anymore. And I think that's what bothers me most. At least when I was angry at the agency, it gave me some fire to feel alive. But I've lost that sense of purpose again. I feel like I'm back to how I was before Rose knocked on the door. Truly dead. I thought coming back after my suspension might give me some peace, even if it was only a false sense of it. But even a problem like Bentley can't help but feel trivial. And Ace is in bad shape. I want him to pull through, but all I can think is, what does it really matter?'

Meadows watched him, listening, an unreadable glint in his eye. Kev thought he might have slipped up in mentioning Ace and expected Meadows to circle back to Clyde's earlier idea to undermine the Median's laws. He also wondered if Nat was truly trustworthy, and whether Spector's agreement-via-text might have been a lie. A trap. What if Spector really thought Clyde's idea was as naive and reckless as Meadows did?

'Not every agent takes to this line of work,' Meadows said just before the silence became unbearable. 'I've seen plenty come and go, from all backgrounds, with many skill sets. It's never the risk that breaks them. Some just lose their belief in what they're doing. The Null is a storm cloud that never passes.'

'But we both know we can change that weather.'

'Perhaps. And I thought that would be a balm for this itch of yours.' Meadows shifted in his seat. 'Clyde's only human. Once he crosses over, he'll take you back with him, and neither I nor Trujillo can police your activities. We could try to hunt you down, but at what price? The odds would already be stacked against you. Assuming either of you are lucky enough to leak out from Charon's Nexus pipeline, you're behind enemy lines in a realm filled with endless shit just waiting to swallow you whole. Should you still choose to search for the Firmament Needle, you're only setting yourself up for disappointment. An incalculable number of souls have already met true death, destroyed completely, and that can't be undone. We can't save everyone. That's the cold reality we have to accept. So this urgency you feel to try and play the benevolent god, it will only end in disappointment.' Meadows lightly rapped his knuckles on the smoked-glass desktop with a look of grim resignation. 'This world—*all* worlds, they're on palliative care. So you can either choose to play the caring nurse and administer pain relief and fluff the pillows for the living while you can, or you can waste both your talent and my time by sulking over things you can't change. What's it to be, Agent Carpenter?'

Kev took a deep lungful of nothing. He held Meadows' tired, bloodshot eyes, then made a small gesture to the report on the table, a large visible portion of which was an agency profile photo of Estelle Page and what Kev assumed to be images of the damage report.

'Were you in the middle of torturing yourself?'

Meadows sighed deeply, acknowledging the ghostly presence of Estelle looking up at him. He fully unknotted his tie.

'Just how close were you two?' Kev asked.

'It was nothing romantic, if that's what you're driving at. But I suppose I miss her the way a house misses a load-bearing wall. People called her the Astronomer because she could light up the sky with new constellations, each star a newly activated Spark. Without her, that sky just got a whole lot darker. Losing her is the biggest hit we've ever taken from Cairnwood. The number of viable assets we have now lost is devastating. We're down to blindly stumbling around, locating new Sparks with old-fashioned intelligence-gathering, which is long and laborious.'

'But it's doable,' Kev offered. 'This *is* an intelligence agency.'

'It's doable,' Meadows conceded. 'Anything's doable in this field. For as long as there have been people, there have been curious minds and those willing to sell what they know.'

Kev felt the atmosphere begin to slacken in the office, a mild ease settling between them. 'How did she get involved with Hourglass?'

'Her medical file slid across the right desk. She was a switchboard operator for Bell Canada when her power manifested; she was twenty-one, a little outside of the average age. I still remember her telling me about the night of her first occurrence. She was reading a book in the comfort of her own bed, when—' his palm lightly slapped the glass, '— she was hit with a sudden splitting headache. Before it went away, it became a spotty vision. The spots became sun-dogs, the sun-dogs became crackling pinheads of electricity, then her gaze shone upon her bedroom wall like—and I remember exactly how she said it—"like Rand McNally painted a map out of the stars."' Meadows paused for a thought or two. 'She was no spring chicken—her death was coming sooner than later—but it doesn't make her loss any easier to accept. And sadly, Rand McNally can't help us in her absence.'

'It seems like Ace was close to her,' Kev said, only now realizing how unprecedented this whole conversation was between the two of them. It was settling into borderline amicability, something he never expected to share with Meadows at the best of times.

'She helped him in his early days at Igloo, eased his transition from aspiring hockey superstar to a life in the shadows. She always had a knack for knowing what to say, but what's more was that she always listened. In case you hadn't noticed, Ace isn't the chattiest of personalities, so if you can imagine him as an angry young man not yet out of his teens, I'm sure you have an idea how his adjustment went. It's a good job he was able to bleed out some of that anger through his work.'

Meadows' fingertip slowly tapped against the sheaf of papers.

'Estelle knew how difficult it was for new Sparks. It's a scary, often emotional period in their lives. Most of these individuals see themselves as cursed more than blessed. Some might have experienced a devastating episode that left their family or professional life shattered. Some might have accidentally killed somebody.'

Kev thought about Nat becoming the literal death of the party and knew from the deputy director's faraway gaze that he was thinking of her too.

'Estelle was lucky enough that her blessing was a means of locating others like her, rather than a weapon.'

'Was this the first time anybody made an attempt to kill her?'

'No, there was a previous one, years ago. But it wasn't Cairnwood. It was a fringe group of sorcerers, and it's because of what we did to them that reinforced the point to our enemies of why they shouldn't cross certain lines. We moved her to the Syrup Farm after that.'

'Does that mean it's now guns blazing on all things Cairnwood?'

Meadows tilted back in his chair, hands crossed over his stomach, tired eyes drifting to the tranquility of the beach on the wall. 'It will be, but it's still a slow process. They're so well insulated, well connected, able to hide in plain sight. But from this moment on, any confirmation we receive of a Cairnwood holding or member, we'll wipe them off the map; let the quiet people who run the country deal with the legal and political ramifications.'

Meadows made a beleaguered grumble, and Kev was almost certain he was going to do something as human and vulnerable as yawn. Instead he said, 'This is a frustrating job sometimes. Patience is key.'

Silence softly settled over the room like a blanket over a sleeping man. Kev unfolded his legs and allowed his soles to touch ground. He thought it best to let Meadows get some rest. 'When's the funeral?' he asked, a parting question.

Meadows rolled his head across the headrest, his half-lidded eyes moving from the island to the ghost. 'A few days from now. She didn't have any family outside of the agency, never settled down or had kids. It'll be a small and private affair.'

Kev nodded and was about to quietly see himself out before pulling a TV detective routine, turning back with one final question. 'Do the souls of Sparks carry their power over into the Null?'

Meadows was so immobile and quiet that Kev thought he had fallen asleep with his eyes half open. But then, 'Their souls still hold the Luminary energy, but they can't harness it without their physical bodies.'

Kev felt a vague sense of threat emanating from Meadows—nothing explicit, more like a dozing lion—and he imagined Meadows as a young soldier lying in wait to ambush an enemy in the jungle.

'Good night.' Kev anticipated some sort of censorious remark to spoil an otherwise civil conversation between two opposing schools of thought, anything to remind him that despite his official reinstatement, he carried a black mark on his record.

But instead, all he got was a simple, 'Good night, Agent.'

32

W HEN DAVE CAME TO, HE found gray morning light filtering through the wooded gloom. He was lying shivering in a deep pile of snow, his waking reality a sudden horror that eclipsed the disturbing dream he had escaped. It all came speeding back to him: waking from death, the fight with the big Spark yeti, and then, feeling a big cavernous hole opening up in his stomach, he remembered all of the people he murdered in his high-speed carnage before flipping the truck on a patch of black ice. And much like a bad hangover, the last memories proved the most elusive. How did he get here? Had he stumbled over the guardrail, giddy on death, walking for miles across harsh country? Why hadn't he stolen another car and continued on his journey? He didn't like how that briefly seemed like a good idea. Of course it wasn't. Steal another car to murder more people with! He felt like going to sleep and never waking up. If he had a gun, he'd stick it in his mouth and erase the memories clogging up the inside of his skull like so much ruptured intestines and tire-tread-marked mush. He punched himself in the face over and over, trying to instigate one of those mini red twisters into popping his head like a grape. He had limited success, the blows he landed healing with depressing swiftness. Even the clean, bitter cold air couldn't hide the smoky scent of his singed and frayed coat. It smelled like some hellish brimstone pit, which is surely where he must have escaped from. Ripping his beanie hat from his head, he squeezed it with both hands and screamed into it until he was out of breath, tears stinging his eyes. He had to find Talbot. Better yet, find more of Hourglass. It didn't matter that they were oppressive monsters; if they could kill him, it would spare him the knowledge that he'd just murdered a shitload of innocent people.

Something in his noisy mind turned over, softening the rush of emotions and memory, and he found himself grappling with his identity again. The quiet man inside Dave, the one who had forced him to flee the interstate, drunk on power and wrath, the one who had been the bulwark against the rage sloshing through his head all these years, was losing his grip.

Dave felt a sense of vertigo drop him back down to his knees, chilled and soaking wet in the snow.

His conscience was tuning itself to a psychic transmission from a terrifying broadcast. The Imp King had literally stolen his attention. Dave was psychically back inside the imp's chamber, immobilized, staring at Kerzix's masochistically-hooked smile poised above him, a wall of big, wet teeth cupping the imp's leathery coned head and manic, elongated eyes.

'David, David, David, you're a terrible driver.' A cackle, more like the whimper from a torture victim, ripped from the imp. 'But an entertaining one.'

Dave found his eyes drawn over the shoulder of his new master towards that giant mouth, stretching with silent laughter like a cartoon on mute.

Kerzix seized Dave's chin, long fingers pinching, forcing eye contact. 'Yes, you have brought joy to my heart. You can tell from my smile, see? But your tax collection is still a little light.' He pointed at the large snow-static lips behind him, and the rich, steady flow of soul energy passing through them from clusters of micro-tubes.

Dave wondered if the souls of the innocents he'd murdered had already made the journey here to the big grinning mouth or if they were still in transit.

'I expect some more pratfalls and decapitations before you exit Earth's stage. I will be hosting another of my celebrations of voyeuristic carnage for my loyalists. You could think of it as a prerecorded screening of your tribute to me, straight from your eyes to the big screen. It's customary, an event all my Marotte Marauders perform. And a great honor for them. Unfortunately, at this time, you are my only Marauder active on a living world, so your slaughter will be the big premier.'

Dave tried to force out the awful graphic events his memory was determined to show him over and over. Death without ceremony of so many drivers and passengers. If they were the stars of their own movies, he thought, they died like extras with very little in the way of dramatic importance or dignity, merely alive one minute, dead the next.

'Exactly!' the imp exclaimed as though Dave had just posited a valuable point, but Dave hadn't said a word. But he had thought a few things. Of course, Kerzix was in his mind.

'Your kind like stories. Everybody, *everything*, on every conscious world, enjoys stories. Including this little paradise. They are the cornerstone of civilization. They educate, they *excite*, they make your dumb, inconsequential lives feel something for a short span. And just like the cinematic movies on your idiotic plane, your executions are my entertainment.' The imp paused, reviled at what might be a bad taste in his mouth. 'That whiny part of you, still hoping that you imagined all of those red stains you left along the road? It will learn to accept its place in this new world. Life is nothing but a cruel trick, dressed up in meaning and self-importance. But it always ends the same way: the living belong to us. No heroes. No villains. No melodramatics. Nothing matters. Only the chaos of life and the inevitability of death.'

Dave couldn't bear the thought of hurting another person. This anger … it wasn't what he had wanted. He thought it might be empowering. He was wrong. He'd sooner turn it inwards and allow himself to implode rather than hurt another innocent.

Somehow, Dave found his voice. 'Your chaos … it seems a little organized from what I can see.'

The imp released a cat's hairball hack of amusement and raised one gloved hand, enlarged and alabaster white, holding its index finger and thumb an inch apart. 'Only enough to keep me and my audience happy.' Those hideously bulging eyes quivered with intensity. 'If there's one thing that the living share with me and my subjects, it's the need for a good laugh. And we all find your false idols and desperate prayers amusing.' His hand swiped out, panther quick, seizing Dave's chin again, holding his attention, face-to-face. 'You do have something about you, though. A tenacious spirit. It makes sense, your piddling blood being what it is. But even Luminaries could only hold off the darkness for so long, and you're no Luminary. You're a pale imitation. So stop wasting your energy in trying to fight me, because all you are is another act in my circus. Leave your pitiful defiance at the gate, and go play.'

Dave's vision blurred and stretched into a near-psychedelic tunnel of color and light. It felt like he was being jettisoned from an airlock, back into a body that was his from birth but now a loan from resurrection.

Silly things like morality and guilt quickly melted away like snowflakes, and a chuckle escaped him as he flashed back on some of the shocked faces he'd glimpsed seconds before crushing them under his wheels or smashing them into other toy cars. He pushed through knee-deep snowdrifts, thinking about the fun to be had when he got back to his hometown.

The Marotte Marauder was going to Buffalo to write and direct a blockbuster.

33

T HE CHARACTERS IN THE STAINED glass were not two-dimensional religious icons. Kozlov noticed that the hard way, getting just close enough to see the ugly truth behind the colorful panes. They were long-anguishing victims, all holy men and women of every religion and culture across the cosmos, each one a death in black comedy. Prized deaths, according to Calkarion, those whose demises could only point to the proof that their so-called deities did not exist. Accidents and mishaps ending in broken skulls, choking, punctured hearts, immolation and exsanguination and asphyxiation. These dead hordes pawed at their stained-glass prisons like mimes, watching as Kozlov's caravan thundered through the confusing mirrored avenues. To Kozlov, the place was as vulgar and unnecessary as a golden toilet.

At last, Calkarion decided they should settle down for a rest. It didn't seem like a good spot to Kozlov, but Calkarion wanted to make a few repairs to the carriage, and for the first time, Kozlov saw Calkarion unharness and unwire himself from his spider and clamshell, walking about on his own two legs as he set to inspecting the shell's axles. Kozlov was still wary of bivouacking in this place, but Calkarion had explained that even the craziest of this land's denizens didn't venture into the Alley of Doomed Prophets; with nothing to eat—besides them, of course—predators didn't bother with the place unless they accidentally wandered in and got lost.

And so they rested, taking turns to grab an hour or two of sleep, with the Arkhitektor standing additional watch for each of the sleepers. Kozlov stirred from another spoiled rest to find his friend kneeling outside Calkarion's armored carriage and staring at one of the walls of haunted stained glass.

His old mentor was quietly weeping, muttering prayers to the trapped victims, tears racing down to become lost in his beard. Not wanting to disturb him, Kozlov allowed his friend to commiserate for these suffering souls in peace and tried to fall back asleep, staring directly at the sky above instead of the surrounding glass walls. But seeing his friend so quietly troubled chased away any chance of slumber, and then, hearing the soft trumpeting buzz of Calkarion's snores, he knew he had no chance. He got up and sat next to the Arkhitektor.

'How long do you suppose these poor souls have been trapped like this?' the Arkhitektor asked.

Kozlov stared at one of the prisoners in question, a human male, fort-yish perhaps, with a chronic case of broken neck, vertebrae poking out over his priest collar like tremendous, ossified tumors, and shrugged in-effectually. Not for the first time, he wished the Arkhitektor had not dis-pensed with his given family name, as per ceremonial tradition. It could only be a small token, but by simply being able to talk to him as the man he used to be, rather than the leader saddled with so much pent-up pain and strife, might help instill some small comfort.

'I used to be better at holding on to my pain,' the Arkhitektor con-tinued. 'All those years, and all those excursions I led our sect on through these awful lands, I was able to seal off my emotions. It was like I was dead inside. But now that I'm actually dead, my purpose gone, all I can do is stare at every victim we see in these kingdoms and think of the in-justice.'

'You never lost your purpose,' Kozlov said. 'I wouldn't have made it half as far without you at my side. You have capabilities beyond me, and I can't do this without you.'

He couldn't help but glance at the figures mutely beating and moving within the Gothic church panes: most of them were species of creature so unusual or unknown to his ken that their fatal wounds evaded his un-derstanding. Though there were several humans dotted about, one being a female swami monk of indeterminate age who had suffered appalling head trauma.

'It's getting harder, isn't it?' the Arkhitektor asked. 'I still remember the pains of aging.'

Kozlov didn't dare mention how tired he was feeling, not just physically but spiritually. All this time spent traversing these wilds of hell was sapping his will to the point where he spent most every waking minute locked in a mantra, convincing himself that they'd find their salvation: *soon … soon … soon.*

'My flesh was always weaker than my soul. Same as yours,' Kozlov said. 'That won't stop us.' He still believed these words, even if his old body garnered nothing from such optimism. However, his mentor's increasing melancholia was beginning to weigh on his mind.

The Arkhitektor squinted up to the sky, unable to look at the forsaken priests and prophets any longer. 'Never in the history of our sect has an Arkhitektor made it so far. Every monk takes their oaths and enters, knowing the scale of the challenge facing them. And not since the first Arkhitektor has a member of the sect successfully made it so deep into this dead wilderness, but …' He lowered his gaze to the dusty, glass-jeweled earth. 'Is this success? We still have no idea how near or far the Needle is. The farther we travel, the more I wonder something terrible: What if the monarchs found a way to destroy it?'

Kozlov had done all he could to avoid thinking of such catastrophic outcomes, but that didn't mean they didn't occupy a small region in the back of his mind, and being confronted by his tutor's anguish made it impossible not to imagine the worst. He thought about the wounded and exhausted Luminary soldier who, along with the Firmament Needle, had been carried from the waters by his old nemesis Vor Dushi, Charon's chief minion, to be delivered to the highest seats of the Order of Terminus. If there was a way to destroy the Needle, they would have tortured it out of their captive long ago.

Thinking such useless things brought nothing of value, and it shamed Kozlov a little to see what could only be construed as a hint of weakness showing in the Arkhitektor's otherwise stoic façade. If even he could succumb to doubt in this place, Kozlov knew he wouldn't be impervious either. Not forever.

'I refuse to believe that. To do so means we might as well just give up and die right here, right now.' Kozlov glanced, almost demurely, at a hundred different sufferings trapped behind glass. 'You've seen too much horror. I have too, but I won't let you fall behind now. And I know that you will do the same for me.'

Kozlov cocked his head to their new tribe: Calkarion, slumbering in the shadow of his coach; Quarmalls, sleeping on the wagon's clamshell roof; and Trillik, quietly sitting guard several yards away, the barrier of orange light scanning along its iron tank body as it checked the battery of its psychic dampener.

He returned his focus to the Arkhitektor. 'I have to believe that with the help of these fellow unfortunates, we'll get a lead on where we're going. Trillik will get us inside the stored memories of the Rictus, and we'll find something useful. We just have to stay strong in the face of all of this.'

'That sounds a lot like faith,' the Arkhitektor said with a tired smile. 'This place feeds on that, so don't go offering it a free meal.'

'I like to call it reasoning. I was a rational military man at one time, remember.' He smiled back, still feeling terribly old and fragile in his necronaut armor.

Distant organ music drifted on the air, as quiet and sinister as a child-snatcher's whisper in a dark wood. Kozlov saw Trillik react to the Big Top's music with a few quiet chirps and a few revolutions of its brain wheel. Kozlov glanced up at the stars fixed in the poisonous sky, tilting his head this way and that to try and locate the source of the horrendous music. 'It's impossible to tell which direction it's coming from.'

'We're safe in here,' the Arkhitektor said. 'If the shortcut to Kerzix's stronghold is as close as Calkarion says, we might be able to avoid that thing altogether. As long as we don't advertise our whereabouts.'

Kozlov gave a tired nod.

'Fortune must favor us every once in a while,' the elder monk said. 'You should try and get a little more rest.'

Seeing how his mentor gently repaired the cracks in his conviction, Kozlov agreed and settled down to sleep, but as the organ music continued its haunted lullaby across the landscape beyond these glass alleys of misery, the only thing Kozlov found was a restless anticipation.

34

'**I** WAS STARTING TO THINK you weren't going to show,' Clyde said, his concern blurring into relief at the sight of Ramaliak.

He had fallen asleep in his apartment, fingers slowly, anxiously fretting his blue twine into knots, his body entangled with Nat, then woken in the Median. Time was a hazy concept in this realm, but Clyde felt as though an eternity had passed while he'd waited for his mentor to appear.

'So am I crazy like a fox, or just plain crazy?' he demanded.

Ramaliak didn't answer immediately, taking his time walking through the luminous groves of polyp trees, each and every one a complex weave of shimmering soul threads.

'I wasn't expecting Kev to contact me, especially about what you're proposing,' he said. 'He's quite persuasive when he wants to be.'

'He does love an argument. I think he should have been an attorney in a different life.' Clyde had his back to one of the large polyp-shaped growths, his fingers absently tweezing his own soul thread jutting from his forehead, banding it around his finger like it was a wet noodle. He had chosen this meeting place for its privacy, far from the metropolis and the gazes of Dremel and his coterie.

'I wouldn't say that,' Ramaliak said. 'Despite all the nonsense that's gone on between him and the agency, I believe he has too strong a moral core.' He sat down opposite Clyde, leaning his back against one of the strange trees, hoof hands dangling limply over his knees. He glanced around. 'I see you remembered how to find this place.'

This wasn't just any patch of land, but the resting place of the soul of Clyde's older brother, Stephen. His dad's soul was a short distance away. Both entwined in different polyp trees.

'Seemed prudent. It's a nice place to rest, all things considered.' If Clyde had been awake, he might have felt the hairs on the back of his neck rising up; as it was, he felt a mild uneasiness, knowing the sentinels were watching him from behind cover, barely glimpsed but, according to Ramaliak, very dangerous, vital custodians of the entire realm.

'I figured you would be sick of so many lights by now. Christmas in New York,' Ramaliak said, softly pawing at some of the tightly woven threads, redolent of so many festive LEDs.

'Christmas can be a little tacky. This is, I don't know … *pure.*'

Ramaliak went quiet, and Clyde had an unwelcome suspicion that the coming news wouldn't be good.

'The suspense is killing me, man. You could have blown me off by proxy, but you came here to talk to me. So spit it out. Is my idea doable or terrible?'

The ram head sighed, and one dexterous hoof gently corrected Spector's glasses on his long face. He glanced over his shoulder, through a clearing in the acreage, at the shining stronghold of the Glowing Reel, standing proud and dreamlike along the horizon as though it might hear him.

'I should probably tell you why Dremel and the other council members aren't my biggest fans. They used to be, one time, but …' Ramaliak paused, then seemed to come to a snap decision, deciding to just blurt it out. 'I used to be the monarch.'

Clyde was surprised, but not as much as he would have expected. In all honesty, it made a sort of sense. 'That's a hell of a secret to be carrying around.'

Ramaliak was a study in Spector's human traits: a small human gesture here, a cryptic pose there. 'It's not much of a secret. Those who need to know, know.'

'So how did you end up becoming the king?'

'Ex-king. The same way I became Ramaliak.'

Clyde knew Spector had been a former professional thief before Hourglass took him in, a decision based on an exploit of his at the British Museum: the acquisition of the Sleeping Shepherd. But instead of earning him a black-market fortune, the device had made him a dreamwalker extraordinaire.

'Seems like a low-bar crime to claim the throne.'

Ramaliak smiled, showing a straight bridge of pearly white nubs. 'Yes, achieving noble status normally requires a few good old-fashioned slaughters and back-stabbings to go along with all the thievery, but I happened to turn up at a particularly tumultuous time in their regime. The Reel's former king had been recently killed by a very dangerous entity.'

'And so they just entrust the crown to the first unknown human criminal who comes their way?' Clyde asked incredulously.

'If things were not so disorderly, it would have been a different outcome. But I ousted the demon, which bought me some temporary good will.'

'How did you do that?' Clyde had almost forgotten the reason for their rendezvous entirely, but all this talk of expelling dream demons made the area between his shoulder blades itch.

'I did what all master thieves do: I stole something of value from it.'

'Okay. What?'

'Get ready to laugh. Her heart!'

Clyde made a derisive noise but wasn't sure what to make of Ramaliak's comment. 'You cut it out?'

'Metaphorically. This demon in question was a succubus. Bad luck for the former king, but I've never been easily led around by the dick, so I wasn't so easy to enthrall. I played along, gained her confidence a little more each night, until I found a weakness. And more befitting to my expertise, her weakness was a jewel. Playing the lovesick whelp, who would ever suspect I'd turn the tables and tear her heart out—again, metaphorically. The jewel was surprisingly easy to snatch. Succubi place so much value on wrapping the lustful and loveless around their fingers that their own physical prowess leaves a lot to be desired. So I took revenge on behalf of the Reel's fallen ruler, shook Dremel and the others out of their whimsical stupor, and they deemed me emotionally incorruptible. Saw it as a sign of strength and strong character. And there's a high premium for such qualities in a ruler.'

'They didn't deem you crafty and untrustworthy, being the guy who stole Ramaliak's idol?'

'Between you and me, many of the former monarch's advisors had some emotional and moral shortcomings. I never considered myself more than what I am at heart: a basic man with quick hands and a soft spot for shortcuts. But in fairness, I'm one of the few honorable thieves you're ever likely to meet. And that being said, I did a pretty admirable job in restoring peace amongst the House.'

'Until you took a misstep?'

Ramaliak nodded. 'All that goodwill was achieved in here,' he held a hoof out to either side, encompassing the Median, 'while I slept. But it wasn't long before I was using my new kingly position to do some, let's say, unethical things in the waking world. I had already been scouted by Trujillo, and thanks to the House of Wise Stones, the hoodoo had given the director a pretty detailed breakdown on the scandalous current affairs of the Glowing Reel's previous monarch. Director Trujillo is a diplomat at heart—that's coming straight from the ram's mouth—but he's still an intelligence operative, and doesn't mind getting his hands dirty to neutralize earthbound threats.'

'Like tasking you with stealing the bad ideas of agency enemies.' Clyde thought about the glass vessels in Spector's office at Indigo Mesa, each one containing the pilfered dreams and schemes of a potentially problematic design.

'Correct. That's fine for our—well, *your* line of work.'

'I'm not a spy.'

'It's a fine line, Clyde: soldier, assassin, gathering enemy intel. You've ticked a number of boxes for Hourglass and you should be proud of it. My point is, the agency does what it does to save human lives. But I was fifty-percent agent, fifty-percent ruler of this realm. And even though the Glowing Reel is technically one of the nine Houses of the Order of Terminus, it is supposed to remain neutral, abstaining from the affairs between the living and the dead, including the fate of their currency: mortal souls. And yet there I was, illegally swiping the dreams from the heads of targets for Trujillo, inevitably interfering in those very workings.'

'So they forced you to abdicate the throne?'

'In a manner of speaking. The problem is,' he gestured at his appearance, the ram-headed dream avatar, 'this isn't something I can abdicate. I was in the neighborhood at the right time, laying hands on the Sleeping Shepherd right around the time the former lovesick monarch was crossing over to the Null, going to the special place where all the dead gods go.'

'Which of the Houses collects those?' Clyde asked.

Ramaliak didn't divulge. 'Until I die, this is my responsibility. But Dremel and the rest of my House's council didn't have to like it, so they voted against me. I had the choice to step down, retaining some limited privileges, or they would kill me. That was the impression, anyway.'

'So, was that a long way of saying you won't help me try to (a) wake up Ace and (b) help Bentley kick his imp habit?'

Ramaliak waited a beat. 'No. It was me saying that I'm going to do the sensible and respectful thing, and talk to the council, and then, when they deny my request—which they inevitably will—I'm going to do as you asked anyway. I'm sorry to say that there's nothing I can do to help Ace. And that goes double for you. You don't know how the Weaver's powers work, so you'll likely do more damage. We can only hope Ace is strong enough to pull through with minimal repercussions to his brain. But as for Bentley's soul, there is a way to purify it. It's a good plan, Clyde—well, *plan* is a stretch, but it's a good idea.' The black ram smiled again, an unsettling row of pearls stretching in a pink mouth. 'Good enough to bottle. There is a major caveat involved, though.' Ramaliak's expression became serious.

'Kerzix is a monarch,' Clyde said preemptively. 'Getting close to Bentley's soul means I could be exposing myself, and the Weaver, to the imp's energy.'

'You'll be putting your life at risk, which means Kev's too. If doing this wakes up the Weaver, or word of this reaches Dremel, there will be no hesitation on his part. The council will unanimously agree to cut your thread. Are you prepared to accept that risk?'

Clyde thought about Ace doing all he could to stop Bentley. He thought about Nat possibly confronting Bentley and coming up short. But then he also thought about the fact that if he died doing this, it would mean dragging Kev back to the Null with him.

'I am,' he answered.

. . .

CLYDE AWOKE TO Nat's sleepy, pleasant face hovering over him.

He smiled in relief. Praise be his comic-book gods, neither Spector/Ramaliak nor Nat had sold him out. 'I'm so happy I'm not waking up next to Meadows and a loaded gun.' He quickly glanced about the bedroom to make sure. They were alone, not a heavily armed retrieval team in sight. The twine was tangled between the fingers of his right hand. He pulled it loose and set it on his bedside unit. 'Looks like I can trust Spector—and you, of course.'

'Nice save,' Nat replied. 'You always make that funny noise when you wake up.'

Clyde rubbed his eyes and smiled. 'What kind of funny noise?'

'Like the shock of realizing you just left your phone on the bus. *Huhh!*' She offered him a wry demonstration.

Clyde smiled and pulled her down to him, planting a big kiss on her. 'Making dumb noises was the bedrock of Spector's training.'

'You did that immaterial thing again.'

'I did?'

'Only for a few seconds, but I was getting concerned you might wake up inside the mattress.'

'How long you been watching me?'

'Only a few minutes. Don't stress, you're not that interesting. Cute, though.' She poked him lightly for confirmation. 'And all solid again.'

She pursued his first kiss, throwing her leg over his hips. 'What's the deal with the immaterial thing?'

'I think it's just my body being on the fritz. A hangover from the Coma Weaver.' He didn't want to think of Babylonian night terrors right now. 'Hey, you know how I know you really like me?' he asked with a smile.

'Because I'm kissing you, even with your morning breath?'

Clyde cocked an eyebrow. 'Excuse me? You're not mouthwash-fresh yourself right now.'

'No, I'm pepperoni and green peppers fresh. I just finished the last slice of pizza.'

'Better than Listerine.' He looked askance at the empty pizza box on the corner of the bed. 'But it was cold of you to not leave me any.'

'I think I was kind of generous last night, dude.' She gave him a wicked grin, curved a glossy coil of black and blue hair behind her ear, and leaned down for another kiss.

The early morning light cast the room in a weak, gauzy glow. The sounds of the city coming to life.

'I know you like me,' Clyde resumed, 'because snoring is sometimes a deal-breaker in relationships, and here I am, making weird *Huhh* noises and doing my immaterial thing. You got patience, Mondragon.' Clyde traced his fingers along the waistband of Nat's panties and palmed the warmth of her tattooed thighs. He didn't want to move. He wanted to stay here all day, with her warm body on top of him, and away from the freezing city and its many threats poised over them.

'What did he say?'

'He's in. He'll hit me up on the burner when he's good to go.' Clyde ran his finger along the taut ridge of her spine, up to the nape of her neck. 'You having any doubts about Meadows?'

She rested her palms on his chest, and Clyde was captivated, losing himself in the allure of her mysterious eyes. 'No. Why have this bitchin' dream power of yours if you don't use it for anything useful? If you can help Ace—'

Clyde cut her off with a soft head shake, like a surgeon delivering bad news to a patient's loved ones.

Nat took a composing breath. 'Fuck… Fine, just Bentley then. I still think it's a good idea. Also,' she moved her palm over his heart, a worried look nestling itself in her brow, 'I've been thinking about what you said, about his power. Putting Ace in a coma? *Ace!* And I've seen the way you give me that look, when my eyes go all special-move crackling violet.'

Clyde felt a stab of guilt, having thought he'd done a better job of concealing such concerns.

'I'm not judging, it's cool. What I mean is, I know me and Ace got a system jolt from Charon, but even with that, Bentley still took Ace apart. This guy must be crazy powerful. Fucking force of nature. And he either can't die or is super hard to kill. And now he's crazier than a bag of cats.'

'A bag of cats being ridden by imps.'

Nat took his hand. 'If you and Spector can find a way to kick the imp out of his head or, you know, his soul, then maybe he'll turn himself in.'

'That's the plan. But he won't just get a slap on the wrist. Possessed or not, it's going to be a difficult, messy situation sifting through all the damage he's done.'

'I know…' Nat clung to a few unvoiced thoughts, a serious look entering her dark eyes.

'I'll do whatever it takes to stop him. If we can bring him in, we'll deal with all that shit when it's time,' Clyde said. 'And if I can't help him, then I'll kill him from inside the Median.'

He felt her body tense a little at that, her eyes crackling once, like a solitary lightning flash along a lonely pasture.

He frowned at his own declaration. 'I…I never thought I'd say something like that so casually.'

She squeezed his hand, her smile faltering somewhere between optimism and cynicism. 'I don't think anybody in our line of work thought their lives would turn out the way they did.'

Clyde pulled her close, kissed her deeply, and forced himself not to think about the person he'd become.

35

S TEALING THE CAR HAD BEEN easy. Dave had little knowledge of hot-wiring or whatever it was that savvy car thieves did for newer models, but he did have a newfound lust for relishing his baser desires. All he had had to do was sneak up on one of the diners from the interstate cafe, kill him in the parking lot, and help himself to the van keys before anybody was any the wiser. The dark December morning had helped conceal Dave's activity, and by the time anybody found the corpse, he would be well on his way home.

Ten miles after the kill, Dave still felt the pressure cooker of hate burning him up from within, thinking about the man he'd just murdered. A roofer, to judge by the van, a man with a trade. Probably a family and a close-knit social circle too. He was a man who had some value, who probably received respect from co-workers and friends, who strutted about each day with the easy confidence of somebody who knows where they fit in. Well, fuck you, pal! Where did it all get you? Head blasted outside some shithole dime-a-dozen highway diner. Before pulling out of the parking lot, Dave had been briefly tempted to head inside to buy a coffee and kill a bunch of people, maybe burn the place down. But now that he had a clear goal in mind of how to show fealty to Kerzix, he'd decided to keep the slaughter to a minimum for now, wanting to avoid any unnecessary problems until it was time. A shrieking laugh echoed through his skull. When Dave first heard that laugh during his highway slaughter, he thought it was a real-time laugh, the mad imp excited, cavorting at his subject's growing tribute to random nihilistic death. But he knew differently now; the laughter was an endless loop, like a programmed pattern. Was it some type of incentive? An antagonistic ear-flicking from Kerzix? Who could tell? But somewhere under that cruel canned laughter, Dave felt another small crack appear in the dam of his pent-up fury, a further trickle of remorse and revulsion at what he had done. What he was doing. What he *would* do!

His hands shook on the wheel, only a soft tremor, yet the knowledge that it wasn't a manifestation of his aggression but instead of a deeper guilt was like a crack of daylight to a trapped miner.

He could fight through this. He could regain control. Stop this insanity.

The laugh track dropped a few decibels inside his head, and Dave tried not to panic, not wanting to waste this opportunity of volition. But what could he actually do with it? He thought about trying to alert the cops. Exceed the speed limit until the highway patrol pulled him over. But then what? If he snapped again, he'd kill them all.

He could pull onto the hard shoulder and run. Find a way to attract Hourglass. They'd kill him for sure. He didn't want to die, but he couldn't bear the thought of all those innocent people he'd killed, and those he still might. Maybe death was exactly what he needed—he always felt like he shouldn't have been born anyway. But how was he going to attract Hourglass' attention? Cause enough carnage until he was all over the media again?

He could speed this van straight through the rail. It probably wouldn't kill him, but he might get lucky and end up trapped inside the crumpled vehicle. But no, then he'd only tear through the wreckage and be loose again.

Shit! Shit-shit-shit!

He felt like crying in frustration. Trapped. With no solution to his problem. He swerved the wheel, aiming the nose towards the guardrail.

The laughter became a dull roar inside his head. Kerzix loomed up in his thoughts, those lunatic eyes casting doubt on such soft-hearted nonsense as empathy and grief. Nothing mattered. Life had no meaning. No benevolent god was waiting to accept your hand and deliver you to a final resting place. Life, all life was just one big waiting room outside Erebus. So take your number, grab a seat, and get over it.

Dave righted the wheel, straightening the van in its lane, smiling at the horns honking behind him. He'd lost his tenuous control. His eyes dampened with tears but burned with resentment.

36

T ALBOT NURSED HIS ESPRESSO, PACING in slow circles about his apartment. He would miss this place ... if he uprooted himself, that is. Not just this city, but this apartment. It was his, and it was his castle. A $40 million, five-bedroom Columbus Circle penthouse. He had other properties, of course, but this was his personal favorite. The first upper-echelon home he had bought since moving stateside. From up here on the 75th floor, staring out of any of the 180-degree-view floor-to-ceiling windows, he imagined his gaze could pierce space and time, staring back at his initiation in that cold, damp London bog amidst the sunken cairns of forgotten corpses. He sipped to Gabriel's health, and since it couldn't get any worse due to his immortalized clay state, he reasoned it wasn't an entirely cynical gesture.

But this apartment ... To leave or not to leave?

He glanced at the bottomless bag on his divan. It contained a respectable armory. He still had all of his bank accounts, and most importantly, his reputation within the Cairnwood Society.

The trick was in deciding which of his next moves would suit him best.

For the purposes of personal security, he wanted agents Williams, Carpenter, Hadfield, Tremblay, and Mondragon gutted and hung from the rafters. But thinking calmly and logically, they shouldn't be his primary concern right now. Thanks to Bentley, Tremblay was either dead or out of commission. He now knew he could physically overpower and kill Hadfield if the madwoman ever tried to challenge him again; she had a mouth on her, and he would make sure he dragged out every single scream hidden deep in her lungs. But not yet. Williams was tricky, but he would be easy to deal with if his partner was taken out of the picture. All he had to do was find a way to separate them: kill Carpenter, who, through some fluke, had previously survived a ghost-destroying Exorcist bullet; or go straight for Williams, in which case Carpenter would be sent back into the pit with him. But it was the new girl, Mondragon, who would be the most formidable, with her being a Spark.

He started another leisurely lap of the suite, watching the sun struggle through the snowy cloud banks like a torch beam through heavy cotton.

And of course, he hadn't forgotten about a few other recent local scores he wanted to settle. Leonard Sharp's security consultant Harlan Brink being top of that list. That son of a bitch had blown up his last Jag with Talbot still in it outside Elzinga Asylum, grievously wounding him. And Leonard Sharp, New York's foremost criminal kingpin, highly respected self-made entrepreneur and former Cairnwood lackey, had been central in this little labor uprising against Talbot. But squashing those two would also require the squashing of Hangman and Doll-Face. The irony was delectable: Brink, Hangman, and Doll-Face, a trio of serious threats whom Talbot had helped create to pit against Hourglass, and they had all ultimately ended up unionizing against him.

And now he was full circle, back on the issue of Hourglass.

If he could rely on Bentley's self-control and amenability, he would be open to a partnership and be willing to strike at the Hourglass team as soon as possible, while they were wounded. The pair of them, Talbot thought, complete with the mystical arsenal he'd plundered, filled him with confidence. But confidence had been something he had taken for granted for too many years now, and he knew it to be unwise to underestimate Hourglass again. And then there was the marotte's effect: Talbot knew nothing of Kerzix, but he had heard the stories of several other poor bastards who had fallen under the effects of those scepters. Whatever curse the marottes possessed, he doubted it would share its toys with him, so Bentley was most likely out of the equation.

Talbot was all alone here for the moment. He spent several minutes rehearsing what he could say to the inner circle if he were to contact them, how he could disclose Gabriel's fate and pass on the blame to an unexpected secondary Hourglass attack. Brazen ideas about vying to take over Gabriel's seat fluttered about his head, but deep down he knew the powers-that-be would never go for it. He was too low caste for such a responsibility. They knew where he came from. That meant he would be left alone in this big city until a new Cairnwood member was deigned worthy enough to manage their East Coast enterprises.

He weighed up Gabriel's Cairnwood ring in the palm of his hand, then slipped it back into his pocket, dismissing all notions of contacting the inner circle. Sod them.

He thought of this city as his home, but maybe it really was time to move on. New chapters. New cities. Build, build, build. He needed to embed himself in a new group, prove that he was still cream rising to the top.

It made sense; deep down, he couldn't deny it. Because he was bigger than petty vendettas, wrestling in the dirt with rambunctious Hourglass task forces. They were nothing but the red welts of insect bites. Really, it was the inner circle where he belonged. And where he was needed, even if the high seats didn't see it that way. Somebody needed to seize control from that lunatic recluse Soma Sarkozy, whose grand ambitions carried the bitter scent of apocalyptic ash; Talbot enjoyed the finer things in life too much to risk seeing them all swept away by the mad scholar's schemes. And who said he couldn't be a hero, just like those delusional hypocrites in Hourglass and Avalon and the rest? Why couldn't he be the plucky underdog savior?

He didn't realize how wide his smile had become until he caught his reflection in the glass, a giant ghost floating over the city. He strode over to the kitchen, placed his cup and saucer in the sink, swept up his bottomless bag of warfare and deception, and gave his beloved apartment one final glance. He would leave the inner circle in the dark regarding Gabriel and himself, for a short while at least. It was time to move on. Onwards and upwards.

<h1 style="text-align: center;">37</h1>

THE AIR WAS SO OMINOUS it was practically tactile. Kozlov knew foreboding well. He was a student of self-preservation, having learned danger's quiet guile during his KGB years, his Peklo years, and, of course, his time spent right here in hell.

And right now, he could tell something wasn't right.

They had exited the Alley of Doomed Prophets six miles back, Calkarion's chariot running smoothly after his tinkering with the bashed chassis. The ground had started to gradually alter in texture and color, becoming a glistening, spongy surface. The series of rolling grayish-pink hills they were racing across seemed to run all the way to Kerzix's front door. It took a moment for Kozlov to realize that they were not hills but huge brains, electrical neurons misfiring sporadically. According to Calkarion's translation, these were the architectural ruins to a pantheon from Trillik's world, formed from a dogmatic movement espousing the majesty of a universal set of brains governing the afterlife. No sounds issued from Trillik, the brain collective demonstrating an air of dignified stoicism, perhaps even a bitter renouncement of their old beliefs.

Kozlov still didn't know which had come first, the brains or their mobility machines. But now that he knew of the intimate relationship between the mind and the soul, he had to admire how close this particular species' religion had come to understanding the afterlife; close, but not quite. Although the conscious and subconscious mind was linked to the soul, there wasn't a tribunal of brain deities crafting Shangri-la through logic. There was only the Order of Terminus, reigning over the void left by the defeated Luminaries.

Kozlov tried not to focus on the squishy terrain, surveying their destination—the crashed flying saucer that softly pulsed its emergency lights like garish decorations as it slowly rotated in place amidst other sections of damaged architecture seemingly poised to collapse like an unstable tower of building blocks.

The source of Kozlov's apprehension became audible before long: the atonal calliope music had found them again. Off in the distance, several miles to their left flank, the Big Top crawled along the hemispheres of many damaged brains like a giant striped caterpillar, its flaming eyes leaving locomotive-smoke trails. The tiny entourage on stilts or penny-farthings stuck close to the living tent like parasites on a whale.

'Where's the shortcut?' Kozlov asked, worried that the Big Top would spot them before they reached the hidden tunnel.

Calkarion only replied with 'Near.'

And it was. Just over the next hemisphere was a tunnel in the ridge of spongy tissue. Transport via brain surgery. How fittingly unpleasant. The Big Top still concerned Kozlov, no matter how far away it was. The jester moon had not returned to blot the sky, but that didn't mean there were no other security measures to monitor errant souls or otherworldly intruders.

Calkarion was evidently becoming something of a deft hand at reading human expression during his time with the monks, taking one fleeting over-the-shoulder glance and seemingly understanding Kozlov's concern.

'We keep moving, the Big Top will miss us, and we'll be inside the palace before it's even aware we exist. But we must keep moving.'

Kozlov responded with a weary nod.

The Arkhitektor placed a hand on Kozlov's shoulder, and with their continually shifting role reversal of teacher and student, Kozlov found himself feeling like the student once again: doubtful of his ability to follow through on this endeavor and in quiet need of guidance.

The Arkhitektor raised two fingers as if to tap the side of Kozlov's head. 'I know you too well. Now isn't the time to overthink. You know our strategy. You know the risks, of which there are many. Now is the time for a quiet mind. Calm. Readiness to act.'

Kozlov knew he was right, but that didn't make the advice any easier to embrace. For all of their shared trials, sneaking into an occupied and fully operational enemy stronghold was new; the Eidolon Trench had been a mere transport depot of sorts, and largely abandoned by the long-absent Charon. Infiltrating a monarch's palace, occupied by its rightful owner, no less, was an entirely different premise.

'In case I don't get a chance later, I would like to thank you for this.' The Arkhitektor's words surprised Kozlov, and his reaction must have shown. 'For helping a crazy old hermit make it this far.'

'You're talking like this is the end. This road might keep winding.'

The Arkhitektor stared at the distant keep, a structural amalgamation of various houses of worship from across all realities. He didn't look afraid or repulsed, as he had done during his moment of weakness in the Alley of Doomed Prophets, but in awe at the sight of it. 'Even though I'm appalled ... it's incredible, isn't it? Existence. The grandness of it all. The strangeness of it all. Think of where we started, where we each came from, and look where we are going.'

The demented fortress seemed to burst into revelry at its acknowledgment. From somewhere deep within its manic precinct, a celebration of demonic laughter and noise scoured the foreboding horizon.

'So much faith and hope. And it's all nothing but myths and lies. But what would life be without a little faith and hope?'

'Honest,' Kozlov offered. 'Practical. A lot of people would stop killing one another in the name of fiction.'

'Yes. But they would only dream up other reasons to kill one another.'

'I suppose they would,' Kozlov agreed. 'Perhaps we all do need a little faith. Not in any of this,' his sigil-laden gauntlet fluttered about dismissively at the latest holy ruins, 'but in ourselves to do what's right. To help one another, instead of pleading for clemency from corrupt holy men or crying out for some higher being to fix our mistakes.'

'When it's time ...' The Arkhitektor paused for a moment, the gravity of what he was about to say deserving of it. 'I trust you to be a just and loving god. Even-tempered and patient.'

'Not I, but we,' said Kozlov, referring to his mentor and their new comrades. '*We* will. Together. I don't see a new republic on the horizon. I see a paradise beyond pain and judgement and fealty. A place accepting of a person's strengths and their weaknesses. Somewhere where they are free to pursue their pleasures but also free from the exploitation of others.'

The Arkhitektor slapped his hand on Kozlov's shoulder. 'You continue to prove worthy of my faith, Konstantin.'

Kozlov felt the resurgence of his indomitable spirit rearing up against the hardships coming their way, and he was able to smile. His nose picked up a new smell: something strong, bitter, and somehow dread-inducing. He cast his eyes around for the source, noticing that it was a trail of dark vapor tailing behind the Big Top.

Quarmalls must have picked up the scent too. Making a droning sound, the living pollen farm tracked the wind currents, gathering subtle data on the chemical scent issuing from the Big Top's course and coming to a conclusion.

Trillik responded with several bleeps, performed some strange digital voodoo with its alien computer software, and blipped and bleeped some more for Calkarion to translate. The damnable message was:

'General Sagillis is burning hymnals. As Ringmaster of the Big Top, he burns hymnals when Kerzix has a new Marotte Marauder. The Imp King will soon be broadcasting the slaughter across all the counties of his kingdom. Sagillis is returning to the Big Top for the coming celebration and induction of his new member.'

Calkarion's chassis hissed along at a sharper gait, carrying them over the rolling electrical fields of gargantuan brains, and right up until they slipped through the secret folds of slick brain tissue, Kozlov stared at the trawling tent like it was a bad omen.

38

SALTY'S TAVERN WAS MOSTLY EMPTY this early in the afternoon, apart from the usual full-time losers and crooks. Dave took note of Skimz's BMW in the small lot but paid scant attention to anything else. It was for this reason that he was caught off-guard by the voice:

'David?'

Dave turned quickly to find Talbot, parked a few spaces over from the BMW, leaning against his Jag, his hands in his pockets like it was a casual encounter. 'I saw you on the news last night. I thought you were dead when I left you. Shaking off grenades and bullets. That's interesting. I've never seen such a durable Spark before.' Dave gave no impression that he was listening. 'I was on my way out of New York and took a gamble that you might be heading home.'

Dave cut a brief glance at Talbot, his maddened gaze singing with fury, and judging from Talbot's expression, he knew he was considering the odds of Dave making a move on him next.

'This isn't my home. I was just shat out here. This place won't be anybody's home by the time I'm done with it.'

'That's a very dramatic claim. You know, I wanted to give you a taste of your power, but this, the influence of that clown rattle, I can't imagine it being the liberation you were searching for.'

'Why, because you're not the one in my ear?' Dave showed a wolf's grin.

'No, David. I wanted to show you your untapped potential. By your own admission you have spent your life thus far as a kicked dog in a world of men. But really you were a wolf amongst sheep. But what you're doing here is rabid and senseless. Yes, I admit that I wanted your talents, but that was part of my job. I wear many hats in my line of work, and headhunting is one of them. I understand the basics of what you're experiencing right now, but I have to confess that it's tantamount to liner notes. One thing I have heard is that anyone who breaks one of those marottes like you did is reduced to a martyr for nihilism and death. Does that sound like empowerment to you?'

'Sounds like exactly what you wanted me to be.'

'An angry child, lashing out at the world? I didn't want that. I don't want you to squander your talents. Which is exactly what that marotte will have you doing until you go up like some moronic suicide bomber. This isn't a worthy cause, David. But what I was offering you was, and still can be. Power. That's what you've always wanted. To conquer your fears and master yourself. Not for mindless destruction, but to build yourself a life to be envious of.'

Dave stared at his hands, shaking in their need to destroy something, then back to Talbot. 'What difference does it make? Everyone wants to control me, or kill me, which is the same as controlling me. Why go with you when I feel this good? You'll only want me to attack your problems, and why should I do that when I can attack mine, and feel fucking great doing it? You don't know how I used to feel. Spending every day like a square peg trying to fit into a round hole. Every single night terrified of a meaningless future, certain I'll never find happiness or contentment, just ticking down the days and the years until I die alone. Each morning I'd be so upset when I woke up, because it meant I'd have to go through it all over again. Isn't that the definition of insanity, doing the exact same thing over and over and over and expecting to get a different result? Sounds like a shit life to me. Why bother? Why not just end it all?'

'I know exactly how it feels. My beginnings were far more humbling than yours. I've told you my sorry history. I often still think of that dank grove so long ago, the meeting place of the Cairnwood Society. Of being a young creature getting used to its human host, feasting on the life force of the frogs and vermin in that marshland, all scrabbling upon the ancient bones of conquered kings and knights and statesmen. No matter how fine my suit is, or expensive my car, I always feel the soggy roots of that place snagging on my trouser leg, the taste of moist toad meat and fish repeating on me until I gag. Growing pains, that's all it was in hindsight, and they were worth it. The big difference is, I had to seize my opportunity. Stop the self-pitying, Dave. You were born with a gift. You're a Spark, for Christ's sake. People would kill for that power. Even if you were not born a Spark, you still could have achieved much more than this.' Talbot's gaze swept across the dump of a bar behind Dave.

'You have advantages most mortals could only dream of: power, great and terrible. Last night you stood your ground and traded blows with one of the most dangerous Hourglass agents I have ever encountered. Did you kill him?'

Dave tried to recapture the tactile sensation of the skull cracking behind the hockey mask. 'I don't know.'

'Well, either way, you accomplished something that some former employees of mine, all very dangerous in their own right, failed to do. There is greatness inside you, David. If you have any semblance of control over this new state you're in, why not stay with me?'

The cackling made an echo chamber of Dave's head, trying to drown out any further dissent or arguments, forcing him to clamp his hands to his head, knocking his beanie askew.

'I don't want to hurt you,' Dave spat through clenched teeth. 'You used me, but you treated me with respect.' His teeth started to grind. 'Go! Now! I don't know how long I can hold on.' As if to prove the point, a sudden cheery outburst had him sputtering chuckles. 'I need to kill a whole lot of people, Ed. But I want them to deserve it. I want the choice.'

'That sounds to me like you still have some control,' Talbot reasoned. 'Why not come with me? You'll have two choices: massacre Hourglass, or some of my superiors. I'm going to Chicago for a while to check out a few things. You would come in handy. Either way I'd say they're all deserving targets. What do you say?'

Dave shook his head, and it took a momentous effort to do so. 'No!' Spittle sprayed through clenched teeth. 'It needs to happen soon. Today!' He started to get anxious, too much energy racing through him in need of work. 'It's like an itch inside my head.' His fingers groped furrows into his wax-white face, digging under his beanie to scratch at his scalp.

'Who are you going to kill?' Curiosity, even disappointment set Talbot's features. 'I'm not judging, but it all goes back to utilizing talent. It seems a shame to waste it on a bunch of ants who didn't realize they were crawling over a god.' Talbot opened the car door and plopped behind the wheel. 'Last chance. Want to come with me? You'll no longer be spending your life on the sidelines like some extra in everyone else's stories. You want to make a scene? I can help direct you. I can make you a big star, so big that this silly marotte curse will be nothing more than a footnote in your story. Shut the clown out, David. Nobody likes those grinning arseholes anyway.'

'You know what I've come to realize?' Dave's face was hidden behind a wall of clenching, clawing fingers. The racket in his head went quiet, and Dave finally lowered his hands in exhaustion. 'I never could be a leading man. But I was born to be the bad guy.'

'Perfect. Because I'm planning some bad things.'

Dave began to shake, impatient rage and blackest humor broiling his nerves. 'You should go, while you still can.'

Talbot placed his hands on the wheel, smoothing it in a meditative fashion. 'Well, if you get through this farce, look me up in Chicago, superstar.'

The Jag's engine purred awake, and Talbot crisply swung the car around and was out of the lot, and then shortly out of sight.

Dave turned back to face Salty's entrance, took a deep breath, and marched forth. His entrance generated enough fervor amongst the die-hard clientele that it could have been a Saturday night.

'What. The. Fuck?' Skimz was in his usual spot in the dark corner, a big white guy in big white sneakers and a camouflage coat, vaping and drinking and endlessly talking business into his phone. He was actually in the middle of dealing with a customer when he saw the clown in the long, burned, and dirty coat walk into the bar like he fucking owned the place. 'I'll call you back.' He hung up the phone, shared a few jackal laughs with his ever-present dirtbag pals Tags and Grizz, and the three of them laid their usual stare on Dave, giving him that raw-steak-to-a-hungry-dog look.

Dave stared at each and every pair of eyes in the place until they caved and looked away. That stuck-up gangster-bait bitch barmaid Lorna was the first to fake an interest in a dirty glass. Johnny, the pool-table hustler who was so utterly devoid of basic manners, became fascinated in chalking his cue.

But Skimz wasn't the type of guy to blush when some total fucking zero tried to stare him down, especially when the stupid asshole was wearing face paint.

'Dave...? That you? The fuck... You finally get into Clown College?'

Tags unleashed a bone-vibrating basso laugh. Grizz chittered, eyes glazed.

'Maybe Bozo'll teach you how to pour a decent pint.'

Dave remained quiet, feeling the hot anger swelling up inside his chest. It felt good. He stared unblinking at Skimz, wanting to provoke a response. Violence was cathartic, but to humiliate a chest-puffing thug must be damn near euphoric.

'Don't try to eye-fuck me just because you found your way into your mom's make-up.' Skimz sat up straight in readiness to prove a point, his cornrows turning the color of old straw under the smoky light. 'You look like some faggot incel school shooter. That shit supposed to make you look edgy or scary or some shit? You don't even know the meaning of those words, little boy.'

Dave slowly walked into the middle of the room, each step calm and assured.

'Dave...?' Lorna sounded a little scared but tried to play it off with a shrill cackle, like they were old friends sharing a joke. 'Where have you been? And what's with the face?'

Dave could have asked her the same thing, her own face covered in nearly as much paint as his, except her slutty chic was to hide how haggard and drawn-out she was becoming. Dave could have felt a little sorry for her, despite her harsh mouth, knowing she would likely spend the rest of her life in this minimum-wage shithole, soon to be knocked-up by some asshole like Tags, gaining weight, losing her looks, dying miserable with a broken gangster family.

Dave couldn't give a fuck. That was on her.

A steady flow of insecurities and humiliations poured through him again. Every snide remark, disparaging stare, and physical intimidation he'd experienced in this place had him vibrating. That's when the cherry on the cake waddled into the room from the back office. Bar manager Hank Pelto, gnawing on a pen. He stopped dead when he saw Dave.

'Where the fuck were you last night, asshole? I had to cover your shift.' Pelto's dark little pebble eyes rattled about in such indignation that Dave couldn't help but smirk at the coming shift in power.

'Hold up,' Tags said, grabbing his phone, staring at the screen with his mouth open like he was trying to read. 'Shit, where is it?'

'What?' Grizz asked.

'Last night, that wild shit on the interstate! The fuck's it gone?' Tag's thumbs were scrambling around, trying to find the bystander footage. 'They took it down.'

Grizz sneered at Dave. 'That pile-up? That wasn't this bitch.'

'The fuck do you know, crackhead? I know what I saw, man. Aren't two assholes running around painted up like that. And it wasn't just a pile-up, there was some unreal shit going on out there. Like something from a fuckin' movie or somethin'.' After several more seconds, Tags gave up and put his phone down, pointing at Dave. 'You—that was you on the news, you fuckin' psycho.' He carefully gave Skimz and Tags some sort of nod, a signal that shit was about to go south, something that they had probably used a lot when conducting their strong-arm business tactics.

The three thugs went for their pieces. Dave smiled. Shortly after, they were in pieces. The whole bar was.

. . .

DAVE KICKED OPEN the tavern's door, exiting the building on a gust of smoke, the flames of the burning bar crackling behind him. He felt incredible. Electric! But there was a vein of sadness running through it: for what, he wasn't sure. Was it shame? No, that couldn't be it. He rubbed smoky tears from his eyes, his vision watery, and remembered that he had just been shot twice in the chest. He reached into his coat and let his finger probe the bloody holes in his T-shirt, feeling the wounds already scabbing over. And there was something else. He pulled out his screenplay notebook, now blood-soaked and with a bullet hole punched through it. He stared at it like it was something he had to mop up in the bar's restroom. He thumbed through it, but most of the pages were suctioned together with blood. Such pointless words. Silly thoughts and feelings. Sad attempts to fictionalize his pain and anger and why he never felt like he was a real person in this fucked-up world. He let it fall to the ground and stepped on it. He now knew his place in the world. Strong people always did. They belonged at the top of everything. That was how nature worked. It was undeniable. He kicked it aside and knelt down to scoop up some of the cleaner snow shoveled up against the wall of the bar, washing the fresh blood from his red hands, pinkish water sluicing through his fingers.

The bar's front window cracked open from the heat, spilling a rolling streamer of black smoke into the air. Dave didn't pay any mind to the building being consumed by the hungry flames behind him.

He kept thinking about the damage he'd done to the heads of Skimz and Grizz and Tags and his old boss! Gushed like fountains! Ha! Pour me a drink! The sound of whooshing air and breaking glass could be heard from inside the bar, and the wailing sirens of first responders fast approaching.

Dave felt the heat at his back, a clown fresh from the oven. He needed something else. Something big, something dramatic. Slaughtering everyone in the bar had been satisfying, but Talbot had been right about one thing: he had dreamed too small. Dumb, really. He needed a big cinematic climax, not a small and gritty noir murder scene. It had to be something with a much bigger bang for the Imp King's buck. He needed inspiration. And he knew just where to find it.

39

NAT HAD MADE GOOD ON her promise of buying a new bike, a black Kawasaki Ninja ZX-6R to be precise, and Clyde was petrified. He was petrified all the more when he learned that Kev had been at the Madhouse all night and hadn't yet returned home, because in his absence it meant Nat would—and had—twisted Clyde's arm into being her passenger.

For all of the horrors he had witnessed and personally combatted, he still found the prospect of straddling a mechanical missile and launching himself into the mercy of other road users to be a nightmare scenario; he still disliked airplanes, never mind this! But if there was any comfort to be had as they roared along the interstate towards the Madhouse, it was that Nat handled it like a pro.

. . .

THERE HAD BEEN no changes in Ace's condition, but Clyde thought some of his facial contusions looked a little better, less swelling, perhaps due to his status as a living ice pack. Nat stood with Clyde as he said a few words of encouragement to Ace; according to the doctors, Ace was still able to hear what was said to him, even if he couldn't respond, and Clyde hoped his words would give Ace something, however small, to hold on to, maybe even follow back to consciousness.

'The Null can't have you yet, you big idiot. We all need you here.'

Clyde placed a pin on the bedside table of a big-headed hockey goon, a graduation present of sorts that Ace had bestowed on Clyde after he finished his training at Indigo Mesa all those months ago. Clyde told his comatose friend, his mentor, that he would take the dumb thing back as soon as he woke up.

Nat had compiled a playlist for Ace inspired by the big Swedish rock kick he'd been on lately: Confess, Ghost, Bullet, The Hellacopters, Alien. She pushed a bedside button, signaling Schulz to start streaming the music through a bedside speaker—"Prominence" by Confess—and couldn't help but smile. 'Here you go, you big goofy bastard. The sooner you wake up, the sooner I can turn this crap off.'

With a tight smile, Clyde patted Ace's arm, and they quietly left him to sleep to the lullabies of phallic power ballads.

.   .   .

Clyde found Kev sitting in the waiting area talking to Barros. Rose, Sarge, and Darcy were also present, and the atmosphere was as relaxed as things could get under the circumstances. Clyde was just relieved Kev hadn't done anything stupid last night; when he received the call this morning, his mind had automatically gone to Kev locked up tight in Meadows' custody. Things seemed truly congenial between Kev and Rose, the way it used to be, and having just left Ace's bedside, it eased some of Clyde's burden. Rose finished smiling at something Darcy had said and offered Clyde and Nat a condoling look.

'It's only early,' Rose said. 'Not even twenty-four hours yet. That ugly son of a bitch will wake up when he's had his beauty sleep.'

Rose's choke bruise was still on the harsher side of purple, and she showed some mild discomfort in swallowing a gulp of her pre-workout shake.

Clyde knew Rose meant it as more of her rousing *fuck it, live fast, die young, I'll take all the shit you can throw at me* brand of encouragement, but it felt amiss today. Clyde understood that to handle any sort of military service you had to adopt a level of hardened bravado, some distancing to keep yourself from becoming an emotional wreck when the hard times come along, but he knew her well enough to know that behind it all, she was hurting over Ace. As was he. As they all were.

'He'll wake up, and he'll be more pissed that he lost another tooth than anything else. Wait and see,' Rose prophesied.

Clyde and Nat took a seat.

'I think he might want another shot at Bentley, if anything,' Clyde said, trying on some of that bravado for size. He turned to Kev. 'Late night?'

Kev shrugged. 'Didn't feel like sitting alone in my apartment.'

Clyde felt a spike of guilt. Since getting back from Indigo, he had spent most of his free time with Nat, and even when he and Kev had hung out together, he'd only been partially present, his mind and his heart alike fixed on Nat.

Kev must have read something in his expression, giving him a wise and easy smile. 'I had a little chat with Schulz and Meadows, that's all. Sat with Ace for a bit. Then Rose turned up to get her dude sweat on.'

Rose feigned a brief burst of hilarious laughter, wincing as she took another belt of her shake.

'You back to full strength?' Nat asked her.

Rose sighed, and Barros almost appeared guilty. 'Not quite,' Rose admitted.

'Give it a little more time,' Sarge said, always the team leader and voice of reason. 'I pissed on the shoes of enough friends in the past to know that just saying "we're good" isn't always enough. Give it time. The old bond will harden again.'

Rose smirked with satisfaction, probably thinking about going another round with Talbot as much as reconstituting their frayed camaraderie. Barros' happiness looked a little too forced to Clyde.

'Don't forget the ex-wife, Sarge,' Darcy said, anything to help.

Sarge's patron smile curdled a bit. 'Never do, Darce. Never do.'

It was good seeing how Kev and Barros were part of Rose's team without any of the lingering damage or trust issues, but Clyde was happiest in seeing how they both seemed to exist apart from the larger group. He didn't know what it meant, but it alleviated some of his guilt for spending so much time with Nat.

Kev floated something before Clyde. Something Clyde recognized, and felt the phantom pinch of its touch on the nape of his neck. It was a Free Thinker, a piece of Hourglass tech engineered to ward off external mental influences.

'Think it could work on Bentley?' Kev asked. 'I brought it up with Meadows earlier, and these guys think it's worth a shot.'

Clyde hadn't even thought of it. Perhaps due to his unpleasant memories of Charon attempting to slip between his thoughts, trying to upturn certain aspects of him like they were heavy stones. 'There's a lot of crossover between the schools of mind and soul,' he said. 'The mind is just an extension of the soul thread, so yeah—worth a shot.'

Kev nodded like he'd known all along that Clyde would approve. 'Bentley can't lay a hand on me. If I can slip this on him,' he spun the Free Thinker around a few times as if examining the contraption, 'it might increase our chances of ending this peacefully. Just in case.'

Just in case I fail, Clyde was thinking. Which was fair, and smart.

Clyde had exchanged a few messages with Kev before arriving, confirming Spector's willing participation in stopping the out-of-control Spark. If Kev's idea worked, he and the rest of the team could keep Bentley docile while Clyde and Ramaliak either saved his life or pulled his plug. It was that second part of the plan that remained a lit fuse, because Clyde still wasn't sure how he was going to venture into the Median without Rose—and, by extension, Meadows—learning of it. He couldn't request a sick note when the time came, stopping Bentley from the privacy of his apartment.

'It's a short-term solution, but a good one,' Clyde said of the Free Thinker.

'Also the only solution,' Rose added. 'Even if he's compliant, we still have to bury the guy.' She stood up, finished her shake, and took an invigorating breath. 'Okay, squad, let's go bend some metal. Barros, bring it in, girl.'

Barros parted from Kev with a lingering look and exited with Rose and the rest of the ISU.

Clyde watched his friend's goofy smile evaporate when he noticed him looking at him. Clyde didn't say anything, but checked the time. 'You feeling good about later?'

Kev pondered the question for a few seconds too long.

'Don't tell me you forgot,' Clyde said.

'My family? No, I didn't forget.'

Nat gave Kev an awkward look. 'You don't seem overly jolly.'

Kev rested his hands on his thighs calmly, eyes drifting away in thought. He was on the verge of saying something, but then seemed to find something else to say instead: 'Let's go for a walk.'

. . .

'Even ghosts could use some fresh air, you know,' Kev said. 'I think that's why so many of them are cranky when they're haunting a house. Maybe it's the memory of fresh air, the feel of it on skin.'

'What's going on, man?' Clyde asked, sensing his friend's procrastination.

Kev had them walking around the courtyard, following the salted flagstones wending through the snow-dusted trees. 'Just wanted to talk in private,' he said. 'I mended fences with Schulz, but that doesn't mean I feel comfortable talking in there; never know if he's listening or not.' Kev gave Nat a brief, uncertain look before asking, 'It went well with Spector?'

'Cool,' Clyde replied. 'From the sounds of it, he might even be looking forward to helping. Not so much for Bentley's sake, but I think he gets bored sometimes. Suppressing who he is.'

Kev's expression buoyed in mild amusement. 'No surprise, really. By his own accounts, he was a criminal. So I'm not surprised Spector is game for this plan of yours, but I'm glad he is. I don't want to see anybody else get hurt. Not if there's a chance to handle this quietly.'

Clyde kept his poker face on, but a wary look traveled across Nat's features like a light breeze.

'Just how risky is this plan?' Kev had to ask.

Clyde started them back down the path towards the main complex, spotting movement between the trees, a few agents in black windbreakers crossing from one outbuilding to another. 'Spector's history is a little trickier than you might think.' Clyde gave them the abridged version of Spector's coronation and subsequent renouncement of the Glowing Reel's throne. 'He's going to have to watch his back from Dremel and the rest of the council. But if anyone can do this, well, it's a professional thief.'

'On that note, couldn't he do all of it on his own?'

'Probably. Definitely. But there's no way I'm letting him do that,' Clyde said firmly. 'It was my idea. It's on me to go through with this'

'It's crazy to think what you're capable of now,' Kev said with unfiltered admiration. 'Shit, the both of you. A Spark and a guy who can fuck someone up from the comfort of his own bed. Soon you won't even need me anymore.'

'Don't say that,' Clyde said, chagrined. 'You know that's some bullshit.'

'I don't know . . . ' Kev used a slither of his power to kick a loose stone off the path onto the snow-covered lawn. 'No reason to feel bad about it. Things change. That's life. It's a good thing, really. Might help us when the time comes.'

Clyde parsed Kev's meaning. *When the time comes* meant the opportunity for them to enter the Null, track down Kozlov, and do anything and everything to assist him in his pursuit of the Firmament Needle. Clyde hadn't changed his mind on the matter. Far from it. And if anything, attempting it seemed more feasible than ever with his access to the Median: who knew what else he could do from inside there? But the idea of actually accomplishing this feat seemed to bob and drift further and further away on dangerous tides. It was one thing to risk Dremel's wrath by dealing with Bentley, but it was a whole other magnitude of risk to one day enter the Null to start a potential existential revolution; not exactly something he could do discreetly, and it would leave him no chance of returning to his life, as Dremel would undoubtedly learn of his activities and clip his thread, banishing him permanently to the Null. Do or die. But it was a problem for tomorrow, and he had to survive today first.

'Meanwhile, if this covert op inside the Median lands on your doorstep, we'll both be under lock and key,' Kev said. 'And just when Meadows called off Del and his babysitters club.'

'You mean the *three* of us will be under lock and key,' Nat corrected. 'I'm not pleading the Fifth while you two go down, giving Uncle M the failed-actress routine, all mascara trails and pouty lips.' This earned a slight look of approval from Kev, which slowly bloomed into an appreciative lopsided smirk.

'Don't forget, man,' Clyde added, his head tipping to Nat, 'her pops works at the Philippines Embassy. She can be pretty diplomatic when she has to.'

'And my old drummer Nutsack—R.I.P.—was a fucking prima donna. I talked him down a lot,' she added like it was a valuable reference.

'Might give us some wriggle room if this thing gets too loud,' Clyde said. 'Anyway, I think we've all had enough fresh air. So tell me, are we still meeting up with your family?'

'About that . . . no. I changed my mind.'

Clyde huffed and was about to try and persuade him, but Kev didn't give him the chance.

'It just isn't going to work. I can't square this with them. I was speaking to Barros about it, getting some experienced feedback, and she said she hasn't once considered visiting her family. Neither's the Sarge, neither's Darcy; it's probably for the best in their cases, the way they look and all. There's still a chance I'll see them someday if my ass doesn't get torn up in the Null or shot full of Exorcist rounds; and who knows, hopefully it'll be in some form of heaven. But until that day . . . ' He shook his head.

Clyde glanced at Nat for some of that diplomatic reasoning, but her silence was all the diplomacy that was necessary. This was Kev's decision, and perhaps he was right.

'Shit . . . ' Clyde scratched at his temple, dreading having to call up Aaron again, or Sandy, and explain that his mysterious surprise wasn't going ahead. 'What the hell do I tell them?'

'I wrote a letter,' Kev said. 'Left it at my place. It says some things. Maybe you could give it to them for me?'

Before Clyde could answer, their phones chimed simultaneously with an official alert. On their screens the static-fuzzed face of Schulz delivered a dire message: Bentley had popped up in Buffalo.

Sometimes Clyde hated being saved by the bell.

40

A NNETTE BANCROFT SPILLED HER GLASS of water over her notes when David burst into her office. There had been some muffled disturbances out on the street a few minutes ago, what sounded like a car wreck or two, a lot of screaming and shouting, but the vantage from her window offered nothing. Still, she was already on edge when the crazy man with the painted face burst in, muttering and arguing with himself. Her jaw mouthing empty nothings, it took Annette several moments to identify him as David Bentley.

She had rarely seen her client so triggered before, and the face paint was unnerving yet familiar, and it only took her a delayed second to place it: the shaky phone footage from the interstate. The footage had become something of a flash-in-the-pan phenomenon, if not for the violence, the drama, and the impossible occurrences, then for the speed with which it had suddenly vanished from all digital outlets.

Whatever the circumstances were surrounding that hoax—maybe it was some cheap marketing stunt for one of those idiotic superhero movies Annette detested so much—David was wearing that same face. He looked like he was five minutes away from becoming an active shooter, all jittery energy and . . . was that blood? Had Dave been shot? His coat and beanie hat were singed and frayed in multiple areas. Still ranting quietly to somebody, scratching at his temple like he had an insatiable itch, he stalked over to Annette's desk, searching for a dry note-pad or sheet of paper amongst the water-sodden pages and folders. He grabbed a spare pad and a pen and was about to slide into the patient's chair opposite her desk when she tried to carefully get his attention. 'David? What's happening, David?'

Dave was too preoccupied to answer.

'David, why have you painted your face?'

Dave pawed about for some soaked papers from the desk and rubbed them against his face, then held the sodden mess up for her to see. The paint hadn't smudged; the sopping-wet pages didn't hold a trace of paint or make-up.

Dave collapsed into the chair opposite her and commenced scrawling in the notepad with the fervent desperation of a man afraid of forgetting his thoughts.

Annette continued to silently assess Dave's clothing: the scorch-streaked trench coat and beanie, the dried blood staining his fingers and shirt a dirty brown... Then she noticed the unmistakable bullet holes in the clothing.

'Good God, David, are you hurt?'

Dave hacked a single violent laugh, wagging the pen at her. 'Good God,' he said with a sad chuckle and continued scribbling erratically, engaging in what could either be construed as quiet prayer or bargaining with some internal problem. No, not bargaining, but arguing. Dave tore off the page and scrunched it up, tossing it on the floor. Started again, his mouth still running quietly.

'Have you done something?' Annette asked. *Something* sounded so ominous to her own ears.

Annette carefully got up, came around the desk, and knelt down to retrieve the ball of paper, unfolding it and reading it. She knew how absurd what she was about to say was, but had to try and engage him in some way: 'It's good to see you're still performing the exercises.'

From what she could make out, the discarded page was either a confession or a madman's rambling. Maybe both. A lot of the writing was illegible, with Dave clutching the pen so tightly it was tantamount to using the nib like a shiv to carve up the paper. She could make out certain words: *Kerzix. Imp King. Laughter. Losing control. Scared. Angry. Salty's Tavern. Killed. Burned.*

Annette was aghast and now more than a little frightened of making any sudden movements.

Out in the hallway, several urgent voices could be heard drawing closer with a running gait. A couple of security guards crowded the doorway. Dave didn't hear a word they were saying to him, too focused on trying to concentrate and use the pen as a conduit for the problems in his head.

Annette waved the guards off, noticing one of them had a few minor glass cuts on his face. Had David smashed his way into the lobby? It was business hours, so the doors were open. Had he shattered some of the mirrors in reception?

'David, can you hear me?' she tried.

David made a small guttural sound, a small desperate cry. *Gahh.* He swallowed, rubbed at his red-rimmed eyes, and carried on writing. Then, without looking up: 'I hear you, Anne.'

Annette lifted the page in her hand. 'David, what is this? Have you hurt someone?'

Dave didn't answer her. Instead, a babel of enraged utterances issued forth from him, the argument in his head very much heating up.

'David, if you've hurt someone, I'll have to alert the authorities.'

'I didn't get around to applying for the Parks Department,' Dave said at last. 'But I have been stamping on some weeds.' A sad laugh moaned forth, and he threw Annette a crumbling look. 'You ever watch any were-wolf movies, Anne? Those scenes where the wolf-man begs to be locked up so he can't eat anybody, and the cops and his loved ones, they never listen, or they're too late, and before they know it the werewolf has a full stomach... You ever watch any of those?' Dave's hands flopped about uselessly. 'You can get the authorities, but I don't think it's going to do much good.'

Annette waggled a finger at one of the guards. 'How about we get Dr. Carver?' The guard jogged off in the direction of Carver's office. 'You seem like you could do with a sedative. Something to relax you, and then we can talk this through.'

Dave slumped forward in his chair, and Annette watched a tear run off his nose to splash the carpet. He wet his lips and looked at her like a man on the ledge of a very tall building. 'I'm sorry, Anne. I tried! I really did! I'm sorry.'

Annette held her palms up, crouching down to his eye level, against the warning of the second agitated guard.

'David, it's okay. It's all going to be okay. Tell me what you are sorry for. Let's talk through this. Talk to me.'

'I tried to stay in control, but I can't hold on. I'm not strong enough to hold on.' Dave was trembling in his seat, losing his grip on the notepad.

'I'm never strong enough. Never have been. I just wanted somewhere to fit in, to stop feeling so alone, but I'm just no good with people. I don't get them. I'll never get them, and I get so angry.'

. . .

DEEP INSIDE THE swirling chaos of Dave's thoughts, the laughter rose up like a broken mind chuckling from a dark well's depths. Flashing lights careened inside Dave's head, a dispiriting merry-go-round of bitter memories and hopeless feelings. Between each passing snapshot of misery was a glimpse of the Imp King rising up, a silhouetted nightmarish jester limned by the bluish-silver light of a movie projector. Kerzix spoke inside his head:

You're testing my patience with all this weeping and chain-tugging. Don't think that by carrying some watered-down Luminary blood you can overcome me, mortal. I'm in control, and you're just another soon-to-be gurning butcher. Now get back to work and bring me my harvest. The festivities are about to begin.

Dave had been scribbling on the pad again when he momentarily blacked out. He would have fallen from his chair if Annette hadn't caught him. He made a choking sound, eyes bulging as he nearly swallowed his tongue. And he found his voice again. The quiet one he suppressed for so much of his life. His *real* voice, stripped further of its ambiguous, indecisive nature and thick with the bitter taste of anger and hatred.

Annette glimpsed at the last word he had scrawled for her in huge, jagged letters: *RUN!*

'Don't worry about the medication, Anne. I have the best stuff right here.' Dave buried the pen deep in her neck. 'I think you call it Direct Aggression.'

'Christ!' The remaining guard exclaimed, mouth quivering in shock.

'I'm the only savior here, asshole,' Dave said, turning to meet the guard's charge. The guard was dealt with savagely for his bravery, followed shortly after by his colleague and then Dr. Carver.

Dave stared down at the glassy, shock-widened eyes of Annette Bancroft, and as he watched her final dying moments, the worst tendencies of his Kerzix-galvanized id spoke through him: 'You were wrong to try and tame such a magnificent beast. This vessel is a roaring furnace of potential, and you tried to dowse it with the cold water of simpering and compassion.'

Dave's eye snagged on the Jungian quote amidst the sea of walled certificates: *The difference between a good life and a bad life is how well you walk through the fire.*

Dave wanted to set that fire. Then everybody would see how well he walked through those flames.

Ten minutes later, the Blue Sky Wellness Center was a half-standing slaughterhouse of fifteen corpses, but the Imp King was not yet sated, and his wicked words continued to coax and stimulate the worst traits inside Dave, leading him back to the streets.

41

TALK ABOUT BAD TIMING. CLYDE didn't think Bentley was going to take a few quiet days off between rampages, but he'd been hoping to have a bit more time for him to set his plan his motion. Now he and the team were cutting through the white morning sky in an unmarked chopper, armed and armored, when what he really needed was a pillow, an eye mask, and some noise-canceling headphones.

No one spoke as they listened to Meadows' briefing and updates on Bentley's movements: the massacre at Salty's Tavern, the subsequent one at the counseling center in Buffalo, and it just kept going. Bentley had ripped through approximately a mile's worth of streets, traffic, and police officers, and showed little sign of stopping. More shaky cam footage had been bombarding the media outlets faster than Meadows could yank it down.

The satellite office in Buffalo had been doing all they could, but they were not equipped to deal with a threat of this magnitude. Meanwhile, local police and SWAT were even less equipped to contain Bentley's destructive swath. A SWAT sniper had placed a round through Bentley's head after he exited a razed Catholic church, but a minute later the madman was back on his feet and continuing his murderous rampage.

Clyde wasn't sure what to do.

His plan to quietly deal with Bentley from inside the Median was ruined, and he was actually contemplating telling Rose about the plan but knew that she would inevitably be concerned about a possible inter-plane diplomatic incident, and they had enough on their hands right now with an out-of-control Spark; he didn't need her trying to stonewall him with any of her bureaucratic aggression. They needed to focus on Bentley and avoid taking two steps back into useless intra-squad squabbling.

Was a full-on assault the only option for them now? Clyde couldn't shake the image of something terrible happening to Nat, and got angry with himself for thinking it. She had as good a chance at stopping Bentley as anybody, especially with Kev and the Free Thinker device on hand, but the thought stayed with him.

His burner phone vibrated. He carefully peeked a glimpse, making sure to keep it out of Rose's sight. He carefully got Nat's attention.

'Spector?' she mouthed softly.

Clyde gave a fraction of a nod.

Spector was currently in his office and readying himself to slip back into the deep fathoms of sleep. He needed to know when Clyde was planning on meeting him in the Median.

Clyde texted back, explaining his tricky circumstances.

Spector was quick in his reply, telling him that he was going in now, with a vague mention of a closing window to grab hold of a tool they would need for the job. He also told Clyde he would leave him a map, tucked inside the basin of a spherical monument in the municipal courtyard.

Agitated, Clyde was about to tell him to wait, but knew that the longer they stalled their covert mission, the more damage Bentley could do. He texted back, asking for a rendezvous point.

Spector kept it simple, replying with only two words: Gilded Hypnos.

Great. All he had to do was sneak through the palace grounds overseen by Dremel and the council of regents who didn't trust him, to help their ex-monarch meddle with their kingdom's very power source, breaking several laws, each of which would carry a death sentence.

42

CALKARION'S CHARIOT SPED THROUGH THE trepanned brain tunnel, guided by the electrical network of pulsing neurons. Kozlov felt his stomach tighten during the ride, but not from the unpleasantness of the route; rather, it was the excitement of what lay ahead. Possible answers. Intel on where the Firmament Needle might be kept by the Order's higher authorities. And all he had to do was navigate a piecemeal castle provided by religious and architectural saboteurs and designed by the Order's resident mad king of theological death. Kozlov reserved his optimism for the moment and watched a pinhole of light growing larger as they neared the end of the secret tunnel.

They had Trillik to thank for this route. The former serf of Kerzix had burrowed through this giant brain as part of an assassination carried out while under the influence of one of the imp's marottes. The exquisite cruelty and violence of the murder had won Trillik a coveted role overseeing the Rictus Folly databank. There Trillik had thrived until the day one of the minds in their tank, a hardy specimen, defiant and resistant as diamond, had awakened. And that wakening had roused the others from their controlled state in turn. Stark terror had met their collective return to consciousness, like waking from a trembling nightmare into a reality infinitely worse. They managed to flee before Kerzix or his Big Top general, Sagillis, became aware of their renewed autonomy, out into the godless wastelands of empty fables and myth.

Calkarion slowed their teeth-rattling progress as they reached the threshold of the damp, glistening tunnel that opened onto an antechamber. Under the glow of a few flickering synapses, Trillik climbed down from Calkarion's wagon and slipped a mechanical hand into the wall of brain tissue. With a few jostles, the brain tank folded back a whole section of rubbery brain tissue, revealing a large metal panel. Behind the panel lay what Kozlov assumed to be the cellars or dungeons of Kerzix's palace. It was suitably bizarre and terrible, and after a few moments' inspection, he was still none the wiser as to the purpose of the room beyond basic sadism. Living brains, thousands of them, of different shapes and sizes and functions, all contained within solution tanks like hideous snow globes. Kozlov and the Arkhitektor shared a look of revilement, then confusion when they saw a glowing thread, wispy like neon smoke, drawn taut from each specimen and spooled into a series of alien devices that seemingly delivered their other ends elsewhere within the palace.

Trillik beeped and chirped, and Calkarion translated. Each specimen was a bank of memorized slaughter, every soul thread a film reel featuring an episode starring an unfortunate from some part of the universe who had unwittingly become a marotte martyr, a jester who collected screams and death rather than laughs.

Staring at the glowing thread of each brain, Kozlov, for the first time, laid eyes on the very origin of a soul: the mind, that magnificent miracle of personality and reasoning and untapped mystery.

Kozlov was still curious as to the exact nature of Trillik, and this trophy room only confounded him further. Apparently, the horizon of giant brains beyond this castle's walls belonged to the great philosophers and shamans of their species, but what came first: the living brain-operated tanks, or Kerzix's disgusting collection of jarred brains? He confided to himself that he might never know, the universe being as bafflingly complicated and chaotic as it was. 'Where do these soul threads lead to?'

Calkarion passed the question on to Trillik, who responded quickly.

The brains functioned as a halfway house of sorts, locked between two unfavorable places. The first place, the Median, Kozlov hadn't heard of. But he was familiar with troubled dreams; what mortal creature wasn't? However, the second place he did know; all of them did. It was the Rictus Folly, the Imp King's personal font of dread and celestial intelligence, locked away in his private quarters.

Calkarion's mechanical crane arm whirred about swiftly, drawing out several black boxes from the racks of his shell, each roughly the size of a good lump of C4. He passed several to Trillik and kept the others himself. Together they spent several minutes placing the explosives all around the collection of brains.

'You're killing these poor souls?' the Arkhitektor asked.

Calkarion paused. 'These aren't Trillik's people. They are the brains removed from various beings. Their bodies are all long dead. All they have now is sedation and the memories of their most shameful acts.' Calkarion raised his last explosive charge. 'This is mercy.'

Kozlov made no argument. With the explosives set, none of the party wished to linger in the despairing place a second longer, and so, with a careful mechanical gait, Calkarion led the way up a wide helter-skelter ramp that Kozlov nearly convinced himself would never end, before stopping at a door the size of a small castle keep and shaped like a laughing mouth. The noise outside was chilling. The monstrous celebrants of chaos, vicariously indulging in mass murder. There was no sense in putting this off. Kozlov opened the door, and the light from the courtyard washed over them in the mingling hues of electrical blue flame and the wan, pale-green sky. The carnival atmosphere erupted in volume. He led them out onto an unguarded parapet and glanced down at the nightmarish pageantry in the courtyard below. The crowds of strange beasts had their attention split among a monolithic wall of giant eyeballs, the iris of each a portal to the live-action violence and murder of a Kerzix conscript. They were all alien worlds, but Kozlov's sweeping disgust did catch sight of one that looked like it could be occurring on Earth: somewhere urban, two fists blurring into red tornados, smashing cars and liquidating panicked police officers and pedestrians.

The other half of the chattering mass were watching joyously as something approached the courtyard, entering from the crazed lands beyond the castle walls. Kozlov heard the out-of-tune calliope music and the deep, rolling thuds of some huge shifting body. He watched as the Big Top caterpillar crawled through the huge castle gate—another laughing mouth with a raised portcullis of teeth. The devils all cheered at its arrival, creating a huge berth for its passage. The stilt-men, the offal jugglers, the rolling cannon people, and the perched kite-men all soaked up the impish glee. Once in the heart of the courtyard, the Big Top stopped, its torch-fire eyes smoldering as it moved its head, the large tent-flap mouth hacking and coughing as it spewed forth a tall and gaunt gremlin done up like a militant circus ringmaster.

'Sagillis,' Calkarion said.

With all the practiced and shallow showmanship of a freak-show barker, Sagillis waved its bowler hat towards the procession of escaped souls being vomited forth from the prison tent. Each soul—some human, most not—was hobbled and terrified, having by chance slipped out of Charon's soul-transport tubes.

The crowd jeered as the recaptured souls were poked and beaten by the stilt-walkers and other entertainers, the scaly ringleader luring them before the wall of unblinking eyeballs.

Kozlov watched as Sagillis bent down to grasp a large hatch in the ground and hoist the lid open with his long-nailed hands. The result was like a confetti bomb showering the audience, except the confetti was the freshly harvested souls of the currently active Marotte Martyrs. They cried in confusion and horror as the claws and tentacles and hooks of the horde seized them, pulling them down into their midst to mock and hurt.

Kozlov didn't know if this subterranean tube was part of Charon's fiendish soul-delivery network, but he doubted it. From what he'd learned from Calkarion, it was likely an illegal tap, Kerzix privately siphoning from the other monarchs.

Kozlov uselessly wished he had a way of blocking the tube, blocking the entire network to keep souls from ever entering Erebus. It wouldn't matter. Not when he got his hands on the Needle.

Calkarion told Kozlov and the Arkhitektor of the imminent fate of that poor lot below: devouring, torture, fun and entertainment for the broadcast audience across the rest of Kerzix's kingdom, a grisly finality that would also destroy their final vestiges of consciousness, their vibrant soul threads turning black and truly lifeless within the Median.

Kozlov had seen enough. He wanted this over with. He glanced along the parapet, eyes drawn to the large tower wall with the enormous UFO embedded near the top. He could hear a sound emanating from it. A theremin's eerie cry. 'The king up there?' Kozlov asked.

Calkarion confirmed it, adding some good news. During these raucous events, the security went slack. Kozlov knew from his KGB career that professional conduct started at the top, be it government, military, or sovereign, and when the head of an organization proved to be sloppy, the body quickly followed. Kerzix's madness would be his undoing.

Kozlov led them along the wall, staying low and hoping the kite-men didn't suddenly take to the sky. It would be too taxing for the Arkhitektor to carry all of them vertically to the UFO, particularly with Calkarion's weight, especially if—*when*—combat erupted within the king's chambers. Kozlov had Trillik lead the way. They had reached the tower doorway when Kozlov heard the rapturous noise below fall into a deathly silence. Silent, except for a rhythmic, oily, springing sound.

'We're made,' the Arkhitektor muttered.

Kozlov cast about the castle walls, finding no sentries or cameras, until he witnessed the leering face of Sagillis cresting over the parapet wall, then dropping away, cresting, dropping. The commander of the Marotte Martyrs was pogoing up and down to incredible heights on a construct of femur and coiled metal. Sagillis' face popped up again, and a nape-quivering chuckle burst from the gremlin's mouth. Split-smiled kite-men alighted on the parapet walls opposite like scavenger birds readying to feast. And below them, the blazing eyes of the Big Top reignited as its tent-flap mouth belched a baritone brimstone chuckle. Shuffling towards the wall, it slowly but steadily began to climb, propelled by a legion of clown-shoed feet.

43

DAVE HELPED HIMSELF TO A big bag of popcorn and a large soda. There were specks of blood on the paper bag, but the kernels were clean enough. A large broken mirror behind the stand showed a dozen reflections of a clown in a Santa hat practically dripping in blood. He stepped over the twitching form of Elijah, the once cocky teenager so quick to sneer, and exited the trashed concession stand.

Dave paused in the middle of the Encore's trashed foyer, popcorn and hot dogs and sodas and corpses littering the place; one person's face had been smashed through the screen of an arcade machine. He placed his snacks down for a moment and made a camera screen with his thumbs and index fingers, relishing the destruction he'd wrought like a proud movie director. He moved his hand-frame to encompass the broken glass doors of the lobby. Outside lay a few dented and busted cars, a smoking bus, and a lot of newly arrived police cars, lights flashing. Behind them, cops were animatedly issuing orders and holding their guns on the cinema. Dave was pretty sure one of them had shot him in the head earlier. He remembered a brief blackout, and Kerzix gleefully commentating to someone—to him, probably—about the amazing regenerative capabilities of this Luminary bastard, and then Dave was picking himself up from the street, his face and beanie swimming with gore. That was the moment most of the law focused less on shooting and more on evacuating civilians. Plus, the cops didn't know if he had any hostages in here with him.

Grabbing up his snacks, he walked towards Screen 12, watching the last few frightened and gasping cinemagoers hurrying out the fire-exit doors. That was good; he would have the showing all to himself, with no assholes yapping and talking on their fucking phones during the movie. He sipped his Coke and entered the latest screening of *Scions of Saturn II*.

He dropped into a chair, threw his legs up onto the seat in front, and drained his soda like a big alien bug sucking down brains. He needed inspiration. Something big and bloody enough to satiate his own anger while also silencing Kerzix's demands. A climax big enough for Hollywood. He could just continue walking through town, tearing down cops—and soon enough, feds—until the streets ran red and Kerzix pulled him from this place, but he wanted something more meaningful. But what? Did the meaning really matter anymore? Wasn't visceral spectacle and catharsis more honest and memorable for his whipped animal spirit than some big, contrived event?

He scarfed down a handful of popcorn, tasting the copper tang from his bloody fingers, and smiled as the movie started.

This might be the last movie he ever saw. The thought inspired a brief flicker of sadness in him, but it was swept away soon enough. He would enjoy this final viewing and then finish his performance of the Marotte Martyr.

44

THE HELICOPTER DESCENDED UPON THE focal point of destruction. Clyde and the others had stayed updated about the proceedings during the flight, but news footage always paled compared to seeing the real thing with one's own eyes. The whole block around the Encore Cinema was shut down and crawling with local PD and SWAT, currently operating on orders from on high, all the way down from the government to the police commissioner, to simply stand back and allow a seldom-heard-of agency to perform their archaic duties.

Clyde and the team disembarked from the chopper onto the old cinema's flat roof, its warped and cracked surface rimed with ice and a few frozen puddles. Even with their elevated position from the street, they had all been required to wear headgear to conceal their identities from the circling news choppers, and Kev had donned his full civilian 'outfit.'

There had been talk of smoking Bentley out of the building, but the idea had been quickly dismissed for two reasons: 1) it was still unknown as to whether there were hostages or wounded inside the building, and 2) nobody actually wanted Bentley back out on the streets. They wanted this mess contained. There had been some talk of simply leveling the structure with an air strike, but that was being held as a final option in case the Hourglass team couldn't finish the job.

They gathered around the rooftop's door, readying themselves for anything.

Clyde was trying not to think of Spector waiting for him in the Median, their opportunity for a peaceful resolution slipping away by the second. He couldn't exactly calm his thoughts by fiddling with the blue twine and so was taking deep relaxing breaths, trying to slow his heart rate, and focusing on a fixed point in his mind as he imagined himself slowly sinking all the way down to that deep, hidden place. Rose would bloody his nose if she knew what he was planning, so it was good that the tactical helmet hid his uncertain expression.

Rose gave a quick scan of the sky. The news heli was getting ready for another sweep. She quickly kicked the door off its hinges, throwing a fine-grainy swirl of brick dust into the stairwell beyond. She stormed in, the others right behind her.

Barros materialized and waited at the top of the stairs with Clyde and Kev while Rose started her descent.

Having sensed Barros pull away from her, Rose stopped on the landing, spinning to face them. 'Fuck me with a cactus, what's up with you pricks lately?' she started to bark before dropping her voice to a harsh whisper. 'We don't have time for this!'

Kev shared a quiet look with Barros, who dropped her stoic act.

'You're like my damn sister, and I love you,' Barros said, 'but I still have some doubts about us. Opinions and people change, and I'm not sure where my head's at right now with this job. Because of that, you still might not be as strong as you used to be, and I can't stand the thought of you biting off more than you can chew. If Bentley is too strong for you, it'll be my fault.'

Rose removed her helmet. 'It's not your fault. We're just working through something.'

Sarge and Darcy appeared.

'I don't think this is something I can work through,' Barros admitted, a tremor of concern shooting across her face. 'I'm feeling at odds with all of this now. Not the job, not *this* job, but the whole Hourglass agenda. I've been thinking about it more and more since me and Kev got chewed out, and I can't deny that it all seems pointless. Small potatoes, when we officially know that the real fight, the one that's worth so much more than stamping down mid-tier occultists and monsters, is over in the Null. That's where the war should be fought. This is just … boot camp.'

Rose rolled her eyes so far back she almost lost them in her skull. 'Do you seriously want to rehash this shit now? Right fucking here?!'

'No,' Barros said simply. 'It can wait. But after what went down with Talbot, I think you should ease off the gas a little. Employ a more subtle strategy for stopping Bentley.'

'We can wake him up with the Free Thinker,' Rose argued. 'Might not even have to make a fist.'

Kev removed the Free Thinker from his deep coat pocket. 'And if this doesn't work on him?' From his tone of voice, the piece of sophisticated tech seemed like a Hail Mary.

Rose gave Kev a searing look, then a full-on death stare at Clyde when he said, 'I think I have a good chance at stopping him from within.' He didn't dare mention Spector's role, even though he knew it might help sell the strategy. 'It could all be over before Bentley or Kerzix even know what's happening. No violence, no chance of any of you landing in the ER or the morgue.'

Rose stepped to Clyde square-on, eyes boring into his with challenge.

'So the fate of our whole truce with the Order and the lives of every single person not just on Earth but across the universe go into jeopardy because you kind-of-sort-of learned a new trick? Because your old man had the bad luck of staining his soul with some fucking dream parasite? Bentley has an imp on his back, and it isn't one of Santa's elves: it's one of the fucking monarchs. A *full-strength* monarch. And you think you're capable of playing god in there and beating him? Spitting in his eye? You're playing around with forces you couldn't possibly understand.'

'And you do?' Clyde asked calmly.

'Of course I don't. I don't know dick about the Median. But you're far too relaxed about messing around inside that place. What about Spector, and that council who have already taken issue with your very existence? It's a shit idea, Clyde.'

Clyde didn't bother answering. His and Spector's plan was already in motion, and by now Spector would have most likely performed any number of acts that would have him up before a tribunal of Dremel and the rest of his parliament. Clyde wouldn't let him take all the risks alone. Not that he'd tell Rose this; it was obvious her stubbornness was unscalable.

'I'm strong enough.' Rose clenched her jaw. 'We all are.' Sarge, eyes clouded in thought, nodded reluctantly to himself and quietly sided with Rose. Darcy followed suit but looked a little guilty about it.

Barros didn't look pleased, but she didn't look too surprised either.

'We stick to the plan. Kev, you hold this motherfucker in place, slap the Thinker on him. If we can't liberate him from Kerzix's control, then Kev keeps holding him while Nat and the rest of us become the stick to Bentley's piñata. After that, he's the Null's problem. We bag his corpse and roll out.'

There was a small part of Clyde that strategy still appealed to. It was more straightforward and presented less chance of doing untold damage to the entire hierarchy of life, dreams, and death.

And after what Bentley did to Ace, a part of him wouldn't mind seeing Bentley dead. Thinking this once more made him confront how easily he now measured up the lives of others. Bentley was a threat, sure, but he was also a victim of much larger and sinister powers, and the thought of simply ending his life out of revenge rather than trying to save it left a bitter taste in his mouth. Clyde had to believe he could spare his life as well as Nat's and Rose's.

'Lead the way,' Clyde said. Rose gave him a calculating look, then marched down the next flight of stairs and into the cinema's third floor, an area that still stank of ancient cigarette smoke, with a balding carpet, walls in dire need of a new paint job, a manager's office, and some miscellaneous side rooms. Bentley would be on one of the lower floors. Where the action was. Clyde felt each second slipping away from him and didn't have the faintest idea how he was going to break away into the Median. As Rose hurried down the corridor, desperation took hold. He buckled over, eyes scrunched shut in pain, and used some of his siphoned kinetic power to induce a small nosebleed. That part was the most worrisome. What if he pulped his nose and sinuses like an overripe tomato? Or caused some hemorrhaging? Flexing his jaws, he really tried to sell it, knowing the bloody nose might convince her. To Rose's credit, she looked genuinely concerned for Clyde, rushing to his side.

'Clyde?'

'Head hurts,' he strung out.

'Fuck!' Rose glanced around at the rest of the team. The ISU looked as worried as she did, but Kev and Nat took a second or two longer to catch up to this unexpected twist.

Clyde knew they would both pick up on this improvised high-school-drama plan of his.

'I won't have you going in there like this,' Rose said. 'C'mon, we'll get you back into the bird to wait this out.'

'I'm fine here. Just let me rest up a little.'

And that was the line that spelled doom for Clyde. Rose released his arm, staring at him with a smoldering intensity. 'Oh, dumb fucking me. You son of a bitch. You going to rest your eyes for a little while, huh? Fuck, you had me for a moment.'

Clyde carefully turned on the taps in his nose again, leaking a little more blood and using the back of his hand to staunch the flow.

'That's a bad habit you got there, Clyde. Using your TK to knock a few blood vessels around?'

Clyde didn't answer. He didn't want to strain Rose's trust any longer, as those issues were already dangerously close to irreparably riveting the team down the middle. But he couldn't stop now, and the atmosphere wasn't conducive to calm meditation. He was too jacked up with adrenaline and too inexperienced with his meditative techniques to possibly slip peacefully into sleep. He would have to take a more drastic route.

He sent a fractional pulse through his body, the convulsion knocking him unconscious.

. . .

CLYDE'S LIMP BODY fell into some old cardboard boxes filled with ancient movie cans and rolled-up posters. Nat and Kev rushed to his side. That wasn't Clyde acting.

Rose glared down at them in contempt, chiefly Nat. 'What's Meadows going to do with him when he hears about this? What will he do with all of you?'

Nat didn't say anything.

'Fuck this. He's breathing, leave him. We do this now, or I'll call Meadows and tell him there's three—' Rose snapped an undecided glance at Barros, 'maybe four traitors on the team.'

Kev squeezed Clyde's hand. 'Good luck in there, man. See you when you wake up.' He stood, ready to follow in Rose's bullish wake.

Nat kissed Clyde softly in the lips and, without a word, followed Kev and the rest of the team as they set to searching the movie theater for Bentley.

45

CLYDE STUMBLED THROUGH GRAVITY'S MOLASSES, shambling across the glowing terrain towards the shining city. He felt groggier than he had in a long time, not since his first descents into this sacred realm. Cutting off his blood flow had worked faster than his meditative exercises. However, he wouldn't be in a rush to try it again.

He entered the boundary of the coruscating city, his eyes primed for any of the stealthy guardians keeping quiet vigil but seeing nothing until he neared the ornate grounds of the council's building. Through the arches and cloisters, he could see the stunning soul loom slowly rotating away in the far distance and also caught his first true glimpse of one of the fleet-footed guardians that had until now only teased his peripheral vision. There were several of them, stuck high to the building's exterior by hooked hands, gently moving along the wall's woven soul threads like spiders crawling across fiberoptic harp strings. Clyde knew these guileful creatures must sense him. Even worse was the fact that they were finally in the open for him to see. Were they making a statement? Had they been issued an order from Dremel to pose a hostile presence, perhaps?

Lithe and multi-limbed—with two of their anterior appendages ending in thread-clipping shears—they were cheetah-toned with hoary flesh and diamond-shaped heads, the latter feature confirming why Ramaliak called them diamond-heads. Clyde wondered if they would try to stop him if he attempted to enter the council's building.

Most likely.

Had the council prohibited his entry?

Again, most likely.

But what of Ramaliak? Had he been caught, causing an alarm to be raised amongst his former advisors? Clyde didn't want to imagine the damage he might have caused by involving Ramaliak in this reckless plan, but before panic could set in, he noticed the large, decorative monument sitting in the heart of the courtyard, a dry basin hosting a big, colorful sphere of knitted souls, rotating gently.

That must be the place Spector had texted him about. Furtively glancing around at the surrounding municipal buildings, Clyde approached the monument. True to Spector's word, Clyde found something behind the basin's lip. It didn't look like a map, but it was a device he recognized well: the Sleeping Shepherd, the ancient metronomic device Spector had stolen from the British Museum and that had subsequently made him its heir.

It took him a few seconds to discover that it was only a replica of the original, a dream-borne copy left behind by Ramaliak. This was starting to feel a little off, and Clyde was fearing a trap. So now what? Holding it in his hands, the quietly beating machine rebuffed him like a surfer by a gentle tide, hit with a psychic direction by way of a clear visual cue. Clyde had to keep himself from smiling, not from pride but the lingering incredulity at what he had become. Nat was right: how many other people got to experience marvels such as this? Here he stood, visiting forbidden landmarks of a dream world few conscious minds would ever know existed.

The image he received was of the holiest of holies: the Gilded Hypnos and Obsidian Extremis, the conjoined pyramids, one shining like molten gold and the other a winged black-glass temple, gorging on the perpetual swirling mist of soul-charge particulate of deceased mortals passing over from life to the waiting terrors of Erebus.

Clyde wasn't keen on setting foot in such a prohibited place, but once you've crossed certain lines, there is little sense in arguing inches. Subsequent images passed through his thoughts as the device showed him the clearest route. The first stop was to a bridge known as Ram's Crossing; it was a bit of a jog, but on the plus side, time and physical exertion took ambiguous taxes in this realm.

He glanced about, evaluating the challenge that lay ahead, noting the number of diamond-heads calmly traversing the woven architecture climbing and spiraling all around him. There were large gaps between their patrols, with most of the guardians cluttering the council's chambers and surrounding ministries. Clyde started off at a light pace down the wide, glowing avenue that ran parallel to the council's building, making sure none of the now brazen diamond-heads were following him, then angled down a warren of curving turquoise alleyways before breaking out beyond the council's square. As he exited the municipality proper, the buildings slowly regressed in size and complexity until Clyde was running along the phosphorescent trails of the outland wilderness. Fields of souls braided into reeds waved upright in a nonexistent breeze like heather. Before too long, Clyde was on the Ram's Crossing. The bridge looked longer than Brooklyn's, suspended over black fathoms of empty space.

He kept his eyes trained on the Glowing Reel in the distance, impossibly huge and blazoned like a celestial event against the black sky. Just west of the reel, the conjoined pyramids looked both stunningly beautiful and sinister in comparison, the great black wings of the Extremis beating slowly like they were underwater.

.　.　.

CLYDE STARTED ACROSS the lonely bridge, unaware of the lone figure slinking along the underside of the walkway, silent as smoke. A diamond-head.

46

THE MOVIE WAS REACHING ITS big third-act climax, and it wasn't until Dave experienced those same old chills that he realized Kerzix's incessant goading for further violence had been briefly drowned out by the sheer excitement and emotional heft of watching his favorite big-screen heroes rise to the hardest of challenges, risking life and limb for a purpose much greater than themselves.

The hair rose on Dave's arms at the cinematic crescendo, and he felt something unexpected but familiar. A minor tremor ran through his numbed heart. A surge of so much repressed emotion that tears sprang to his eyes. How pathetic was that? But it was a gush of empathy and catharsis greater than any drug. His arms and now nape crawled with goose flesh, and for one fleeting moment he felt a nascent purpose beyond the childish lashing-out of hatred and violence, and a feeling other than self-pity and displacement. He felt hope.

And yet, same as every other time, he knew the beautiful moment would never last. The warm sentiment would soon be excoriated by the usual storm of bitter, barren ash.

The Imp King's obnoxious chuckle echoed through his mind. The magic of cinema and its showcasing of humanity's virtues against darkness quickly paled before a feeling of absolute nihilism.

'Don't fool yourself,' Kerzix whispered. 'You only fool for me. I allowed you a little intermission, but it's now time to wash love's sickening sugar-high from your thoughts before I gag. Bring me the last of my tributes and earn your place amongst my top heathens. You'll be a lord at my house, indulging all that itching barbarism of yours against an endless sea of the pious and the lost.'

Dave felt a sharp pang of sadness as the big-screen brand of happiness and camaraderie, a bond he could never truly experience, was getting ready to leave him.

Inside his skull was a decrepit carousel of Kerzix's design: instead of glossy wooden horses there was a fly-blown horse carcass carrying a Christian crusader, a giant rotting elephant slumped with a Buddhist monk, a jet bike with some holographic religious banner and a decaying armored alien, and some type of ruptured squid painted in luminous symbols with a magma-vent priest straddling a saddle made of pink coral.

'Stop tormenting yourself with these water-weak fantasies and fables, David. They'll rot your brain.' The king of despair appeared, walking between the spinning dead parade of religious zealots and persecutors. 'What have real people ever brought you but misery?' He hung onto the pole impaling each rider and extended one chunky white-gloved hand for Dave to reach out, grasp, and rejoin the fun. 'Nobody will ever save you, David. No heroes from the fictional dreck of your earthen entertainment. No divinity from the dogmas of your pathetic species. I'm your only god, David. I belong to the only pantheon left standing in existence. Nothing is more powerful than death.'

The carousel started to increase its speed, fast enough to induce a sense of centrifugal inertia in Dave. He wondered if his body might vomit on itself. Kerzix's gaze grew ravenously covetous, and those long fingers extended further, further, insisting upon Dave, and from up the king's frilly sleeve a barrage of memories spewed forth like Polaroids, each one failure upon failure, humiliation upon humiliation. Breaking what little remained of Dave's sinking spirit.

'Only I can offer you a place to belong.'

Dave slowly reached out towards Kerzix's enticing grasp. He was broken, exhausted, lost, and angry, but also absolutely disgusted to the point of catatonia at the works his rage had produced.

Over the soaring emotional heft of the movie's score, Dave opened his eyes. They were burning with tears and a feral light.

47

IT WAS A STANDOFF THEY couldn't possibly win, and Kozlov knew it. This was to be a running scrap, bloody and desperate, right up until they breached Kerzix's inner sanctum inside the crashed UFO. He was huddled over the swiveling turret on the roof of Calkarion's shell, which had inclined at a near 45-degree angle to allow the muzzle to poke through the crenelation of the parapet. It was a precipitous position for Kozlov, but he was well braced against the cannon's handles as he lined up the barrel sight on the Big Top scurrying vertically up the rampart.

Kozlov had been expecting some variety of ballistic munitions when he squeezed the trigger but was instead treated to an unruly barrage of whipping high-energy lines that moved like jagged lightning and were the color of molten steel. The lethal whips tore into the Big Top's face, but the assault didn't prove as deadly as Kozlov first anticipated. The material of the striped tent wasn't canvas but some type of armored flesh that did an impressive job of weathering the burn.

The attack still seemed to hurt the Big Top, but was more like a case of moderate sunburn than the melting death Kozlov had hoped for.

'We have ourselves a sideshow,' the pogoing Sagillis celebrated with his scratchy voice. 'Big Top, release my acrobats!'

The Big Top's heavy mouth flaps blew open with a discordant organ howl of fury—what Kozlov had taken for calliope music turned out to be the living tent's atonal breathing—and an exhalation of gravity-defying daredevils fired skywards to alight along the rampart's edge, surrounding Kozlov's band, while others remained in the air. In suitably morbid amusement, Kozlov saw that they were all actual bat-men, a species of dark and furry humanoids with rustling wing spans and painted smiles. The Arkhitektor seized hold of one of them as it tried to dive-bomb Kozlov, altering its trajectory just enough to make it impact into one of its shrieking brethren perched on the wall.

Calkarion produced several more mysterious marvels of engineering: a pair of rifles locked into firing positions, housed within his spider-ride's large metal pincers, and a third one held snugly in his own hands. The three muzzles unloaded a spectacular array of explosive spheres, raining plasma down onto the hordes below before giving the Big Top special attention.

Trillik charged through the grounded kite-flyers trying to bar their approach to the UFO tower, its robust iron limbs swinging and shattering bones, dense manacles zapping out agonizing electrical impulses. It made it to another of the laughing-mouth doors, this one locked tight with its barrier of clenched teeth. Trillik's rack of brains whizzed around several times, the mind with the knowledge of how to bypass the gate's security taking charge.

The iron brute inserted an electrical prod into a cavity along the gate's gumline, exposing an arcane security lock of mismatched symbols in need of pairing up. Trillik solved the puzzle without delay, parting the bared teeth.

A siren blared out from on high, and Kozlov glanced up to see an array of emergency lights flashing in urgent sequence along the UFO's discus body. Staring down at them through the circumferential window of the saucer was a silhouette, lean-boned but with puffy dress-shoulders and a wriggling headdress: Kerzix, watching as the carnival of chaos and death breached his tower door.

Kozlov resumed the energy fusillade at the Big Top's murder circus and noticed, in horror, how fast the living tent was now moving, its dozens of clown feet running up the wall towards them, tent eyes blazing like Lucifer's torment, a new sharp keening sound to the discordant calliope music. The Big Top floundered up the last four meters.

Before he could bark at Calkarion to get them the hell away from there, Kozlov felt the vehicle burst into life, the horseman's three-pronged assault now gunning down threats from all angles. Things scaled the walls in a rising tide of delirious giggles and dead eyes while cannon-men who had positioned themselves along the opposite rampart wall blasted themselves over the courtyard like bright and colorful kamikaze fireworks, attempting to hit their liege's enemies in showers of napalm embers and cooked meat.

Calkarion's spider chassis skittered with agility and grace along the rampart towards Trillik's entry point, the big wheels of the clamshell speed-bumping over the piling clown devils and shot-down acrobats. Behind them, the rampart shook with the crash landing of the Big Top, a candy-striped whale beaching itself along the high wall.

Kozlov watched over his shoulder as those blazing eyes sought them out and the mouth flaps draped open, promising only psychosis.

Shadows swirled about in the pale-green sky as more kite-men weaved away from Kozlov and Calkarion's surface-to-air assault, circling to regroup for an imminent bombardment. Their plans stalled when a cloud of confetti started to blot them out of the sky, obscuring their view. It wasn't confetti, Kozlov quickly realized. It was pollen. Kozlov had lost track of Quarmalls in all of this madness, having lost sight of him as soon as they made their frantic charge along the rampart for the tower. Now his searching gaze found him. Quarmalls hadn't moved. He'd stayed behind, standing his ground, smack-bang in the middle of the rampart between his retreating allies and the encroaching Big Top. Kozlov tried to yell out to him, to tell him not to do what he knew he was going to do. Quarmalls, waving his ringlet arms around in wide circles, showered more and more of his pollen stores into the air, blinding, disorienting, and even inflicting caustic damage to some of the species of conscripted jester. Kozlov was losing sight of the tent charging after them like a runaway steam train as the dispersing pollen started to swell into a solid wall of obscuring color, but a closing gap still remained, just long enough for him to see Quarmalls' depleted body begin to judder, his dandelion head sprinkling its seeds away on the breeze, and the last of his body's pollen content erupting like a powder keg, his empty tubule frame collapsing in a springy heap. The calliope music seemed to scream, if such a thing were possible.

'An honorable end,' the Arkhitektor said, snatching an incoming can-non-man out of the air. The flying bomber had several lit belts of dyna-mite and other powdered explosives around his torso. The Arkhitektor redirected the bomb-man towards the wall of giant eyeballs still relaying their live-action snuff films. Several of the eyes ruptured like squashed grapes; others scarred over instantly, blinded like cataracts. With a great strain, he pulled with everything he had, toppling the eye-frame over, each remaining eyeball landing with a squelch that could be heard over the din of war. Several of the eyeballs rolled loose from their veiny bear-ings, bouldering through stilt-men and other bizarre sideshows.

Sagillis was keeping pace with the invading party, barking orders as his pogo steered him clear of the giant rolling eyeballs bowling over his forces. Calkarion ground to a sharp halt, the sudden lurching motion nearly tossing Kozlov from the wagon's roof. Kozlov was about to voice his displeasure but then saw the fury in the horse-man's stare as he con-verged his three cannon muzzles on the gremlin war general, still hop-ping ludicrously on his grisly pogo stick. Kozlov knew there must still be some unresolved issue at play between Calkarion and his former slave master. Calkarion fired, timing his salvo so that it would hit Sagillis as he bounced to his apex. But Sagillis impressively corkscrewed between the hail of plasma-ball shot with smug showmanship and landed deci-sively upon the rampart to bar their way, utterly fearless, or utterly psy-chotic. He let his pogo stick fall to the ground.

'Calkarion. Trillik. Welcome back, traitors,' Sagillis said. 'It's nice of you to martyr yourselves in such fashion. None of you were worth the trouble of hunting down after you ran away from my circus.' The gremlin waved a scaly claw to the destruction his ex-employees had wrought. 'Not a bad effort. I suppose you whelps were stronger than I gave you credit for. But for the jolly pleasure of my king,' he said, one sharp yellow nail pointing up to the shadow of the imp lord dancing about the space-ship in frustration, or perhaps it was mad merriment, 'I'll be disembow-eling all of you now.'

The Arkhitektor, plainly impatient with this prince of fools, hauled Sagillis over with an invisible lasso of force and began to squeeze.

But if Sagillis was in pain, he didn't show it.

It was impossible to make any sort of meaningful eye contact with a walking tank full of brains from any distance, but Kozlov hoped his own species was easier to understand; he nodded and, thankfully, Trillik took his meaning, turning its back on them and entering the rampart tower to climb the stairs up to where the Rictus Folly and the monarch of unanswered prayers waited.

'You can either help us in fighting alongside us or by dying,' Kozlov told Sagillis.

'A human!' Sagillis wheezed laughter. 'What a small universe this is. My lord is having a word in my ear as we speak. Turns out I have another matter to attend to on your dying idiotic rock.'

The Arkhitektor continued to squeeze. 'This end is too good for you,' he said.

'This isn't my end,' Sagillis said. 'It's yours. I'll be going now. But please, make yourselves at home.' Just before the gremlin blipped out of sight, it pointed over their shoulders.

Kozlov turned, teeth bared in anger, expecting that they had come this far only to fall from some mischievous miscreant's sneak attack.

Through the last trails of bright pollen and acrid smoke, two torchlights burned bright like dragon eyes through a battleground pall, and with a hungry speed the Big Top, scarred and blistered, darted forth, its entrance flaps peeling back to show a dark and hypnotic gullet. The huge mouth of the tent swallowed them all whole.

48

LYDE WAS AWESTRUCK BY THE interior of the Gilded Hypnos. Having climbed the glowing golden steps of the pyramid to the colonnaded plateau, he'd craned his neck dramatically to stare up at the vast, beating black wings of the Obsidian Extremis and the rainbow mist girding the two pyramid tips until he grew disoriented; such heights made him think about the time he was a little kid seeing the Empire State Building for the first time, staring up at it from street level and trying to imagine he was wall-crawling it like Spider-Man. Thankfully Spector's directions didn't require him to climb the exteriors of these staggering structures. After walking between the two rows of looming judgmental statues to enter the Hypnos, he'd thought he would have seen enough to prepare him for what lay within. He was wrong.

A veritable army of weird alien statues, sculpted from unknown elements and giant in proportion, stood on glowing plinths around the perimeter of the chamber, those with obvious eyes glaring defiantly as though at their imprisonment. His anxious gaze sought out the Coma Weaver amongst their number, but there were so many, and the chamber so vast, that he didn't have time to stand around and gawp. When he managed to finally tear his gaze from the imposing monuments, he saw the small form of Ramaliak in the center of the chamber, standing before what appeared to be an expansive, waist-high model city of translucent geometric shapes; over to his right was some sort of small glass altar, or rather, some type of glass table.

Clyde descended the steep stairs and made his way to the perimeter of the translucent dream machines, which rang with a pleasant symphony of ethereal glassy notes.

Ramaliak turned at Clyde's approach.

'What is all this?' Clyde asked. The glass structures were even more beautiful up close, a crystal city imbued with its own pale lucent glow, bound within a shimmering membranous dome.

'This is the Oneiroic Hemisphere.' Ramaliak ran a hoof along the semi-transparent membrane of the Hemisphere with the sound of a wet finger rimming a wine glass. 'Collectively, those translucent polyhedrons are responsible for regulating the memory catalogues and the sheer raw phantasmagoric power fueling the subconscious plane, those dual dreaming layers that protectively envelop the Median's core. Individually, those translucent boxes are small in construction, but are mighty batteries; proof, if it were needed, that great things can come in small packages.'

He then pointed a hoof straight up.

Perhaps a mile above them and the sweeping crystalline vastness, the tip of the Hypnos vanished into the strobing rainbow mists of the newly deceased.

'The crossover,' Ramaliak said. 'With each new death, a length of the deceased's soul thread is clipped from the Median and exported into Erebus.' Clyde watched the cloud of coalescing souls, stunned by the morbid beauty of the process. 'Each of them is funneled through vents in the Hypnos' peak, into the vacuum of the Obsidian Extremis.'

Clyde's humility in the presence of such an event darkened as he watched the silent beating of the inverted black pyramid's giant wings.

'The Extremis,' Ramaliak said, noticing Clyde's disquietude. 'The origin point of Charon's entire soul transportation network.'

Clyde forced his eyes from the Extremis back to the rainbow palette of clipped souls, wondering which of them were Bentley's victims.

'Why are we in here? Isn't Bentley's thread out there somewhere?' Clyde asked, gesturing towards the nigh infinity of threaded souls out beyond the Hypnos' entrance.

His trained eyes, no longer focusing on the splendor around him, caught a flicker of movement in the corner of the chamber. There was nothing there. It must have been a trick of light.

Ramaliak's hoof brought up a pair of shearing pincers as if in answer, holding them out for Clyde to accept. 'These once belonged to a diamond-head.'

Clyde accepted the tool and inspected it in muted uncertainty. 'Once belonged? How exactly did you come by this thing?'

'Never mind that,' Ramaliak said dismissively. 'Okay, there's two parts to this process. Kerzix's poison runs deep. You'll need to scrape away the infection from Mr. Bentley's thread—you won't miss it; it looks like cords of dark, oily filth. Those pincers will scrape any clots away like butter.'

'What if I accidentally cut his thread?'

'It's easy, Clyde. I wouldn't let you do it if I didn't trust you.'

Clyde glanced at the elegantly curved scimitar pincers in his hand. 'And what are you going to do?'

'My part is a little trickier. I have to enter here to check the dream circuitry, so to speak,' he said, gesturing to the Oneiroic Hemisphere. 'Sift through Bentley's memory file, try to make sure Kerzix hasn't introduced any deeply embedded indoctrination—the sort of suggestions, or sometimes even altered memories, a psychic invader can implant to stoke certain tendencies in their subjects. Think of it this way: if you're cutting away the rotten tissue, I'm the antibiotic making sure nothing malignant remains after surgery. If we're going to do this, we should at least be thorough. But that doesn't mean I'll be taking my sweet time either. I'll need to replace Bentley's thread before it's reported absent. Don't want Dremel coming down here.'

'I'm not planning on dragging things out either,' Clyde said. 'Any minute now, Rose will be taking aim at Bentley's head, and vice versa.'

'Over there.' Ramaliak's hoof pointed to the translucent table, where lay a single neon-blue soul thread with a lot of slack in its length, as though it had been expertly teased out of its woven tapestry and then neatly clipped. Sections of it were coated in dark viscous smears as advertised.

'You cut it from its stitching? Why isn't he dead, and why isn't it getting sucked up into—' Clyde was about to point up to the converging pyramid tips when Ramaliak interjected.

'A thread can be removed for limited periods of time, like putting a severed limb on ice. It can be mended back into its stitching. If done quickly. Now,' those big mammalian eyes leaned in close to Clyde, 'we're on a clock, remember?'

Clyde grasped the diamond-head's severed shears tightly and took hold of Bentley's soul thread like it was a venom-loaded snake, hoping Kerzix's malign influence couldn't somehow jump from Bentley to infect him. Being cursed with one dream parasite was problematic enough.

He started to gingerly scrape one of the shears' keen crescent edges against a large grayish stain. Ramaliak was right: the nasty stuff came away easily enough. Clyde went to work on another large stain, trying not to think about his unconscious body lying defenseless in the cinema. To say nothing of the physical threat Bentley posed to Nat and Rose. He was almost tempted to cut the line altogether, just to put an end to it all.

But he didn't. Instead, he worked harder. Whittling away at Kerzix's corruption.

. . .

CLYDE WAS SO engrossed in his task that he didn't see the diamond-head prowling closer, padding silently, its sightless head drawn to the criminal.

49

DAVE DIDN'T KNOW WHAT HAD happened. It was all so fast. One moment he was being pulled under the black tide of anger, the impish voice gurgling through the frenzy, and the next he was back in the dark cinema, being ripped from his seat by unseen hands and dangled over the amphitheater's balcony, aloft like a dark star backlit by cinematic heroics. Dave didn't know what the hell was holding him in mid-air, locking his limbs in place, but his body started to turn around, allowing him to see the cause of his problems. There were six problems, but he didn't recognize four of them: a stranger heavily concealed in mismatched clothing, and waiting in the shadowy aisle, three awfully mutilated ghosts. But Dave remembered the two women: one was the tattooed Filipina who'd chased after him in his apartment building; the other was the jacked blonde who'd hit him with a grenade launcher. And she was just as quick on the trigger now. Not a grenade this time, but a shotgun blast.

Dave felt his body buck. The impact was like the time those pushing and shoving assholes in high school accidentally bumped him in front of a teacher's car for a few good laughs; a brief warm numbness, and then pain.

But that was then. This was now. How many times had he been shot today? He could soak up anything that was thrown at him and tear through these inferiors like paper. His blood rained down onto the empty seats below the balcony, and Dave smiled as the wounds healed over.

'Don't let them cage you,' Kerzix derided. 'You have an audience, so do something! Put those gifts to some use and give us an encore.'

Dave's smile turned to teeth-baring hatred as he tried to break free of the invisible restraints, but his hatred and power were not quite enough, and the Imp King admonished him again. Belittled him to stoke his fury.

Meanwhile, the platinum-blonde killer jacked another round into the large barrel and blasted him again as Agent Hobo continued to hold him in place with a confident hand gesture. Something gleamed metallically in his other hand. This unknown object left Hobo's hand and floated towards Dave.

Shotgun Blonde ripped another blast through Dave's body, earning a few condemnatory glances from Tattoo and Hobo; the three ghosts hovering in the wings didn't offer much of a reaction to the proceedings. Dave had lost sight of Hobo's floating metal device.

Another shotgun blast.

Blood showered down, flecked the large screen. Wounds healed. Dave tensed and flexed, and for a moment he thought Agent Hobo was loosening his grip on him, but he wasn't. Dave knew it was all his own doing. He was a Spark, for fuck's sake! Talbot had told him how powerful their progenitors were. Cosmic beings created to repel the forces of death and annihilation. He wasn't a Luminary, but even a Spark sure as shit wasn't going to be beaten like this!

Fists clenched, his arms strained against the inertia, moved a few inches, and then a few more. Shoulders, knees, torso, all began to slowly thrum with repressed motion.

His hand started to vibrate, the first traces of coruscating rouge ribboning his knuckles and forearms.

Something cold and sharp sank into the back of his neck, not biting deep enough to hurt but certainly enough to be uncomfortable. And suddenly his thoughts started to flicker and discombobulate, the chuckling imp's voice sliding in and out like a weak radio signal, a crackly susurrus.

Kerzix was still ranting and raving, trying to press Dave's inadequacies, but Dave couldn't fully hear the Imp King's tirade; he did, however, manage to catch a couple of fragments of the excited babbling, something about their connection being tampered with, and how invaders were storming his royal tower.

The raspy voice told Dave one more thing: there was assistance inbound to aid him in murdering his group of would-be assassins. This was to be the end of the line for Dave's earthly servitude. One final tribute of souls, and what a tribute it would be.

Dave tried to argue back, not wanting the help, not wanting to choke on any more bile and hate, only wanting for everything to end. The psychic confusion was becoming too much to bear, and Dave found himself sliding uncontrollably towards catatonia. But before the black hole could swallow him, whatever it was that had clamped itself to the nape of his neck faltered, not powerful enough to keep Kerzix from delivering one final almighty twist of the key.

Dave let out a furious scream like a trapped animal.

A shotgun blast punched through his chest.

He renewed his efforts to break the invisible hold, hands wreathed in ruby trails.

Shotgun blast.

A tear opened in the air behind Dave, a portal superimposed over the movie screen. The tear in reality revealed a pulsing darkness within, through which a horrid creature catapulted. Sagillis landed perfectly onto the brass rail of the balcony amphitheater, yellow cat's-eyes sizing up the Hourglass agents. The unexpected visitor's arrival threw the agents for a moment, but not as much as what followed in its wake: a giant writhing tent, bursting through the hole like a violent birthing, stretching the fabric of the portal, the leathery tent peeling open to cough forth a battalion of gurning horrors scrabbling over the balcony seats and packing out the house.

With one final animalistic roar, Dave broke Agent Hobo's hold on him. Kerzix's poison tongue slithered along Dave's brain, speaking of how spineless and submissive his enemies thought he was. He grabbed the brass rail before he could fall onto the seats below, then heaved himself up and over the rail, feeling some of the bullets still lodged in his body. He just about managed to land in a crouch, coughing a single mouthful of black blood onto the old carpet before tearing the device from the back of his neck and showing it to his enemies before smashing it to pieces with a single blow.

50

ALL WAS DARKNESS. **A**ND **THEN** Kozlov's weary eyes started to make out the forms moving about inside the tent. Two exhaustingly long files of big-footed oddities. Clowns, he realized, only unlike the garish paint and pageantry of the Marotte Marauders, these travelers were naturally corpse-white or pastel-blue-skinned, wild tangles of luridly colored hair, grotesquely engorged noses, large bulbous eyes perfect for low-light environments, and split-wide mouths. Kozlov suspected that this species, wherever they originated from, were the inspiration for the entire sub-culture of entertainers throughout human history.

He had been expecting death inside the innards of this tent, but the procession of clowns merely continued to stand in two parallel lines, marching when necessary and standing still when not; they didn't even pay any attention to the newcomers. But death was in here; it just needed a moment to prepare. Kozlov noted the dense but malleable ground, muscular and living, not unlike a giant tongue. Then, as if to confirm his suspicions, fire-breathers spat gouts of flame into the featureless void, illuminating the sodden, straw-carpeted mouth. The balls of fire shone in the enlarged glassy eyes of several scores of murderous entertainers who were now uncovered from the shadows. The source of the odious stench also became clear. It wasn't the tent's innards, and it wasn't the enslaved clowns caught somewhere between life and death. The reek belonged to the creature issuing a great roar from the furthest depths of the throat. The thing lumbered towards Kozlov and his companions, its hideousness finally ignited into stark relief with another belch from the fire-eaters: it was two-headed, six-pawed, and powerful enough to shatter bone and shred flesh with a single bite or swipe, a grizzly bear fit for hell itself. At first glance, Kozlov thought the beast's tamer was saddled on the animal's back until he discovered there were no legs dangling against the monster's powerful flanks. The tamer was a nascent growth protruding from the beast's spine, an emaciated chalk-white thing with a lumpen head and a patented smile of oversized yellow teeth.

The last defenses of the Big Top were encroaching towards Kozlov, the Arkhitektor, and Calkarion when they just as suddenly appeared to stop, heads tilting as though tuning in to some important decree only they could hear.

From what seemed to be an impossibly far-away distance, the tent's flaps drew open, revealing a tiny light of freedom. With a confused babble of whoops and manic hollering—and in one instance, a dual raw-throated bear roar—the final regiment of carnival horrors raced forth towards this unknown calling. Kozlov and his companions attempted to follow after them but found themselves running in space, helpless as the mob disappeared from view. The drapes closed, and once again they were left with only the mechanically-moving mime procession.

A torch beam clicked on from Calkarion's chariot, passing along the puffy-sleeved arms, chests, and shoulders of the ambulatory clowns. After a few false starts, the beam found what it was searching for: a sort of dangling ripcord, but not one of leather, nylon, or even rope; this one glistened, slick and engorged.

Calkarion's oscillating chest screen lit up marquee-bright in the shadows. 'Because of my mechanical knowhow, I used to ride alone, but I have been in here once before. That cord is our only way out of this place.'

'Is that what I think it is?' the Arkhitektor asked. It seemed like it could be the tent's epiglottis.

'Is this an actual stomach?' Kozlov asked. 'We pull that, it vomits us out. What about stomach acid?'

'Big Top doesn't consume for sustenance. There's no stomach; this is only a vehicle for Sagillis' forces. That cord is a kill switch, put there by

Sagillis so he could have his transport team here destroy the vehicle when he grows bored of it; he enjoys creating new rides to parade throughout Kerzix's lands.' A complicated look shadowed Calkarion's face. 'Pulling that cord isn't enough. It needs to be held until the last moment. First, mobility will stop, then the entire system will start to shut down. The kill switch is specially designed for the clown procession—at the last second, they'll vanish through a built-in trapdoor bespoke only for them. After that, the Big Top's crude mind will cease functioning, and the structural integrity will collapse. The full weight of the tent is denser than you might think, an armored material. We'll be crushed.'

'Then I'll do it,' the Arkhitektor said without delay.

'You don't understand,' Calkarion replied. 'Even a spirit can't survive the process. Shutting down the ride creates a secondary trapdoor after the clowns are ejected. The second trapdoor becomes a vacuum for everything else inside, a high-pressure pinhole that evacuates everything, flesh or no flesh, into unknown space.'

The Arkhitektor grunted disdainfully. 'Changes nothing. You two need to help Trillik. Get the Needle's location. You continue on. That's all that matters.'

'I won't let you die here, not after everything we've been through,' Kozlov argued.

'Have you become so accustomed to my presence that you have forgotten? I'm already dead, Konstantin. Been dead a long time now. We both knew this journey would demand the most from us. I'd be proud to end it here, should it mean you can carry on that much further. To the bloody end.'

Was that true? Kozlov wondered. Had he spent so much time carrying his mentor's spirit around inside him that it scared him to accept that from this moment on, he would truly be alone? Pushing through hell's adversities without his most trusted and reliable friend. His chest hurt, and he almost allowed an unbecoming expression of love and despair to crack his composure. That wasn't what his life's lessons had instilled in him. He grumbled something, feeling older and frailer than ever, and even without words, the Arkhitektor understood what his protégé felt.

'You were my greatest pupil. You did the Rising Path proud. Now you must go and see our crusade through.' The senior monk met Calkarion's warm equine gaze. 'Thank you. You have been a noble companion. I hope you find the atonement you're searching for, but know that you are a hero to me. Your people would be proud of you. You both look out for each other.' The Arkhitektor raised his hand in farewell, then slid an invisible grip around the kill switch dangling high above the acrobats' high wires. 'Get ready.'

Angry and pained, Kozlov jumped upon the back of Calkarion's chariot, not wanting to look away from the man who had shaped him more than any other.

'Konstantin?' the Arkhitektor called. 'One last thing.'

Kozlov clenched his jaws tight to stymie the weakness of sorrow.

'Liev. That was my civilian name. A lifetime ago.' With that, the Arkhitektor pulled the kill switch.

All at once, the hacienda of black mirth and monsters started to come apart at the seams. The two clown columns dropped out of existence, and the tent's mouth flaps hung open in slack dementia. It seemed so far away, but Calkarion revved the engine, and the metal spider arms scurried forth with reckless speed along the giant tongue. Making it to the mouth seemed impossible as the tongue started to spasm and roll like a foul sea, Calkarion's forelegs and wheels straining for traction. A jarring shudder slammed the vehicle, pitching Kozlov over the side. One heavy gauntlet lashed out blindly, barely managing to snatch hold of a bar welded to the shell's aft. A bolt of pain raced along his right shoulder from the sudden impact of hanging on as his legs dragged along the rough, shifting tongue. Grunting in strain, he was trying to climb his way back aboard. Heaped on the roof, ignoring the pain in his shoulder, Kozlov raised a hand in farewell to his friend, snarling back the hot pressure of tears welling in his eyes as he watched Liev shrink in the distance. Reaching the mouth, the escape vehicle launched outwards, not back onto the parapet of the monarch's palace but into an entirely different but no less deadly melee. Kozlov thought it was a theater at first before realizing it was a cinema. And taking stock of the two sides warring with each other, his attention was drawn first to the cinema screen, overlaid with a shrinking portal showing Kerzix's stronghold, and then the familiar faces of several American agents who had once saved him and Liev from a terrible beast.

51

CLYDE WAS MAKING STEADY PROGRESS, each cut easily scraping away more of the carbon-colored tendrils. They fell to the ground, corroding into nothing. He had no way of knowing if his efforts had yet to make any difference to Bentley's self-control in the waking world, and several times he felt his emotions getting the better of him, envisioning Ace lying in his hospital bed, becoming a vegetable; imagining Bentley killing Nat or Rose; and he had to pause a moment before he cut through Bentley's line.

It was during one such pause that something slammed into his back, almost severing Bentley's thread for him.

It didn't so much hurt as confound; Clyde wasn't sure if pain was even possible for immaterial forms. Physics were debatable in a realm of the subconscious mind, so perhaps it was purely a matter of primeval emotion and mood, but Clyde felt the dreadful weight pinning his back. His panicked peripheral vision told him it was a diamond-head. He caught a fleeting glimpse of its hooked limbs—and one of its paired shears—expertly, delicately latching for purchase on the temple's woven floor. He opened his mouth to call out for Ramaliak, then reconsidered. Ramaliak had done enough so far. Risked enough for him already. Besides, Clyde wanted to see if a mortal tinged with a Babylonian dream demon could slay a diamond-head. The creature's weight on his back didn't seem to be moving, and it had already had ample time to destroy him had it chosen to do so. But it seemed to be waiting, crouched like a guard dog awaiting its master's edict.

Was it sending out an alert? Calling for reinforcements?

Clyde reached out to grab the fallen diamond-head claws, but they were out of reach, no matter how much he strained. Worse, he couldn't push himself up beneath the guardian's weight. Panic started to set in. Thoughts of either being slain right here and now by this beast, or by Dremel and his cohorts. Worse still, he imagined the trouble that would come down on Ramaliak. Thought about Bentley rampaging, hurting Nat.

A tingle shot through Clyde, deep enough to send shudders through his entire body. He didn't know what it was. But it somehow created enough space for him to roll onto his shoulder, and then his back.

His right hand was gloved in cold white flame. Without thinking, he pushed the burning hand into the diamond-head's abdomen, dragging it across, eviscerating it. Despite lacking a mouth, the thing shrieked— an odd sound, almost digital—and reared backwards. No viscera spilled out, only a blanket of cold orange embers trailing away on an unfelt breeze, which quickly became a full-body cascade until there was absolutely no sign a diamond-head had ever been there. Except, Clyde noticed tensely, for its two soul-cleaving tools. What the hell could he do with them? Bury them? Give them to Ramaliak for safekeeping? He glanced at his hand. Normal again.

If it was to be a problem, it would be one he would deal with later. He got back to his feet, casting around for more diamond-heads but finding none. There was no sign of Ramaliak either.

He grabbed Bentley's soul, holding it taut, but before he could set to work slicing off the rest of the corruption, another tingling surfaced in his fingers, his arm, shoulder, right into the core of his very being. He didn't know why he did it, why he was risking it again, but he placed the diamond-head's cleaver on the ground and held his free hand over the soul thread. His memory of waking the Hangman from Charon's psychic grip at Elzinga Asylum crept through his thoughts, and Clyde watched in astonishment as his hand seemed to operate on some primal instinct, fingers glowing with white fire, gently singeing and unknotting the corrupt windings of Kerzix from the stuff of Bentley's thread.

52

KEV HAD SEEN WEIRD, AND he had seen weird. Correction: he thought he had seen weird until now. But he had never watched a living circus tent burst into this reality and regurgitate an inter-species squad of murderous entertainers. Yet if there was one thing he had learned since joining Hourglass, it was to file away any questions until after the danger had passed.

The balcony was a cramped environment in which to fight, made worse by the poor lighting, number of combatants, and multitudes of seats. So the first thing he did was tear out an entire row of seats in a screech and bang of breaking metal and crash them into the gremlin leaping and slicing about the place like an enthusiastic crackpot dictator. Out of the twenty-some hurled seats, only the last one hit, but the heavy plastic seat back smashed the circus ringleader into the high ceiling, creating a shower of plaster and relief molding. Kev used the seat to hold the gremlin in place, watching it squirm and try to free itself. The creature was tougher than Kev had expected from its scrawny build, but at least he'd made a lot more room for his team to do their job. The movie's big CGI climax was drowned out by Rose's angry shotgun, still bleeding Bentley but not stopping him, and the ISU yelling commands as they punched and dragged the long-suffering souls from the bodies of the outlandish killers closing in. To the team's relief, the souls of these savage lunatics were not under any higher form of protection, allowing the ghost unit to knock and drag out as many of them as they could. The relief was short-lived, as the blood-chilling two-headed roar of the devil bear introduced itself.

Kev finished crushing the gremlin against the ceiling, satisfied to see that he had at least squeezed some blood from it instead of only damaging more of the decorative ceiling molding. He brought the gremlin down, like a fairground hammer, straight into the fiendishly ugly head of the bear-rider, breaking their skulls, or at the very least knocking them both out. But even with the rider flopping about on the two-headed bear's back like a superfluous appendage, the brutal animal was still on the offensive.

Nat was using the audible chaos to charge herself up into a stadium rock show on two legs. Her bass pulsed like an otherworldly rifle, light and lethal sonic booms breaking the ranks of the giggling maniacs climbing over the corpses of their fellow entertainers. She didn't seem to hear the bear barreling down on her from the other side of the balcony, its tremendous charging weight lost amidst the sonic quaking of her bass. Kev stopped it in its tracks, flipping it into the air seconds before one huge swiping claw would have separated Nat's head from her shoulders. Kev was about to see if he could choke a living tent with a two-headed bear when he was forced to do a double-take: speeding out of the now sagging and deflating tent was somebody he had been wanting to see again since the completion of his first assignment—Konstantin Kozlov. ..and riding a hybrid horse-man-metallic-spider-vehicle, no less. The bold entrance had the metal spider thing awkwardly scrabbling into a bad turn, the hefty weight of the armored clamshell crashing through a large swath of seats and smashing a hole through the balcony's rear wall.

The excitement of this unexpected arrival didn't last long. Kev watched a shadowy figure leap across the piles of dead clowns towards Nat, one clenched fist lit-up like a crimson lightbulb in the flashing gloom. Natalie managed to turn her head just enough to slip the worst of the impact but still collapsed under the devastating power of Bentley's fist. He was on top of her, frantic and hyped, his entire forearm now channeling his dreadful capacity for destruction, readying its awful true potential. Kev didn't know if Clyde was remotely even close to success or not, but the chance to spare David Bentley's soul had passed. Nat was in danger. And Kev was going to break Bentley's neck like a chicken.

Bentley's fist was poised like a red lantern. And then the lantern suddenly went out. And even in the flickering shadows, Kev saw the doubt and confusion wash over Bentley's face.

.   .   .

THE EFFECT WAS akin to being startled out of a nightmare. Reality was a cold, gray wall of shame and horror at the things he knew himself to have done. So much death. Cold-blooded murder. Dave's face twisted in disbelief as he stared down at the young woman he was kneeling over, about to strike her with the unwanted power from dead gods. Then he recognized her. Paused. Her eyes flashed violet, and a ripple shook the air, launching him in a twelve-foot-high arc. He scraped the ceiling and came down, away from the shattered balcony and into the dark, empty seats and the dead scattered sideshow below.

.   .   .

CLYDE DROPPED THE last of the vile, smoldering cutlets to the floor with exhaustion, watching them wither away into nothing, hoping this had been worth it. The cold burn left his fingers. He stared up at the never-ending cosmic light show swirling into the great maw at the apogee of the Hypnos and wondered if the reason he felt so tired was something to do with his coming into contact with Kerzix's corruptive influence, or perhaps just being in the vicinity of such a sacred and powerful place as this. The cause of it dawned on him, bolstered by gut reaction. It was the diamond-head's scarring. He was fortunate to have cut short the creature's mauling before it had managed to destroy his dream avatar—and ergo, his soul—which would have cast his soul into Erebus, leaving his lifeless body in the Encore Cinema for his team to take home in a bodybag.

Feeling woozy, with a sensation like lightning running a jagged circuit along his back and shoulders, he glanced at his ordinary-looking hands as though they belonged to someone else. Then, from within the membrane encapsulating the Oneiroic Hemisphere, the goat-man materialized as if from thin air.

Before Clyde could express joy and relief at his friend's return, he was stricken with an awful sense of being watched. Glancing around, he found it wasn't another diamond-head creeping up on him. His gaze, almost magnetically, was pulled to a repugnant form deep in the ranks of the perimeter statues. Even separated by the vast space between them, he recognized it at once. Much larger than Trujillo's file photo. Its crooked body, multiple limbs, and many merciless eyes. The Weaver. Frozen in some form of stasis of unknown mineral or energy. Frozen … but could he feel it? Its eyes needling him, scraping across his soul? Or was it simply his fear?

Ramaliak's voice traveled to him from what sounded like worlds away, and Clyde felt a rush of vertigo that put him on his knees. Something started to gingerly probe at Clyde's back—hooves, Clyde realized. New sensations, pleasant and unpleasant alike, raced up and down his back. Clyde didn't know what was happening, but he thought he heard Ramaliak tell him he was going to be okay.

With a tremendous head-rush through darkness and neon glitter, Clyde opened his eyes to what felt like the worst hangover he had ever had. He had no idea where he was, his sight so gummy it could pass for conjunctivitis, but with a quick rub from his thumb and forefinger it passed quickly, allowing him to make out a few old movie posters framed on the gray tile walls. He pushed himself up, finding dry blood crusting his nostrils and upper lip, but he'd left the back pain in the Median. That was a relief, but at the same time, he was anxious to call Spector and find out if they were in the clear, or if they had just fucked things up spectacularly. But for now, he ran, charging down the corridor, searching for his team.

. . .

KEV SAW THE look of confusion on the Russian monk's face and imagined his own must be identical at seeing Kozlov come riding in on a mechanical horse-man like a fugitive from a sci-fi western. Clyde probably would have loved this, Kev thought.

'New York?' Kozlov asked, recognizing Kev and surveying the slaughtered remains of Sagillis' nomadic war party.

The sounds of combat had left the screening room in a cloistered ring-ing din, with only the dramatic score of the movie's closing credits to fill the ambience.

'I've been dying to see you again,' Kev admitted, not hiding his excite-ment.

'Me too.' Rose jacked her last shotgun round into the chamber, bring-ing the barrel down on Kozlov. 'You're making some very big waves in the Null. It was a mistake to let you go last time. Not today. By authority of Hourglass, you're to stand down now.'

'I don't recognize your authority,' Kozlov said plainly. 'But I recognize your face too. Most of your faces,' he added, spreading his glance from Rose across the whole ISU, but seemed to draw a blank on Nat. 'You have my gratitude, but I'm sorry to say I won't be repaying you by sur-rendering.'

Kev stared past Kozlov to the portal window showing a rampart tower capped by a busted-up flying saucer. 'You heading back?' he asked the monk and his alien steed.

'The fuck he is,' Rose grated, her shotgun not wavering an inch. 'We've had enough rocky roads lately, and your pissing about with the biggest dogs in the graveyard is really going to fuck things up for everyone. And I'm talking *everyone.*'

'Don't attempt to educate me on what I'm doing,' Kozlov sneered. With a gauntleted gesture, he waved at the piles of Kerzix's broken fools. 'You're making enough problems without me.'

'These assholes invaded here.'

Calkarion's oscillating board lit up. 'Kerzix will send more if we don't stop him now.'

'Are you sure you're on the right side?' Rose asked, examining the clown paint on the strange bugle-horned horse head. Calkarion didn't dignify her question, but instead, the nimble mechanical forelegs of his ride were busy lining him and Kozlov up to face the portal, which now appeared to be constricting slowly.

'One more move!' Rose yelled, tracking Kozlov's head with the shotgun.

The gears of the spider legs started to turn. Rose squeezed the trigger, or she tried to. It was locked in position. There was only one explanation.

'Kev!' she shouted. 'You're really fucking up here! We can't let them carry on. If word of this gets out to the highest seats in the Order, it'll be the end of everything. They'll wage war.'

'Then we had better be quiet.' Kev yanked the shotgun from her hands, making sure to keep the trigger rigid so Rose's incredible strength would sooner break the trigger than get a shot off. He looked to Nat, seeing the uncertainty in her eyes. 'Tell Clyde I'm sorry I couldn't wait. Good luck to you guys. Look out for each other. Maybe I'll see you in a better place one day.'

'Kev . . . ?' Nat looked like she wanted to say more but couldn't find the words.

Rose launched herself at Kozlov, trying to stop him with her bare hands, but Kev stopped her in her tracks. Sarge and Darcy swept towards Kev, their expressions indicating to Kev that they were none too happy to be doing so. Barros was quicker, throwing a sucker punch and an elbow at the pair of them, stunning more than hurting them but providing the brief window Kev needed. Calkarion's mech chariot launched itself off the balcony, taking Kozlov and Kev with it. And not only them. Barros was there too, along for the ride as the chariot pierced the closing membrane between this world and the Null.

. . .

CLYDE FELT SOMETHING on his way to Screen 12. It was an unnerving sensation, a tenuous fluttering rooted somewhere deep in his mind that gave him an instant sinking sensation. He had felt it before, and knew what it meant.

Kev.

He sprinted for Screen 12 and burst through the doors just in time to see Kev riding on the back of some strange vehicle with Barros, speeding along a stone rampart towards an even stranger tower. Then the portal sealed shut, and all he could see was the last of the movie's credits rolling up the screen. Clyde wanted to believe his eyes were playing tricks on him, but his heart knew they weren't. Kev was gone. His best friend had left him, but for where? Was that the Null he'd ridden off into? If so, unlike last time, he wasn't in the company of an Hourglass agent with

hoodoo-powered tracking minerals in her blood, meaning Director Trujillo and his hoodoo clan couldn't zero in on his position to perform a
swift exfiltration. Kev and Barros were on their own over there.

In the gloom of the theater, Clyde picked out piles of bodies that
could have been the result of a conjoined circus and freak show explosion. His eyes tracked a small movement from within the rows of seats.
Not everything down here was dead. Bentley staggered up onto un-
steady legs, one hand braced on a seat back. His other hand was lifting
some hideous scaly creature up by its flamboyant formal vest. It looked
like a gremlin. Whatever it was, it appeared to be in worse shape than
Bentley.

. . .

CLARITY HAD RETURNED for Dave. His latest physical wounds had
healed, but he figured that if he so much as jogged, he would rattle like
a coin purse with all the bullets he was carrying inside him. But that
meant nothing compared to the absolute disgust he felt at himself and
at the manipulator still cackling inside his head, still trying to goad his
worst impulses into furious fits of anger. But for some inexplicable reason, Dave found it much easier to ignore Kerzix now.

He lifted Sagillis off the floor, finding the creature heavier than it
looked, and saw the craven inner workings of its nasty little mind playing
out in its crafty yet fearful eyes. It was trying to barter, wheel and deal,
every desperate trick it could think of. Dave wasn't listening to it. Without
drama, he loaded up one single, devastating shot, and his knuckles burst
out the back of its scaled head in a small eruption of viscous goo.

Dave dropped Sagillis' slack body and saw an unfamiliar, solitary
man standing in the aisle watching him, soon flanked by the remnants
of the Hourglass team as they made their way from the balcony amphitheater. They could kill him here and now. And he didn't care. It would
be doing him a favor. Then he remembered that it would mean his soul
would be sent straight back to Erebus. Back to Kerzix...or someplace
even worse.

He closed his eyes and held his hands in supplication, hoping the tattooed Spark had the power to do what so many others couldn't.

Instead, he felt his arms twist behind his back, the young black guy cuffing his wrists sharply.

'I'm sorry about hitting you.' Dave could hardly look the female Spark in the eye.

She shrugged it off. 'I've taken worse shots in mosh pits.'

53

'**I** **NEVER EXPECTED TO SEE** either of you again,' Kozlov shouted so that Kev could hear him over the shuddering bangs of Calkarion's vehicle as it clambered up Kerzix's tower with a daring enthusiasm that bordered on reckless. 'Too late for either of you to turn back. I hope you know what you're doing.'

'Something worthwhile,' Kev said. He and Barros were trailing after the vehicle, keeping watch for any aerial attacks. 'You're looking for the Needle. We're in.'

Kozlov, harnessed inside the shell, gave the newcomers a terse briefing of the madness they had just entered. 'We have no intention of fighting Kerzix, and most likely wouldn't stand a chance against him,' he finished. 'This strike is about distraction and discretion.'

'You need to look up the word discretion,' Barros said.

'Not us,' Kozlov said, his voice warbling from the spider's shuddering vertical ascent. 'We're the distraction. We have an ally on the inside, a former security officer of Kerzix's crown.'

The mech arachnid's forelegs were splayed out like the tense fingers of a mountaineer, digging deep into the masonry and carrying them upward with impressive speed. At this rate they would be banging on the flying saucer's observation window in no time.

Kozlov saw the numerous lights along the saucer's rim start to flicker more sporadically than usual, and even the tower and surrounding lights along the ramparts below seemed to be hit with an alarming power surge.

'Where the hell is he taking us?' Barros asked.

As if in answer, Trillik leaned out of an aperture in the tower, the glass tank catching the light from the green sky. It looked like it was about to jump out to its death. Calkarion jinked the vehicle at an almost 45-degree angle around the tower, coming up alongside Trillik.

The brain tank grabbed hold of the passing ride with one big robotic hand, securing itself to the shell's roof with a heavy bang, and Calkarion swung the ride into a stomach-flipping descent back down the tower. Kozlov held on tight to a makeshift guardrail, teeth bared at the frightening descent, his gauntlets wringing a metallic groan from the bar.

'That's it?' Barros yelled over the rattle and thunder. 'That's the distraction?'

Suddenly, everything darkened. Every light source that wasn't a naked flame or the chartreuse sky died.

Trillik's screeching cry of victory reminded Kozlov of a digital meltdown.

Kozlov felt another lurch of gravity as Kev gestured with one ghostly hand and pried Calkarion's entire vehicle off the wall and eased it onto the grounds of the massive courtyard below, now lit only by blue flame and poisonous sky.

'Where the hell are we going?' Kev asked. 'Wouldn't it be better if I carried us over the castle walls?'

'The underground routes will better conceal us,' Kozlov replied. 'We don't want the imp to see which direction we're heading in.'

The ragged remains of the monarch's forces had started to regroup, forming up to charge.

'More of these fuckers?' Barros grunted.

Calkarion's gaze ignored the charging mob, settling on a fixed section of the palace wall close to the tower. Kozlov knew what the horseman was staring at. Calkarion raised one dark hand, a black cylinder clutched within. With one button press, the ground rumbled, shaking the shadowy battlements and foundations, rattling the wagon, and sending the circus mob toppling like dominoes. Kerzix's entire library of suffering and death was no more. The horseman let rip with a triumphant cry from his bugle-mouth, a proud declaration of rebellion that matched the trembling crescendo.

'Old scores settled,' Kozlov explained to Kev and Barros.

Amongst the courtyard of corpses that had once been the circus mob, a large number of souls were standing over the dead, frightened and confused expressions on their faces—at least those that were human. The Big Top's refugees were liberated once more to try and find a way out of this place.

'What about them?' Kev asked of the souls busy scattering in a dozen directions out of the courtyard.

Kozlov's expression conveyed everything he felt. He didn't wish them luck, not through cynicism, but pragmatism. They were lost. Lost until this entire system was brought down in the name of something better.

Calkarion got them moving again, slowly at first, his eyes lingering on the exploded ruin of the castle cellar. He gained speed, driving them towards a sloping path barred by a tall, toothy portcullis. Trillik tapped a few prompts on a small touchscreen on his arm, raising the gate.

The slope led them away from the giggling Bosch hellscape into a massive underground tunnel worryingly reminiscent of a reddish-pink throat.

'Where the fuck's he taking us?' Barros exclaimed. 'This is a mouth!'

Kozlov held up a hand to calm further outbursts. 'It's not the first one, believe me. According to Trillik, it's one of Kerzix's escape tunnels.'

'As long as it doesn't end up as an asshole,' Kev said. 'Okay, so what happened back there? Did the brain-can get the Needle's location?'

The gullet started to pulse and gag, growing darker by the second until Calkarion lit the headlights of his vehicle. The fleshy ground led downwards.

Trillik clambered down to the side of the speeding vehicle like a daring hijacker, and Kozlov looked at the whirling brain tanks expectantly. His shoulders were tight, strung out in anticipation of its coming report. The brains settled down in their giant jar, and it ran its digital garble past Calkarion.

'Something wrong?' Barros asked.

Kozlov stayed mute, barely able to swallow past the dry lump.

'The last account of the Firmament Needle was its transportation to the Metacarpus Hold,' Calkarion said. 'No records exist of this location's whereabouts.'

Kozlov knew nothing of the Metacarpus Hold and could only suspect that it would be a site close to the heart of the Order of Terminus.

'Shit . . . ' Kev sounded breathless. 'Don't suppose you've heard of that place in your travels?'

Kozlov shook his head tiredly. 'No. But we'll keep searching.'

'I thought that seemed too easy,' Kev said sardonically.

'Easy?' Kozlov asked with a threatening grumble.

Kev must have caught the offhand presumption of his comment. 'Not what I meant. I can only imagine what you've been through since we last met.'

'No offense taken. You both helped save my soul and those of my brethren, may they rest in peace.'

After a respectful pause, Barros asked, 'All of them?'

Kozlov's face scrunched tight, composed itself. 'I just lost my last comrade.'

'We understand all too well, believe me,' said Kev.

The winding intestinal passages finally ended, and a strange incandescence began to permeate the tunnel. Calkarion killed the torch beams as the way transitioned into an enormous expansive tunnel of stunning decadence and surprising beauty. The walls were composed of—or at least layered with—heavy sheets of solid ruby.

This passageway didn't look like an escape tunnel, but rather for Kerzix's vainglorious contributions to secular entertainment. Arranged about the length of the passage were various mementos and commemorations of many sickening attacks from his ever-changing Marotte Marauders across time and space: statues, paintings, types of living media unknown to humanity composed of liquids, lights, and strange matter. Some of the works involved the Big Top perched on a burning hillside, with Sagillis and others celebrating the bloodshed of the pious, and several larger pieces depicted the Marotte Marauders' furious battles against glowing figures of a pure and refined air: Luminaries, Kozlov suspected.

Kev turned to Barros. 'Rose was wrong. She and all the agency brass.'

'Damnit, Rosie,' Barros said as if to herself. 'You always were a stubborn bitch when you wanted to be. Jesus. I've had my doubts since we first learned the Needle really existed, but seeing all of this … where we are … They really are just wasting their time. Peacekeeping. Balancing the books for an average lifespan. Pointless. They should all be here with us. This is the real fight.'

'Then I guess we'll have to fight in their name,' Kev said.

Kozlov listened to them and felt their war-honored bond. And it made the pain of Liev's sacrifice all the more poignant now that he'd lost his oldest friend. He held in that sharp stab of mourning. One day he would use it to impale whosoever barred his way to the Needle's final resting place.

'Does Kerzix know we're going for the Needle?' Kev asked.

'Before that blackout at the tower, Trillik leaked the news of Kerzix's cheating his fellow monarchs out of a small fortune in souls. That's a capital offense amongst their ruling class. They'll hunt him down for this. Destroy him, divide his kingdom.'

'Shame we can't see it, but a win is a win,' Kev said.

'It'll keep him busy,' Kozlov said. 'Trillik also corrupted the imp's communications network, then covered their tracks. That will mask our intentions and keep the imp in the dark for a while.'

Kozlov settled back in his seat, finally feeling the extravagant corridor start to incline as they left the morbid trophy room behind, leading them to the mouth of the tunnel—an actual gigantic mouth, which Kozlov recognized as one of the numerous cackling maws he had witnessed dotted about the landscape.

They vomited from the mouth to find themselves in the wilds, maybe a mile from the castle. In all directions, endemic vitriol was being poured over every conceivable and inconceivable religious sect in the universe: further acts of arson, desecration, blasphemy, murder, torment, and hunting; some in intimate groups, others with more spectacle.

Kozlov was more than ready to put this place behind him, knowing that even though his friend and mentor was now truly gone, he would always be by his side.

He glanced up at the imp's tower, the UFO now dark and lifeless, the castle quiet as the grave. He was still expecting to see that UFO spring to life somehow, whisking the disgraced monarch away to some redoubt far away. It didn't. Whatever Kerzix was doing now, he was broken, his empire decimated, his prized fortune of souls lost, and his head essentially on the chopping block.

'Keep the faith, Kerzix,' Kozlov muttered.

'What?' Kev asked.

Kozlov turned back to his party. 'The Metacarpus Hold could be anywhere.' He nodded to Kev and Barros. 'Pick a direction.'

'We're really doing this, aren't we?' Barros said to Kev. Finally, she gestured towards a distant forest, which looked to be the quieter of the various directions, for what that was worth.

Calkarion's engine grumbled; the repaired chassis had started to squeak again, but the vehicle started off for parts unknown. With any luck, Kozlov thought, it would reach a safe location before any major repairs would be necessary.

54

C HRISTMAS EVE ARRIVED WITH LITTLE enthusiasm for Clyde, and it was with a heavy heart that he knocked on the Carpenters' front door. Standing on the porch, the Christmas lights warded off the wan afternoon cast while a wash of memories swept through him of the times he had spent here growing up: hanging out in the backyard with Kev on summer evenings, chilling with him in his bedroom to watch a movie, skipping class occasionally to play video games; he and Kev, just two kids growing up, unaware of how minuscule their youthful problems actually were. Wanting to escape high school. Trying to pick up girls at parties. Figuring out what sort of bullshit part-time job they could tolerate in their youthful exuberance. Most of all, Clyde remembered the comfort he felt here, Kev helping to guide him through the dark, dull haze of his brother's death when Clyde needed a break from his mom, not because of any problem existing between them, but because she threw herself back into her work at the Bay Ridge Veterans Affairs Medical Center, and the last thing he wanted was for any reminder of soldiers being killed or as good as.

When the front door clicked open, Clyde's heavy heart was joined by an uncertain tongue. Having missed their scheduled Sunday afternoon catch-up on account of Bentley's rampage, Clyde had called Aaron up to apologize profusely, blaming it on his phone battery dying and getting caught in an endless gridlock.

Clyde wanted to be mad at Kev for that, but how could he be?

It was a terrible excuse, but Aaron and Sandy had been nothing but forgiving and asked if he wanted to reschedule for today, which, despite being Christmas Eve, was no problem for the one they considered to be a surrogate second son of sorts. Still, seeing Aaron threw him off balance a little, unsure of what he would make of Clyde's news; it certainly wouldn't match introducing them to their lost child. He gripped the envelope in his hand tight, hoping this wasn't a ridiculous idea.

'Clyde,' Aaron said softly, as though he, too, was on the spot, surprised to find Clyde on his doorstep. He ushered Clyde into his home.

He bore a striking resemblance to Kev, but perhaps a little taller and leaner, his short curly hair grayer, but Clyde clearly saw Kev in him, and who he might have one day grown into. His seasonal sweater was more conservative than the ones Clyde remembered; Sandra enjoyed outfitting her clan in horrid Xmas knitwear as part humorous ribbing, part obligation.

Clyde found the house to be a warm and cheery solace amidst the freezing neighborhood. The savory smells of a family feast wafted in from the kitchen, followed by Sandy's voice calling out to him in welcome, as if he had last been here only yesterday.

'How have you been?' Aaron asked. 'How's your mom?'

'I'm okay, yeah. And she's good, thanks, still at Bay Ridge.'

'I expect nothing less,' Aaron said, a warm, poignant smile briefly touching his lips. 'You can always tell when somebody has found their calling in life. It takes over them. Hers is a worthy one.'

Clyde couldn't help but feel like a little boy again, not the grown man who had faced down hell. 'How's Rhi? She still on the way to becoming a nurse?'

Aaron made an embarrassed half-turn towards the kitchen at the end of the hall, as though he had forgotten his manners. 'She's actually coming down with her new boyfriend soon for dinner. You should stay. You know how Sandy is, how she goes overboard with the food. We'll end up wrapping most of it up to take down to the shelter.'

Clyde was hungry, but he couldn't impose on them. Besides, he had his own plans. 'Thanks, but I can't stay.' The envelope in his hand was starting to itch. He held it out a little uncertainly. 'I thought you might like this—*hope* you might like it. It's not a Christmas card. I found it when moving some old boxes around the other day,' he lied.

Aaron stared dumbly at the envelope for a moment, accepting it as Sandy sidled up next to him, wiping her hands on an apron rich in a history of grease and oven burns.

Clyde had his arm twisted into staying for a coffee at the very least, but it didn't take much twisting. He was sitting in a cream-colored armchair in the living room, and it was just as festively decadent as he always remembered, but it wasn't the wealth of decorations that held his focus, but the damp-eyed stoicism of Aaron and Sandy as they sat shoulder-to-shoulder on the couch, reading their departed son's letter. Clyde had read it after collecting it from Kev's apartment and sticking it in an envelope. It wasn't a formal letter, but more like an entry into a diary Kev never actually kept; a collection of his thoughts from his first year at college:

The ancient Greeks had a word—well, they had many words!—but eudaimonia is loosely considered the pursuit of a good life, driven by virtue. I have been reading the great Stoic philosopher Seneca, whose thoughts on humanity's prodigal attitude towards time and our ugly coveting of material possessions have resonated with me deeply. Fitting really; since I started this college course to try and do something with my squandered life—I know, I'm not even out of my twenties yet, but time is still precious, just ask Seneca. What will I do with a BA in Philosophy? Who the hell knows, but what I do know is that it must be better than slogging away in one dead-end job after another. And I'm happy! All the frustration, all the time and energy I've wasted by drifting aimlessly since leaving high school, I'm now harnessing towards something worthwhile. Most importantly, I think it will make my mom and dad and Rhi proud of me. I always lacked the drive that they have. They are smart. They are doers.

Mom and Pops do an incredible job at humoring me, but I know they want more from me, expect more from me. And I don't blame them.

I see how hard my mom works, and how stressful her job is, but I also see the purpose it gives her. Educating the youth is her calling; she's a natural teacher, and I always remember her unflappable calm and endless patience in helping me with my math homework and English homework, and a million other things; but I'll always suck at her beloved IT skills!

And my dad ... a software engineer—Damn! Was I adopted? Well, while I've ironically never been good with computers, he's also a problem solver, and while he's more technically minded than me, I've finally figured out a major problem of my own: myself. I know what I want to do with my time now.

Rhi, I'm so proud of her too, and in writing this, I realize that I should tell her this more often; but I'm sure she knows, she's no dummy. She's going to be an amazing nurse when she graduates, but her bedside manner will probably need some work. She pretends to hate me, but she's fooling nobody but herself.

And, of course, I can't overlook Clyde. Every day, I'm blown away by his talent, admiring his determination, and his passion for his art. But also, for his endless support and friendship, regardless of the weather. I'll never be able to fill the void Stephen left, but Clyde will always have a second brother in me.

These four people mean more to me than anything else in this world, and each day I think of them and their virtues, and it gives me the motivation to push on. It feels good to finally have a purpose, and a passion of my own. Yes, I wasted a few years there, but hey, I still have the time to do something. Hopefully, it's something that will make up for lost time, make my existence matter, and who knows, perhaps I can help some people along the way.

No matter what hardships or doubts I will have to face from this day forth, I will face them with equanimity, forever carrying these four people in my heart and soul.

Clyde thought his friend had done a good job—that was why he read it twice, the second time through a veil of tears—of carefully saying what he had to without dispelling the illusion around his death. But unlike Aaron and Sandy, Clyde could read clearly through the lines, knowing that Kev's talk of college and finding his purpose really meant the Null and, well, attempting to establish an entire alternative metaphysical realm of existence. Clyde already knew Kev's exit from this world was blind chance, but he also knew if it wasn't during the battle at the Encore Cinema, then it would be some other way. Kev wanted more. Clyde imagined his friend sitting there in his apartment, being observed by neighboring Hourglass agents as he put these words to paper, trying to find the best and most eloquent way to express his love and gratitude to his parents and Rhi, and Clyde too—which surprised him, as though Kev might have had some doubts about Clyde's chances of making it back from the Median—while at the same time keeping it light enough not to cause harm; a mild cut, perhaps, for honesty and sincerity, but not a mortal wound.

Clyde stared into the warmth of the electric fire under the mantel, still feeling like a cracked teacup, everything having leaked out of him, leaving him empty. Some sappy Christmas movie was playing quietly on the TV, reminding him again that this stupid holiday was nothing more than a tinsel-covered marketing stunt for people chasing the one product they can't buy, a fluffy slice of domestic warmth and contentment that won't abandon them come January 1st.

'Thank you for this, Clyde.' It was Sandy, dabbing at her eyes and letting her glasses hang by their chain. 'It's nice to know he was happy in his purpose. I just wish he had been able to see it through.'

Clyde swallowed a lump. 'Me too.' He wondered where Kev and Barros were now. What they were caught up in. He still felt the thread that linked him and Kev quiver every so often. Had he failed his friend? Since returning from Indigo, had he been so swept up in his thoughts of Nat that he missed his friend's signals? They were meant to head into the Null together, hell or high water. And damn the consequences and Trujillo and the hoodoo and anyone or anything else. But when ... ? In taking that opportunity, Clyde knew Kev was only being true to himself. He didn't know how yet, but he would find a way to reach his friend, and he'd be there with him when they found the means to take the fear out of death.

Aaron looked down at the photo accompanying his son's letter. An old Christmas photo of the Carpenter clan at the Rockefeller ice rink, with a teenage Clyde and Kev huddled in the middle. Aaron seemed to be studying it as if searching for some hidden meaning. 'I'm going to frame this. It's going on the mantel.'

'Are you sure you can't stay for dinner?' Sandy asked, her expression imploring.

Clyde decided he could spare a couple of hours for them. For Kev. For himself.

. . .

THE TAXI PULLED up outside Clyde's mom's apartment building. Clyde jostled the Christmas present aside to reach for the money in his jacket pocket. Nat beat him to it, the chains on her leather jacket jangling as she slapped the fare, plus a generous tip, through the partition into the cabbie's hand.

They could have used an agency drop-off, but post-work hours Clyde was doing his damn best to steer clear of anything Hourglass. He hadn't noticed any spooks tailing him for over a week now. Either they were being discreet, or no complications had arisen concerning his activities with Spector.

Still, the days following David Bentley's apprehension had passed in a dull blur of agency scrutiny from Meadows, and more than a few awkward talks with Rose. The actions of Kev and Barros had unavoidably cast a degree of suspicion on Clyde through association, but Nat had gone to the wall to defend him, her closeness to Meadows working against the deputy director on this occasion. There had been some vague words coming from on high, of Trujillo and the hoodoo considering counter-actions to hunt down Kozlov and his new additions, seeing as how the obsessed monk had so far beaten the odds and managed to survive this long on his dangerous quest. Whether Trujillo would make good on this threat or not remained to be seen. Either way, Meadows, and Rose of course, continued to regard Clyde like he was a fox in the henhouse, despite his being as shocked at Kev's actions as they were—more than that, he was heartbroken. But that was the price you paid when your best friend had developed a habit of spitting on agency policy.

'Have a Merry Christmas,' the cabbie said. He was wearing a Santa hat, so they must have struck it lucky and found one of the unappreciated hacks who still found some joy in life. But then, Nat's tip really was quite generous. She was a good sport about paying for the inflated holiday fares.

'You too, dude.' Nat hopped out of the cab.

Clyde joined her on the curb. 'Thanks for this.'

'The cab?' Clyde knew she was messing with him. 'It's cool. I'm not as shit-scared of meeting your family as you are of meeting mine.'

'Not meeting your family. Having dinner with the family *friend*,' Clyde emphasized.

She gave him a *you're weird* look. 'You know we don't have Meadows 'round to carve the turkey, right?'

'I'm way past worrying about Meadows.' He kissed her. 'Let's forget about work right now.'

'Done.'

Clyde started towards the building's salted steps. It was true. He didn't know exactly when it had happened, but somewhere between his and Spector's covert op and losing his best friend for the second time—he had tried pulling Kev back, but despite being soul-bound, Kev still had autonomy—he decided he wasn't going to worry about crossing Meadows anymore. Honestly, his sensibilities about everything in his life were so mixed-up that he felt almost insulated from his actions.

After all, no procedural consequences had arisen for Clyde's Median-related activities at the Encore Cinema that day. There was no proof that he had intentionally knocked himself out to enter the dream world, and Rose's suspicion alone wouldn't stand. Meaning Meadows had arranged a series of medical check-ups, which only concluded that it seemed to be a result of stress; with Spector adding his carefully worded expertise, dismissing it as a flare-up, a potential side effect of his mind's activities.

But nothing to be too concerned over.

Aside from that, Nat was the only one who had seen up close the change in Bentley, how he suddenly seemed to break out of his violent fugue. She had attributed it to Clyde and Ramaliak's intervention, but there was no evidence to validate this to Meadows. The change in Bentley could have been down to whatever was going on with Kerzix and Kozlov.

If Meadows still harbored suspicions about Clyde or Spector, he was sitting on them for now.

As for Dremel and the rest of the Glowing Reel council, they hadn't paid him any nocturnal visits. And he was still alive, meaning they hadn't dispatched a diamond-head to clip his soul thread . . . yet. However, Spector did tell him to keep away from the Median for a while, just to make sure their actions had blown over without attracting further attention. He'd also heard that Bentley was still painted-up like some circus reject, and he didn't know if that was a problem or not: was Bentley truly back to normal? Had Clyde missed some lingering presence, leaving a bit of Kerzix still embedded deep in Bentley's soul like a cancer cell in a body, waiting to metastasize? All Clyde could do was play dumb on the matter and hope his actions hadn't been in vain.

'This season's tough on a lot of people,' Clyde said. 'Outside of work, my mom doesn't have many people in her life. I want to show her a nice time. Add a little comfort and normalcy to her Christmas after all that

Bentley stuff on the news. Holiday's bad enough without a super-powered maniac and a triple-digit body count.'

While the Mondragon family were already well acquainted with some of the more mysterious aspects of the universe, Clyde's mom was one of the many who had watched their understanding of the world fly away in tatters, never to return, when Bentley's second rampage was broadcast across every media outlet, garnering a substantial degree of perturbed acceptance not only amongst conspiracy theorists but swaths of the global community. The world had changed overnight after watching an unkillable lunatic punching holes in everything he came across.

Nat, seemingly touched by the sentiment, gave him a kiss of her own as he reached for the buzzer. The kiss was electric, teasing, but no way was Clyde going to be fucking her in his childhood bedroom with his mom down the hall. He almost smiled. It was the most pedestrian problem he had faced in a long while.

That didn't make him any less anxious, though. For Clyde was anticipating his mom's embarrassing stories of him as a little kid, which he knew Nat would enjoy at his expense.

If nothing else, the pending humiliations of introducing Nat to his mom would help keep his mind off worrying about Kev and, in turn, help her stop worrying about her only remaining son going through life alone and loveless.

If she only knew the real troubles he had.

55

The Fish Tank sat at the bottom of the Hudson River, and it didn't hold goldfish. It was a facility that held the worst offenders who still held some potential value to Hourglass. It was a place where enemies with useful knowledge had that knowledge viciously removed, or where those with a sharp enough edge might one day be pointed at a bigger, worthier target.

Ace swilled from the can of Moosehead he had brought along with him, but the Christmas tunes playing over the PA dampened his enjoyment somewhat.

'You should lay off that shit for a few days,' Rose said. 'You're fresh from a coma, for fuck's sake.'

Ace had woken up a week after Bentley's apprehension. Groggy, but with his mental acuity no worse for wear. His injuries were mending nicely too. Against the physician's orders, he had demanded somebody immediately get him a six-pack of Moosehead from his on-site stash. Clyde had obliged, sneaking them in with Natalie, after Rose, Sarge, and Darcy had left. Ace had almost wept and came awkwardly close to declaring his love of Clyde from his hospital bed.

'Never felt better,' he insisted. He made a face, though. 'But the atmosphere's ruining the taste a little.' The networks of dense plastic tunnels were rendered almost opaque by the murky river water rushing past on all sides, and all Ace could see outside were the muddy halos of safety lights anchored to the surrounding river bed, and the occasional torch beams of an agency submersible patrolling the facility's perimeter. The prison was staffed by a mixture of human agents, and those in the water-filled heavy rubber and plastic suits whose faces were sealed behind portal windows: sub-marinas; various species of oceanic sub-humans with fealty to Hourglass. Good troopers, loyal and lethal.

The fish-man escorted Ace and Rose into the Fish Tank's massive, three-tiered central hub that could be best described as three ship helms stacked on top of one another; the spokes of each helm were tunnels leading to various other sections of the complex, such as the security command center and a general population cell block for lower-risk offenders. In between the "spokes" of each helm were the cells of the more high-risk prisoners. Formidable iron doors that also resembled helms were fitted with a wide central window for inmate observation. Besides the stout construction material, the doors, and the stone and steel cells themselves, were outfitted with various traditional and nontraditional security features to suit a wide range of prisoner attributes, should one start acting out.

Ace pulled something from his inside pocket and held it out to Rose. 'Give him this for me.' She accepted it with an amused snort.

'You stopped off to get this?' Rose asked. 'Glad the coma didn't improve your maturity. You sure you don't want a few words with him?'

Ace gave one more sour-faced swig of beer. 'Not really in the mood. I'll just tap on his glass when you're ready to leave.'

Rose signaled to the guard, who spun the spokes of the chamber door, pulling it open like an iron space capsule.

■　■　■

DAVE LAY ON his hard bed, staring at the ceiling. It beat staring out at featureless freezing water. He didn't bother turning to see who his guest was. It was impossible to tell the time of day under the river, but he had started to gauge mealtimes by the rising peaks of his constant hunger. It wasn't dinnertime yet, so he figured it must be the same couple of sadistic guards who stopped by to knock him about every other day—one a norm, the other one of those things in the sleek armored diving suits—satisfying their curiosity as to how much blunt-force trauma the clown could soak up before dying. Dave figured he'd starve to death before those assholes succeeded. When Dave was first processed by Hourglass, a pathologist—not a surgeon or even a back-alley quack, but an actual pathologist—had been brought in to dig out enough lead from his body to melt down and make a radiation shield. Using a pathologist made sense in a sick sort of way, as Dave knew he was alive, but he sure felt dead.

'Bentley.'

The female voice threw him. Someone new.

He turned his head...and almost wished it was the two thugs. Rose was slowly approaching him, and over her shoulder he saw Ace waiting outside the door, his eyes hard. Another surge of shame rolled through Dave. Penitence and self-loathing were new hobbies of his now, and he felt, for the first time in his life, that all his insecurities and rage and self-doubt had found the right target in himself. He wanted to say sorry to Ace but felt too ashamed to call out. Too much energy to raise his voice. But at least somebody had survived his attacks.

Dave sat up, putting his back to the river view.

Rose stopped by the red DO NOT CROSS line painted on the floor, staring at the bald clown in a red jumpsuit. Dave wasn't shackled, but if he crossed the line, it triggered an unwanted response.

It seemed like they were just going to wait in silence forever until one of them spoke.

She was the guest, so she must have something to say.

Dave then realized she must be waiting for a personal apology. Of course. He cleared his throat, but she spoke over him, surprising him.

'I'm sorry,' she said. Dave was speechless, and his expression must have said so. 'We wanted to help you, but...things didn't work out. I don't know what you might have done under Talbot's influence. You might have done all that shit anyway, or maybe you would have seen sense and not killed a shit-ton of people. Who knows? But it was my actions that got you caught up with Kerzix. That's on me. I have to live with that.'

Astounded, Dave didn't know what to say. It didn't let him off the hook; he would never let that happen. Would he have killed all those people without the imp on his shoulder? No, he wouldn't have. Never. Even in his bleakest power fantasies, he knew that was all they were, fantasies of an angry outsider, and that actually harming his perceived enemies was entirely different in real life. Still, he couldn't deny that he'd been aware of Talbot slowly charming him into taking a shadowy fork in the road. Getting a little drunk on his first sips of power. Who was to say he wouldn't have developed a taste for it over time?

'Can't you find a way to just kill me?' he asked, surprised that his voice almost cracked into a sob. He thought about Ace, and the damage he'd done to him, envying his mortality.

'We could encase you in concrete and drop you in the river, but you don't get off that easy. There are forces out there that pose a threat to global security. *Mortal* security. Your friendly former benefactor Talbot and his employers are one such group who have the greed and stupidity to unbalance the scales.' She was pacing a little along the painted line. 'We've come close to that ourselves a couple of times lately, and it's becoming a bad habit.'

'Talbot ...' Dave sifted through the fragments of that hellish day. 'He asked me to go with him ... to ... *Chicago*. I think he said Chicago. Wanted me to dirty my hands with him. Something about ...?' His expression grew more clouded. 'I don't know. I think he was talking about taking over the Cairnwood group there, or something.'

'That matches with the rumblings we've been hearing. I don't know if he's a cockroach or a cat with nine lives, but one of these days he's going to end, badly. And I'm hoping I'm there to see it.'

'Seems like I got my hands dirty enough all by myself, huh?' Dave flexed his fingers. The power was still in him. Nothing short of death and the liberation of his soul from his body could snuff it, but the Fish Tank had ways and means to attenuate it.

'Spare me the pity party,' Rose practically hissed. 'They say you've really kicked that laughing fuck out of your head. That true? No other voices?'

Dave hadn't heard a peep from Kerzix since that day at the cinema. He wasn't sure of the monster's fate and could only pray that it was dead. Mentally, he was a free man, but the *experts* didn't know why his face was still the way it was. And the imp had left something else too: a brain full of unwanted memories. Dave spent every day torturing himself with the morbid recollections of the people he'd killed, his hands doing terrible things to their soft bodies. The pain and fear and hope dying in their eyes. He nodded at her question.

'You don't need me to tell you that this place is no white-collar country-club prison. You're here to sit and live with what you've done. I don't know squat about prison rehabilitation rates, but what I do know is that the boss wants you here for a different reason. You threw your life away, Bentley. I know there are some extenuating circumstances—boy, do I! Not too many people have extenuating circumstances like you, but they're the cards you've been dealt. Tough shit.' She threw a brief glance at Ace, then stopped pacing the line, hands behind her back, chest out proudly. 'Employment can be a tricky issue with our agency strike teams, and there might come a time when your attributes could help us in restoring further imbalances. If that time comes, you might get a temporary reprieve from the fishies outside.'

Dave kept his mouth shut. What was there to say? He certainly wasn't going to act grateful. It wouldn't be intended as a favor if such a thing came to pass, nor would he accept it if it was. He was here to suffer. And that's what he wanted.

'Anyway, it might never happen.' She tossed Ace's present to him. 'Ace doesn't want you getting hungry.'

Dave glanced at it. A small box of fish food. By the time he looked up, she was gone, and the door was already sealing him back in.

Darlene Love's "All Alone on Christmas" played over the prison wing's PA system. He turned from the door, staring forlornly at the freezing depths of the Hudson River, seeing the clown reflected back at him, thinking about the festive atmosphere in the city above and the path that led him to this. Life was wasted on him, but he wished the best for all of those lucky enough to have somewhere to belong. He lay back on his bed with his fingers laced behind his head, staring at the fish food resting on his chest. A small laugh bubbled up from somewhere deep in his chest, brewing steadily into an eye-watering riot.

At least he wasn't angry anymore.

56

T ALBOT COULDN'T REMEMBER THE LAST time he had dressed so casually. It took him a moment to realize that actually, he never had. He had gone straight from rags to riches, shunning the middle ground altogether. Now here he was, in beige khakis, gray loafers, and a gray long-sleeve button-up shirt, sipping a hot chocolate and rereading the notes he'd collected so far with notepad and pen at a bustling cafe in the Chicago Loop. He felt positively bohemian. Even his typically dark, stylishly upscale hair was mussed and casual.

It was another new day in a new city, and soon it would be a brand new year. Ripe with potential. The New Year's Eve crowds—those who were not working the holiday—were scurrying all around out on the streets in manic preparation for the evening's festivities. He could feel the heady brew of excitement and opportunity in the air.

But not for him. For him, it was to be a sober affair, but by no means maudlin. It was undeniable that his position within Cairnwood had slipped more than ever. Three successive failures already had him hanging on to his mid-tier position by his fingernails. Marginalized. Doubted. But now with Gabriel out of the picture, a mystery that nobody could explain, least of all Talbot, he was now lacking the former weight and support of an esteemed inner circle member for the first time in his career. Had he lost his edge? Burned out? Talbot was content for the local establishment to believe so. Let them cast quiet aspersions on him behind his back. It would only strengthen his position.

When weak, act strong.

When strong…act weak.

Having formally introduced himself upon his arrival in Chicago, extending the expected formalities and respect to the local Cairnwood players, not wanting to step on any toes being the new guy in this town, he had sensed a strained sense of charity from his new contemporaries, as though he was only to be measured by his recent disappointments rather than the rest of his career.

And so, while he graciously accepted the offer to take some time to orient himself with his new surroundings—most likely because the Chicago branch viewed him as a liability or nuisance—he took in the multitudes of culture and energy of this magnificent city, realizing he could be very happy here. He visited the Art Institute, Willis Tower, the Millennium Park's Cloud Gate sculpture. He got right into the tourist spirit. But it wasn't all rest and relaxation. He was already pondering the downfall of his new rivals.

His pen lightly tapped the page listing the local power players. Bulletpoints of historical importance. Possible weaknesses. Strengths, whether hearsay or fact.

Talbot felt refreshed. And why not? A new year was dawning. Time for reinvention. His own man, away from Gabriel's overbearing clutches. Admittedly, Gabriel's absence would be substituted by new observers once Talbot had acclimated to the new group, at least until he erased some of the black marks on his name, but they wouldn't be members of the inner circle. Soon enough, sure. In time. But for now, he would play along with his new sense of freedom. Hence his recent shopping spree. A wardrobe full of casual Friday. Gone were the cufflinks and sharp suits. In were the khakis and jeans, and even, through a sudden burst of explorative impulse, a bright Hawaiian shirt of palm fronds and tangerine sky, despite the season! It seemed more modern. Many of today's nouveau riche favored dressing down. It was like role-playing to them. The everyman. A way to blend in with the lower classes.

Except Talbot wasn't role-playing. For him it was strategy. Let this new bunch of stuffed-shirt Cairnwood sycophants treat him like he was ready for euthanasia. A has-been whose recent spate of professional embarrassments had sent him over the edge. He still had a very deep bag full of very dangerous weaponry hidden away in a safe place. And now he had the names and faces of the people he would be climbing over to eventually secure a seat at the big table. It wouldn't be easy, or quick. But he would get there.

In the past he had thought of such ambitions with the internal voice of a cocky, self-assured upstart; now it was one of cold, ponderous sobriety and—dare he admit it?—fear. It now went beyond the allure of profit and influence, and into basic common sense and sanity. Soma Sarkozy was demented, and his veiled ambition to court the dead gods of Erebus stank a little too much like subservience at best, and absolute destruction at worst. Assuming the Order of Terminus didn't simply burn Sarkozy like some oversized penny-dreadful dreck, being subservient to another line of power-mongering managers held little appeal to Talbot. He knew very little about Sarkozy. The scholar was a myth. But he did know that he founded Cairnwood, and was thus an inevitably tremendous threat. Worse still, his deeper connections and motivations were inscrutable. Was it possible that the rest of the inner circle knew all of the detailed workings of Sarkozy's ultimate plot and wholeheartedly had faith in it, or were they too blinded by their ancient ties and loyalty, and a hunger for more and ever more power?

Power. It was an appetite Talbot still shared with them, albeit his unglamorous upbringing had conditioned him for lean winters. He knew what it was to struggle, and endure, and to see the harsh reality of a difficult situation. Gabriel and the others, all they had known was full stomachs and a drunken gluttony. And Talbot wasn't prepared to risk allowing Sarkozy to blindly set the table for what could be their last meal. Yes, it would take time and caution and hard work, but Talbot would find a way into the group's innermost workings to assess the risk of Sarkozy's master plan. And if the scholar was as warped as Talbot feared—his pen hand briefly took on a coat of deep-green pigment—then he would feast.

Talbot returned the notepad and pen to the pocket of his jacket hung across the back of his chair. He finished the thick, sweet dregs of his cocoa and decided to have another stroll around his new stomping ground. He had a good few hours to kill yet before the Navy Pier fireworks rang in a new era.

EPILOGUE

I**T WAS LATE WHEN THE** phone vibrated, coaxing Clyde from a restless sleep of some undefinable dread and the ethereal melody of a glass harp. The Oneiroic Hemisphere?

Christmas and New Year had been and gone. It was now the second week of January, but finding sleep had been a crapshoot since Kev's disappearance, whose absence had left Clyde feeling like a piece of himself was missing. A sensation that wasn't helped by the fact he was still living across the hall from Kev's apartment, now empty, lifeless, and back on the market. But what was worse was the fact that he couldn't even sense him through their bound threads anymore. He was sure Kev's soul was still "alive," but for how much longer? Each day had become a slow, grinding agony of wondering if today would be the day that Kev got his soul utterly destroyed.

At first he thought a few nights at his mom's might change how he felt about his living situation and alleviate some of his depression, but even after a great meal, a few beers, lots of lighthearted conversation, and—despite his previous hesitance—an excellent introduction between Nat and his old bed, he still found himself unable to lose himself in the gentle seas of sleep. Even Spector's trick with the yarn wasn't cutting it, leading Clyde to believe that it wasn't a magic bullet but a mere gimmick used to focus on something other than his busy thoughts.

Didn't really matter what stupid distraction he used; if his mind didn't want to rest, it didn't want to rest. The wounding of his dream avatar had also provided a few sporadic and strange sensations whenever he did manage to fall into sleep, but it was nothing he was unable to adapt to: a few phantom pains along the back and shoulders; the occasional weirder-than-normal dream; some emotional imbalances upon waking, predominantly grief.

He reached over to the bedside unit, trying not to disturb Nat, who was sprawled out in a New Bomb Turks T-shirt. It took him a few dopey seconds to realize it wasn't his phone that was vibrating, but the burner Kev had bought.

Spector.

At this hour?

He opened the message, feeling a constriction in his throat.

A tightness formed in his chest, his muscles stressing.

We need to talk. It's awake.

Clyde didn't need clarification on what *It* was. It could only be one thing: the Coma Weaver. He remembered its lifeless eyes, like a cluster of poisonous berries, watching him from its frozen posture upon its glowing plinth. Clyde had pushed and pushed, and that little open-handed soul surgery he'd performed on Bentley's thread must have awoken the being that had stained his bloodline.

He looked over his shoulder at Nat. She was still, her eyelids twitching, lost in an unconscious dream world that Clyde now feared almost more than the Null itself.

A world that a great many sleepers might soon come to fear.